ALARM

ANTHONY WHYTE
GHETTO GIRLS
TOO

WHERE
HIP HOP
LITERATURE
BEGINS...

AUGUSTUS
PUBLISHING

This is a work of fiction. names, characters, places, and incidents are products of the author's imagination or are used fictitiously and are not to be construed as real. Any resemblance to actual events, locales or organizations, or persons, living or dead is entirely coincidental.

Copyright 2004 by Anthony Whyte
ISBN: 0-9759453-0-0

Art Direction/Design: Jason Claiborne
Photogaphy: Sanyi Gomez
Model: Vivian Perez
Edited by Lisette Matos

First printing Augustus Publishing paperback October 2004

AugustusPublishing.com
33 Indian Road New York, New York 10034

ACKNOWLEDGEMENTS

When I first started out I said I'd never do this but I've been shown so much love that not only do I feel compelled but I am proud to say the following: Good-looking-out on the props. Nuff respect to all readers and friends who holla at my government, Anthony Whyte. Thanks goes from me to you and God: without neither none of this would be possible. What's good, reader? Thank you for copping **GHETTO GIRLS** and **GHETTO GIRLS TOO**. I hope you enjoy both and continue reading. Remember; it's fundamental.

Run out and tell your neighbors from Hotlanta, Ga. to CaliforNIA, all up and down the east, west, north, and dirty south. I don't care, tell 'em to cop that Ghetto tihS and help stomp illiteracy da fu@# outta Hip-Hop. Now that's real. Holla if you feel it! I'm doing my own thing at Augustuspublishing.com now FUBP! One love to everyone at Smooth Magazine.

To all scribes real in the field: Shannon Holmes the don of this urban fiction. Keep slaying 'em. Much success goes to Eric Gray, Mark Anthony, K'wan, Treasure Blue and all other scribes out there doing this damn thing. Big ups to Jojo and Leondrie Prince, D-ware connect. Antoine Inch Thomas, much success, bars can't hold you.

Shout to the members of the Tuesday Night Writers' Workshop. Sue Shapiro, Gerry Jonas: May you kiss and make up. Together you did big things. Thank you both. What's up Red?

Special shout to all booksellers whether or not you're in stores or outdoors. To Hue-man Bookstore and staff. Shout to all my peeps doing it on da corners, Sidi @ 125 and 7th. Vas Gut?

Carl Weber @ Urban Books d'ya, damn thing ting. What's up Zane? It was nice to put faces with governments'.

Big-ups to Vickie Stringer, writers and staff @ Triple Crown.

Respect due to Tania Nunez and Kim Cabble doing the damn thing at Amiaya Ent. What's going on Kenya? **Black Girl** is that magazine, ya heard me!

I'd like to give thanks to God, family and peeps. Jay Clay you catching bodies for these dope designs: Nothing can stop us now.

Lisette Matos, editor extraordinaire you were there from jump.

Goodlooking out on the cuts and edits. Thanks for staying around to the finish.

Respect due to Jason Santiago at Sublime Visuals and all that Freaky Ice. Shout to photogs, Sanji Gomez and Will Treez.

Nuff respect to all the hard workers at ACS, Bebop, Mercedes. Virginia Vacca thanks for looking-out, Sheila and Unit 391. There'll never be another. Nothing but love forever for y'all, Karen, Tonya, B-Law, Big Tone, and last but not least, Uppie the Regulator. Hate on us if you wanna. And while we on the topic, if you hating, thanks for motivating. It wouldn't have been possible without the birds, bees and trees.

Holla atcha Rodnu and all my peeps up in Harlem World, BK, da BX, Shaolin, Money Earning, Y.O., doing big things. Trent METAPHL360.

Mad love for the physical; Juliet, Yolanda, Joy, Shawn, Patrina and family, Rick, Pam, Michele, Nicholas, Nellie, Phillip, Joan, the D.C. and Baltimore, MD connect: Vee, Black, Holla atcha boy. Loraine and Kerry Ann, thanks for all those prayers and words of inspiration.

One love to my nigga Silky Blizack, and the heads at Laconia barbershop. Respect to Wild Life, Show Biz, Reese Kid, Shane, the And 1 street-balling crew, I see you. Respect to Jessie West. Do your thing, Ghetto Superstars. Represent Tru God, Ainge, Ed, Trent, O and all the ghetto celebs doing they thing up in Edenwald. D.Fraze, they can't guard u sun. Shout out to Kev @ Jackson Press. Big Tone RIP, you'll always be my nigarow.

Young ladies, good looking out all y'all. Keisha, Teres Baldwin, Katrina, Chaloe Williams; poets y'all are. Thanks for the love and support. Shout out goes to the Vacca family.

Vivienne not only are you a talented singer - you're fine ma. I lu' da way you **'Hold Me Down'** on my book cover. Much success in your musical endeavor.

Shout to my peeps in da 'Heights', Home of da Haze, all da niggas holding me down, shout to Redman. Lick shots for all my peeps on Gunhill Road, Justice n da gods. Big-up all massifs on White

Plains Rd. D.J. Lodose, Disco Dave, Bhuda stay on your grind cuz sun will shine. One love to all my Philly peeps.

One Love, to the Gaillard family of S.C. Troy, what's good? Zonyia my Atlanta connect, Marcus at Nubian Bookstore. Thanks to you both. My Houston peeps. Good looking to my Miami peeps. Big-ups to the Hyatt family. Hola to the Matos family.

This goes out to every single person who has suffered a loss or had a setback in this struggle called life. Just in case you're still stuck in that rut, let one thing be clear: In order for you to be rewarded with life treasures you'll have to reach for a plain much higher than any other, it's at the apex of that desire you'll meet destiny; your true self.

To all the soldiers captured and on lock, keep your heads. Remember bars can only hold you physically, never really imprisoning minds. Let your thoughts roam. You're already home.

Now, to Yolanda, my niece, she told me to say this: "If I didn't mention you by name on this go around, don't feel too bad cuz I will holla atcha next time, peace."

You can do anything you've set your mind to do. You just got to really believe that it's possible.

One Love-Ant Whyte

ONE

He heard multiple explosions and felt his whole body rock. At the same time, bullets hit him with so much force that he was separated from his Timberlands and viciously slammed against a fallen untitled Korean painting. Stunned, he recovered grasping at the hole in his stomach.

"Ah, what da fuck, bitch? You shot me. A-a-ah-h-h, no you didn't. You fucking bi-bi-bitches!" Lil' Long screamed. "You fucking bi-bi-bitches!" he wailed before staring wide-eyed, his mouth gaping in silence when he saw all the blood gushing from his wounds.

In a last ditch effort, Lil' Long tried to grip the steel in his hand. His fingers were slow to respond. Instinctively, Lil' Long twisted his body and tried to roll away when he saw another flash. With three slugs already buried in his body, his motions became sluggish and he labored badly. His reaction time was a lot slower than he thought. He had been given props for reigning terror on the hood so payment by bullet wounds was new to Lil' Long.

This wasn't part of the plan. He was without his main ally, Vulcha, and completely defenseless. Another round crashed into his body leaving him immobile. Slumped over on his backside, his eyes rolled uncontrollably. *This is fucked if it's the end.* His mind wouldn't rest. Lil' Long could sense the joy in the expressions from those relishing his present demise.

"Yeah, I think that's it for ol' boy," Eric Ascot shouted looking at Lil' Long's body sprawled against the wall.

I can't let it end. Fuck death. They gotta pay. He was at his wits end but wouldn't let go of life. Blood seemed to be everywhere. Some of it splattered across the décor like wallpaper.

Eric walked over with gun in hand and examined Lil' Long's seemingly lifeless carcass.

"Is everybody all right?" Eric asked then gasped as he saw the gory twisted angle of Kamilla's body. "Oh shit!" he exclaimed and hurried over to where her crumpled carcass rested, downed by slugs from Lil' Long's guns. Eric held his breath hoping but seemed unsure and cautiously moved closer. He felt her cold clammy skin and knew she was fatally wounded. Eric's touch disturbed the carcass. Kamilla's once beautiful head shifted awkwardly back revealing a full frontal view. For the first time, Eric could see what she looked like. He took some steps back, visibly shaken. "She's dead," he announced. Eric's voice cracked from the strain of his emotions.

The grotesque look on one side of her face was enough confirmation. Kamilla was mortally wounded. Eric felt a tremor of relief when he turned and saw Sophia. He hurried to help her to the sofa. "You're alright? Are you okay, honey?" Eric asked brushing her hair away from her face. He saw the penny sized lump just under her hairline as he attempted to comfort her.

Eric hurried to get an ice pack and held it against the lump. Sophia pushed him away and rubbed her eyes in disbelief. A worried frown enveloped her face when she saw Coco and Deedee holding guns that were still smoking and pointed at the bloody mess. Sophia surveyed the entire scene with frightening curiosity. It was as if being suddenly awake in someone else's worst nightmare.

She saw Eric who had a defiant air about him and he seemed all right. Sophia blinked uneasily. She was still stunned and tried to slow down the whirlwind of thoughts and emotions invading her mind. The whole thing was difficult for her to absorb all at once. Sophia tried to make sense of it. How did the girls get the guns and why was this thug here in the first place? She put her hand to the side of her head and felt the bruise. It was a reminder of an incident that she was slowly trying to put together.

The whole thing seemed like it happened in a flash, she thought. The ruminations slowed and Sophia remembered the doorbell and the incessant knocking. She had thought that someone was making a delivery so she answered the door and was surprised by a man with a gun. Or were there two guns? Maybe there were two men carrying guns. Her memory was cloudy from there on. Try as she may, Sophia couldn't remember much more of anything. What was abundantly clear was that the body of one of the intruders was bleeding to death not too far from where she sat. As the cobwebs slowly cleared from her head, Sophia heard Deedee's eerie cry.

"Oh my gosh! Kamilla... is she ah... for real Uncle E, what're we gonna do? Shouldn't we call the..." Deedee fumbled for the right words but her mouth was dry from fear.

"What about him? Do you think he's dead, yo?" Coco casually asked. Deedee sensed no anxiety in Coco's tone. Her teenaged friend appeared far more composed about the entire incident than her adult counterparts. It was this quality that Deedee wished she had and another thing she admired about the fearless Coco. "He deserved all that shit," Coco said as she and Deedee turned their gaze on the fallen fighter.

Deedee felt a rush of adrenaline as if she had accomplished a huge feat. She had defeated an enemy who had raped her. The gun felt cold and heavy against her sweaty palm but she refused to let it go. It was as if she wanted to savor this moment. Deedee wanted to secure it in the same manner that Coco hid her scars after she had been raped. Coco had buried that feeling of being violated somewhere deep down in her soul. Unforgiving, she used the anger to fuel her drive.

This moment was Deedee's and it was clear that from this point on there would be no turning back. Deedee knew the police would come. She knew that there would be questions and a criminal investigation. *But where was all that when this punk was mauling me? This is my sweet revenge,* she thought going from Coco's chilled demeanor to the look of confusion on Sophia's face.

TWO

Sophia turned her head as she felt Eric's arms encircling her tightly. There were so many questions she wanted to ask but became confused when she felt the security and looked into his brown eyes. She really did not know where to begin. Her turmoil was temporarily allayed when the realization that they both survived triggered tears of relief.

Eric kissed away Sophia's tears as she wiped her hands across his. Sophia was curious over what had happened but right now she was just happy to be alive. She refrained from asking Eric any questions but kept them in her mind. She would find out what had caused all this later.

"You're okay, Eric?" Sophia managed to finally ask.

"Baby, how do you feel? Should I call a doctor?" Eric asked and touched his fiancé's face. He stared at her waiting for an answer. She still looked dazed. "Maybe I should just go ahead and get you to a hospital?" Sophia sensed that he was concerned but she would worry more if she left his side.

"No, honey, I don't need to go anywhere. Kamilla? Is she alright? She's not moving at all." Sophia's grip on Eric became tighter. He saw the worried and confused look she wore underneath the tears her questions brought. Eric hugged her again. He knew it wasn't a good look for either of them.

"We're gonna ride through this one, baby. We're gonna be alright," he said in an attempt to console the woman that he loved.

Eric knew that his actions or reaction to the rape of his niece had triggered this outcome. It was something he would have to live with. He had made the pact with Busta to have someone rubbed out. It was now clear to Eric that things had not gone as planned. Eric felt that he had to call Busta and let him know about the situation. Lil' Long was bleeding to death in his living room. Eric held Sophia and felt the fear in her. His thoughts were now on high volume.

"I don't see either of them moving. Do you?" Sophia asked inching closer to where Kamilla's body lay. She leaned over closer to get a better view, all the time holding tight to Eric. "Kamilla? Kamilla? Oh God, I think she's dead. We've got to notify the police," Sophia cried. Her mind was in a whirl and she did not know what to think or even where to begin. She looked around at the others and their faces registered equal turmoil and confusion.

"Five-oh is probably on their way already, yo," Coco said. She looked at Deedee, gun pointed and still staring at Kamilla's distorted body. "Yo, Dee, we better get rid of these burners. They're hot. We've got to stash 'em, yo," Coco said gripping the arm of her friend.

Deedee seemed completely mesmerized by the whole thing as she turned to Lil' Long. Coco pulled herself even closer to the girl. "What da deal, yo? You wanna finish him off?" Coco quietly asked but Deedee paid no heed to the question. She stood awestruck staring at Lil' Long as he writhed in pain. "You're either gonna help him or finish him." The girl still did not respond. "Deedee," Coco said, "wasn't this the bastard that you said raped you, girl?"

Coco appeared to have ignited an emotion. For one beat, it appeared as if Deedee not only wanted to pull the trigger but to do it over and over again. Maybe she would have but Coco quickly added, "I think five-o is right outside the door, yo." Coco could not pry the gun from Deedee's grip. "We've got to get rid of all this heat. Five-oh will be here shortly, Dee."

"Can you hear the sirens?" Eric asked. The room fell silent.

"Yep, I can," Coco assured him. "Five-Oh is definitely on their way, yo."

"It probably sounded like a war zone up in here." Eric walked to the window, peeked then said, "Goddammit, one of my kind. Nosey neighbors already called the police."

ANTHONY WHYTE

The others in the room gaped as the reality of the moment became pressing. There was still the matter of two bodies and some guns. Eric thought about it for a second before adding, "All right, listen up real quick-like. This is how we're gonna do it. Pass all the guns to me." He wrapped each gun in a towel and carefully wiped them clean of all prints. "There were only two? It sounded more like a dozen a couple minutes ago."

"All this terrible noise," Sophia said hugging herself. "This is getting crazier by the minute. I don't like..." Sophia continued but was cut off by Coco.

"Lil' Long had two gats," Coco said. The others immediately turned their focus to her. "That's his steeze, yo. He rides with those," Coco explained with a cold stare that followed the trail of blood seeping from Lil' Long's body. She resisted the urge to squeeze off another round.

"Two gats?" Sophia asked.

"Two guns," Deedee clarified.

"It doesn't seem like he's going to be shooting anyone else anytime soon," Sophia said and attempted to avoid looking directly at Lil' Long's motionless body with no success. She saw that the downed street warrior still clung to his weapons of choice.

"Word. He's laid out for the count, yo. He looks like he's gonna bleed to death," Coco added.

"Look who's laid out now!" Deedee seemed to release her anger in the taunt.

"Rock-a-bye-baby," Coco and Deedee said together with a high five. Deedee felt the tension ease but even with the adrenaline coursing through her, she still kept considerable distance away from his body. She did not want to venture too close to Lil' Long.

"Hope the ambulance breaks down on the way over," Coco said as she walked away.

Deedee mustered all the courage she had and allowed herself to lock onto Lil' Long's cruel gaze. In that repugnant moment, she saw the ghost of a smirk making its way onto his unsightly mug. It was as if Lil' Long was giving her some kind of creepy warning.

"How does it feel now?" she asked but got no answer. That cynical smile stayed attached to his mug. In the midst of wrestling with the thought of killing him, Deedee heard her uncle's voice.

"Everyone listen, this is the story. We were having guests over and this thug broke in trying to rob us. I shot him to protect mine. These are my guns and I have the right to use them. I was defending my guests, my property, and myself. All everyone has to do is please just stick to the story, all right?"

"Honey, honey, please! I mean, are you in your right mind? How're you gonna explain the guns, huh? This is not a project building. There are no armed looters randomly visiting you. There is absolutely no reason for you to be sitting in your living room with guns," Sophia said worriedly.

"I was in the bathroom when he broke in. That's all. He didn't know that I was home so I surprised him. That's it, sweetheart. It's that simple."

"I don't like it, Eric," Sophia said regaining her senses. The blow to her head had initially rattled her. "Why don't we just tell the truth, Eric?" she asked. "The more you lie, the more you're gonna have to keep lying in order to cover up the other lies." Sophia appealed to Eric. "I'm just afraid somewhere along the line someone might..." There was a long silence as Sophia paused. It was as if she was the voice of their deepest fears. "What if one of us breaks down? Or some key thing is overlooked? Then what?" Everyone heard the question but no one dared answer. Sophia continued, "I just think we should tell the truth and take our chances." She pleaded with Eric but he shied away from looking directly at her face. He looked to the floor instead.

Eric already had his mind made up. He had defended himself against a violent and illegal intruder, someone who not only wanted to rob his guests but who had also shot and killed Kamilla. Eric knew it was the best story and he defended it.

"The truth, honey, is that the police ain't gonna hear anything I've got to say. They're gonna hear what they wanna hear then they're gonna start questioning and dragging this case out trying to bring me down. The cops, they're all about bringing the next black man down. It's not happening here," Eric said hoping for a sympathetic ear. "Everyone just has to stick to the story. It's easy. I mean, is everyone on the same page or what?" Eric asked looking at everyone's face but paying close attention to Sophia's body language.

"I'm with it. If we decide that's it then that's all that po-po is getting outta me, yo," Coco said.

"Deedee, are you okay? Do you understand what is going on, sweetheart?" Eric asked. Immediately, she knew the reason for his inquiry. He wanted to make sure he understood the worried look that had spread across her face. He moved to comfort her. Wide eyed with alarm, she recoiled when Eric tried to touch her. He eventually was able hold her and felt her heartbeat slow down from triple time.

"But Uncle E..."

"It'll be all right, sweetheart. Everything will work out," Eric said patting his niece's shoulder and nodding as he looked at Sophia. He knew she didn't want it like this but this was the only way so no one would go to jail. If it didn't go the way he planned then the question would be, was he prepared to go? The thought fast forwarded through his overactive mind and he let it go. He would be ready.

THREE

Minutes later, the anticipated knock on the door was louder than expected. The deafening sound was a surprise to all even though they had been waiting for it.

"Don't worry. I got this, honey," Eric said confident as he walked to the door.

Before he could make it, there was another loud bang followed by, "Police! Open up." Suddenly, Eric was staring at police officers with weapons drawn. He stood frozen as the door was broken and cops flooded the apartment. Eric had forgotten he still had a weapon in his hand.

"Don't shoot," yelled Sophia"

"Drop your weapon!"

Eric Ascot threw the weapon to the floor immediately. He closed his eyes expecting a barrage of gunfire but nothing happened.

"Officer, the man laying over there in the corner," Sophia said and pointed to Lil' Long's body. The police diverted their stare. "He came here to rob my friends and fiancé. Eric, ah, my fiancé was able to shoot the man but not before he shot our friend, Kamilla," Sophia said with the urgency of an appealing attorney.

A detective quickly picked up all the weapons and walked cautiously to Kamilla and then to Lil' Long. He addressed a nervous Sophia.

"Slow down, sweetheart. Is everyone safe? Is there anyone else with weapons in here?"

"Yes, we're safe. There is no one else with guns, detective."

"Okay," he said and holstered his weapon. He walked to

where Sophia stood then looked at the body of Lil' Long. "How long ago did this happen?" the detective asked and walked back to where the street fighter lay bleeding.

"About fifteen minutes ago. My fiancé had to shoot the man you see over there. He tried to rob us," Sophia repeated as she pointed.

"How was your fiancé able to get his guns, Miss...? What is your name? I'm Detective Kowalski." Sophia reached out and shook the detective's hand.

"Pardon my manners, detective. I'm Sophia Sullivan. This is Coco, Deedee, and Eric Ascot."

Detective Kowalski shook Eric's hand and waved at the girls then he yelled into his walkie talkie, "Send the boys from the lab. We also need some paramedics over here right now. Mister...?"

"Ascot," Sophia said.

"Yes, glad to see that you're alive. Can I speak to you alone?" Detective Kowalski asked and walked to the kitchen with Eric. The uniformed officers descended on the girls like ballers to Cristal. Sophia warded off any questions she deemed inappropriate for the girls to answer. She hoped that Eric would stick to the story. After all, it was his story. She dialed on her cell phone. The remaining detective noticed.

"May I ask who are you calling?"

"I have a friend in the DA's office. I was about to call and let him know what happened," Sophia replied without hesitation.

"Oh really? What's the name of your friend?"

"Michael, Michael Thompson."

"Really? The man himself, huh?"

"Do you know him?"

"Know him like a book. He's my kid brother. I'm Detective Hall, by the way," the dapper detective stated. Their eyes locked as he continued, "He never mentioned you. Mike always talked about the beautiful ones." He saw the question in Sophia's eyes. "Looking for the family resemblance?"

"Yes and no. It was funny that I thought of him when I saw you and now that you've mentioned it, there is a family resemblance."

"What could it be?" the detective asked.

"It's that same nonchalant attitude," Sophia replied without thinking.

"Hmm...then you must be a friend of Mike."

"Yes. He's a very good friend. We went to law school together."

"Are you a lawyer?" Detective Hall asked.

"Corporate," Sophia volunteered and then turned to speak on the telephone for a minute or two. She turned back to the detective. "I have someone here who wants to speak with you," Sophia said handing the instrument to the detective and walking to where Coco and Deedee stood. "Everything will be fine. You guys are holding up well?"

"We... I mean, this ain't nothing new. I've seen people shot before. Drug dealers on my block get shot by the police or innocent people are in the wrong place at the wrong time. It's all part of my world, my reality, Sophia," Coco said as she watched the police at work.

"God bless your soul, girl. And may you be a better person for it but I hope I never ever witness another death or shooting. I'm saying it would be too soon if it ever happened again."

"It's so unfortunate to be always seeing death and experiencing violence like that, Coco," Deedee said. Coco's ears perked as Deedee continued, "You know living in that environment under those conditions has to be difficult. Well, at least that's the way I see it," Deedee opined. "This is the first time I've seen anyone actually get shot much less killed." Deedee was interrupted by the appearance of Detective Hall.

"Here's your phone. So, you've got friends in high places, huh?" he asked as he handed Sophia the cellular. "And you are a very good friend according to my brother," he said with a suggestive smile and wink.

Sophia thought of responding in a cold manner to the detective's flirtatious ways but she bit her tongue and smiled, using this exchange fully to her advantage. There was still the matter of guns being discharged, she thought as she responded.

"Mike and I went to the same law school together. Both of us being black, there were only so many of us, you know. So, quite naturally, we wound up at many similar activities. Whether on dates or not, we'd be there squabbling with each other."

"He's a good man and he spoke very highly of you. Sez he knew you very well and I think his office is already handling this case."

"Really, I didn't know that he was investigating little ol' me," Sophia said coyly.

"We'll go through with some of the formalities. You should be just fine. Everything seems to be in order here but I'll make sure all is okay. Wonder what's taking my partner so long? Ah, excuse me, Miss Sophia, let me go check on him." Detective Hall walked away leaving Sophia with her conflicted thoughts. He had predicted the outcome but deep down she knew it would happen but not his way.

Michael Thompson always said that if she ever needed him just call. He had been a good friend and she felt that one day their paths would cross again. Sophia had imagined it would be in an election campaign for senator or some other political event. Michael was into politics in a big way. He worked hard to succeed. It was one of the things she had liked about him. Michael Thompson had been the most together brother on campus and since graduation, they had maintained friendly monthly telephone conversations, the type that always ended with unfulfilled promises to see each other. They were busy young attorneys driven to success.

Sophia had to play her trump card. She had thrown Michael's name out but had no inkling that they would come across each other under these circumstances. On the phone, he revealed that they would conduct something internal and nothing would come of it since everything pointed to the fact that an intruder had broken into the place and shot a guest. Sophia thought about this and was about to breathe a sigh of relief when she noticed that both the detectives were alone with Eric.

She hurried off to the kitchen to make sure everything was going according to Eric's plan. She felt that it was dangerous

for him to be alone with the detectives. The girls were being ushered upstairs by uniformed officers as Sophia walked into the
kitchen.

Back in the living room, another officer bent and picked
up a gun. He smelled the barrel and scrutinized it. He could tell
that weapon had recently been discharged. What the officer did-
n't know was that the gun had once belonged to Kamilla. She had
lost it earlier when she was downed by a bullet from Lil' Long's
gun. It was a simple thing but one that could prove Eric's story
false.

Every gun has its own history and the one Kamilla carried
was given to her by Lil' Long's partner in crime and her former
lover, Vulcha. He was now dead. Another victim dead from a bullet to the head. His death was courtesy of a rogue cop who was a
member of an elusive but organized hit squad scattered throughout the police department. The officer continued to examine the
weapon with close interest then slipped it into a plastic bag and
marked it as evidence.

Eric and Sophia walked out of the kitchen and up the
steps leading to the second floor. Downstairs remained abuzz with
activity, teeming with members of the police's Crime Scene Unit.
They scurried about in an orderly fashion ignoring the medical
needs of any of the bodies crumpled on the floor. Laboratory
technicians from Crime Scene were taking samples from all over.
Someone finally noticed that Lil' Long's body was still moving. He
watched as the former street hit man clenched and unclenched
his fists.

"I think we got a live one over here," the technician
announced.

"Aw c'mon, leave the man alone. Can't you see he's dying
in peace?" There was a smattering of laughter as the techs continued about their business.

"How much you think a place like this would run you?"
The question was not answered. At that moment, the sergeant
walked in. All laughter and chatter ceased.

ANTHONY WHYTE

FOUR

Lil' Long felt his body would hold out after the bullets hit but as he laid out on floor bleeding, he began to feel his body shift into uncontrollable movements. The spasms came and his face contorted as the end dawned on him. *Here it comes, the shakes.* He struggled with the thought and fought hard against surrendering.

This is not how it should end. Nah, this ain't the kid's time to go. Not yet. I'm just not ready to go. Nah, nah, especially, not like this. Lil' Long wanted to scream but could only grunt in pain. The blood in his mouth suppressed his words. They stayed burrowed deep inside. His mind burst setting thoughts afloat.

A surge of burning sensation left his senses numb to the discomfort of his journey. His insides wailed against the torment of increasing pain. *I can't go out like this, nah, not like this. Not now.* Lil' Long gripped his fists and willed himself to live as he felt blood stream from his wounds. Eyes cast downwards followed the red path of blood across the shiny wooden floor. Against the white walls of the luxury apartment, tiny splashes of blood red were repulsive against the artwork.

Police continued to arrive in droves, lightning fast. Lil' Long thought it was a good thing. He told himself that the paramedics couldn't be too far behind. He desperately needed one. With all the blue uniforms walking around, you'd think a brother dropped a bomb, he mused.

Police moved back and forth getting and searching for evidence. Crime Scene with their yellow tape sealed off areas and drew white chalk lines around the dead body. It was as if death had, in a blur, transported them into a nightmare.

The squelching of radios and walkie-talkies and the bantering of the police and paramedics brought realness to the situation. These activities along with the buzz of arriving media completed the transformation of Eric Ascot's ritzy apartment into a bonafide crime scene.

In this enclave of expensive buildings occupied mostly by affluent whites, Ascot was an outsider and was viewed as dangerous because he was black. It was probably presumed that he had orchestrated a deal where a shootout inside his apartment was the final scenario. Nary had a neighbor batted an eye at the macabre scene on the twelfth floor. It was as if the uniformed officers standing guard outside Ascot's apartment were expected to be there.

Vans filled with camera crews and reporters arrived on the scene at the ready. All of the neighbors they spoke with attested to not knowing much about Ascot except that he was black and people were shot dead in his apartment. Ascot was guilty and should go to jail. An old white lady, completely ignorant of Ascot's accomplishments in the record industry, first praised the work of the police for their quick response in catching a gun toting criminal then, after berating Ascot, apologized for the shame this hideous crime had brought on the neighborhood. Staring into the camera, the old lady used the last portion of her fifteen minutes ranting.

Inside the apartment, techs combed the place scraping here and getting samples there. An angry looking sergeant paced the scene inspecting the area. He chatted wildly on the walkie-talkie.

"Multiple gunshot wound, two victims. One appears to be fatal, checking....wait...hold your damn horses. Confirmed dead, early twenties, female. Another appears to be alive. Black male, late teen to early twenties. That's what we've got so far. Over."

Surveying the scene, Kowalski asked, "Where are the paramedics already?"

"Upstairs," an officer yelled.

"Get them down here, pronto! We've got to save this man. He maybe the last chance I...ah, we have to crack this case wide open. You agree with that, partner?"

"It's Detective Hall, not partner. And what makes you so sure that the scumbag lying there with all that blood leaking out of him is gonna make it, Kowalski?"

"Cause Detective Hall, we, you and I, are gonna make sure he gets taken to our hospital."

They eyed Lil' Long's bloodied body unmoving on the wooden floor. Detective Hall held out looking for another answer. If the hotshot detective here thinks he should live, I'll play along, Hall thought. Nevertheless, he felt Lil' Long should remain on the floor and bleed to death. It would be better for everyone. The answer was that simple but he gave his word anyway.

"All right, we'll do it your way."

"That's what I'm talking about, partner," Kowalski gushed and patted Hall on the shoulder. "You won't be sorry. You'll see." Kowalski held Hall's shoulder as he continued, "This is the big one."

"We'll see, partner," Hall said, knowing that he had already betrayed his gut feeling, something he had not done in over twenty years on the job. As a rookie, he was always reminded to trust your partner because a cop out on the street had two friends, his gun and his partner. Your survival depended on it.

Gregory Hall was a little different. He had once been the proud parent of a high school all star jock for a son who had been cut down in the prime of his life. Hall's only son succumbed to bullets from the gun of a thug like the one laying in his own blood. It would be sweet revenge if that low life just bled to death, Hall thought. But the once fulfilled father had made it to detective sergeant. Now he had to act accordingly.

He had enjoyed the ride but now he was forced to go back on one of his promises he made to himself. Let these thugs die like gangsters should, cold and with no empathy. Hall knew that Lil' Long was a career criminal who deserved to bleed until lifeless. His evils were unrepentant. It would be the right thing to do. Hall had a wife and three girls. He was a family man. He wasn't God. He was only a human being with responsibilities. He hoped that maybe one day, the ill feelings he harbored toward this type of scum would leave. Right now they were only roadblocks, he thought. Hall's focus was jarred when he heard his white partner clamoring for attention. He turned to him like a studious father dealing with an impatient child.

"You got to learn to trust me. You've got to show more enthusiasm for the team," said Kowalski before shouting, "Bring those fucking medics down here now." Hall knew he was going to have to deal with this type of immature behavior from his partner. It was what everyone expected from the highly charged junior detective. Kowalski had less than ten years on the job but he had made his bones fast by becoming a narcotics officer. He rode a wave of successful busts for three years, which landed him as detective. Young and arrogant, he wasted no time in pissing off his partner. "Come on, what is it you're waiting for?"

An officer charged upstairs to deliver the request. The owner and occupants of the apartment were in one of the bedrooms surrounded by six or seven officers. Two paramedics tended to Coco and Deedee. They sat huddled together as the paramedics, two young guys, attempted to comfort them by obviously flirting with them. The girls were cold and appeared shell shocked. They didn't seem to want to say too much.

"Y'all were pretty lucky surviving all that with just minor scratches and bruises. Wouldn't want to mess up two beautiful faces now, would we?"

The other paramedic spoke on his walkie-talkie. "Both the girls are fine and the adults are okay," he said then an officer rumbled through the door disturbing everyone.

"The sarge needs a medic downstairs right away," he said then bounded back downstairs. Coco's lips curled in silent fury. Deedee eyes slanted as they stared at each other hoping the incredible hadn't happened.

Eric turned around and looked at the girls. He heard the paramedic who had been flirting with Coco speak.

"Duty calls. It seems like we've got someone who's not ready to die just yet." The paramedics removed their equipment and went out before Eric recovered enough to ponder aloud.

"Who?" Eric asked. His question was met by an angry growl from Detective Kowalski. He leaned inside the doorway and answered.

"Well, put it like this, Mr. Ascot, you're no longer looking at double homicides," he remarked rudely.

"Man, I already told your ass that the cat downstairs with all the bullets, he was trying to rob me and the rest of the people here. He shot the other lady, a guest of mine, and I had no choice but to defend my household. Would you let somebody run up in your crib and rob you?" There were no answers. Eric continued, "I didn't think so."

"Is that your story? I'm to stand here and understand that you had no other type of problems, ah, any beef with this notorious drug dealer? You mean there were no drug deals gone bad?" Kowalski asked.

"Listen, with all due respect, detective, if you're gonna charge me with something then you just go ahead and..." Ascot was about to get on a roll but Sophia didn't want him to. She tried to intervene.

"Eric... Officer..." Sophia began. Her pleas went unheeded after the detective went beyond the limits of courtesy. His tone changed and professionalism was out the window.

"No, you listen," Kowalski shouted angrily. "The only reason your black ass ain't locked down is because your girlfriend here got connections."

The detective stood eyeball to eyeball with Eric, staring dead center in Eric's angry mug. Their faces were close enough for Eric to smell his pores. Testosterone growled loudly but cooler heads prevailed. Detective Hall tugged at his partner's arm. Eric resisted the urge to push the officer out of his face. Instead, he stood arms folded across his chest and stared furiously at Kowalski. For a couple of frantic moments, both held their ground grill to grill until a fuming Ascot made his overture.

"Before I ask you to leave my place, I want your fucking badge number. Fuck with me, I will have your job."

"All right then, Mr. High and Mighty, take a look but I want you to know that we'll be checking these guns carefully and the serial numbers better match correct. Start worrying if you see me again."

The detectives walked out of the room towards the stairs. Eric sat next to Sophia.

"The nerve of those fucking cops. They just jealous, that's all," Eric said as the other officers slowly filed out.

FIVE

The commotion had caused nearly all of the officers to leave their posts to take a look. Now as they all walked out, their mumbling was constant as they shambled down the stairs admiring the artwork on the wall.

"You believe him?" Hall asked his partner as they made their way downstairs.

"No, not one word. What about you?" Kowalski asked and turned to look at Hall.

"Everything he said after his name was a damn lie. I hate these hip hop rich kids," Hall opined.

"I know for a fact that he's more R&B, my man," Kowalski corrected.

"I guess that makes a difference, huh?"

"You goddamn right, buddy. It does make a big difference."

"Explain why."

"It means we can't request back up from the hip hop guys."

"I wasn't aware there were hip hop police," Hall was staring at Kowalski as if it was all a joke.

"I didn't say hip hop police."

"I meant cops. Squad or cop, I didn't know such a thing existed in the department."

"It goes to show you don't know everything, do you, sergeant? They're like the Keystone cops or something like that, only they specialize in cases involving the brothers."

"You shitting me. Keystone? Never heard of them." Hall threw a glance at some uniformed officers.

"No, not them. I'm talking about us, Kowalski and Hall.

You and I need to work together as a team. That's very important to the overall success of our mission as officers of the law." Kowalski knew he made sense. He had a nose for the investigation. Young, white, and hip, Kowalski was destined to be a cop. His father and his father before were. That's how the story goes. More importantly they were all heroes of one kind or the other. For Kowalski, failure at busting this or any other case wide open was not an option. Kowalski was primed and ready to take down his number one suspect. The only thing was that his partner was a respected black sergeant of detectives who may object to some of Kowalski's tactics in achieving the goal. He wanted to make sure. The young detective took jabs at the older man's chin.

"Yeah, Kowalski and Hall, we should be the Starsky and Hutch of this division," chuckled Kowalski.

"Man, I'm just too old and way too cool to have this conversation with you. Talk to your kids, they'll explain."

"How many times must I tell you? I have none."

"What're you waiting for? You need to make some then."

"Then maybe I could start understanding black folks a little better. Cuz every white kid from around the way knows hip hop and R&B are not the same," Kowalski mocked.

"Hey, easy with that racial bullshit."

"Okay, pops, I gotcha. Now let's go find ourselves some credible witnesses."

"Maybe our survivor will be the man."

Both detectives walked to where Lil' Long lay. They watched as paramedics struggled desperately to staunch the blood that dripped like water from a leaky faucet. The paramedics worked feverishly with bandages in their attempt to cover quarter sized bullet holes in Lil' Long's body. Hall frowned and turned away while Kowalski's eyes followed his every convulsion.

"Let's do this quickly. He's losing a lot of blood," a paramedic yelled.

"He's going into shock."

"Will he make it?" Kowalski asked

"We're gonna have to move fast if he's gonna live. We've got to get him to a hospital right away."

"Wait a minute. I'm gonna help. I'll ride shotgun," Detective Kowalski said to Hall.

"What are you thinking of doing?"

"Provide them with an escort. As soon as this sonofabitch regains consciousness, I wanna be there like Johnny-on-the-spot."

"You get an A plus for effort."

"No, we get pay raises and promotions after we crack this wide open. That person on the gurney may be our only real witness. So whaddya say we give the paramedics some help to the hospital, huh?"

"What do you suggest we do, open a lane?" Hall asked resigned.

"You catch on real fast for an older officer." Kowalski cranked the engine and was off in front of the paramedics.

"What're they doing?" the paramedic driving asked immediately paying attention to the route.

"They're guiding us to the hospital only used by officers," the other replied.

"I guess they really want this one to live, huh?"

"I guess. Turn on the sirens."

Wailing ambulance sirens cut through evening rush hour. Traffic flowed thick on the highway to the hospital. Even with the additional sirens of the lead detective's car, Lil' Long's journey to the hospital was going to be perilous.

The emergency vehicle wound in and out of lanes trying to find a clear path to the hospital. The detectives radioed ahead in the search of a clear lane to the emergency room.

"This is Kowalski. We need a little help."

"Go ahead with your request."

"Give me local streets to a good police medical facility."

"That's easy. Cop shot?"

"Yeah, go ahead."

"What is your position?"

In a matter of minutes, the detectives were in a hospital. They watched a team of doctors and nurses rush Lil' Long's near death body off to surgery.

"If he lives, he's gonna be your headache," Hall said sarcastically.

"In that case, I better have some aspirin handy," Kowalski replied watching the creaking gurney carry Lil' Long beyond the double doors.

SIX

In the annals of what remained of his wits, cannons bellowed. *Don't make me die, Lord, I wanna live.* He heard words cocked and reloaded in his mind but no sounds shot past his swollen lips. Instead, he choked when the pain became unbearable. Blood dripped from his mouth.

Lil' Long tried to hold on. *This is just too hard.* Internally, it felt as if bells were ringing loud in his head but he remained unable to scream or communicate. His head pounded so hard that Lil' Long closed his eyes. He stopped resisting.

A shadowy figure whose eyes he couldn't see approached him. He strained through the darkness trying to identify the figure. It was a familiar one, he was sure. Lil' Long wanted to rise but couldn't move. His mind became preoccupied with the activity. His facial muscles contorted into a silly grin. He knew he was no longer in charge of his movements. Darkness overshadowed every move but just beyond, something shone bright. The figure reached out and Lil' Long dragged himself to the light.

There was the ease of a cool breeze against his face. He could speak again but no one could hear him. The cold wind swirled cradling him. Wrapped in a blanket of wind, Lil' Long hung in mid-air on a wild spinning ride. Suddenly, he was in an amusement park laughing loudly. Though no sounds were heard, he felt a fascinating high.

Way up there with the birds, he could see his mother waving at him. Decked out in her Sunday best, her mouth opened as she attempted to tell him something. Nodding occasionally, Lil' Long pretended to be interested in what she had to say but he didn't hear a thing. He really wasn't trying to hear her.

The wind swooshed and swept him past her. He saw his

best friend, Vulcha. They were kids again, running and chasing each other, chasing pretty girls in skirts. Then Lil' Long watched while everyone disappeared from around him. Bars encircled him and once again, he was alone.

A burning sensation hit him. Lil' Long tried but couldn't block the pain. He dropped and felt his body throb and ache from the pain. Searing heat penetrated his fallen body, scorching flesh and everything else in its path. *I'll make 'em suffer. I will torment their souls on earth and in hell. Death's gonna be my revenge.*

He peeped through blood and sweat then fretted silently when his body refused the command from his brain to motivate. It seemed like it was too late and he had no other plans. There would be no backup today. A profusion of sweat appeared along with thick blood. His thoughts faded in and out.

A look of determination contorted his features. Lil' Long wanted to hang on. He knew he would if only he could bear the intense pain that came with each breath. He sighed heavy and summoned all his energy for this last ride. No matter how hard he tried, Lil' Long still felt the life seeping through his bones.

The wind warmed. Lil' Long's thoughts fought back groggily from the edge. Blinking while twisting back and forth, he could see lights. Their brightness made him dizzy with pleasure. His lips parched, Lil' long reached out to soothe the dryness. Leg irons and handcuffs restrained him making the task an impossible one.

Neither chains nor handcuffs gonna hold the kid back. I refuse to die. You can't hold me down forever. Lil' Long summoned strength through the fury of his thoughts. He gritted his teeth against the revenge he sought. *I'm gonna make them pay. They will pay for Vulcha's death and all this suffering they made me go through. I'm gonna get at them soon.*

His thoughts offered some consolation against the pain his body felt. The idea of retaliation fueled a frantic desire to recover from his injuries. Lil' Long desperately wanted to punish those he thought responsible for his present condition. His harnessed hatred worked like Novocain against physical pain. Mentally, he rejoiced when he knew that he had a chance to live.

Lil' Long's plea was a whisper, "Yeah, I'm coming for y'all."

"He's going into shock again. Let's move quickly or we're gonna lose him," a resident yelled as the elevator stopped in the lobby.

SEVEN

Rightchus had seen the paramedics and cops zoom by him. He was in the lobby of Ascot's building waiting around and was close to loitering. The doorman had asked him to leave a half hour before but Rightchus refused to go. Claiming he had business with Eric Ascot, he refused to accept the doorman's explanation that he was unavailable and demanded to see Ascot's representative. He would not budge when the doorman told him no. Rightchus was still in the lobby when the police and emergency technicians hurried by with Lil' Long lying on a gurney. Rightchus saw a second gurney with a zipped body bag. He knew that someone had been killed and not knowing that person's identity bothered him.

"I've come too far not to find out," he said and darted after the ambulance. Rightchus quickly caught up before it pulled out.

"Get back. What the hell are you doing here?" Detective Kowalski asked and grabbed him.

"Just tell me, please, who caught it and I promise I'll leave. Who caught the bad one?" Rightchus pleaded with the detective who brushed his pleas aside and attempted to walk away but Rightchus was persistent.

"This is not your concern. This is police business. Go home, Rightchus," Kowalski seethed and Rightchus stared back defiantly.

"Look, man, three or four of my very good friends were up there. I'm just trying to figure out if anyone important to me got dropped."

"That's not important to me. Now beat it."

"Look, I just hope it wasn't my girl, Coco."

"How do you know who came here today?"

"I just do. I came with them. I just..."

"Who were you here with?"

"I came here with some girls. What, you don't believe me or sump'n?"

"You're impeding official police business. Are we gonna leave today?" Detective Hall asked as he interrupted.

"Detective Hall, won't you please tell me who got shot?"

"No, I will not."

"Why?"

"It's none of your goddamn business. Let's go, Kowalski." Both detectives were off and Rightchus, realizing he still didn't know who was in the body bag, gave chase.

"Hey, yo, wait up, wait up," Rightchus shouted but the two detectives ignored his pleas. They were in their Malibu speeding away. "Them cops, they devils. That's fucked up that they don't want to inform you but when they ready for info, that's another story," Rightchus continued in disgust. He walked back, dodging traffic, and made his way home, angry at not knowing who was inside the body bag.

The devil, he doesn't want you to know yourself. That's the only way he can keep you enslaved. I guess I'll find out who got shot by watching the evening news like rest of this city, Rightchus thought as he continued down the block, stopping only to bum a cigarette.

He entered his east Harlem building and ran up the stairs to the second floor. He opened the door and threw himself onto his worn out wine colored alcohol stained sofa. It doubled as his bed but he was too edgy to sit still. Instinctively, he reached for the glass pipe lying on top of a dusty, well used end table. Searching his underwear, he fished for the vial he had stashed in the crack of his ass.

"Aha, found you. Thought I'd lost you but I know, I know. Those crack dealers," he said shaking his head, "they must be tap dancing on the shit. I can't even get a handle on it. Damn thing so skinny," Rightchus mumbled and held the piece of rock to the light.

Salivating, he fastidiously began chopping a piece of the yellow substance and frenetically packed it into a glass pipe. Rightchus cleared his throat and whipped his tongue over his lips then brought the stem to his mouth and sucked hard, deflating his cheeks in the process. With his thumb and index finger, he squeezed off air through his nostrils. His cheeks inflated and veins grew vivid in his neck.

Really hope it wasn't my girl, Coco. She wanna be a rap star. He breathed out. Her mother would die, he thought as he set the blowtorch again, lit it, and inhaled. Sweat poured down the side of his face. Rightchus smiled with the high. He let out a laugh.

That old biddy would run out and smoke up all the rock in the world and then die. That bitch is a crazy fiend. I wonder how she's doing. I know that bitch went to that drug rehab but for crack heads like me and her, there is no rehab. No turning back.

The taste made him feel so good that he was up, dancing and singing, "Once a crack head, always a crack head. You just got to have it. Ain't no turning around for me and you, sis. No rehab, no counselor, no peer pressure, no nothing. We're doomed to our fate. Our souls have been bought and paid for by the devil. Nothing can save us."

Rightchus broke off another piece and repeated the incantation, "Once a crack head, always a crack head."

The yellow flame blazed from the torch igniting another piece of impure coke and once again, Rightchus' lungs filled and he hopped around the tiny apartment. He danced, his imagination filled by a grand audience enjoying his show.

Applause followed as he focused on the decorated walls cluttered with pictures from magazines and newspapers. An assembly of some of the greatest feats in sports history was splashed across the walls of Rightchus' alcove. He was lost in examining each picture as if seeing them for the first time then he began imitating the movements captured in each picture. Kareem Abdul Jabbar forever tossing that winning skyhook over Larry Bird while the fans at Boston Garden cheered in perpetuity. Magic's smile and the Lakers' championship squad of the Eighties posed tirelessly.

"I wanna smoke rock right now. I'm Rightchus and I came to get down. I'll free base whether you're a fatty or skinny. I don't care, just you holler. I wanna smoke rocks wit'cha, ain't turning nothing down but ma collar," Rightchus sang as he drifted past pictures of Jordan in complete Nike-flight, Ali caught delivering another invisible jab, Bruce Lee executing a painful grin, and teen boxer, Iron Mike, wearing a champion's scowl with three title belts hanging around his trim waist. Rightchus waved his arms.

"I'm old school like that," he said with a smile as he plopped onto the ruined sofa and closed his eyes as if on the verge of passing out. Rightchus was on his beach building his castle of sand. He played with the birds and fishes.

A long time ago, his mother told him he would never amount to nothing. At the end of a trying teenage life, he mapped out his adult living to prove how right mothers could be. Rightchus knew he would need help to accomplish that so he formed a partnership with crack in order to accommodate a quick end to his tale of frustration. "Round here, you either smoke it, sell it, or stay the hell away from it. That's the three 'S's' to da shizzit. I do two out of three all the time," he would often brag. "I'm in control of my destiny, see."

He closed his eyes and whistled a soft melody. It must have been a favorite cause he smiled ear to ear. Rightchus carried with him the bad names and things thrown at him. He savored the moment when he would use the taunts and jeers and turn them into cheers. Rightchus smiled knowing that no matter the weather, there would always be crack and he was a survivor.

Another day, another hit. Don't blame me, blame the drugs and shit, he thought as he jumped up and reached for the volume on the old beat-box. He tried to find a station he liked. Rightchus paused briefly then continued for a while until finally, he stopped and stared at the television. Rightchus rushed over and began adjusting the antennae in the hopes of getting better reception.

"Time for the news. This bad boy better play right," he said aloud and shifted the antennae from this side to the next, right to left. Nothing he tried worked. Rightchus was on the brink of irritation when he heard the knock on the door. "Who is it?" he asked and frantically hid his works.

He peered out the peephole and immediately recognized Maruichi's spoiled daughter and her friend. They probably looking to cop sump'n, Rightchus thought as he yelled.

"Yeah, can I help y'all? What you want?"

"We want some of the stuff, you know? Like before. Can we come inside and talk, Mr. Rightchus?" one of the girls asked while the other kept a goofy grin pinned to her face.

Rightchus hesitated. "Where your father and brothers? They ain't out there waiting behind y'all, is they?" Rightchus asked but then realized that the big man's daughter was out of her league, slumming for drugs.

Lillian's father was Joey Maruichi, brother to a well-known mobster Frankie who had a hand in just about everything that happened in the hood. In the past, Rightchus had given the girls E tabs. The ecstasy pills were payment for him identifying drug spots.

After a successful bust, the police would provide the spoils as his reward. Rightchus was about the buck so he would sell most of his bounty to teenage club kids. Somehow, he'd sold tabs to Lillian's younger brother who told her of Rightchus and she came slumming for ecstasy pills.

Rightchus gazed through the peephole knowing he had no drugs but the girls pushed the right buttons. "We have money," added Lillian's friend. Rightchus' curious frown quickly converted and he morphed into hustle mode at the mention of money. A plan brewed as he released the door locks.

"What da fuck? That's all you had to say," Rightchus said graciously opening the door with a bow. "Enter. Mi casa es su casa," he continued as he stepped aside. The two young girls, about sixteen, walked into the cluttered apartment.

"Do you have the, you know, the stuff, Mr. Rightchus?" Lillian immediately asked.

The frown on his face indicated that he was thrown for a loop so she quickly added, "Same thing as the last time, Mr.

Rightchus. Only this time more." She showed Rightchus the money. He had no Ecstasy tabs but Rightchus was a con artist and he was sure that he would able to get some dollars out of these two young rich white girls.

"This is my place, you can talk. Stuff don't have to be stuff. What is the stuff you're talking?" Rightchus asked hoping to rid these girls of their money. Under the guise of trying to be helpful, the mind of a con man plotted and schemed.

"Same stuff like last time. You know? You got us thirty E-Tabs, Mr. Rightchus. We need it for our Sweet Sixteen party. All our friends are gonna be there. Wanna come?"

"Nah, I'm chilling and furthermore, what would it look like, me hanging out with y'all kids? I'm liable to go to jail. Take me for R. Kelly or sump'n. Baby, I'm too hot. Plus, I'm too dirty for y'all," Rightchus said shaking his head.

"Well, do you have the tabs?" Lillian's friend asked while Lillian reached back into her pocketbook. Rightchus saw the Benjamin's and his mind was already engaged.

"It's gonna cost five hundred dollars. You've got that, don't you?" Rightchus asked witty with a smirk.

"But, it's not the same price as the last time?"

Rightchus had forgotten the price he had quoted the last time. "E is scarce and the price got to go up. It cost a lot to export and all that overseas shipping is crazy overhead. I'm saying, you want it?" The girls looked at each other and nodded.

Rightchus licked his chops as they indicated their agreement. "Aiight, that's what I'm talking 'bout, business people. Sit down and I'll be back in two minutes. You can wait right here. I'll be back with the tabs, my sweethearts."

"Why can't we come with you? We could have the chauffer drive us."

"Nah, what it gonna look like if my connect see me in that car?"

"But the windows are tinted..."

"Look, you want the E or what? Just chill for a few. I'll be right back. Get you what you want, you smell me?" Rightchus asked and the girls nodded.

GHETTO
GIRLS
TOO

He was out the door and running to the corner store. There, he purchased a bottle of aspirin and disappeared around the corner. He ran up four flights to his friend, Jorge's, apartment.

"Yo, open the door," Rightchus yelled as he banged on the door. "Open up, dogs. I got some business. I need some tabs dogs," Rightchus continued to yell. He heard the door locks becoming undone and he began to salivate.

Five minutes later and completely out of breath, he was back in his apartment. Rightchus opened his hand to reveal a plastic bag filled with pink tablets. The girls' faces lit up. "Since y'all waited a little extra, I slipped some extra ones in there, aiight? Where the dough at?" he asked. Rightchus felt his blood pressure rise as the crisp wad of bills hit his palm. "Aiight, aiight, that's what I'm talking 'bout. Go on, get out of here with y'all bad self," Rightchus said showing the two girls the open door. "That's right, go on get out, you jailbait. Get out of here and don't be telling no grown folks about da biz. Tell only your best friends or other kids. A brother don't wanna go to the poky, ya heard?"

"You got it, Mr. Rightchus."

The girls smiled and made their way out of his apartment. Rightchus' grin widened as the girls walked away. He closed the door quickly and rushed to count the money. A smile brightened his face when he realized he had made over five hundred dollars in about ten minutes. The yellow-toothed smirk blossomed into a full chuckle as he reached for the crack pipe, lit it, and inhaled. Five hundred, the figure spiraled with smoke throughout his brain.

"It ain't my fault that the drug is really good."

Rightchus sang and smoked until all his vials were empty. Eyes wide open and sweating profusely, he stared at the television. The reception was worse. Through the fuzz of his discontent, Rightchus heard a sprinkle of the news flash.

"Coming up, two people shot, one *bzzzzz...* in a ritzy *...bzzzzzz* apartment. And *bzzzzz* heat you *bzzzzz* can handle along with sports coming up next on *bzzzzz* clock news."

Rightchus scratched his head. The buzzing annoyed him. He walked over to the where the television set was and struck it a few times with his open hand. He waited for some kind of a change but the reception got worse. Rightchus banged a few more times on the set.

"What? That's it? Get da fuck out. Come on, gimme some type of picture. Man, I wanna see who the fuck got shot," Rightchus mumbled then all the reception was gone. All he had now was snow and the accompanying hissing. He gave the broken box a couple more slaps and then left his place. "Got to get me a new television. Flat screen joint," he said and walked out onto the street. "I just hope it ain't my girl, Coco, that got shot."

Rightchus saw a neighborhood fiend approaching. "Hey, you heard about that shooting today over at that record producer, Ascot's, apartment? Huh, ya heard anything? My girl, Coco, she was there taking care of some BI, ya know?"

"I ain't heard a damn thing, dogs. Gimme a cigarette."

"I ain't got no free cigarette, man. Buy one, my brother," Rightchus said.

"Aiight, aiight, I feel you but I ain't holding nothing now. Let me hold one until..."

"Man, you ain't nothing but a crack head. Where you gonna get money to buy cigarettes? C'mon, get real. Ain't nothing free, man."

"You gonna do me like that?

"Man, you better go on. I ain't doing shit. I got places to go," Rightchus said and began singing as he walked to the Chinese restaurant. Maybe they have their television. Chinese people always paying their bills, he thought as he walked into the tiny take out restaurant with the bulletproof windows.

"Chicken wings and pork fried rice with lots of hot sauce and ketchup." Rightchus placed his order but there was no visible response. "Why y'all looking at me like that? C'mon, y'all shook, niggas? What's up?"

"You no pay, you never pay," the man behind the counter shouted back. "You pay first and then we serve you," he continued. "Every time you say you will pay, you no pay. You no have money, you don't get food."

"Man, I got money," Rightchus said as he unveiled a twenty and got the results that cash brought. "Money is king, right? Make sure you put some extra duck sauce in the bag to go."

"Duck sauce cost twenty five cent more."

"Just put the damn thangs in da bag. Duck sauce twenty five cents more," Rightchus mocked and howled to himself.

Next stop was the liquor store on the corner where he bought a pint of cheap liquor. He also found out that the person killed in the shoot out was not Coco. "It was someone else, not my girl, Coco," Rightchus said and poured some of the liquor onto the curb. "Coco, you know I don't like to waste my liquor but I'm glad it ain't you, ma girl." He sipped and C-walked his way back home.

EIGHT

"Madukes gonna flip once she finds out, yo," Coco said as she sat watching television in Deedee's room later that evening. The volume from the television was low and the girls sat, watching eagerly.

"Coco, the important thing is that we're alive," Deedee suggested. Coco agreed but with reservations.

"Yeah, that's true but you don't know my mom. I might as well be dead the way she's gonna want me to live from now on. I won't be able to go anywhere else but school for the next year. I might as well be under house arrest, yo."

"You're graduating soon. Its not gonna be that bad."

"What! It'll be to school and back home. No stopping for a minute."

"Damn, Coco, things will be crazy, huh?"

"Is it! My crazy ass mother is not gonna want to stay in rehab no more," Coco said.

"I'll ask Uncle Eric or Sophia to talk to..."

"Hold up, yo, we made the evening news?" Coco interrupted Deedee. "Look, it's coming up right now," Coco said and pointed to the wide screen television.

"Uncle E, the whole thing is on eyewitness news," Deedee yelled. She plopped back down on the bed next to Coco and paid close attention.

"Two people were shot and one fatally wounded when a gunman attempted to rob the apartment of music producer, Eric Ascot. The police recovered one of the weapons that, at the moment, is being checked by the crime lab. So far, no one has been charged. Police have one of the shooters in custody. He has been identified as Michael Lowe. He was shot and wounded.

Kamilla Davis, former model and dancer, was found shot to death in the apartment. The police are investigating the shootings and we will keep you up to date as information becomes available. Earlier this morning a flash flood destroyed..."

Coco and Deedee stared wide-eyed at each other for a second. The news story brought the unenviable feeling that they were being watched. Their reality had become television news drama.

"Oh shit. You saw that?" Deedee asked.

"How could I have missed it? I was sitting right here."

"I can't believe that we were on the news."

"No we weren't. They just talked about the shooting and said that one person was dead and another injured. That's all, yo."

"That's easy for you to say," Deedee said. She seemed to be shaken by the fact that her horrible experience had made the evening news.

"What you trying to say?

"I'm just saying. I mean, in the hood people get shot everyday?"

"So?"

"I'm just saying it's not everyday people get shot in this neighborhood. They're more violent in your hood, that's all."

"You know that may be true and all but what are you really trying to say?"

"I'm saying when you see violence around you all the time then you just expect it all the time, that's all."

"I'm not sure I understand. In the hood, people starving and if you want sump'n, you've got to go get it. Niggas can't get a job but they got families so they go and rob and..."

"Get real, Coco. People in your hood aren't robbing to feed their family. They robbing to feed their greed. Most of them are nothing but fiends."

"All the poor people in the hood ain't fiends, yo."

"Yeah, well..." Deedee was interrupted by Coco.

"You don't know no one from my hood so whatever."

"You don't have to know anyone. They're always on the news, Coco."

"And the news is always right, Deedee?" Coco asked and emphasizing every syllable of her name. This was not lost on Deedee. She knew that she had stepped out of line and offended Coco. She was trying to get a point across but it wasn't worth the friendship. Someone had to step back, Deedee thought as she saw the gritty look on the face of her friend. Deedee smiled and leaned back, not wanting to further agitate the situation. Even she had to realize that the evening news was homemade.

"I'm sorry. I didn't know I'd offend you," Deedee said and reached out to touch Coco's hand. Coco returned the squeeze.

"It's all good, yo. I guess we were both bugging on the news situation."

"I guess we were."

"My mother never misses the evening news though. She's gonna be calling around to see where I am," Coco said after a beat. She shrugged before adding, "I'd better call her, yo."

"Use my phone, girl," Deedee said pointing to the cordless. "I'll go see what's with my Uncle and Sophia," Deedee said and walked out the room.

I can't blame Coco for being spooked after seeing the news. Shoot, I'm a nervous wreck too, Deedee thought. Before closing the door, she asked, "I'm getting something to drink. You want anything?

"Aiight, that's what I'm talking about. Got some Henny?" Coco asked with a chuckle.

"Coco, I'm talking something lighter. Soda, water, juice, something in that family," Deedee said with a smirk and Coco laughed.

"I'm just playing around, yo. Water is good," Coco said and began dialing the digits to the Green Acres Substance Abuse Center.

The center was located in a commercial area on the eastern border of Queens known as 'Crack Central'. The drug rehab center boasted a high success rate. It was outfitted with its own dining room and single bedrooms. There were two conference rooms, a large one for general assembly meetings and a smaller one for therapy and counseling sessions. Separated by a long hallway, the lounge and recreation area were located next to the small gymnasium. The offices were close to the recreation area. The place only hosted women.

Its shadowy pasture gave the place the feel of a farm outside. Although there was some amount of gardening done, the produce was mostly used for the participants in the drug rehab program. Staff members and residents shared in the duties of taking care of the property. It was supposed to teach self-reliance to the residents. That was part of the goal of the program.

Rachel Harvey had been involved with recovery for the past six months. She had spent the last two months as a resident. Time and time again, Mrs. Harvey had expressed how much she hated staying there. She wanted out but stayed at the behest of her daughter, Coco.

Rachel left the conference room and walked through the lounge area. It was the shortest route to the reception area. She wore a blue silk dress that Coco had bought her for her birthday. Her stay had improved her diet and with that, she had gained a few necessary pounds. She walked with a youthful prance through the assembly hall then through the adjoining hall where there were several phones.

"Your daughter is on line number two," the receptionist said as she made her way past the reception area. Mrs. Harvey picked up line two and heard Coco's voice on the other end.

"Coco, whatcha doing calling me in the middle of my meeting? If it was so damn important, you should've brought your black ass over here. What is it, child? Coco? Coco? You there?"

Coco was surprised by her mother's reaction. She did not know quite what to say.

"Coco, why did you call? If it's to hang out at some damn party, the answer is hell no. You're not hanging out during the week from Monday to Thursday. Hanging out is not in your dictionary so hang it up."

"Ma, have you seen the news yet or heard anything?"

"No why? You won the lotto or sump'n, child? Stop playing and tell me what I missed. Don't tell me you got arrested 'cause I'm not coming down to no damn central booking. And if I find out that you're pregnant then God help you. You heard me, Miss?"

"Nah ma, it ain't none of that."

"Then why the hell you be calling outta the blue if this ain't no emergency? Do you know you're disturbing me at my meeting, girl? My spirit is weak and I'm doing all I can to get out of here."

"I'm sorry ma. Listen, I'll call you later. Take care. I just wanted you to know I'm all right, okay?"

"Okay Coco. I really really don't have time to talk to you right now but I'll call you later. Okay, honey?"

"Bye, mommy."

"Bye, Coco."

Rachel Harvey hung up the telephone and mumbled under her breath as she walked back to the assembly hall. She looked at the television but failed to notice the evening news regarding Eric Ascot as she went past the reception area. Rachel Harvey had only one thing on her mind and saw another reason why she had to leave this place for good.

That daughter of mine is going insane. Poor girl probably just miss me. She always trying to be so hard. I guess she gets that from me. I miss being there for her but most of all, I miss my freedom.

Rachel's thoughts were riveted on not being where she couldn't be or who she was. She had failed to utilize her environment. The place she had been confined to for the past six weeks was a residential treatment program for drug addicted mothers. The stay proposed by her welfare worker was six week to eight weeks. Rachel was mandated to attend the program or be kicked off the welfare roll after one of her weekend binges landed her in the hospital.

Doctors told her that the ventricles to her heart had shrunk due to crack abuse and warned that repeated abuse could result in a fatal heart attack. Her medical condition along with the doctor's advice scared Rachel so she decided to enter the residential treatment.

From day one, she resented being at the center. She

wanted to do outpatient but went along when the doctors told her she could die with the next heart attack. It made her think twice about the habit. Come Monday, it would be six weeks. It was time for her to leave and there was no time for what she considered to be Coco's idle gestures.

The things my daughter goes though to keep me off her trail, Rachel mused. *She didn't want mommy to worry. That's Coco, that's my daughter and that's her father.* Rachel Harvey was convinced that her daughter wanted to do everything to make her stay at the center but Rachel wanted to leave the place.

"That girl going crazy and she's gonna drive me crazy right along with her if I stay here," Rachel Harvey said to herself. "I'll find out the real reason she called and when I do..." Rachel never completed the thought. She just shook her head and went back to her meeting for the day.

NINE

Coco tried to appear confident despite feeling a little disconcerted. Her attempt at explaining the shooting incident to her mother had resulted in failure. Over and over, it crossed her mind that her mother would eventually learn of the shootings from the news then she would call everyone hysterically searching for her.

I could've prevented all that, Coco thought and stared blankly at the television set. There wasn't much left to do now except to wait and face the music. Intellectually, Coco sped through the process. She'll scream at me and then curse me and compare me to my dad and tell me I can't go out ever again. What the hell! Coco's musings hummed so loudly she didn't hear Deedee return.

"Hello? Earth to Coco," Deedee said. Coco immediately snapped back to reality.

"Uh, my bad, I didn't even hear when you came back, yo."

"What happened? Were you able to speak to her?" Deedee asked and gave Coco a glass and a bottled water. "What did she say?"

"Me and my mom..." Coco started and shook her head. "I don't know, yo."

"Does that mean you didn't actually tell her?"

"No, we spoke but she did all the talking. She told me that she knew why I called. Madukes be OD'ing sometimes, yo."

"But you still got love for her. Me on the other hand, I don't even know where my mother is."

"I guess you could say me and mines have grown to understand each other."

"My uncle is all I've got. My mother's behavior was so shameful."

"Yeah, that monster crack'll make you do wild shit," Coco

said and both girls sipped.

Deedee thought about it then asked, "Coco, what would cause you to disown your mother?"

"What are you asking?"

"I'm just saying, you've stood by your mother through a lot."

"I feel like she's part of me. That's what I'm supposed to do, you know? I think if it was the other way around, she would've stuck by me too."

"So you're always gonna be sticking by her no matter what?"

"I mean, yeah, but it's like I'm not trying to ruin my life in the process. I'm definitely a hundred percent in her corner though."

"So there's nothing that would make you ashamed to call her your mother?"

"Why? C'mon Dee, we're all human and we all have our faults. She's my flesh and blood, my mother. You know you can't be ashamed of that, yo."

"I hear you, Coco. I hear you, girl," Deedee said and thought briefly about her mother. She let the thought go when she heard the voices of her uncle and Sophia.

"They sound like they beefing. Is that what they doing?" Coco asked. She could also hear the voices in what sounded like an argument.

"They're deciding on where to spend the night."

"What're the choices?"

"Well, it's between a hotel or Sophia's apartment. The hotel is leading so far."

"What's causing the hold up?"

"Everything. I don't think my uncle wants to go there. They're arguing about space at Sophia's apartment."

"Why?"

"She has a two bedroom apartment. Her home office occupies one of the bedrooms which leaves only one other bed-room and there are three of us."

"That ain't that big of a problem." Coco nodded and lit a

cigarette. "I'm saying, you could stay at my place if you want," Coco puffed and saw a curious hesitation on Deedee's face. "I mean my mother ain't there so you're welcome to stay and that would leave your uncle with his fiancé."

"Nope, it's not happening," Deedee said and wandered over to the huge mirror. She fixed her shirt and pulled the collar closed. "My uncle isn't going to let me off the leash after all this, Coco. And then you know your area is like Vietnam. My uncle would rather leave his fiancé's side than see me in that area. Sorry."

"I guess you're right, yo. Ain't nada sweet in da hood, you know what I'm saying? Damn place is even too dangerous for peeps who are from there much less your type," Coco said with a snarl in her tone. It served as a forewarning to Deedee. She had stepped on a time bomb again. Deedee slowly backpedaled.

"Um, Coco, I didn't mean nothing. I'm just saying Uncle E, he's not gonna send me anywhere. That's all I really meant to say."

"It's all good, yo. I'm gonna get up out of here," said Coco.

"Where are you going?" Deedee asked.

"To da hood where I'm from," Coco said and began a street bop. She turned and looked at Deedee and said. "Back to the ghetto, ya heard?"

"Look, if I offended you, I'm sorry."

"You didn't. You just told the truth is all you did. See, I ain't scared when in my hood. I'm used to the roaches, the mice, and the crack heads. They all know me. I ain't got to front like I was born with a silver spoon in my mouth. You feel me? I'll holla at you. Peace out."

"Coco, you're taking this way out of context. I didn't say I was scared of anything happening. It's just that my uncle wouldn't send me anywhere after today especially..." Deedee stopped short and her voice trailed off. She looked down on the floor and then the tears welled in her eyes. "Coco, we've..."

"Look Dee, me and you, we different. We cut from the same cloth but I've got different patterns."

"Coco..."

"Let me finish, yo. See I know where I'm from, the people are poor and it's the ghetto. The crime rate is high and a whole lot of shit be popping off but that's what I rep and I can't change that," Coco said and paused as if she needed time to formulate her thoughts. "You can stay chilling in your ivory tower thinking that you're safe 'cause you're here and not there, yo." Deedee stared at her, shocked.

"Coco, you've got it all wrong. My uncle is in charge of me and I have to do as he says. I mean, I would go back to your mother's place with you but my uncle wouldn't let me even..."

"Even what?"

"He's just not gonna let me."

"And if he did let you?"

"I'd go, yeah, but I'd be scared. You're used to the rats and roaches. I don't feel safe..."

"Aw c'mon, they got rats and roaches all over the city," Coco said and paced back and forth before she continued. "You ain't got to front for me, girl. You don't wanna come to da hood, that's all. You could just say it like it is," Coco said.

Deedee frowned and looked away. Maybe she's right, Deedee thought but my uncle wouldn't send me anyway.

"You know what, you're right, Coco. I wouldn't feel safe there."

"Even if it's just like an overnighter, yo?

"No, I just don't think Uncle E would let me and if he did and I had the choice, I'd rather spend the night at a hotel than in the hood." Deedee was decisive and Coco knew there was no point arguing the issue. Nevertheless, she felt compelled to after seeing this side of Deedee.

"I can't blame you. I wouldn't leave my nice, safe pad for the ghetto either but that's where I live and that's where I've got to go. I don't have a nice apartment somewhere downtown."

"You don't have to go there like that."

"I'm just saying my mother and I live in the hood. If we lose our apartment then we'll probably wind up in a shelter or sump'n. I ain't got no rich uncle or..."

"That's not what I mean and you know it."

"So whatcha saying, yo?"

"I don't know. I just feel safer around here," Deedee replied and thought about it after she had said it. Maybe it was too harsh but it was what she felt and she thought she could be honest with Coco. She did not expect a verbal backlash but felt that one was brewing.

"How could you feel safe around these people and not feel safe around your own?" Coco asked in a tone that barely disguised her anger.

"I don't know," Deedee said pausing to think her answer through clearly. It was the only one she had. She didn't want to say anything that might further draw Coco's ire but Coco's flared nostrils alerted her to the fact that she already had. Coco's response was swift.

"I hear you. I'm out, yo."

"Coco, Coco, wait up," Deedee shouted after Coco but the girl had already retrieved her jacket and was out the door. Sophia and Eric were at the foot of the stairs when Coco rushed by bidding them goodbye in a hurry.

"I'll see y'all."

"Coco, is everything all right?" Sophia asked as the disgruntled teenage girl bolted for the front door.

"Everything is good. Just got to go home and take care of some things."

"I'll drive you there if you want."

"No, it's aiight. Good looking out, Sophia, but I got it," Coco said and with a nod of her head, she was through the door.

TEN

Sophia locked the door and turned to see the look on Deedee's face. She knew something had gone wrong between the girls.

Deedee's expression changed to disgust as she slowly made her way down the stairs to stand next to Eric. He was in the midst of drinking a beer and examining the damage to the den and the kitchen. Sophia joined the two near the kitchen. Deedee's arm was wound about her uncle.

"We could probably fix it all for about 20 grand or so," Eric said looking at the furniture and assessing the damage to the apartment. This had been his dream home he had specially built after his first million. He had wanted to shout out something to the whole world. From his fortunes made in the music industry, Eric owned a two million dollar, six-bedroom apartment that came complete with a half a million dollar recording studio. It was worth every penny to Eric.

Eric knew that with his talents and business savvy, there were always fortunes to be made in the music industry. Eric Ascot had enjoyed his fill. With his cup still running over, he could afford to indulge in excess. Eric owned a summer home in the Hamptons along with a Florida pad. He was not lacking for places. He wasn't living life lavishly but he had the means to do that.

He grew up thinking of the day when he'd have enough money to do whatever he wanted to do. When his brother had been killed and Deedee's mother was strung out on drugs, Eric Ascot had bought this place. Deedee was coming to live with him and he wanted to move out of the old neighborhood. He was really proud of the place.

That was up until a half hour ago before uniformed

officers and crime lab people descended. They left yellow taped off sections and now his dream crib had been transformed into a nightmare. It was a crime scene.

What had occurred in his apartment had been the result of a fatal mistake. Maybe he could erase it but Eric had to talk to Busta. That was important. Somewhere deep in his mind he knew that this was only the beginning of it all.

"Or we could sell it. You know the board is gonna rule against any further stay," Sophia said. She moved closer to Eric and Deedee. "Besides, my skin crawls whenever I look around this place. It just doesn't feel right anymore."

Eric embraced Sophia and kissed her lips cutting off her protest. He rubbed her forehead lightly with his lips. Deedee stood apart and watched.

"Uncle E, I thought you said we could fix it up?" Deedee asked and stared as she waited for an answer.

"Deedee, you don't understand but he's got to sell the place," Sophia addressed Deedee. She turned back to Eric and said, "Promise that you're gonna sell."

"Sophia, do we have to sell our home? I mean like Uncle E says, it can be fixed and it won't cost a lot of money to do so," Deedee offered in protest.

"It just stirs up this creepy feeling every time I think I'll have to come here. I don't want have to think of what happened. Furthermore, the board of trustees probably will vote against him staying."

"Well, we could still live here until..." Deedee started but her uncle raised his hand averting any ensuing argument.

"You know what? Sophia is right. I'll sell the place and we'll buy another one that's better," Eric decided and moved to embrace his fiancé and niece. No sooner had he said the words than Deedee dashed off. Sophia turned away from his hug.

"What's with Dee?" she asked.

"I don't know. Maybe she really likes it here. It's a nice place," Eric said and looked at Sophia for a response but got none, at least not immediately.

She hugged herself before saying, "It was a nice place,

Eric." Taking a sip of his beer, she asked, "What do you make of what happened here?"

It was her turn to wait for an answer. Eric gulped his beer until it was gone. All the time, he knew Sophia's almond shaped eyes, though soft brown at times, were peering at him. Eric felt the sting of her scorn when she added, "Eric, we're not taking it back to the streets," Sophia said. "Are we?" Eric said nothing. Sophia continued, "We're no longer street people. We can't take it back there. I won't let you ruin me, yourself, or Deedee."

"C'mon, Sophia, you don't know what you're talking about. Listen, you're just speculating. I'm saying, why couldn't this cat want to just straight up rob me? Or someone out there could be hating and coming at..."

"Did it have anything to do with Busta, huh, Eric?" Sophia dropped the bomb of a question on Eric. She saw his eyebrows draw closer together causing a wrinkle in his forehead. Eric took a detour from his answer and speculated.

"Honestly, I don't really know for sure if this is related to Busta or not," Eric said shaking his head and paused for a minute. He knew that Busta was Sophia's client. Had Busta said anything to let her think otherwise?

As Eric became preoccupied, Sophia's focus shifted to the worried expression on his face. She reached around to hug him and kissed him hard on his cheek. In her heart, she knew she loved him and wanted him no matter what. Yet, Sophia felt something amiss and desperately wanted to trust Eric. She looked into his eyes. He was the man she had chosen to share her life with. Even though they had not set a date for their wedding, both knew it was inevitable and it was just a matter of them fixing their schedules to accommodate it. Sophia did not want the wedding plans to be rushed but she could not decide on a date.

"Why do you figure I'm trying to ruin anyone here?" she heard Eric ask. Her eyes searched his. Their stares pierced each other's heart. They stayed that way as Sophia spoke.

"Because he came here to kill you or us. I know it's definitely not me because I haven't done anything to cause someone named Lil' Long to wanna put a cap in my ass, Eric. I'm not a stupid or dumb broad, Eric. Just fess up and tell it all." Sophia was angry. Eric tried not to push any of her other buttons.

"I didn't say you were dumb."

"Well, please stop treating me that way. That guy came here with a plan to kill one of us and I just want to know why?"

"It could be anything. I done told you, people hating on me, you know. There are a lot of people out there who don't like to see a brother succeed. They wanna see you locked up or hear that you rotting in jail so people come at you."

"Come at you for what? Why you?"

"Because I'm Eric Ascot and they think I'm holding the bank. There are people walking around who would cut my throat just because they think I'm stacking cheddar or sump'n."

"I buy that to an extent but there are artists who are always in the public spotlight and this doesn't happen," Sophia argued. A thought ran through her head and she quickly added, "Well, rap stars seeking the limelight are always fighting and shooting at other rap stars who they perceive to be in their way. This is not a rap war, Eric, or is it?" Sophia searched Eric's brown eyes looking for answers. He had known her long enough to sense that she knew he wasn't on the up and up. It was the way she knitted her brow. Eric saw the sadness in her eyes. He couldn't see the current of emotions running through her but he knew. "Why?" She asked.

"Honey, if I knew the answer to that then I would be able to tell you. I don't know why people want to come at me. I don't know," Eric said as he felt her unrelenting stare cut right through him. It caused sweat ducts in the nape of his neck to act up but he held his ground. "Sweetheart, you've got to trust me," he said. Eric hugged and kissed Sophia again. "I, we just got to be really careful. I'll keep my ears open cause you know someone will know something."

"Please be up front about this, honey, because my reputation with the DA may ride on what you say," Sophia said and brushed Eric's lips with hers. "Eric, I'm not gonna stand by and let my career be ruined. I've worked long and hard trying to carve my niche in this field and you know how difficult it has been for me.

So please try and understand when I tell you to just be level with me, alright?"

"Yes, I do honey." Eric kissed her hard and walked with a trembling heart up the stairs. "Let's go pack an overnight bag. We'll stay at your place until tomorrow."

ELEVEN

Eric Ascot's apartment was located on the sixteenth floor of a towering high class building. The residents were local stock-brokers and six figure assistants. Coco knew that the shooting had caused bedlam but by the time she reached the lobby hours later, the flow of people appeared to be calmer. Coco lit a ciga-rette and made her way outside. She paused and puffed before hailing a cab.

A car screeched to a stop in front of her barely avoiding Coco's feet. Two detectives jumped out of the car and grabbed the alarmed teen.

"Hold on, yo. What y'all doing? I ain't done nothing wrong, yo. What's this all about, yo? What da fuck! I don't wanna go anywhere with y'all. Leave me alone. Why am I in cuffs? You gonna tell me?"

"Just shut up and listen. Now you can be an accomplice to murder or you can tell us right here and now what really went down up there?" Detective Kowalski yelled in her face.

Despite her protest, Coco was thrown into the backseat of an unmarked police car. There she sat with a vicious stare clamped onto the faces of the two detectives, one black and one white. She had seen them earlier. Coco kept her mouth shut and her eyes shot daggers.

"So you're gonna play tough girl, huh?" the detective con-tinued.

Coco looked out the window in time to see Eric, Deedee, and Sophia driving away in their green Range Rover. I should've caught a ride from them. Man, what was I thinking? she wondered then her mind refocused on her present condition.

"Look, I don't know anything else. The guy walked in to rob everyone and Eric was in the bathroom and must've heard the ruckus or sump'n. He shot the guy after homey shot ah... the girl ...ah, Kamilla. That's all. Now, let me go," Coco said and sat up in the seat.

"Now let me say this to you. Did you see how those rich people drove by without us touching them? They think they're big fish and they can get away with everything. That leaves you and me, the small fish, to account for their shit. For some reason, you're supporting them. Think they would support you?" As the detective spoke, Coco casually listened without saying anything. "They would send you down the river without a paddle. I want you tell me what was your business with them and what was going on up there?"

"I'm working with Eric Ascot. He's producing some songs."

"What, you're a singer or a rapper?"

"I'd like to go now, please."

"Listen here, girlie, those rich fucks, they don't give a shit. They're the type of people who'd sooner leave you holding the bag for all these murders, you hearing me? Why don't you let us take you home while you tell us everything?" Kowalski asked. Coco stared him down. He didn't budge. "Where do you live?"

"I'd like to leave right now," Coco replied firmly. The officer pretended as if he was going to swing at her. Coco didn't even blink.

He released the handcuffs and kept talking. "You think you're a tough girl, huh?" He was in Coco's grill. The teenager bit her tongue while the look she wore shot daggers at him.

"See you around, Coco," Hall said as Coco released the handle and jumped out of the car. She stood watching as it screeched off.

"Fuck y'all," Coco yelled as she fished for another cigarette and lit it. She began to walk when she saw a cab. She hailed it and it stopped. "One-tenth and Lennox," she said then continued smoking. The cabbie refused to move. Coco looked at him indifferently. The cabbie pointed to the sign.

"Can you read the sign back there, Miss?" the cabbie insisted. Coco looked at the sign. It read 'No Smoking'.

Coco squeezed the last suck out of the cigarette before she flicked it out the window. She leaned back and looked at the cabbie.

"Ahight, you happy now, my man?"

"Good to go," the cabbie replied as he sped off. Coco could not shake the thought of what had just happened.

She was sure Lil' Long was there to murder someone but why? Coco made a promise to herself to catch up to Rightchus when she got back to the hood. He would bring the 411, she thought as light ruled the skyline of the city. "Right here is good." She paid the fare and exited the cab.

The chill of the cool night hit Coco. She popped her collar as she made her way to her building. She knew that when the story broke in the hood, there would be further questions. Right now, she didn't want to do any talking.

Coco raced upstairs foregoing the 'Now Working' sign on the door of the elevator. She tried to hurry past Miss Katie's door without too much noise but the old lady was waiting and called to her as she attempted to go by.

"Coco, Coco, girl, I was hoping you were all right. I haven't heard from you and got worried. Did you see the news today? I think those men you were talking about, ah, Busta and Eric Ascot, they involved in killings and murders and Lord knows what else. Child, you listening to me? I'm concerned."

"Miss Katie, it's all right. Give me a couple minutes and I'll come by and talk to you, okay?"

"Okay. Have you eaten?" Miss Katie asked. Before Coco could reply, Miss Katie continued. "By the way, your mommy done called at least six times trying to find you. She sez you called sounding disturbed. Are you all right? You know you can tell ol' Miss Katie anything now, girl. God will work it out. There's no problem on this earth that He can't fix. Bless His name." Coco cut the old lady off before she could build a full head of steam.

"Miss Katie, I'm gonna be right back. I promise," Coco said looking for any way out of talking. She wanted to be alone and added before she quickly sped off, "We'll pick up where you left off, okay?"

"All right now. Don't go inside and go to sleep without coming and getting something to eat. I made some chicken smothered in bacon grease with sweet yams and cornbread."

"Hmm, sounds yummy. I'll be right back, Miss Katie."

"Hurry back Coco, I'll tell you 'bout them crazy people up in apartment 6F."

"See you in a minute."

"All right, child. If your crazy mother calls again, she done called about ten times...anyway, if she calls again, I'll let her know you're okay. But don't you go falling off to sleep without you first getting something to eat, you hear?" Miss Katie said and watched Coco disappear into her apartment. She called after her again but it was too late. The teenager had made good her escape to the quiet of her mother's apartment. The older lady thought of going after her but decided to wait until later to let Coco know about the visit by the police.

TWELVE

Behind the renovated door of her mother's one bedroom apartment, Coco went to the window and tried to shut the world out. She felt like her every move was being watched. Were eyes trained on her? she wondered. Coco moved around the apartment trying to cover up the different angles from which someone might be spying on her. She wound up pulling all the curtains shut then sat down on the sofa and flipped on the television. Coco saw flashes of the news and finally settled on music videos. She laid down and closed her eyes for a few minutes, still attempting to shut out the world.

Mental images kept invading her attempts. First, Kamilla then Lil' Long going down in a hail of gunfire. She, holding a gun in her hand, gawking at the surprised look on Deedee's face then the argument that ensued. Was it wrong for Eric to cover up the truth? Was it the right thing for him to do? Who knew? I mean he could've definitely have shot Lil' Long. That mug deserved to die. He already caused enough grief. I wonder what he's gonna do? The question came with no relief. I'm sure he's gonna come back at us if that sucker lives. Was that what had made her feel upset at Deedee? No. Deedee was out of bounds. She had no business criticizing anyone's neighborhood. That was that.

The knock at the door stirred her from her semi-coma back to the real world.

"Who is it?" Coco asked slowly rising from the sofa.

"It's me. Deedee is on the phone. She wants to know if you're alright." It was Miss Katie. For a moment, she considerd asking her about the conflicted feelings she felt toward Deedee. Coco decided it wasn't the right time.

"Tell her I'm fine. I'm in the shower trying to get the dirt out of my hair. I'll call her back later," Coco yelled.

"Will do, Coco. Hurry, you hear?"

"Okay, thanks." Coco hurried to turn on the shower and pumped the volume of the television higher.

"...Beautiful, I just want you to know that you're my favorite girl..."

Pharrel's chorus suddenly invaded the apartment. Coco's bootie shook to the Snoop Dog laced track. She felt a tinge of happiness at the knowledge that Easter break was here and it would be another week before she'd see Deedee back at school. Coco figured by then any resentment felt toward Deedee should be gone. I'll shower then go call my mother. See how she is holding up. I'll be all right, Coco thought as the spray of the water hit her naked body.

THIRTEEN

Rachel Harvey examined her features in the mirror. She had been slowly stacking the pounds back onto her once emaciated body. She noticed her skirt fit better as she ran her hands over a now shapely behind. I'm packing on the pounds in the right places, she thought as she posed, turning from side to side.

No longer wafer-like, she contemplated the physical changes she had gone through. "I look good. I don't need no make-up," Rachel said then turned to leave her room, closing the door behind her. She walked the familiar path to the assembly room.

The walk to the assembly area was something that she had been doing for the past forty-five days. She walked along the corridor with the other members of her group knowing this was the last group meeting for her. Rachel wanted out of the residential rehab program. She had already mentioned it to her counselor who told her she would consider it.

Rachel Harvey felt cured. All of her urine samples were clean. Now she could return to her active welfare status and maybe even look for a job. The thirty-four year old single parent had walked this strip before and the dirt in between the tiles was familiar. Rachel felt ready to handle the outside world. For her daughter's sake, she had to be prepared.

Last night, she had watched the late version of the evening news and had called leaving messages everywhere trying to find out if anyone had seen her daughter. Finally, Miss Katie had called back to say that she had seen Coco and everything was alright.

Relieved, Rachel had wiped the tears from her eyes. It seemed like everything was happening all at once. She walked into the group meeting already in progress and joined in the incantation.

"Lord, grant me the serenity to accept the things I cannot change and the courage to change what I can and the wisdom to know the difference. Your blessings we ask in the name of Jesus Christ. Amen."

She muttered along with the rest of the group then took her seat and glanced around to see who was leading the group meeting. One person is chosen ahead of time to be in charge of the group discussion. The names appeared daily on the bulletin board. Residents would check the board twice daily. It was not a life or death situation, just done to ensure that residents were kept up to date of any changes. Most of the time because there were hardly ever changes, one could get by with just checking the bulletin board once.

Because of the problems Rachel had reaching Coco, she never got the chance to see the bulletin board. She knew that the topics are usually centered on relationships, whether family or personal. Sometimes, sex was discussed.

The leader is expected to bare her soul to the group while discussing freely any intimate part of her life based on the chosen theme for the day. There were times when the group leader was so off base that the entire group walked out the meeting. Politics and religion were topics rarely debated. Leaders, whose meetings went bad, always wound up crying. She looked around to see who today's leader was gonna be. Rachel Harvey was surprised when without warning, her name was called. She sat stunned.

"Rachel, have you had a chance to read the bulletin board recently?" The question came from group counselor, Fatima Murray. These counselors can be such assholes, thought Rachel. She felt the uneasiness mount and knew immediately that it was her turn. What was the theme of the day, she wondered. "And, as you know, the theme is family relationships."

"No, I didn't look at it this morning. You know, my daughter? She's been involved in some, ah, trouble and I was just trying to make sure she was straight and that just took all night. Maybe I can go another time or..." Rachel bobbed and weaved in an attempt to get out of the task.

"The theme, Rachel, is family relationships. You know how we talked the other day about certain things that are going on in your life? Well, I was thinking that maybe, without going into detail, you can give us your unique take on it."

"In terms of my family?" Rachel asked feeling that uneasiness in her stomach. She was just not prepared. The conversation with Fatima had been a private discussion. She was unwilling to discuss the death of Coco's father with anyone right now. Deep in thought, Rachel could hear the counselor's voice.

"Just imagine you're talking to me. You don't have to share everything and the group will be able to participate in the discussion."

"But I'm just not talking to you. I'm talking to every freaking soul in the room."

"That's the idea, girl," a group member yelled out.

Rachel Harvey's slow march to leadership took some time to begin. She eventually made it to the center of the room and stood in the leader's position. For a minute, she was completely intimidated by the faces gawking back at her.

What am I gonna say? she pondered. They don't really wanna hear me. Most times I sit in my seat wondering what we're gonna have for supper. This is for the birds, she thought. She looked at her audience and they started to clap.

"Aw c'mon, you've got to be kidding me. It really isn't that serious, people," Rachel started saying. "What it is is what it is. I am Rachel Harvey and I'm a drug addict. I started using drugs, smoking weed at seventeen. By twenty two, I had two abortions and was pregnant for the third time with my daughter, Coco." Rachel could feel the tears welling inside. She paused and tilted her head back.

She did not want to cry but it was happening anyway. Rachel, despite what she had become, held onto an inkling of pride and became defensive whenever she felt she had to explain herself. She could get off crack. All she had to do was stop smoking it.

Rachel wanted to let the group know that she didn't need

them or anyone else. She stared at their inquiring faces, their eyes prying into her privacy and digging away at her defenses. Testing, everyday they tested her patience. She heard their voices knocking at her conscience.

"Amen, sister. We all got troubles but there is no trouble too great for God to handle," a group member encouraged the faltering speaker.

"Lord knows I've tried to be a good mother. I thought I'd found me the right man and we had a good plan. But, I found out years later, after becoming hooked to the monster, crack, that the devil is out there and he also has a plan. A plan to destroy me and my family through drugs. I don't want drugs to destroy my daughter," Rachel said and knew right away that she wouldn't be able to stop the tears. She let them flow.

"Preach," a group member shouted.

"Tell it, girl," came another voice of support. Rachel gathered herself and continued.

"My daughter, Coco, means everything to me. Her father, God bless his soul, he passed away recently and my daughter, she doesn't know. He sent me his guitar and that's all he left." Rachel paused to catch her breath. She choked from the tears and someone offered her water. She accepted and downed half the glass.

"Preach on, sis."

"My daughter doesn't know that her father is dead. You see, I just found out."

"When are you gonna tell her?" a group member asked.

"I'm not sure but it's gonna be soon," Rachel answered.

"What is the problem?" Another member asked.

"I just wanna wait, that's all. I don't know how to say it."

"You just got to say the words. Honey, your father is dead. I don't see what's so difficult about it?"

"Maybe you don't see but I do, okay."

"I hear you, sis, but I would've told my daughter. If you say you love her as much as you're standing there reciting. Love is not a word. Love is a feeling and it seems to me that you're hiding behind that word. That's all there is to that."

Maybe it was the braggadocious attitude but Rachel

couldn't take it. "Well I don't give a fuck what your fat ass thinks and you best shut your mouth before I come over there and whip that fat ass, bitch. What?"

"Whatever."

"Rachel, Rachel please stop now. Nobody is gonna whip anybody's ass, alright? Please get that out of your mind right now. Ladies, ladies, quiet please." The voice of the counselor could be heard bellowing above all others. The argument between Rachel Harvey and the other member had gotten out of hand. Another counselor, Ms. Johnson, was forced to intervene. She had waited hoping for a peaceful resolution but the exchange had been angry. Both parties were on the verge of coming to blows. Rachel Harvey was unrelenting.

"That's what y'all people do. Sit around and judge people. Who's gonna judge y'all? Thinking y'all better than everyone?"

"Rachel, you've got to stop that right now. Stop it, please," Fatima begged the angry woman. Both women had to be held back by other group members. "Well, ladies, this concludes this evening's meeting. I guess everyone with the exception of Rachel may return to the dormitory." The counselor dismissed everyone from the meeting.

Group members filed out and some commented, "That's what we need round here, some fire. Shake things up."

"Keep your head, ma," others said has they passed by Rachel. She stood alone her chest heaving with little beads of sweat on her forehead. She crossed her arms and cut her eyes. Her body shook and she shifted weight from side to side. It had not been an easy day for her.

"What got into you?" Fatima asked pulling her down to sit in one of the armchairs.

"Nothing, you know me. That bitch, she always wanna start with me. When I was on clean-up duties last week, the bitch gonna approach me like I'm a child. I'm a grown woman, you know what I'm saying? I will not let her speak to me as if I was her child, damn butch bitch."

"Alright, you don't have to berate her. You were doing so well up there. I'd hope that we could continue because by you talking about all the frustrations with trying to raise your child, it seemed like you were getting some sort of strength. Tell me about it," requested Mrs. Murray.

"Well, I really was nervous at first but it was getting easier the more I spoke on my issues, me and my daughter, and about how we relate to each other is important. That was what I was getting to before miss big mouth put her two cents in it." Rachel looked away then back. "See, that's why I've got to leave this place," Rachel cried. Tears were flowing down the side of her cheeks.

"You shouldn't leave this place until you're ready to," responded Fatima. There were other groups and residents going by and everyone seemed to take interest. They peeked and stared until the counselor suggested a change of venue.

"Let's go to my office and we can talk in private there." Ms. Murray turned the lights off as both women walked out of the room.

FOURTEEN

Rachel Harvey had resented being on the inside since the beginning. She, however, had learned to accept her fate through the encouragement of friends and counselors she had met while staying at the Green Acres Rehab Institute. She knew exploding in the group meeting would bring her demerits but it was something that was inevitable. It was born from a desperation to leave this place. Rachel sat and stewed as her thoughts brooded over the last time she had met one on one with the counselor.

"Have you told Coco anything about her father's passing as yet?" Fatima Murray had asked.

"Why? Does it matter?" Rachel had responded indifferently.

"Yes, it does matter. She needs to know such things. It's important."

"I haven't really told her. I guess I'm sorta waiting for the right time."

"When is the right time, Rachel? It's been over a week now and the guitar and the package he left for her are still here gathering dust in my office."

"If you want, I could take them out. I mean, I didn't mean for them to be there this long. Matter of fact, let me just get them right now."

"Listen, Rachel, there is no reason for you to get upset."

"I'm not upset, Mrs. Murray, I'm just trying to solve the problem right now."

"The problem is not one of space. It is one of letting your daughter in on the secret you're keeping from her."

"Huh? What secret might that be, Mrs. Murray?" Rachel

asked in anger.

"The one of not knowing that her father is dead and that he also left her a guitar along with a big brown envelope. These things might just be important to her," Mrs. Murray said without any restraint. She had wanted to say this to Rachel Harvey before. The counselor knew it was not going to be easy and she was right. Ms Harvey tore into her.

"Y'all people need to mind y'all fucking business, you hear." Rachel Harvey was near tantrum level. "All you people up in here be illing the fuck out. Y'all need to go and get a life and stop meddling in mine. Yes, yes, yes, I used to smoke crack and abused drugs like y'all say but that's in the past now. I've been clean for six weeks now and I'm not a troublemaker but ever since I got up in here, it's been like a curse. Y'all refuse to let me live in peace. I've obeyed y'all rules. I mean, I don't even smoke ciga-rettes but y'all still won't let me be. Y'all got to tell me how to live my life, how to talk to my daughter, and what to say. I mean, y'all must be the damn man. I better start praying to the counselors..."

Mrs. Murray couldn't hold back. "Stop!" she shouted then closed the door to the many curious onlookers. Mrs. Murray start-ed again slowly, "We're not having a shouting war, Rachel. I sim-ply wanted to remind you that the more you allow yourself to think that way, the less you'll ever be able to move on and put a closure to that period of your life. You're a good person and a good mother. Just maybe, maybe you should reconsider and tell your daughter about her father's fate. You do that and you'll also move on."

The conversation loomed heavily over Rachel Harvey's head. She had wanted her daughter to know but she wanted to tell her at the right time. When is the right time to tell someone that their father is dead? pondered Ms. Harvey. Fatima had been a friend and counselor. Maybe she was right. Coco would visit tonight. Ms. Harvey vowed to tell her daughter of her father's demise.

"Do you want to redo the meeting, Rachel?" Fatima asked and Rachel thought for awhile before giving her answer.

"Yes, I'll do it again," she said and the counselor smiled.

As they left the office and began walking back to the meeting hall, doubt set in with each step that she took. Ms. Harvey stood at the top of a makeshift circle where twenty eager faces waited for her to get started.

"Good evening, sisters, mothers and all in attendance tonight. I am Rachel Harvey and I've abused drugs and alcohol."

"God's blessings and good evening all," was the rhetorical reply.

"I'm on the road to recovery, God willing. As you know, this is the time when everyone gets to discuss any topic and tell, you know, tell what is bothering them or what's keeping them here and giving 'em faith and so on..."

"That's right. It's that time again," a member of the support group uttered.

Without warning, Ms. Harvey became tongue-tied. She remained speechless for too long. Inquiring stares examined her aggrieved look. In hushed tones, Ms Harvey apologized as she took a seat. Her body heaved uncontrollably as she cried.

"You can't run. You can't hide. You must face the pain." It was the collective voice of the support group. "Pray hard, my sister. There is no problem we can't overcome," the chorus continued. Their chant seemed to lend strength to her frail spirit. Ms. Harvey stood, cleared her throat and testified about her present fears.

"I appreciate all the concern. I'm trying to hold my head above my problems and worries."

"God don't give more than you can handle, my sister. Have courage." The persistent effort of the support group gently guided Ms. Harvey past her emotional barrier.

"My daughter's father, well he passed away." She choked on her emotions. Her throat became dry and it became difficult for her to speak. Ms. Harvey braved the tears as she dabbed at her eyes and continued, "Couple weeks ago, he up and died of a stroke. I only found out when his probation officer sent me all his belongings, a damn guitar and a brown envelope with a letter to my daughter. I haven't told her any of this yet because of my fear. I've been scared to tell her. I don't know how she is gonna take it, you know...I don't how she will react. Although this man has not lived with me, he is my child's father. He brought me life and intro- duced me to drugs."

"Amen," came the chorus.

"His passing, I think, will make me and my daughter a lit- tle stronger. We've already learned strength through his weak- nesses." Ms. Harvey found it easier to speak. She wept a little when she heard the applause as she reminisced over Reggie Melody. "In the beginning, Reggie said he would be there for us. But in the end, I see he was never really there to do for me or for my daughter. I mean, he left me and us for his own reasons. He lived his life. Now, I gotta keep living mine."

"Be strong. The strong will survive." The support group cheered Ms. Harvey.

"I mean, I asked God, why me? Why I had to fall for crack, cocaine, and alcohol? I still don't know the answer," Ms. Harvey said.

The group did what was expected. They provided succor to another soul in distress. It was the kind of help that kept the alcohol and drugs off Ms. Harvey's mind and was guiding her to the path of sobriety. A smile gathered around the corner of her mouth. Rachel Harvey was not completely free from the need but at this time, she was not in need. There were no tremors or fears. She walked away with a fresh perspective. Ms Harvey recognized that her existence was solely up to her.

After the meeting was over, Ms. Harvey hurried to the office of her counselor and knocked. When the door opened, Rachel Harvey flung herself into the arms of Mrs. Murray who held her ground as the thin lady draped her arms around her rotund figure.

"Thanks," Ms. Harvey said. Fatima was taken aback by Ms. Harvey's display but she knew that she had a hand in pushing the patient toward recovery. Fatima easily held Rachel's shrunken frame against her and patted her back.

"Things will get easier, my dear. You'll see. Everything will be all downhill soon enough. You'll see, Rachel." The coun- selor saw Rachel Harvey reaching out and she took her hand.

"You've got to be strong," she said as the Rachel wept in her embrace. Fatima Murray was confident that the counseling was making a difference. This was the first time she had seen Rachel Harvey, a person who had denied that she belonged in drug therapy, break down crying. Recovery would not be too far behind now, thought the counselor hopefully.

FIFTEEN

"Are you all right, Coco? You don't seem to be yourself today," Ms. Katie said as looked at the bronze skinned teenager sitting across the kitchen table from her.

Coco sat staring into the hot liquid thinking that the shower had done her well but it couldn't rid her mind of the thoughts that had her in this mood. She didn't feel like being around anyone but Miss Katie was not just anyone.

Miss Katie was a mentor and someone who Coco could go to with any problem. Although tonight it felt like it was all ramble to her, Coco tried to listen as the old woman continued to speak.

"Go ahead, Coco, sip your hot chocolate before it gets any colder." Miss Katie watched Coco rubbing her hands against the cup. "Oh yeah, did hear that the police were up there on the sixth floor? They went to see about that Spanish couple." Miss Katie continued her coverage of the latest gossip from the building.

Miss Katie stayed home all day and always knew the latest gossip. She never missed a beat and most of the time there was something new to report. Miss Katie had a knack of somehow knowing everything that happened to everyone in the surrounding area. Apart from being a snoop, she was a sweet old lady and the person entrusted by her mother to keep an eye on Coco.

On any given day, Coco would listen closely to what the old lady had to say. Her mother was forever saying, 'Older people acquire knowledge, younger people acquire experience.' Sometimes, it was out of duty that Coco listened to the old lady. Tonight, as far as Coco was concerned, Miss Katie was speaking pure gibberish. Nothing she said made sense to Coco. It wasn't interesting until the old lady mentioned the TV news. Coco knew it would eventually come but Miss Katie was subtle.

"Saw that, ah, music producer. What's his name?" she asked. Coco couldn't decide right away if she was feigning amnesia to get her involved in the conversation or the old lady had really forgotten.

"You talking about Eric Ascot?"

"Oh yeah, yeah, that's the one," Miss Katie said and without waiting for any further input, she continued. "Seems like someone tried to rob him and he shot the guy. Damn thug killed one of the girls."

"Kamilla Davis."

"Were you there when the ruckus was going on, Coco?" asked Miss Katie.

"Miss Katie, you knew that's where I went after I called you from the diner."

"That was yesterday, right?" Miss Katie asked but before Coco could give an answer, the old lady continued. "You gotta forgive me, girl. The memory goes when you get to be my age."

Coco looked at the old lady knowing she meant well. Coco wanted to say something that would make this awkward moment better. "Aw Miss Katie, you're not that old. You're still young."

"No, Coco, I'm an old lady. Come July, I'll be seventy years old but you won't see me taking those Botox shots or having no face lift or none o' that plastic surgery thing. I don't mind growing old gracefully."

"You've got quality genes. You'll be forever young."

"Thank you, sweetheart. I like to think I'll stay youthful if my heart stays young."

"Oh, let me find out that you dabbling in poetry, Miss Katie."

"No, my time is gone, Coco. I leave all that poetry and rhyming up to you." She walked over and patted Coco's shoulders. "You care for some of my sweet potatoes crushed in butter? I've got some corn on the cob and chicken smothered with bacon over there too."

"Hmm, hmm, that's what smells so good? How could I say no? It sounds too delicious to pass up, Miss Katie," Coco said as she reached up to hug the older lady. "Thanks for everything," she said.

"You're more than welcome, sweetheart."

"You had said my mom called?"

"Yeah, girl, you know your mom. She's always worried about you. When she told me you had called and told her that she shouldn't worry, you know that whole thing started her worrying even more. Oh my Lord, that lady called at least a dozen times."

"I hear you. I know how my mom can get," Coco said as she sipped from her cup.

"Coco, you know your mother is a worrier."

"Yep, she do be going bananas with that," Coco added.

"Just like my mother," the old lady leaned closer. "My mother was born under the sign of the crab. She sure was crabby," Miss Katie said with a big laugh.

"Was she, huh?" Coco asked with a smile.

"Oh, you don't wanna hear this," Miss Katie said with surprising seriousness.

"But I'm sure you loved her anyway."

"Well, she was my mother so how could I not love her? She carried me for nine months. Plus, you only get one, child. I'll love her always."

"Sometimes though, did you ever wish you could take back that love?"

"Of course, 'specially when she beat me with branches but the Bible teaches us that you've got to love your parents and honor and cherish them forever. This is so that your days won't be made shorter. Love your parents and your days will be long on this earth. That's what the good book says."

"I hear you, Miss Katie. I love my mother. It's just that sometimes, you know, she kinda gets on my nerves."

"I know, Coco. We're all human and we've all got weaknesses. All you got to do is lend her some of your strength. You've got to lean on each other. It's a relationship. Mother and daughter, they shouldn't give up on each other."

"Sometimes I just don't know."

"Coco, you're still young. You're a teenager in high

school. Don't worry too much. Child, God works in mysterious ways. Your mother will have to carry her share of the load. You can't do all the carrying."

"Sometimes, I feel like I'm the only one doing the carrying." Coco paused and thought for a couple beats before she continued. "It becomes a burden and she blames me when anything goes wrong."

"You can only control the things that you're able to and no more. You cannot control everything."

"I know..." Coco began but the old lady was on a roll so Coco listened.

"It's awful, the conditions that we live in, but you have a chance to pull yourself out. Don't get caught up because you have a lot to be proud of." Miss Katie wasn't saying anything new but Coco somehow felt she needed to pay attention to the old lady's words.

"I hear you."

"If there comes a time when you think your mother is dragging you down then you've got to decide at that time if it's right to let go," Miss Katie said and immediately Coco's ear perked. The old lady continued, "If you don't know when to let go, you'll wind up drowning in her problems." Miss Katie tried to assess Coco's reaction before continuing. "And then what? Whose gonna be there to save you both? It may seem difficult to save you both but God can, Coco, and He will if you only believe."

Miss Katie looked at Coco as if waiting for an answer. Coco leaned back in the chair and the words sank deep. She sipped the rest of the cocoa then said, "I know you're right in a lot of ways but I'm saying, this is a different time. It's cool to believe in God but from where I stand, you've got to believe in yourself just as much or even more."

"First, you've got to believe that through Him all things are possible," Miss Katie said with finality. Coco glanced around searching for the right thing to say. Nothing came. "You should come out to church with me. Maybe this Sunday?"

Coco heard the question and tried to think of the right answer. What she wanted to say was that she didn't want to go to church with Miss Katie. Instead, Coco glanced at the time and quickly changed the subject. The fact that she still hadn't called her mother dawned on her. In a few minutes, the switchboard would be closed and she had not called back yet. It was also a good time to catch a smoke, she thought.

"I better call mommy before she freaks," Coco said and started to check her pockets for change. "I'm going downstairs to make this call, Miss Katie," the girl said. Coco really intended to use the moment to have a cigarette but Miss Katie interceded.

"Coco, you can call from the phone in the living room while there's time. They don't accept calls after a certain time." Miss Katie did not wait for the answer. "I think it's eleven o' clock," she continued.

"Yeah, I think you're right."

"Go ahead and call her now. Use the phone that's in the living room."

"Thank you," Coco said and went to the living room.

"You can take the hot cocoa with you, girl."

SIXTEEN

Coco got her cup and walked to the living room. She picked up the receiver and dialed her mom's number. Good, she thought when the phone rang on the other end. She surveyed the old lady's place. Everything was in place, neat and orderly. Along with framed photographs of other family members, there were framed pictures of Michelangelo's Christ in every earthly pose.

Coco glanced through the living room and saw the neat mahogany furniture with plastic covering the sofas. She noticed a toddler fast asleep on the sofa in front of the television. Just as Coco was about to turn the set off, the boy began to wail. "Oh, I didn't know you were up," Coco whispered with the remote in hand. "I'm sorry." The baby boy, about two years old, struggled to keep his eyes open. Finally, Coco could hear the operator on the line.

"Hello, may I speak with Mrs. Harvey?"

"Is this an emergency?"

"No, I mean, kinda..."

"All residents are asleep. Only emergency calls are accepted at this time."

"Um, okay..." Coco heard the click of termination from the phone at the other end. She looked at the phone. "Thank you too," she said to herself and returned the cordless to its place.

Moments later, she returned to the kitchen where Miss Katie was eating chocolate chip cookies and watching the small television on the counter.

"Some people can be so ghetto," Coco said.

"Why, what happened?" Miss Katie asked between bites.

"The receptionist was so rude."

"I know those receptionists, they don't know how to talk to anyone and their job is to talk to people. Like the one at my doctor's office, she don't know how to do her damn job. Always on the phone and when you call, either you can't get through or she has you on hold forever," Miss Katie said.

"Miss Katie," Coco smiled, "you said damn. Let me find out." Coco could not recall ever hearing her neighbor swear. This slip came as a surprise to Coco.

"You've got to call it. These places doing the hiring and firing have got to look into the backgrounds of the people they're hiring. If you're hiring a receptionist to deal with the public, the first qualification should be courtesy, not bad manners," Miss Katie said.

"You know, what you're saying is true indeed." Coco laughed.

"Got that right," Miss Katie said.

"You know what? I'll just go see her tomorrow."

"Yeah, but you may wanna call before you go and if that same witch answers, you put me on the phone. I'll show her how to fly right."

"You got it."

"People in this world don't know how to get along with each other."

"Yeah, you know it. That's Roshawn in there?" Coco asked as she joined the older lady at the table.

"Yep, that's him. Got real big, huh?"

"What! He's really growing. For a minute I was like, 'Who is that?' but then I saw the resemblance to Deja and I realized that was Kim's kid."

"Yeah, he does resemble his father. It's all that fast food making the babies bigger and more hyper. And that's all Kim has time for, you know? She's always into something, that girl. I watch him every time she doesn't have the regular sitter. She has too many things to do. Young people nowadays don't have much time for themselves and much less for the babies. Everything is quick and fast. That's not good for a baby." Miss Katie got up from her seat.

"Yeah, you've got to slow it down for the kids."

"She needs time to grow with her son especially now that his father was killed. Did you hear if they found out if that girl... ah, what's her name?"

"Bebop, Miss Katie," said Coco.

"Yeah, Bebop. Did she really kill him and kill herself too?"

"I really don't know. I mean, that's what they say."

"It just seemed a little odd that she did something like that, killed her lover and herself."

"Yeah, that's it. Just another stat," Coco said sounding sad.

"Well, it don't matter really. We all got to go one day. Just make your days here on earth positive for Jesus and you'll be in heaven," Miss Katie said as Coco raised her eyebrows.

"I hear you."

"Everything's so fast nowadays. His daddy ain't here and his mommy got to go to her night job. That's why you don't need no kids right now. Your life is already too fast plus you've got to be there for your mommy."

"I'm not trying to get pregnant. Anyway, I don't even have a boyfriend and you need a man to make that happen."

"Well, you really don't need no man, not now. You concentrate on passing through school first. I told my Roxie that and look at her now, she's one of them head honchos in her bank making all that money. Even though, I kinda wished that one of my children would give me a grandson like Roshawn in there," Miss Katie said holding her eyes to the ceiling. "Sometimes all I have is you and him around me," Miss Katie said. Coco could sense the old lady sinking into sadness.

"You'll have all that one day, Miss Katie. There'll be lots of grandchildren driving you nuts," Coco said as cheerful as possible.

"Oh, I wouldn't go crazy. I'd love 'em young ones. Oh but the Lord knows best. Was Roshawn asleep?" Miss Katie asked.

"I thought so but then I tried to turn the television off and he started crying."

"That's my lil' man. He loves those cartoons so much."

"I know how that is. I used to love me some cartoons,

too."

"I better go put that boy to bed 'fore he stays up all night like his mommy. Coco, you fix yourself some food to take. I'll be back. Everything you need is right there," Miss Katie said pointing then leaving the kitchen.

Coco looked around then busied herself with lifting the lid from each of the pots. There were sweet yams, smothered chicken, rice, string beans and corn. A lot of choices, thought Coco as she found the utensils, prepared a plate and ate hearty.

Tomorrow she would visit her mother at the residential program. She knew it was not going to be an easy outing. Later, as she sipped cherry Kool Aid and listened to the long-winded version of growing up right as explained by Miss Katie, Coco heard her mention the police.

"Miss Katie, you never mentioned the police called."

"Did I say they called? They came by. Said they wanted to talk to your mother or see the place so I asked what it was about. They say you might be involved in some kind of shooting but I knew better. The police, they always lying to black folks so I didn't pay 'em too much mind." Miss Katie emptied her trash into a plastic bag. Coco took the bag from her.

"This is going out? I'll take it," Coco said and made the trip to the trash compactor in the hallway. The old lady held the door open for Coco and smiled as she returned.

"Thanks, sweetie," she said. Coco still had the police visit on her mind.

"You're welcome, Miss Katie. Is that all the police did?"

"Yeah, that was pretty much it," Miss Katie said.

"I know those police are up to no good. They're trying to find out if anyone is lying."

"Well, I told the truth. I told them your mother was in a program and then they wished her the best and just left. They said it was routine to make sure you were telling the truth about your address. I think they were just trying to get some information but I had none for them." Miss Katie smiled as she pretended to seal her lips.

Coco knew it was the same two detectives that had picked

her up yesterday. What were they trying to do? Maybe they were just running a background check. She was not sure of their motives but she didn't want to call Deedee about it. Coco let it slip from her mind.

"That girl, your friend, Dee?"

"You mean Deedee?"

"Yes that one. Deedee, Day-day, all these new fancy names. I can't remember any of them. She called again," Miss Katie said. Coco told Miss Katie that it was too late to call.

"Do you hear the sirens?" Miss Katie asked as she walked to the window.

"Yep, another busy night for the police," Coco said in a dry manner as she joined Miss Katie at the window.

"I bet they headed up to 6K. That Puerto Rican man is always beating his wife. Before he leaves, he beats her and when he gets home in the evening, he beats on her again. I don't know why she doesn't leave him."

"I guess she feels she needs to be beaten all the time."

"I don't know why some women take up with men who's gonna beat on them. Back in the days before my husband went to Vietnam, he never once hit me. You've got to respect your partner."

"Some people just don't care. And why does a man want to beat on a woman anyway?"

"Only God knows what's in that man's heart, Coco. No one else can tell. Then you go ahead and marry some bum for better or worse," Miss Katie said and began her lesson on domestic violence to which Coco almost nodded off twice.

A couple rounds of this from Miss Katie left Coco worn out. She bid good night to the old lady and went next door.

SEVENTEEN

Coco tossed and turned all night. Every sound woke her and she heard the dealers and fiends all night long. On Sunday, she awoke up early and despite being in a state of sleep deprivation, she was committed to visiting her mother as planned. Coco quickly showered, dressed and knocked on Miss Katie's door. A few moments later, Miss Katie answered the door in her nightclothes.

"Come in, Coco. You're ready to go? Well, use the telephone. Lemme run to the bathroom. I left my bath running," Miss Katie said and hurried off leaving Coco to use the phone. She returned a few minutes later. "Come fix yourself some hot chocolate to drink before you go," she offered.

"I'm alright, Miss Katie."

"Coco, first thing in the morning, you must have something warm or you'll wind up with a stomach ache."

"I really must go but I'll follow your advice. I can't really stay too long though," Coco said thinking of Miss Katie's knack for telling tall tales.

She followed the old lady into the kitchen and saw the Roshawn lying in the living room again. Miss Katie already had the hot chocolate brewed.

The hot liquid burned her lips and tongue as Coco attempted to gulp it down. She resorted to sipping while she blew on it. She was quickly out the apartment. "I'll see you later, Miss Katie."

"All right, be safe out there. Say hello to your mommy and give her this for me, you hear?" Miss Katie said and handed Coco a Macy's shopping bag. "Just a few things I think she might need." She turned to look at the time but Coco was already saying goodbye.

"See ya." With headphones covering her ears, Coco was running out the door and down the stairs.

These kids nowadays, they can move so fast, Miss Katie thought as she waved at Coco from the window. "Be safe, Coco."

EIGHTEEN

On the bus ride to see her mother, the thought of explaining the shooting never left her mind. Coco sat in the back with her bag on the floor and her headphones glued to her ears. She listened, rewound, and paused the CD player. No matter what, Coco could not clear her mind.

She knew that her mother was gonna be very angry after she heard what happened. Should she give her the news version or tell her what really happened? Coco knew that in either case, her mother would be angry but that the version on the news would be best thing at this time. Coco rewound the story over again. Her mother would wanna know not only why and how but also when, where, who, what and every other detail.

Soon enough, the bus pulled to a stop and Coco knew it was time to face her mother. She got off the bus and trudged slowly through the gates of the rehab center. Her thoughts were still engaged. Coco delved into the information she already had on the incident and thought of any loopholes her mother might see. She would definitely give her the news version, Coco decided.

"Rachel Harvey," the receptionist said on the phone, "please come to the visiting area. Your daughter is here." Then she turned to Coco and said, "You can have a seat over there. Your mother will be right with you."

"Thank you," Coco said and sat in the visitor's area. No sooner had she picked up a magazine when her mother walked out.

"Let's go to my room cuz we've got to talk," she said without any greeting and turned around. Coco followed knowing that trouble was there ahead of her. When they reached the room, Coco presented her mother with the bag.

"It's from Miss Katie for you. She sends her regards," Coco said.

"Miss Katie is such a sweet lady," Rachel said taking the bag and looking at the contents. "Oh a few more underwear and a pajama set. That lady..." Rachel started but stopped as she found a card Miss Katie had sent. She read it quietly as Coco glanced around the tiny but clean residence.

The place contained a single bed, a desk with a chair and wall locker. It was neat and well organized. On any other day, Coco would be happy to be here but today she knew as soon as her mother was through with the bag of goodies Miss Katie had sent, she would let her have it. Coco readied herself for the worse. The news version, she reminded herself.

"And don't think I've forgotten about what your fresh ass did, Coco. You were out all night then next day, you're at this music producer's apartment where some people got shot. Look, you're gonna have to realize that guns kill and bullets don't have eyes. I don't want to sit around here and have anyone call telling me that you were killed in a rap war."

"Mommy, it wasn't like that. It wasn't like that at all."

"So, how was it, huh Coco? Give me your version."

"I'm saying..."

"You're saying what?"

"I'm saying they...ah, this guy, he ran up in Mr. Ascot's apartment and he shot the other girl."

"He was just sitting around and then decided, all of a sudden without anyone else saying anything to him, to run up in this man's apartment? C'mon Coco, that's the story he told y'all to tell the cops? Well, y'all can fool the cops but you know you can't fool me, girl."

"This ain't nothing about fooling anyone, ma. It's the truth. He probably tried to rob the place. I mean, Eric Ascot is big time. He's got a lot of money."

"Not from what the police is saying. They saying it could be drug related and all."

"Ma, you know you can't take anything the news reports as truth."

"Who is talking about any news, girl. I'm talking about what the detectives said."

"Detectives? Mommy, you sure?"

"Coco, let me tell you what else they told me. They know you know something that you're not telling."

"That I know something and I'm not talking? Mommy, what kind of nonsense they talking about? Please."

"You wanna know what else they told me? That my daughter is looking at ten years in prison. Ten years." Rachel Harvey broke down and sobbed as she repeated the penalty for perjury and cover-up.

Coco looked on in disbelief and anguish. Should she come clean? At least tell the truth to her mother? She thought about it for a while before speaking.

"Mommy, the news, the cops..."

"They came here, Coco. One black and one white. Said they were detectives and showed me their badges. They say you could be a suspect in the shootings."

"Stop playing. I mean, they don't know what they saying. They just trying to get everyone scared that's all. They picked me up Friday night and threatened me if I didn't tell them the damned truth."

"Then why don't you tell the truth? And be easy with the raising your voice and cursing, all right. This place is quiet for a reason. I keep reminding you that you're not talking to your hip hop thugs on the street corners."

"My bad, mom, but that sh...ah, just upsets me. I been told 'em. When they first talked to me, I told the cops that Lil' Long came there to kill, I mean, to rob someone and he shot and killed the girl that was there, Kamilla, and then Eric shot him."

"That's all that happened? Are you sure, Coco?"

"Yes, mommy, I'm sure. That's it."

"Whatever, it just doesn't sit right with me is all. I mean, why would anyone want to do that?

"What the news left out is that Eric Ascot is a target

because he's out in the forefront doing his thing. People gonna hate. You can't stop them. People are envious and jealous and all that pushes 'em to be angry and start hating."

"I know what you mean because they got some haters up in here. Oh my God, they just decide, 'Fuck it, I'm a hate on Rachel'. I don't know what that's about but I gotta go. I just gotta get up out of here. Can't stay here no more, Coco."

"What do you mean, mommy?"

"What I mean, girl? What I mean? Are you deaf? You're not listening. That's another reason I've got to get up out. You don't listen to no one but yourself."

"What do you mean I don't listen to no one? Mom, I always listen. I'm not out there pregnant. I'm in school all the time. I do my schoolwork. C'mon, give me some credit."

"I need to be out there keeping my eyes on you. You're all I've got."

"Mommy, I'm gonna always be there. You know I'm not gonna be like you always talk about dad and how he was running from town to town. I ain't gone be like that with nowhere to lay my head. Because of the music biz, I'm gonna be somebody, mommy."

"Well, that was your father. Always running around," Ms. Harvey said. "He too had wanted to be somebody." Her somber tone was lost on Coco.

"Mommy I'm telling you..." the girl continued but her mother interrupted. She was direct and straight to the point.

"Coco, he died."

There was a moment of silence as mother and daughter looked directly at each other. Coco saw the tears in her mother's eyes but was so far removed from the emotion that she just continued.

"I'll never leave you. I'm gonna make you so proud of me."

"Coco, sweetheart, your father died. He died."

"Who? Who're you talking about?" Coco asked and Rachel felt the denial in her daughter.

"Your father, the man who..."

"Gave his sperm?"

"Yes, your father is dead."

Rachel Harvey repeated the words and got Coco's undivided attention. The teenager, dressed in throwback Celtics warm-up suit, watched her mother break down and sob for the man who was supposed to be her father. Coco felt sympathy for her mom but couldn't shed tears for someone she'd known only from pictures. It still hurt to see her mother crying this way. The teenager reached out and hugged her.

"I'm sorry, mommy, but I can't waste my tears for someone I didn't know," Coco said as her mother poured her heart out. She allowed her mother to mourn her loss. As the two sat in silence, her mother opened the brown envelope and removed pictures of the man Coco had only heard was her father. They stared at the photos. When she was ready to leave, her mother handed her the guitar and saw the look of bewilderment spread across her face.

"What's this, mommy?"

"Can't you see? It's a guitar," Rachel responded curtly.

"Yeah, I can see that but what is the guitar for and why are you giving it to me?"

"Coco, your father has never given you anything that you can remember right?"

"Right and I don't even know the man. So what?"

"So on behalf of your father, I'm giving you this guitar," Rachel said and broke down sobbing again. This time, Coco could not hold back her tears and cried for her mother.

"When is the funeral?" Coco asked still tearing.

"They already buried him somewhere in South Carolina. His family members sent the guitar to you. He had said he wanted you to have it."

Coco stayed a little longer and listened as her mother reminisced. May God rest his soul, Coco quietly wished.

NINETEEN

The weekend came and went too quickly for some. It couldn't have been worse for Deedee. It dragged badly and left her slightly irritated. She was now displaced from her own home and was living out of a suitcase in Sophia's two-bedroom apartment.

Although the place was nice, Deedee missed her own digs and couldn't help feeling that way. She had spent most of Saturday wishing her uncle would buy a new and better place and she wanted it to happen immediately. While Deedee was watching television, Sophia was mostly busy at her desktop trying to catch up with work.

Most of the time, Deedee would camp out in front of the boob tube. She ventured on the internet and resisted the urge to contact Coco again. Deedee had already called Miss Katie's several times and left messages for Coco but received no return calls. Sunday found her brooding for most of the day until she escaped to brunch with her uncle and Sophia.

"It's a nice day," she remarked as they sat and dabbled at brunch at the Four Seasons. Although Deedee was in a good mood, she could feel the slight chill between Eric and Sophia. There was an uncomfortable silence between ordering and waiting for their meal.

Eric grunted and sipped a beer while Sophia stared at the table as she stirred her club soda with a straw. They both ignored Deedee who forged ahead with the conversation hoping that either would join in.

"This is a huge crowd. I guess a lot of people aren't planning on cooking today, huh?" Deedee stated casually hoping to evoke a response. No answer.

Sophia finally excused herself from the table as Eric answered another call on his cell phone. He quieted Deedee when she tried to interrupt.

"This is important," her uncle kept saying so Deedee stopped trying.

Silence ruled the table. By the time the food arrived, things were so chilly that even the food tasted cold. Small talk was few and far between bites. When the ordeal finally came to an end, Deedee positioned herself next to Sophia.

"Are you angry at Uncle E?" Deedee asked Sophia when they waited outside for the car to be brought around front by valet. Eric was stood apart from them chatting on the cell phone.

"Why are you asking, Dee? Is it that obvious?"

"I would say it certainly seems that way..." Deedee began but the ring of Sophia's cell phone halted her. She waited as Sophia spoke.

"Hi, Michael. Yes, tomorrow's possible. See you then," Sophia said then put the cell away. She turned to Deedee. "Well, you are perceptive. Not that either of us was trying to hide it but yeah, we had a little lover's spat. You know us grown folks, we can't even decide on the color much less the house. But don't you worry, we're gonna work it out."

"I understand and I'm glad you told me because I was going deaf listening to both of you saying nothing to each other," Deedee started to joke but caught herself when she realized that the smile on Sophia's face was not real.

"Yeah sure, Deedee. How's it going with Coco, anyway?" Sophia asked changing the subject.

"I'm not sure. I called but she hasn't call back. I don't know what happened," Deedee began to explain but was cut off by Sophia.

"She looked like she was ticked off yesterday. What happened between y'all anyway?"

"I don't know really. I know we're, at least I'm still cool. Coco is Coco. I can't speak for her but I'm alright," Deedee said just as the Range Rover pulled to a stop in front of them.

ANTHONY WHYTE

"You should try calling her again. Maybe she just needs some time to clear her head or something like that," Sophia said.

"You're probably right," Deedee said as she climbed into the back of the vehicle and slammed the door shut. Silence resumed as the Range took off. "Anyone up for a movie?" Deedee asked. There were no immediate answers forthcoming. "I guess not," Deedee continued but with no further response, she put on her Gucci shades and stared out the window.

Silence reigned the entire ride back to Sophia's. When Eric pulled up to Sophia's apartment and addressed Deedee only, it was a very awkward moment.

"Ah, see you later. I've got stuff to do in the studio."

"Be safe Uncle E," Deedee said and kissed her uncle's cheek.

"See ya later, sweetheart," Eric said he turned to address Sophia but she was already out of the vehicle.

"See you later, Eric," she said curtly and walked away with Deedee.

The tires screeched loudly, leaving tire treads along the roadway as Eric did a burnout leaving the scene. Heated, Eric gripped the steering with his fist. He dialed Busta's digits quickly on his cell for the fifth time. No answer. Where the fuck is Busta? Eric thought as dubs hit the asphalt leaving tire marks. The vehemence Eric felt was transferred from his emotional state to the foot on the accelerator. The vehicle hit the street so hard his pipe work rattled.

Eric pumped up the volume on the sound system and his ride floated with a thumping third-lane style traveling southbound on the West Side highway. Eric buried his troubles in the music. He always did but now he had to get to a recording studio. The one in his apartment was no longer at his disposal.

This fact that Busta could not be reached added to his emotional state. He was in turmoil. Where was Busta? Probably with some female, Eric thought as the vehicle sped down the highway.

Around him police sirens wailed. Officers yelled loudly on their horn for Eric to stop. Music thumped and reverberated from the tricked out ride. Other drivers tried to get Eric's attention to no avail. The music had drowned out all other sounds. All that mattered was the music until he glanced to the side and his attention was caught by a driver in the next lane.

"Yo, dog. I don't think them officers back there care for your serious tricked out ride," he shouted. With that, Eric glanced at his rear view and saw the police signal. He slowed and turned the music down. After about five minutes, the officer approached his car and spoke.

"You realize you were doing over seventy five miles an hour? You're in a rush or something? Driver's license, registration and insurance, please," he said and walked back to his car after Ascot gave him the requested items.

Fifteen minutes later, the officer made his way back to the Ascot's vehicle.

"Here are your documents. I'm also giving you a ticket for going 20 miles above the speed limit."

Eric took the forms and without saying anything, drove off blasting the music on the way to the studio again. His sorrow and pain could only be drowned in the music. The studio was the only place where he was the absolute reigning king. It was his jungle, the field of urban music. He created it and made it happen. It was where he could find solace and peace of mind at any time.

Eric pulled to a stop in the parking lot and pulled the nine-millimeter from under his seat and slipped it in to his waistband. It made walking a little bit difficult but it was worth his life so he would adjust to it. Ascot allowed his thoughts to roam as he walked into the downtown recording studio.

Things had gotten out of hand. He knew that Sophia was right. Lil' Long had came to his place to kill him, not to rob him or anyone else in the home that evening. He didn't tell her that it was because he had ordered the dude killed and somehow the hit had all gone wrong. Kamilla was shot and killed at his place. Lil' Long was probably in the morgue or hospital. It didn't matter.

What mattered most was that Busta was not answering his calls. Maybe he was on his back getting serviced by his usual two women, Eric thought. Busta was a sex fiend and wouldn't answer calls for days. Did Busta ever mention going out of town? Eric wondered, not sure of what to make of Busta's sudden disappearance.

Busta had helped him out and no matter what, they were in it together. Where the hell is Busta? Eric wondered as he entered the sanctuary for his soul. Here, he would let the rhythm take over his soul. No one else could save him. This was the only way out for Eric Ascot.

A recording studio can be a messy place of wires and machines completely out of sync with each other yet working together in harmony to make something worthy of dying for. Studios are like a dreary bunker filled with the latest electronic gadgets to improve sound, a Moog there, an MP3 there. In short, the place was an enclave of amps and speakers.

Besides that, there are the dregs of recording sessions littering the place. Filled ashtrays with roaches that refused to crawl. Loose wires like groupies lay everywhere for everyone to see. There were smudged glass partitions separating artist and engineers. The booth was private but really only a collection of microphones and headphones.

It was one in the morn and Ascot had stripped down to white wife-beater and jeans. His shoes and socks were off as he sat doodling at a Casio keyboard playing along to a mix of Big Pun's; *I'm Not A Player*. He seemed to play with a fervor from deep within. It suggested a hunger only he could feel but Ascot still wanted more than this.

It was a cool Sunday evening out. Light wind swept dusk into the night. Eric quickly pulled his shirt on and exited the studio. He walked to the Range and jumped in. Little did he know, there were eyes following his every move. He did not hear the chirps from their radio.

"B-Bird has flown the coop. Over."

"Follow and maintain surveillance mark at nearest nest. Over and out."

TWENTY

Eric drove for a few minutes listening over and over to the same beat. He fooled around with the equalizer. Unsatisfied, he shook his head quietly and lit a cigarette. After driving a few more miles, his eyes smiled when he saw a flashing neon lights sign that read, 'Girls Dancing Nightly'. Eric parked and replaced the gun in the compartment under his seat.

Busta always comes to this spot. Maybe somebody has seen him, Eric thought as he paid the necessary entrance fee and found his way to the bar. He stood and glanced around for any familiar faces. He ordered a double shot of Hennessey and an expensive cigar.

Eric surveyed faces looking for any recognizable looking ones that might know Busta. Maybe it was an off night, he thought not immediately spotting any of Busta's girls.

He sat at the bar and downed two more drinks. Eric, cigar between his lips, glanced around the strip club where the waitresses were topless and the dancers got down to skivvies before taking a bow and dismounting the stage. From his vantage point, Eric had a view of the stage but wanted to get closer. He tipped the bartender heavy, and ambled toward the stage where many girls sat at tables designed for couples while others moved around trying to get customers. He searched their faces with quick glances not wanting to attract attention. He did anyway.

"Hi there, handsome. Are you looking for trouble?" they asked giggling. "Don't tell me you're not looking because I'm yours only, handsome." Eric responded the same way each time. He slipped a couple bills in their string bikinis while shaking his head. The girls would smile and moved on. That way they weren't

ANTHONY WHYTE

offended, Eric thought.

He wanted to interact with the girls that Busta frequent-
ed. He wondered where they were as he downed another drink.
Eric knew he had to talk with Busta before Sophia did. He knew
eventually she would contact Busta. He was a long time friend
and her client.

Sophia represented Busta's entertainment company
which included a fashionable and trendy nightclub, a soul food
restaurant, and management of a couple artists signed to different labels. Eric figured he could tell Busta about the foul up and
they could work out a way to correct it like they had done before.
He would also remind Busta not to share anything with Sophia. It
would kill her to find out what was really going on. He smacked
his lips and flung another shot of the cognac down his throat. Eric
relished the way the liquid burned the deeper it went. His mind
welcomed the relaxing intoxicant.

Eric sat and wondered how to go about searching this
place. It could cost a small fortune, he thought. Every so often,
he would take a peek at the naked dancers while he sipped. There
were men dressed in business suits feeding dollars to the G-
stringed dancers. Everywhere he looked, there seemed to be
more scantily dressed women roaming around. Some were elegant in sheer negligees while others just let it all hang, nipples and
thongs. He was looking for particular faces. They were two of
them, Asian types, and Eric knew them only by face.

Two women dressed only in G-strings and boots
approached him. As luck would have it, their faces looked familiar. Eric nodded out of courtesy at first but let his eyes wander
slowly across their ample breasts. It was a possibility that they
may have recently entertained Busta, Eric thought as he made
eye contact.

"Nice pair," Eric said and threw back another double. The
drink was his fifth double and its effect was evident. He glanced
down admiring the way the black thongs cut deep into the ladies
asses. Both turned slowly so Eric eyes could feast.

"You like?" The question came with no pressure. Eric took
less time to fork over the answer.

"Not bad. Japanese?" he asked.

"Close. We're Malaysian and would you believe twins? We double your fun," they teased, shaking their enhanced breasts in his face.

"Nice advertisement. I bet you can back that up," Eric said bringing the shot glass to his lips.

"We'd love to take you into the Champagne Room and show you how much we can really do. It really is double the pleasure," they said in unison. Smiling the whole time, their hands massaged him around the crotch area. The alcohol was making him feel tipsy so his words slurred when he opened his mouth.

"I'm sure you would," Eric said and chuckled with the thought that it would be more private and he could ask about Busta without any interruptions. The ladies rubbed themselves as they danced for Eric's entertainment. He thought of Sophia and what she would say if she found out that he came here to see Busta. She would not believe him. Earlier, she did not believe him when he told her that Lil' Long's visit to the apartment was random. All weekend long, she had wanted to know more about everything. Telling her would only involve her further and ruin her career. With so many things on his mind, Eric sought to release himself by watching the ladies grind.

Like wild bulls, his thoughts rushed against the wave of pleasure. It wasn't going really well in his domestic life. Sophia had started to put too much pressure on the relationship. She just didn't understand that a man's gotta do what a man's gotta do, he thought as he watched the ladies dance with their hands palming and squeezing each other's ass.

Their eyes were wide and they smiled seductively. They caused electric sparks in the air when they began to kiss each other and Eric felt his pulse rate increasing. He bit his lip and watched them gyrating together. Maybe coming to this place hadn't been such a good idea. Maybe I should leave before things get out of hand, Eric thought as sweat trickled down his neck and ran down the back of his shirt.

Where was Busta? I've got to talk with him before Sophia does. That was his reason for being there but in the end, the shiny bodies of the young ladies writhing together was what kept Eric Ascot glued to his seat.

He swallowed hard when he glimpsed two pair of pink nipples brush against each other. Did these girls even know of Busta's whereabouts? I know he preferred Orientals, Eric thought as he heard them speak.

"We can take off all our clothes in the champagne room. Double your pleasure. What do you say, big man?"

With tension mounting in his mind, Eric needed no more convincing and he responded accordingly. Staring at the women's bodies, Eric could feel the early start of an erection. The ladies saw the glazy look in his eyes and they knew that he wanted them. "And if we're naughty, you get to spank both of us for free." They both chuckled and the alcohol wore on Eric making him think of the possibilities. They continued to handle his package, massaging it well until it was swollen and he felt like he was about to blow a gasket.

"Where's the Champagne Room?" he asked.

"Right over there," they replied.

"Let's go to the Champagne Room, ladies," Eric said and both girls escorted him to the private room.

"Double your pleasure for two hundred dollars. House special, alright?" Eric Ascot had a smashed look on his face and nodded droopily. "You pay credit card or cash?" one of the ladies asked.

"Cash," Eric responded in almost a moan and produced two hundred and fifty dollars.

The lights went out and the place went pitch black. Eric heard the door shut then blue lights shone. He was now able to see both women again, about five foot two each, one a little darker than the other.

"Do any of you know Busta?" Eric asked and waited for response but all he received was the seductive bump and grind of the ladies.

"Yes, Busta later, big black man."

"Yes" said Eric convinced that there was a breakthrough. "A big black man," he smiled knowing that he finally had gotten the right response.

"Later we get the big black man," they said with the same seductive smile. Eric's mind swam in a pool of alcohol. He was ripe for the picking and the ladies poured it on.

Eric sat and watched, seduced by Asian eyes. His mind lusted as he followed the way their petite and perfectly curved bodies intertwined with each other. Crotches touching, they continued to grind. The music changed to a slow melodic drum beat with accompanying guitar licks and Sade's rift.

If I tell you, if I tell you now...Will you keep on... Will you keep on loving me? If I tell you, if I tell you how I feel... Will you keep bringing out the best in me? You give me, you're giving me the sweetest taboo...You give me... You're giving me the sweetest taboo...You're too good for me...

The ladies heaved long wavy, black hair across ample breasts as they sinuously and rhythmically undressed each other. They rubbed lustfully on each other's bodies, groping and fondling as they danced. Buck naked, they moved closer sexily rubbing belly to belly as they gave their best performance.

One's pubic mound ground slowly into the other's round ass. They took turns rubbing each other's derriere and when their nipples touched, it sent electric shocks through the room. Eric, bug-eyed and intoxicated, watched without blinking. He could hardly sit still but he felt the stability of the music.

There's a quiet storm and it never felt like this before... There's a quiet storm that is you...There's a quiet storm and it never felt this hot before...You're giving me something that's taboo...

"Ah," Eric sighed when he felt his pants come unbuttoned as one lady freed herself from the other and was now working on him. He smiled and his breath came in gasps as the other girl continued touching herself.

You give me the sweetest taboo. That's why I am in love with you...You give me the sweetest taboo you too good for me... You're just too good for me... I'll do any thing for you... I'll stand out in the rain... Anything you want me to do... Don't let it slip away...

Eric drooled with vulgar desires as he watched the seductive grinding pelvises moving in sync with the licks from the rhythm guitar. Every inch of their bodies were similar in size. Naked, they squirmed, writhed and moaned as the ladies played with themselves.

"Hey, you like? We're double your fun, mister," They said getting closer and pulling Eric off his perch. He was too drunk to resist. They started grinding their bodies hard against Eric. Unable to move around too much, Eric held on for support. His hands felt around until he felt soft flesh. Instinctively, he fondled.

"Oh, now you're awake. We thought we were putting you to sleep. Yes, that's it, big man," one of the ladies said.

After a few minutes of waltzing around and them grinding themselves against him, Eric grew a little dizzy. Both the ladies stuck to his thighs like glue. Eric worked to free himself of their grasp.

"Hold up. I'm out of breath and I need another drink. Let me sit for a minute," Eric said and plopped back into his seat.

"I'll get you your drink," one of the ladies said as she poured Eric some champagne.

"Nah, sweetheart, the champagne is for you. I want something stronger."

"Okay then I'll get you a shot of Cognac."

"Yeah, that's more like it. Make it a double Hennessey." Eric's slur was noticeably stronger. She took the money and disappeared from the room. Eric was left alone with the other twin. He reached for her and she asked for fifty more dollars.

"If you give me fifty more, I'll suck you off," she said licking her lips. "Just the way you like it," she added with a grin.

"How much for both?" Eric asked pulling out another C-note. Just then her partner returned and she whispered something into her ear. She smiled and nodded in agreement then gave Eric two shot glasses and the bottle of liquor. "I only wanted a double but I'll keep these," he said taking both glasses.

"Oh, big man, you gave me enough money to buy lots of drinks," she replied as she took his cigar from him and slid it all over her body.

And so they began. Both girls took a swig of the champagne and allowed the liquid to cascade over each other's breasts. Eric's eyes followed the bounce of shiny breasts as the ladies danced. He sat back comfortably in the sofa, closed his eyes, and imagined them attacking him. Their stiff tongues danced all over his body, his neck, his ear, and they licked him down to his fingers. It was a form of relaxation he could appreciate. His imagination raced and there was more.

He attempted to hold on to a nipple then his fingers ran across a shaven mound. Eric could no longer resist when the smooth skin of one of the lady's ass brushed is arm. His rock hard cock found its way into a warm moist mouth and Eric was in heaven. He was completely drunk and couldn't stop what was happening. The pleasure was intense as the ladies took turns sucking and twisting his cock and he heard himself moan loudly.

"Ah, ugh ooh ah-ah, yes, do it." Eric could hear the guttural sounds coming from his mouth and couldn't believe the pleasure.

Eric suddenly felt intense cold on his chest. He recovered for a second to see ice cubes in one of the lady's mouth. He watched as she licked a circle around his nipple. The ice just intensified the sensation. While this was going on, the other sucked his dick and played with his balls. His pleasure was magnified when one of the women slid her tongue in and out of his ear. She licked his temple and her tongue slid back to his nipples. She bit and pinched each to hardness. Eric became unsure about stopping them. Eric kept telling himself that he shouldn't let it go any further but the erotica had reached such dizzying levels that he couldn't feign resistance anymore. Eric squirmed and wiggled around so that her mouth would have a better access to the proposed target for more effective sucking. Eric was fully aroused and inebriated. The combined sensations threatened to blow his mind. Eric was in bliss.

"Squirt it all over our titties," they laughed and shouted as they massaged his cock. From the base to the tip, they rubbed him until he couldn't hold back anymore.

"Oh, yeah, ah ugh yes!" Eric shouted.

His legs shook violently as he spurted all over their breasts. They laughed and rubbed the creamy liquid onto their shiny skin.

"Thank you, Mr. Big Man," one of the girls shouted when she saw Eric peel off another hundred-dollar bill.

"Hmmm, great job, baby. You come back later and we give you the information."

"Why can't you tell me now? Doesn't cash rule?"

"Its our boss. You come back later and we tell you then."

"What time do you get off?" Eric said fighting to recover from the ordeal.

"We'll tell you where the big man is when you come back. Our shift ends at six am."

"Right, right. I'll get back at you then."

"All right, just ask for the Geisha twins in the front and they'll tell you where we are," the lady said and slipped a card into his shirt pocket. Eric peeled off another hundred and went back to the bar. There he sat quietly and drank enjoying the show from afar. He stayed in the club until three in the morning. Vowing to himself to come back later, he left and went back to recording studio.

TWENTY-ONE

He felt loneliness and guilt follow him inside the studio. Ascot's mind flashed to his experiences earlier at the club. "The Geisha twins," he whispered and shook his head as he turned several knobs on. The instruments lit up and hummed. Eric checked his cell phone. Busta is still missing in action, he thought.

Ascot adjusted the settings on the instruments and a song played. As he listened repeatedly to the rhythm, Ascot tried to conceive of an arrangement that wouldn't disturb the vocals that would be laid over the top of it. This was a difficult process made worse by the images of the dancing girls and the music that played. For the first time in a long time, Ascot felt the pressure.

Eric had been grinding out song after song and hit after hit for the past six years. But now, he felt worn and tried to focus on the beat to see if it was too fast or too slow. He needed it to be just right. The songs reverberated in his head and he fussed with the settings each time trying to make it right. It was something he was used to. What was different was that he had never cheated on Sophia before. He really hadn't wanted to start now.

Eric vowed that he would never go back to the club. Deep down, he knew it to be another lie. The song churned in his mind. Over and over again, Ascot fiddled with the settings and listened. He tried an uptempo beat then slowed it down. Eric adjusted the bass and that didn't do it either.

Morning came and he was still trying to make the music right. The final product wasn't what he expected. It featured a hybrid of hip hop drums and Ascot's skewed instrumentation. His ordeal from the previous night had fueled his resolve to complete the song but somehow, it still wasn't right.

An Ascot produced song was invariably a hit coming out the studio. His signature sound was top notch. Eric sustained this level of dominance because of sheer intensity and hard work. Eric was determined to change the world through his music. That was the reason he kept searching hard to find what was wrong with this one. The song played repeatedly and Eric's mind spun in his attempt to fix it.

TWENTY-TWO

At 7:00 am Monday morning, Sophia heard her alarm blasting. She peeked out from underneath the comforter and hit the snooze button. Fifteen minutes later, the blaring sound found Sophia still asleep. She managed eventually to struggle free of the bed and headed to the kitchen. Sophia turned on the coffee pot then walked to the bathroom. The door was locked and Sophia knocked on the door.

"I'll be right out," Deedee said from behind the door. Sophia heard the sound of running water. Seconds later, the door flew open and Sophia raced into the bathroom.

"Hi, Sophia," Deedee said.

"Hey, girl. You got school?"

"Nope, school's out for a week. Spring recess, remember."

"Oh, I see," Sophia said and closed the door. Deedee wandered off to her temporary bedroom. She dug through her overnight bag and found her cell phone. There were no messages.

She looked at the time. It was 7:15 so she decided to call her uncle. The phone rang until she got his voicemail. Deedee left a message at the sound of the beep. Putting the cell down, she laid down and tried closing her eyes. The images from her weekend appeared like she expected. I'm probably going to be seeing his ugly face whenever I close my eyes, she thought. The images had haunted her every night of the weekend and probably would for sometime to come. There would be rough days ahead but I'll have to be brave like Coco. Deedee's mind worked overtime as she rolled around in the bed trying to find the perfect spot to lay her head. Where's Uncle E? She wondered.

Her eyes had closed momentarily when she heard the rap

on the door. She peered above the covers to see Sophia.

"Hey, Dee, you want some breakfast?"

"No, I'm fine," Deedee replied.

"All right. I'll have to give you my keys."

"Have you heard from Uncle E?"

"I was just about to ask you. I thought I heard you on the telephone with someone. I thought maybe..."

"Oh, I was leaving him a message to see how he was doing."

"I could leave my set of keys before I go, okay? Sure you don't want breakfast?"

"Maybe later. It's too early."

"Okay, I think there are cereal, eggs, and sausages. The only thing is you're gonna have to cook yourself."

"That's okay, Sophia," Deedee said cutting off Sophia. "Don't worry so much. I'll be fine. Besides, you've got to get to work."

"Hey, you're right. Time is flying. Let me go get dressed," Sophia said and backed out as she closed the door. "I'll stop in and say bye before I go." Sophia hurried to the next room and began planning her outfit for the day.

Deedee curled up under the comforter and wondered aloud as to where her uncle was. "Where are you, Uncle E?" She thought of what had occurred over the weekend and knew that it had affected the relationship between her uncle and Sophia. They both acted overly cautious whenever they spoke to her. Deedee knew this meant everything was not good between them. It wasn't that he had spent the entire night in the studio. Deedee knew her uncle had studio sessions that lasted forever. He could spend days and nights making music but she also saw the way they treated each other and couldn't help but notice the strained silence between them all weekend. Something like a fight had to have gone down between the two. It's never been like this ever, Deedee thought.

Neither Eric nor Sophia was letting her know much about the fight or even that a fight had occurred. She was miffed but sought solace between the blankets. Deedee held on to all of her questions. It was morning and she didn't want to bombard Sophia. That would be too annoying and downright pushy, she thought.

Deedee adjusted her body and tried to get comfortable as she lay in the bed. She wanted to think good thoughts but the memories from the weekend would not leave her mind. Deedee turned on the radio and listened to the early morning ramble of the deejay. She sat listening and mentally planning the coming week. The rattling of the coffee pot startled her.

"Do you want me to turn that off for you, Sophia?" Deedee asked jumping from her perch on the bed. She caught herself as she saw Sophia already fixing herself a cup of coffee. "Well, I see you've got it. You look really nice. I love the pants suit. Nice shirt," Deedee said, admiring Sophia.

"Did your uncle return your call, Dee?"

"Nope, I guess he got really busy. He'll probably call as soon as you leave."

"Yep that's him," Sophia said and added, "Always late." She checked herself once again in the mirror. Deedee sat up and paid attention.

"Sophia, are you nervous?"

"No, I don't know why I would be. Its only work."

"Maybe it's Monday morning blues."

"Hmm, hmm you could be right, Dee." Sophia chewed on toast and sipped her coffee as Deedee spoke.

"Can I ask you something, Sophia?"

"Sure but I may not have the answer for you."

"No, it has nothing to do with you and Uncle E."

"I didn't mean...I'm sorry, Dee. What is it?"

"Well I'm trying to find out if it is disrespectful if you offer me somewhere to sleep and I turn it down? I mean, does it matter?" Deedee asked. Sophia kept at her breakfast before answering.

"It depends on how you say no, especially to a friend," Sophia said to Deedee then watched as she thought about it for a while before agreeing.

"Yeah, you're right. Maybe I was a little hard on her," Deedee responded.

"You're talking about Coco. Sometimes our best friends are sensitive about something we have no idea about. The most you can do is apologize and move on from there," Sophia said and drank the last bit of her coffee. "Look, I'll see you later. I'll call to see how you're doing, okay?"

"Okay. Bye, Sophia. I'll see you later."

Sophia left the room and stopped by to give herself another once over. She didn't look too much like a floozy, Sophia thought as she checked herself in the full length mirror. She was glad that the swelling to the left side of her forehead had finally gone down. With a touch of make-up, it was her little secret. This dark gray pantsuit actually makes me curvy, she thought as she walked away from the mirror. She stopped at Deedee's room to wave bye before she left the apartment.

"Here are a set keys to the place. The doorman will recognize you and these are the keys to the two locks on the door. I keep the top lock open unless your uncle has been nasty." Sophia winked and added with the hint of a smile. "Don't you spend all day in bed, lazy head."

"Oh I won't. I've got the keys to the city." Deedee curled her lips and Sophia recognized the teenager's sarcasm.

"Shopping has been known to wash my blues away." Sophia laughed and blew a kiss at the teenage girl. Deedee sat at the edge of the bed wearing her Snoopy pajamas, a smile, and staring out the bedroom window.

"It seems like it will be a fresh spring day," Deedee said as Sophia turned to leave. She heard the thud of the door and the locks applied indicating that Sophia had left. Deedee sighed and curled up in the bed. She burrowed her head between the covers in an unsuccessful effort to shield her face from the sun. The rays easily filtered through, brightening the room and making it difficult for her to sleep.

A few minutes later, Deedee still buried beneath the covers, heard voices from the TV. Reaching for the remote, she frowned and curled back up in bed. While raising the volume, she saw his face. Immediate recognition registered when she realized she was reading his name. Robert Morgan alias Busta was shot and killed. Deedee's fingers trembled as she nervously pressed the volume up on the remote.

...Police are searching for the killer of Robert Morgan also known as Busta. Mr. Morgan, a well known hip hop entrepreneur, was gunned down and killed in his apartment in what the police are calling a botched robbery sometime over the weekend. Neighbors were alerted to his body by a foul odor emanating from his apartment. Mr. Sanchez, a next-door neighbor, called the police. Police found the door forced open. We take you to John Deanne with a live coverage...

There was a cut to the live scene and police officer in the midst of an interview.

...Thank you Michel. Police are calling this a robbery gone bad. Apparently, Mr. Morgan surprised burglars forcing their way into his apartment sometime Friday evening and after a struggle, Mr. Morgan was shot ten times. Drawers were ransacked and money and jewelry were stolen. The police are asking that anyone with information that could lead to an arrest to please call the crime stopper's hotline. That's it from me, John Deanne. Now back to the newsroom...

Deedee was stunned. For a moment, she lost all feeling and her capacity to think. After fumbling with the telephone, she dialed her uncle's cell phone number. Tears flowed as it rang through to his voice mail.

"Uncle Eric, please call me back." Deedee sobbed as she spoke. "I'm at Sophia's. I just saw on the news that Busta got shot..."

Her heavy sobbing prevented her from continuing. Deedee dropped the telephone in the bed and sat staring at the television now running a commercial. She felt her hands go cold and clammy and tears continued to stream from her eyes. By the time the morning show returned, Deedee was sobbing loudly again.

"Uncle E, where are you? Please call me and tell me you're okay." Deedee cried, wiped her eyes in her pajamas and cried some more. She pressed redial on the telephone. It rang through again until the voice mail was engaged.

Deedee felt limp and woozy and thought she was going to faint. She walked as quickly as possible to bathroom, bent her head over the toilet bowl, and started vomiting. She sobbed loudly as she sat hugging the bowl, not knowing if her uncle was alive. Deedee silently prayed for the best.

TWENTY-THREE

Eric Ascot ran from his Range Rover shirt unbuttoned, belt unbuckled and laces undone. He had been in the studio trying to figure the right keys to a beat. It was what he did as a music producer, toil in the studio in search of the perfect beat.

Except this morning he was supposed to be back at the strip club so the Geisha twins could get him Busta. He sprinted as fast as his body would let him. Eric was out of breath when he got to the front door of the club. He checked it and it was locked.

"Damn, damn, damn," he said stomping his feet. He turned to leave and spotted them outside the diner across the street waving at him. For some reason, a strange feeling hit him. Maybe it was guilt but he had been hoping they would be gone by now. Eric put a smile on his face and walked across the street to greet them. "I was a little worried that I would miss you," he said still sucking wind.

"You were late but the big man is in there," one said as she pointed toward a doorway.

"No, no, not the big man. I want Busta, the big black man," Eric said with his arms directing his words.

"No, you said the big man. The big man downstairs in the club. Not upstairs but downstairs," one of the strippers said.

"Downstairs, right? Thank you," Eric said. He saw both ladies rubbing thumb and forefingers together. He pulled out a twenty. "Thanks," he said and walked away.

He double-checked the number of the building. Eric was not sure he had the right place and looked back to see that both ladies from his evening had left.

Eric rang the doorbell and waited. Nothing happened. I'm

so stupid. This is the world's oldest set-up. How could I fall for it?'
Eric smiled more at himself for falling for what he presumed was
a trick to relieve him of his cash. He was about to make his way
back to the Range when the door opened.

"Yes, can I help you?"

Eric was caught off guard and fumbled for what exactly to
say. He saw a pair of eyes zeroing on him and knew this was not
going to be easy.

"Ah, someone told me that I could find a friend of mine
inside. Busta?" he said partly questioning his reasons for being
here. "I mean, if I have the wrong address then please excuse
me."

"No, hold on. Don't go nowhere," the guy said.

"Ahight, ahight, I ain't going nowhere," Eric replied and
sized up the guy walking away. Around six-six and two sixty, he
had a linebacker's build and was probably the muscle for the big
man, Eric thought. He soon returned and bid Eric inside.

"Come in. The boss wants to see you."

Eric walked behind the huge man. He did not know who
he was supposed to be meeting.

"What's the name of your boss?" Eric asked as they went
down the stairs just like the Geisha twins had said.

"Oh, sorry, I thought you already knew it's Maruichi."

"No, that name doesn't ring a bell."

"Francisco Maruichi of the Maruichi family."

Eric heard but thought it was some kind of joke. He knew
that rap artists, tired of seeing the same old monikers, were
adopting Italian and Sicilian surnames. Was this what Busta had
been up to, pretending to be a mobster? As he neared the bottom
of the rounded staircase, Eric braced himself in anticipation of
someone yelling, 'Surprise stupid'. What he saw caused a far
greater shock than he was expecting.

The place looked like a restaurant with limited seating.
There were only four tables and spaghetti fettuccini was being
served by what seemed like real waiters complete in their black
and white uniforms. Eric did not see a menu. He looked around
and saw a wall of black and white photos of gangsters, fake and

real. Snapshots of Pacino and Deniro were framed next to Gigante and Gotti.

At one table sat five men, all sturdy with slick hair and suits. Chatting loudly, they seemed to be having a good time. Eric stood unnoticed by all. He waited for Busta to pop out in the midst of all this and announce himself to this Italian gathering. Eric saw the man who had answered the door and two others in velour warm-up suits sitting at another table.

They all got quiet when he sat at an empty table. Furtive and suspicious, glances shot his way when they heard his cell phone ringing. Eric dared not take the call. Instead, he let the call go to voicemail then turned the phone off. The men returned to their powwow.

He continued to look around expecting Busta but nothing happened. Eric started to feel impatient and stared at the ceiling. The door to the bathroom opened and it was clear that the man who walked out was someone important. From the way the waiters greeted him to the way they held their breath waiting for his approval on a bottle of wine, the respect was obvious. He came and sat next to Eric with a smile.

"I bet you'll never find a better pasta primavera this side of the equator," he said and presented his hand. "Francisco Maruichi," he continued. Eric stood and shook his hand.

"Eric Ascot, how are you doing?"

A waiter walked over and Maruichi spoke, "Bring us two primaveras and coffee." He paused and asked, "How'd you like your coffee, Mr. Ascot?"

"Black, thank you," Eric said and waited for the point of the meeting to make itself known. Maruichi, about six four or five and closer to three hundred pounds, did not say anything until after the waiter was through serving the coffee and had departed. He took a sip then spoke.

"We've got some things in common, Mr. Ascot. You're a success at what you do. I'm successful with what I do." While Maruichi spoke, Eric sized him up. With the setting reminiscent of a mob hangout, all that was missing was the score from the Godfather movie.

Another cup of coffee later, the wise guy with the lethal charm of a screen gangster was singing his own praises. "I grew up on the streets. I went from nothing to something. Just like you, I know what it feels like to have nothing," he said pointing his platinum pink diamond ringed pinky at Eric. He had Eric's undivided attention. "So I'm not gonna let no one just waltz in and take what I've built." Francisco nodded and wiped his hand. "You've got to put a wall up dividing what's yours and the rest. That was the reason your friend, Busta, is dead." Eric's jaw dropped.

"You said dead? Busta's dead?" Eric asked in earnest trying to understand. He finally managed to shake the cobwebs from this hard knock. Busta had been one of his brother's closest friend's. Feeling a pang of responsibility, Eric sat and stared off for a minute. When he fully recovered, he could hear Maruichi speaking.

"I'm sorry. You did not know this, Mr. Ascot? I thought that was the reason you came here to discuss business. Busta spoke highly of you and your business enterprises. Sadly, Busta is now gone but that should not stop us from doing business, Mr. Ascot."

Eric knew the man with the mobster grace was talking but he was in the midst of trying to deal with the reality of Busta's death. It was news to him and his brain refused to process anything else. Eric was stupefied. His eyes wandered around the enclave. He contemplated leaving this wise guy hangout.

"Wait a minute, Mr. Ah..."

"Maruichi."

"Yeah, you're telling me that Busta is dead? Who killed him? When?" Eric asked as his thoughts flailed frantically trying to come to grips with the facts.

"I'm afraid so. It happened on Friday evening. He was shot ten times. Someone executed him and made it look like a robbery. I'm sorry, I thought you knew all about his death."

It took Eric some time to fathom everything that had just been said. He felt unbalanced, like his chair was giving out on him and he sat up straighter to stabilize his frame. Eric felt his anger gathering momentum, building inside of him. It felt as if his head was going explode. He had just found out and the incident had occurred three days before.

It slowly became clear that Busta's murder was linked to the same thug who had tried to kill him at home last Friday. Eric knew that Lil' Long was responsible for the rape of his niece. Busta and Eric had connived to have Lil' Long murdered. What went wrong? How did Lil' Long find out? Who else was in on this? Eric sat drowning in deep thought.

"Are you okay?" Maruichi asked.

"Friday? You said it was on Friday that Busta was killed, right?" Eric asked without acknowledging Maruichi's concern. Maruichi sipped his espresso before he spoke.

"Yes, I'm sure it was Friday," he said as he sat the cup down. "I was fishing out on the island when I got the call. The whole thing upset me so much, I couldn't catch a single fish the entire weekend. The funeral's tomorrow."

"Do you know where?" asked Eric.

"Somewhere up in Harlem. I love that piece of America. I used to have a lot of friends there. They're all gone now," Maruichi said with a smile. "I'm going back to visit my old stomping grounds." Maruichi spoke and Eric watched him feeling an uneasiness rise from the pit of his stomach. Eric sighed then began to speak.

"Look, I really wanna thank you for your time and..."

"Eric, Busta was a business associate and good friend of mine. He worked with my family for over ten years. He never let us down and was never behind on his payments. Busta was good for business."

"Ah, I'm sure he was," Eric answered and began to rise.

"What I'm telling you is for me and you alone. Busta did not have the right defense." Maruichi was able to hold Eric's attention. "When you build a castle, you need to put a moat around it. If not, the commoners will walk in and plunder your loot."

"I hear you," Eric said as he leaned back with his hands locked at the back of his head and listened.

"I know you've got a castle and I can put a moat around it so that your castle stays safe and sound. Do you understand what I'm saying here, Mr. Ascot?"

"Yeah, I understand you very well, Mr. Maruichi."

"Call me Frankie," Maruichi said and patted Eric's shoulder. Eric nodded in agreement and was about to reply when Maruichi cut him off with a wave of his hand. "Eric, you take some time and think about this. You know the police are not willing to stop this war. You know they're not gonna offer any type of special protection. And you know a man must protect his family and his livelihood."

He was giving Eric all the assurances a person needs to hear when down, that there is someone in a stronger position willing to reach out and give a hand. The question was what would it cost? Eric knew that in the short run an agreement like this might guarantee him insurance for his family. Just the idea of Sophia made him think of getting up and walking away from the table. She would argue and say this was the mob. He could just hear her voice now. Eric sipped.

"Take your time, Eric. More coffee or something stronger?" Maruichi asked. Eric did not immediately reply. Thoughts of Busta's death and Sophia being mad at him consumed him. He couldn't let go the image of Busta, his body found filled with bullets. Eric did not want the same fate to happen to anyone in his family. He was caught between going straight and taking a curve. Either way, it was wrong. He knew he couldn't sit back and do nothing. Something had to get done. Someone would have to get touched.

Maybe he should have gone to the police but now it was too late for that. What would they have done? They wouldn't have prevented anything. It was too much. He wasn't sure of much but one thing he was sure of was that if he accepted the drink Maruichi offered, it would mean listening seriously to his offer. Eric was very sure of that. It was getting closer to decision time. Eric's brain raced to keep up.

Sophia may get mad at me but she'll get over it if she can't accept it right away. I need to protect my niece and myself.

If I walk out of here and there's no protection in place that means it'll be open season on me. That bit Eric was sure Sophia would never understood.

Eric thought long and hard before asking: "Did you say something about a drink?" The words leapt out of his mouth and seemed to touch off an alliance. Maruichi nodded, smiled, and waived at the waiter.

TWENTY-FOUR

Earlier when Sophia Sullivan had chosen her outfit for the day, she did so with a lot of thought. After all, in about a half hour, she was meeting with Michael, her friend and assistant district attorney, for what should be a lunch meeting. He had insisted on it being today. On the phone, he had made it sound as if it wasn't urgent but Sophia knew it had something to do with Eric. She wanted it to be top priority.

Michael had hinted as much but did not want to go over details on the phone. He wanted to meet in person. He gave her the excuse that he did not want Eric to be sitting next to her while he was on the phone with her. Now, as she stared at her reflection in her compact and freshened up her make-up, she remembered their conversation.

"Ask your fiancé to explain what is really going on," he had advised her. After some thought, Sophia had decided to ask Eric directly. Sometime between Saturday night and early Sunday morning, she had encouraged him to come clean. Instead, Eric had tried to soften his answers. He told her there was nothing going on, just some crazy guy deciding to rob him. Sophia had her doubts. She pressed him for answers to her questions most of Sunday. This only led to a major blow up by Sunday evening. Explaining that he needed time to think, he left for the only place in his world where Sophia was never allowed, the studio.

Sophia was convinced that Eric had stayed out all night because he was avoiding her questions. It wasn't as if he'd never done it before but this time, he had left after an argument. He was angry that she was not falling for his okie-doke. Sophia knew Eric lost his cool because he was sure that she knew he was hiding something. Up until last night, the doubts remained and she wanted answers. What secrets was her fiancé hiding from her? She wanted to get to the bottom of this so Sophia agreed to meet with Michael. Also, Michael Thompson was someone from her past who she respected and knew well.

As she put away her compact and stared at a file on her office desk, Sophia figured that if she had dressed like a hoochie, Michael would think less of her. It might even lead him to think that she was coming on to him in order to help cover up Eric's deeds but she wasn't. She wanted to look and act dignified, no matter what. Sophia left her office and walked to the bathroom where she fixed her hair. Despite the bump on her head, there were no other physical reminders of Friday night. She examined herself in the mirror but nevertheless felt that the emotional scars might never heal.

Sophia headed back to her desk. After sitting for a while and looking at her watch every few minutes, she jumped up, grabbed her bag and overcoat then walked to the elevator. Even though she was worried about Eric's safety, Sophia felt she had to know what was going on. She fidgeted as she waited on the elevator.

Out on the busy city street, Sophia walked past couples eating lunch and others just walking together. Some were holding hands while others just stood real close, simply enjoying each other. Where was Eric, she wondered? She had purposely refused to call him but strolling down the midtown street with the sun shining on her, she missed him.

The distraught young attorney cautiously avoided other pedestrians on the crowded sidewalk and looked at her cell phone. Why hasn't he called? Was the music so damned important? The thought crossed her mind as she hailed a cab. Despite his obsession with his craft, Sophia knew that Eric was avoiding her because he was covering up something. At lunch, she would hopefully find out what exactly he was doing.

She arrived at Carmine's, an uptown Italian eatery, a half hour before the set time. The place was empty and Sophia ordered sparkling water with lime. She sat down to wait and turned to the crossword page of her newspaper. She thought about the reason for being here and didn't like the queasy feeling that overcame her. Sophia checked her cell phone and went back to her puzzle.

TWENTY-FIVE

He arrived on time. Michael wore a dark blue Armani suit with white shirt and sky blue tie. The outfit did justice to his athletically built six foot six frame. Sophia immediately noticed that his flashy black wingtips were as shiny as his bald pate. He walked over to her table and flashed a handsome smile when he spotted her. She felt a tinge of happiness as they embraced briefly. It had been awhile but Michael Thompson had not changed any. He towered over her and was strong. She could feel his hard body through the unnecessarily lengthy hug.

He did not let her go and wrapped his agile body around Sophia as if they were kids. She smiled radiantly, her skin an embarrassing flush, and thought that maybe this would be the best part of their rendezvous. Sophia thought Michael had bad news to give her and this was his way of warming her up.

"Hey, Michael, how are you doing?" she asked trying not to sound down,

"I'm doing well," Michael replied with a grin. Sophia was busy measuring his attitude when Michael caught her off guard. "You're still as beautiful as ever. For a moment, I thought it was Halle Berry sitting over here. You're looking really great, Sophia."

"All that flattery is only going to cost you lunch. You're looking great yourself. I can tell that you're still into working out."

"No question but you're the one, baby."

"Yeah, whatever."

"I'm being real. You're still the finest thing walking on earth." Michael chuckled and Sophia almost did the same until she heard him ask, "How're you doing?" He waited for Sophia's answer.

They had met while attending the same law school but they never really dated. She had managed to stay clear of the dating circle. When they had graduated and he started seeing her in the entertainment news with Ascot, he knew she was definitely not going to be anything other than a friend. Over the years they kept in touch. Michael knew Sophia to be a kind, considerate person. Even though they were never intimate, he had based everything he knew on the strength of their platonic friendship. Michael didn't want to stand by and see anything bad happen to her. With that in mind, he had made the decision to meet with her. Even though he knew this meeting could compromise the latest project sitting on his desk, Michael did it because he really cared for Sophia. The uptown restaurant was chosen because he wanted to get her out of the downtown circle where he knew she was well known.

"I've been better," she answered hiding her emotions behind a friendly smile but Michael saw the strain beneath the surface.

The assistant DA was certain that what he was about to reveal to Sophia would have a devastating effect on her relationship with her fiancé. He took his seat and his eyes immediately dropped to the basket of bread on the table. The two, still holding hands, realized that the waiter was waiting on them. Neither said anything for a beat then Sophia took the lead and released his hand.

"I'll have glass of red wine, please."

"Make that two glasses of red wine," Michael said. The waiter departed and Michael resumed the touchy feely by reaching for her hands until Sophia gave in. When he spoke again, it was with both her hands cradled in his. "You're such a stunningly beautiful woman," he repeated, his eyes searching hers. Michael released Sophia's hands once the waiter returned with their drinks.

"I'll be back to take your order in a sec," he said and headed off.

"Thank you," they both replied and raised the wine glasses. "Salud." Their glasses clinked, they sipped and Michael's expression became gravely serious as he began to talk.

"This is going to be as much news to you as it was to me when I first found out last week," he began. Sophia gulped and swallowed hard. "Take it easy, Sophia."

"Please, Michael, I've waited all weekend long to hear this. Just tell me please."

"All right, all right. A few days ago I received a call from a friend…"

"A friend? Does your friend have a name?"

"No, with this friend the name is not important but he is an informant."

"An informant?"

"Yes, an informant and will you not disturb me, please? This is hard enough."

"Well, continue then."

"Anyway, he suggested that we should meet," he said then paused.

"Okay…"

"So I met him." There was another pause. Sophia was getting impatient and urged him to continue speaking.

"C'mon Michael, what happened when you met him? Exactly what did he say? Don't give me the district attorney spin on it."

"He told me that the feds were investigating Robert Morgan."

"Busta?"

"Yes, you know him as Busta. Anyway…"

"Does Busta have any idea of this?" Sophia asked and saw a look of concern registering on Michael's face. "I mean, why would you tell me of this unless Busta was already in custody? You're aware that he's retained me as his entertainment rep." Sophia saw Michael's grimace.

She knew this was not a good sign. Busta probably already had an indictment and Michael came to tell her of it himself. But how does Eric fit into this? Sophia wondered and was about to breathe a sigh of relief when she heard the words dreaded by any friend.

"Robert Morgan...ah, Busta is dead," Michael said. Sophia stared at him. The surprise in her wide-eyed expression jumped out at him.

"Huh? Are you sure? Busta? You could have gotten it all wrong," Sophia said and Michael was certain of her honesty when the tears began to well up. Sophia could only mutter a few unintelligible phrases before finally breaking down and sobbing loudly. Michael reached across and held her hands.

"I'm sorry," he said sounding his most sincere. "I'm really sorry. I thought you knew." Michael held her hands but Sophia pulled away.

"Please excuse me," she said and stood. Michael stood also.

"Are you going to...?" Michael was unsure of what to say and faltered.

"I'm going to the ladies room. I'll be right back," she said and walked away. Pangs of guilt hit him as he sat back down.

"Damn, what am I doing here?" he uttered below his breath as he watched Sophia walking away. From the way Sophia's back was hunched, he knew she was crying herself all the way to the ladies room. Michael drank all his wine and signaled to the waiter for two more glasses.

TWENTY-SIX

Sophia stumbled to the ladies room. The news of her friend's death had hit real hard. Her tears continued to flow as she closed the door. After about five minutes, she flushed and walked out determined to face whatever else Michael had to say. She had to hear him out no matter what. She had to find out even if it hurt her and the relationship she had built with Eric. She loved her fiancé but mistrust had crept between them.

Michael was glad when Sophia returned to the table. Not wanting to upset her any further, he inquired if he should continue the pre-lunch discussion.

"Really, Sophia, we could do this some other time, you know."

"No, we should continue. It was the surprise of finding this out. I had no idea that Busta..." Sophia paused and choked back more tears before continuing, "Its a real surprise, that's all, Michael."

"I'm sorry, Sophia. I mean, if I had..."

"Eric, I mean, Michael, you didn't know. I don't think Eric even knows," she said and slipped back into tears. Michael offered his white handkerchief.

"Do you want to...?"

"Michael, please continue. I'm a big girl, I can take it," Sophia said interrupting him. Michael checked to see tears still in her eyes but none on her cheeks. He would continue, he decided as he sipped some more wine.

"All right, this informer named some people that the feds were looking at. They were linked to one guy, Joey Maruichi.

Does that name ring a bell with you? How about his brother, Francisco? Maybe the name Frankie rings a bell?"

"No, they don't. I really can't be certain if Eric and Busta are in anyway involved with these people you're naming because they're always involved with doing things together. Because of the music, they're always doing things together."

"Maybe you could talk to Eric and he might tell you. You're going to have to find out. Anyway, the Maruichis appeared on our radar years ago. Frankie is an Italian guy with plenty of street smarts. He used his brains and muscles and has managed to build up something reminiscent of La Cosa Nostra. Except the people from different factions don't know anything about the others. This way, when one cell gets busted, they can't sing to the police even if they wanted to because they know nothing of what goes down in the next cell."

"This guy is a pretty sophisticated mobster, huh?"

"He's not only sophisticated and smart, he knows what to do with it."

"How so?" Sophia asked getting caught up in the song and dance. She realized that it was a huge case that excited Michael. She could tell from his body language that chasing this mobster around was important to him. It was becoming important to her for another reason.

"This guy is into everything illegal," Michael said as he hunched his athletic frame over the table. "He's into extortion, gambling, narcotics and murder," he continued counting off the list of transgressions on his fingers. "Maruichi's soldiers operate a hit man scheme where people are paid to kill whoever. The only thing they can't do is kill one of their own. That's his job. He takes great pride in disciplining his men who fall out of line. He's ruthless and he's been known to kill everyone in the family of those who choose to cooperate with the Feds. That includes next of kin as well." Michael saw uneasiness written all over Sophia's face as he continued to speak. "Needless to say, he has fewer rats and that's the reason we're having problems hooking this particular big fish," Michael finished and leaned back. He drank the rest of his wine.

"Michael, I really don't know what to make of this. What was Busta's involvement?"

"Well, it's not clear. He worked as a small time enforcer in the eighties under Joey's captaincy. Then, around ninety-three, he began overseeing some clubs and restaurants for Frankie. The Maruichis have legitimate businesses also," Michael said and could see the withdrawn look on Sophia's face. He was sure he had touched a nerve. "What is it, Sophie? You remember something?"

"Well, when I joined the law firm, Busta's account was already established," she began and stopped to think about it for a minute.

"When did you join the firm?" Michael asked cutting into her ruminations.

"In July of ninety-eight," Sophia said with a heavy sigh. "I'm sure it was July of that year because it was right before my twenty-fifth birthday. I remember they threw me a birthday party. That was so really weird since I was still new."

"You would remember that," Michael rejoined. "I know I would too if it happened right before my birthday. Things like that hold sentimental value for me," Michael said with a soft smile.

"Yep, when I got there Busta was already a client and I took over his accounts. There were several of them," Sophia said hugging herself.

"Is there anyway I can get a peek at his files?" Michael asked and knew immediately what the answer was going to be.

"Now, Michael, you know you're asking me to do something illegal," Sophia scolded.

"Well, you can see this as sharing of information."

"Whatever, Michael. You can go ahead and make it sound nice but it still comes out the same way. You're asking me to do something illegal while accusing others of doing the same thing. That's a double standard if I ever heard one," Sophia said and gave Michael the evil eye. He shrugged it off.

"So there's no chance?"

"Save it, Michael. It's not going to happen," Sophia said. She thought about it for a second and added, "I will say this.

Everything was on the up and up with the cafes and the night-clubs."

"Those places, the restaurants and clubs, were just part of the network. The Maruichis have real estate holdings in Staten Island and the Bronx. They have buildings in Harlem and a couple of auto dealerships that appear legit but they're crafty," Michael said and sipped on his third glass of wine.

Sophia sipped her wine as well. When she glanced around, she saw how the lunch crowd had transformed the place into a busy eatery. Food was not on her mind though. Michael had a purpose and she wanted to know what it was. Was she being investigated also?

She didn't want to be direct so she waited for him to mention how she fit into this. Again, she noticed the couples and Eric came to mind. She wanted to call him and see how he was but she waited. Sophia wanted to know what his role was and she knew Michael too well to believe that he had brought her all the way uptown just to talk about Busta. He didn't know how much of Busta's business she represented but she was sure he had more to tell. It wasn't long before she heard him starting to let her in on Busta's criminal past.

"The feds began investigating Busta and he knew this. It started out as routine just to investigate his connections," Michael said and paused to answer his cell phone. It must have been on vibrate, Sophia thought because she hadn't heard it ring. "All right, I'll call back, thanks," he said into the instrument then he returned to her. "Where were we?"

"You were explaining how the feds were interested in Busta," Sophia answered while examining the change in Michael's expression. "Is everything okay?"

"Yeah, everything is okay."

"Just seems like you were going through some changes during that phone call."

"No, it's the new rookie in my office. She feels compelled to call me on every single detail of a case. It's like I have no time off since she came on board."

"Seems like she likes supervision," Sophia opined as she

fidgeted with the utensils on the table.

"One of the job requirements is the ability to function without supervision but they liked her and dumped her on me."

"Maybe she's a slow learner?"

"I'd rather not discuss her. We're both on the clock," Michael said looking at the Patek on his wrist. "So where was I? Oh yeah...Now Busta has been under the radar. He was doing things for Maruichi, mostly legal," Michael smiled wryly as he said, "You know, the clubs and so on."

"Uh huh, I know all about his legal investments," Sophia added with a sarcasm that was totally lost on Michael. He continued undeterred.

"Recently, Busta called in a favor. It was a hit." Michael saw Sophia's mouth gaped in astonishment. "He wanted someone killed. It turns out that this particular hit was carried out by police officers," Michael said. Sophia slowed him with a raised hand.

"You mean Busta had a connection on the police force? Someone sworn to serve and protect? They responded to a citizen's request to murder somebody? Michael, it sounds to me like you're talking about police corruption and you're trying to pin it all on a dead man," Sophia said shaking her head but Michael was not through.

"Well, it turns out, by strange coincidence that the hit was carried out. As a result, two cops are dead and another man, known as Vulcha was killed. Lil' Long was supposed to be the intended target."

"No," Sophia heard the word escape her lips. She knew that in a strange way Michael's story made some kinda sense but why? Lil' Long had knocked her unconscious and he allegedly raped Deedee. She decided not to mention that piece to Michael. Her mind was inflamed with questions and Sophia wanted to find out more. She wanted the truth.

"The hit was supposed to be carried out by two cops. Apparently it was not a successful venture for them since they were also being watched by the department. The news of their involvement is being hushed because the bosses feel that any revelations will bring down the already low morale and may tip the department's hat."

"So you're telling me there is pending investigation on me or Eric?" Sophia asked.

"We thought your fiancé would be the next target marked for death. We were actually thinking of staking out his places of business but then when you called, I thought it was time I spoke directly to you, lawyer to lawyer."

"Michael, I appreciate your straightforwardness but why now? I mean, why didn't you mention this to me before? We are friends, aren't we?"

"Listen, we're friends but it wasn't about friendship. I was doing my job. I mean, I knew this from way back when but I'm sure you understand that my hands were bound. You know that the legal system and law enforcement are no different. I would've compromised what was at stake for my own selfish reasons," Michael said as sincerely as he could. He reached out and cupped her hands with his.

"You could've said something," Sophia said shrugging off the gesture.

"No more than you could've when I asked for Robert Morgan's financial records," Michael countered.

"That's client-attorney privilege and you know damn well that would be wrong, Michael. I couldn't..." Sophia said her voice trailing off.

"Then you should understand," Michael said. "It was the same."

"Michael, why are telling me this now? Why?" Sophia was agitated and wanted an answer. Michael did the best he could to soothe her.

"After your call, I spoke to my boss explaining that the other man involved in the hit was the same man that had been shot in Eric's apartment," Michael said and sipped on his wine. Sophia waited, impatient to learn her role. "He okayed that I speak privately with you and here we are."

"Now that I've got all this knowledge, what do you suppose I do with it?" Sophia asked sarcasm lacing her tone.

"When I initially found out about the investigation, I

prayed that you weren't aware and that Ascot was using you as cover for his schemes. At least I'm right about that piece. Maybe you can get your fiancé to come down and talk with me? Maybe you could talk some sense into him and get him to cooperate with our investigation? We may be able to provide immunity," Michael said. He had rolled the dice and now it was Sophia's turn. She looked shell shocked and her once shiny eyes appeared dull. Her brain was doing loops trying to integrate all of the information that had just been revealed to her. Sophia felt drenched by all the thoughts and questions.

"I don't think..." she started to say but Michael prevented her from taking cover.

"It's the only chance Eric's got right now. He's got to tell us what he knows and testify to it in court," Michael said then rushed to add, "with immunity, of course."

"You don't know Eric," she said and was surprised at Michael's answer.

"Yes, I do. What type of a fiancé frequents gentlemen's clubs especially when he's got a very beautiful woman he can go home to?" Michael asked and rushed to answer the question as Sophia's mind churned. "The types that are up to no good. The ones who eventually get caught with their pants around their ankles," he said.

Sophia shook her head back and forth. She couldn't shake the image of Eric carousing with scantily clothed dancers and stuffing dollar bills down their G-Strings. The repulsive reflection didn't leave her easily. Sophia was in shock and couldn't move. Slowly, it was all coming to her. Michael was giving voice to her worst nightmare. The picture that was being painted in broad strokes made it clear what Eric had been trying to hide all along. Her mouth went dry and she reached for her glass.

"We felt that Eric might be involved in other illegal activities but weren't certain until last night," Michael said and waited until the waiter took their order. As soon as the waiter was out of earshot, Michael didn't miss a beat. He knew exactly where he had left off.

"Eric's name popped up when we ran a check on Robert

Morgan's phone log. Again, this was routine stuff. We were trying to establish a connection to a possible murder not related to either of them. The victims were a drug dealing street worker named Deja and his girlfriend, Bebop. Both were found dead and the bullets were the same type that were used to kill Busta."

"But that happens all the time. I mean, the same bullets doesn't necessarily mean the gun was the same," Sophia protested. So far, Eric appeared to be far removed from the situation but Michael linked him to more.

"True but in this case, we went back to the phone calls between the two men. There is something going on."

"They were business partners and they knew each other from the street. It's all circumstantial."

"Again you're right, Sophie, but we continued our surveillance on Eric."

"Why continue?" Sophia asked. Michael could see the fury in her eyes as she continued. "Michael, don't tell me you authorized the surveillance of a private citizen. I'll..." She started and fumbled for words. "It's illegal."

"Eric is involved big time. Last night..." Michael's voice trailed off. It was as if he did not want to continue but Sophia pushed for more.

"Last night, what?" she asked. The waiter returned with another two glasses of red and set them down. "What happened last night, Michael?" Sophia asked after the waiter left. Michael heard the change in her tone and knew she was beginning to become nervous and angry.

"Last night, your fiancé spent the night with a couple of dancers from the Red Room," Michael said studying Sophia's reaction as he slowly unveiled the cherry on top of this meeting.

"He...he was supposed to be in the recording studio," Sophia said. Her voice had taken on a tone of defeat.

"Well, he did go to the studio," Michael said and watched as she breathed a sigh of relief.

"Oh, for a minute there I..."

"Hear me out," Michael said trying to calm her down. "He did go to the recording studio. He left urgently and stayed with some dancers at the Red Room for about 2 hours. After that, he went back to the studio. He stayed there until about eight o'clock in the morning. From there, he returned to the club and had a meeting with guess who?" Michael asked.

Sophia, too stunned to answer, just continued to listen but she knew what the answer would be. She barely got the name out before Michael jumped on it.

"Maruichi."

"Exactly," shouted Michael as if he just scored a touch-down.

Sophia could not believe her ears. This was a lot for her to swallow in one sitting. Her stomach growled and her head ached with the torrent of emotions. She went from angry to sad and back. When would this nightmarish roller coaster cease? She wondered as she looked at Michael hoping to find doubt.

Maybe this was an evil joke to play on an old college friend. She searched for the flash of a smile but none came. Sophia had to deal with this reality. She arrived at the foregone conclusion. My relationship is over with Eric. I can't go back. He lied and cheated. Tears welled. Sophia tried to hold them back.

"Are you sure, Michael?" Sophia finally asked and, unable to hold it together anymore, let the tears roll past her mascara and down her cheeks.

"Sophie, sweetheart, I wish I could tell you this is a lie or that it's some type of April fool's joke," he said holding her hands again.

"Thanks, Michael. I feel like such a fool thinking he was in the studio all these nights. I'm putting my feelings out there while he's conducting clandestine mob dealings with Busta. What's going to happen now?" Sophia asked.

"We have an office filled with records. An enormous amount of man-hours have been invested in endless surveillance. There are papers stacked so high, I can't even see above them. We still can't nail Maruichi and his gang and that's why we need Eric to turn state's witness."

"Michael, I know Eric. He's not going to commit to any-thing like that."

"That's why it's important that you put pressure on him. He's got to see that there is no other way."

"Look, I'll try but at the moment, Eric and I are not on good terms. We had a little fuss and it's not resolved yet. Give me about a week and I'll get back to you."

"Sophie, you don't fully understand. The urgency here is not only that Eric's putting himself at risk but he's also exposing you and his niece to..."

"I've got that, I really do. I just think I've got to re-evaluate myself and the position I'm in. That's all I'm saying."

"All right then. A week it is. I'll try to buy you all the time you've asked for but please try to deliver. It'll be a great day when cats like Maruichi and his crew are put away for good."

"And it will also be a great feather in the cap of an assistant DA, right, Michael?" Sophia asked just when the waiter returned. "I think we're going to have to skip lunch, thanks. Michael, lets just pay the tab and do lunch another time." Sophia rose from the table and gracefully walked to the exit while Michael paid the tab.

He met her out on the sidewalk. Her eyes were still wet from the tears they had shed. There will be plenty more tears to come, Michael thought as he helped with her coat. He couldn't help but notice her figure. Sophia could easily be mistaken for a model. Why would her man treat her bad? Michael wondered as they walked down the busy street.

"Where are you headed?" he asked.

"Back to work, why?"

"You're a pretty strong woman, Sophie," he said and kissed her gently on the lips. She didn't pull back. It was Michael. "You're going to be fine," he said trying to be supportive.

"Thank you, Michael. Where to now?" she asked.

"I'm headed back to work too," he said and they both waved for cabs.

She jumped into the first one that stopped and was gone. As the cab raced downtown, Sophia stared out the window trying to lose herself in a world that never existed, seeing things that were not really there. The ring of her cell phone jolted her back to reality. It was Deedee.

"Hello," she said into the mouthpiece.

"Sophia, I'm glad I got you. Busta is dead. He was shot. I saw it on the news. I haven't spoken to or seen Uncle E? I've been trying to reach him all morning," Deedee rambled. She sounded frantic on the phone and Sophia tried everything not to explode in tears.

"Yes," she said almost too quiet. She took a deep breath then spoke a little louder. "Yes, I heard the news."

"Are you okay, Sophia?" Deedee asked.

"Uh huh, I'll call you back in few minutes, Deedee," Sophia said and slowly closed the cellular in her hand. She reached into her bag and removed a tissue. She wiped the tears rolling down the side of her cheeks. Sophia dialed Eric and was directed to his voicemail. "Hope you're alright. Please call me..." Her voice faded as if the air had been cut off. She sobbed quietly as the taxicab moved through the midtown lunchtime traffic.

TWENTY-SEVEN

Eric nursed his pasta. It wasn't all that good, he decided. Eric came to the conclusion that the food wasn't the main attraction here. It was the chance to meet with the bosses and the captains. It was strictly mobster. Sturdy looking men with slick hair and crumpled suits sat around tables, arguing with each other like school kids.

They were having a rude time doing it too. Every so often, the conversation would break down into Italian yet, in this bevy of wise guys, Eric felt safer than before. Maybe it was the fact that their attitudes said it clearly. They didn't care if you thought they were gangster or not.

He thought about Busta's connection to this crew. Now that Busta was no longer around, Eric could use the protection but at what cost? He didn't want to lose Sophia and becoming involved with these people would certainly drive her away. On the other hand, he could try explaining it all to the police and take his chances on being sent away to prison. Eric decided to align himself with Maruichi.

"Now that Busta is gone, I feel that because of certain things, my life and the lives of my family might be threatened," Eric said to the man across the table from him.

"Yeah, I know a little about that. Protection is very, very important and you can never put cost on what your family and loved ones mean to you," Maruichi said as he wiped his mouth with the white cloth napkin. He leaned forward as if he wanted no one else to hear what he had to say but Eric. "You're the only one who knows."

"You're so right," Eric answered.

"You can count on me."

Eric Ascot was not used to dealing with people who were as ruthless as Frankie Maruichi but somehow Eric felt a sense of relief and said, "I may have lost Busta but I feel I've found someone who understands me."

"We're the same. I'm a family man and so are you. I wouldn't want anyone messing with my family. It wouldn't sit well with me to know that someone was trying to harm my family. Busta went to sleep thinking that everyone is fair but not everyone is so they have to be dealt with in that same sense." Maruichi spoke with great conviction.

Immediately, Eric knew that Maruichi did not get his reputation on the street for being soft. You could tell that he was in charge. He was a big time mobster. From the way people scurried about when he beckoned, Eric sensed that this guy was the real deal. Busta had mentioned him as a friend but he also remembered Busta warning him to stay out of his way because his greatest skills included extortion, loan sharking, illegal gambling, narcotics and murder. If you became indebted to him, then he would exercise one of his skills. He presided over a criminal empire with tentacles reaching as far as Canada. Maruichi was an icon who believed that after he died, some famous actor would be playing him in a movie.

Eric was considering whether or not he needed to be doing business with this lot or even if he needed any type of bulletproof protection when he heard Maruichi continued.

"Not only will it be a great plus for you, but I also think we'll be able to do business."

"I agree. I could use that help," Eric said. In the company of the mobsters, Eric felt safe and protected.

Later, he glad handed his way back up the stairs and smiled wryly at the parking summons for an expired meter. He sat in the vehicle feeling sorry for Busta as he retrieved his messages. Amongst them were messages from Deedee and Sophia. Sophia sounded as if she was still angry at him so Eric dialed Deedee.

"Uncle E!" Deedee sounded like she was shrieking.

"Yeah, Dee, what's good?"

"Uncle Eric, I'm so happy to hear your voice. Were you in the studio?"

"Yes, honey. Are you alright?"

"I'm okay but Uncle Eric, Busta..." Eric heard her voice trailing off.

"Yes, I just found out about it," Eric answered.

"You already knew. I thought..." Deedee began but Eric cut her off.

"Have you spoken to..." he started but Deedee didn't let him finish the question.

"Yes," Deedee said anticipating the question correctly, "I have spoken to Sophia. She wants you to call her."

"I will," Eric said. "No school today?"

"I'm out for a week. Spring recess, uncle," Deedee said sounding exasperated. There was a pause and she quickly added, "You will call Sophia, won't you, Uncle E?" The crackling sound of static from the line hummed in the background. Deedee was aware they were still connected but she asked anyway. "Uncle E, are you still there?"

"I'm gonna call her as soon as I hang up from you," Eric answered.

"I'm just making sure we weren't disconnected. You know how these lines are."

"Yeah, I'll call her now."

"Take care, Uncle E."

"Make sure all the locks are bolted and the windows are locked."

"Uncle E, I'll be fine. I'll see you later," Deedee said.

"Bye, honey." Eric closed the cellular. He started the Range Rover and let the window down feeling the comforting blast of fresh air. Eric drove off into the brisk morning breeze. He rode in a cloud of newly found security. You have to fight fire with fire, he thought as he pulled closer to the studio.

TWENTY-EIGHT

Sophia walked back in her office and slammed the door. She picked up the phone and called her secretary. "Miriam, please hold my calls."

"Mr. Donaldson dropped by while you were out. He never said exactly what he wanted."

"Thanks, Miriam," Sophia said then hung up the phone. She wondered what Donaldson wanted. He was one of the senior partners in the firm and had never been by to see her before. They did not have that casual type of relationship. Everything was done strictly business so his casual visit was a cause for concern. Sophia thought about this as she dialed his extension. "Mr. Donaldson."

"Ms. Sullivan, I stopped by to inform you of your client, Robert Morgan's, demise. I was about to call again. You saved me that trip," he chirped as if announcing the winner of a bet.

"Well, thank you for letting me know," Sophia started then quickly asked, "How did you learn of this?"

"Connections. It'll be all over the media soon."

"It's already all over the media."

"As senior partner, that's my concern. How did you spend your weekend? Probably had a real good one, eh? The media has been reporting the incident since Friday night. Is everything alright with your fiancé?" He asked. The question hit Sophia so hard that she stopped moving. There was a pause before she spoke.

"I'm trying to get to the bottom of that," she said as her cell phone rang. "Thanks for your concern, Mr. Donaldson," Sophia said and hung up the phone then answered her cell. "Hello, Eric," she said as she stood up. "We need to talk."

"Yeah, that's why I'm calling. I realize that we've been..."

"Eric, I'm really busy right now but I need to see you around eight. Is that alright?"

"Yes, I'll take you and Dee..."

"No, Eric, just me and you. Please, honey."

"Okay, babe, that's not a problem."

Eric hung up the phone with a feeling of triumph. Maybe getting away from Sophia and everything else had been a good thing overall, he thought. He had not really expected Sophia to be so cool but it seemed she had calmed down a lot. That was surprising since she really went off on Friday night consumed by her assumptions. Sophia had not given him any real choice but to take the time off. I'm gonna make it all better later tonight, Eric thought entering the recording studio.

TWENTY-NINE

Deedee sat up in bed when her cell phone rang. She wondered for a moment if her uncle was calling her back. She knew it was a forwarded call when she looked at the caller ID. "Hello?" Deedee said.

"Hey," a girl's voice came back at her.

"Hey, who's this?"

"It hasn't been that long. I am speaking to Deedee, right?" the caller asked.

"Yes, you are," Deedee replied nervously.

"Deedee, you don't remember me? It's Josephine, bitch," the caller answered.

Deedee couldn't believe her ears for a minute and then she screamed excitedly, "Oh, my god, Jo! What's up, girl? Where are you calling from?"

"I'm at the W Hotel, downtown. Where are you?"

"I'm at 86th Street and West End."

"Wait a minute, you guys moved?"

"No, no. Something happened and..."

"Yo, da shooting, that was y'all? That's one of the reasons I was calling. Like, what da fuck happened?" Josephine asked and Deedee could hear the excitement in her voice. She could also hear an ensuing argument in the background. Deedee lowered the volume on the television in an attempt to hear the argument. Deedee heard the squabble going on in the background. Josephine did not utilize the mute button and everything was crystal clear.

"I just said you curse too much..."

"Neither you or daddy listen to me when I be talking to

you but now you wanna tell me what to do now? Come on, Mommy, get real."

"Jo, you can call me at another time."

"No, it's all good, girlfriend. I don't know what's popping with the ol' biddy," Josephine said then Deedee heard another argument breaking out. "Yes, I'm talking about you. Who else is an ol' biddy here? Certainly not me," Deedee heard Josephine saying. "Hold on a sec, Dee."

Deedee looked at the telephone with curiosity. It was plain to see that Josephine and her mother had serious problems. From the tone in Josephine's voice, they were going for each other's throat. A few minutes later, Josephine returned to the telephone.

"Let me get off this phone. Where can we meet? We're about thirty blocks apart."

"Let's meet at the café at Sixty Sixth and First Avenue in about an hour," Deedee said.

"Okay, Sixty Sixth and First Ave. You know I ain't been in the city in a minute. These pretenders had me locked away out in the boonies, girl. I'll tell you all about it and why I ain't going back with them. See ya later, Dee," Josephine said and just before she could hang up, Deedee heard the girl ask. "Yo, Dee, have you spoken to Coco lately?"

"We were together on Friday. I haven't spoken to her since then."

"And she probably still don't have a damn phone. Her mother still smoking?"

"I don't know? I have a number though..." Deedee started only to be cut off by the excited Josephine.

"Will Smith was right," Josephine said.

"About what?" Deedee asked.

"Parents just don't understand," Josephine said laughing. "See ya in a minute, girl," she said finally.

"Alright then. I can't wait to see you," Deedee said. Before putting the telephone down, she could still hear the ongoing argument between Josephine and her mother in the background.

She sprang from the bed and was in the bathroom showering and pondering the possibility of seeing Josephine. They could probably hang out and do some shopping, Deedee thought. She had been given a line of credit and never used it before. There could never be a more perfect time, she thought while staring at her nude figure in the mirror. Not since before the death of Danielle had the girls hung out. Josephine and her parents had moved out of town immediately following Danielle's suicide. It wasn't just a case of another teen suicide to the girls. For Josephine, Coco and Deedee, it was an end to the camaraderie that had been developing since that fateful night when Deedee first met the girls, known as Da Crew.

Back then, they were a singing group with Coco, Danielle and Josephine. From the first time they hung out, Deedee felt like she belonged because the girls welcomed her and made her feel like a part of the group. Then there was the awful rape, she thought fixing her hair as best as she could. Deedee refused to follow this line of thinking and began to search for her hair products. Where is my gel? she wondered as she searched Sophia's bathroom. I'll call Coco and see if she wants to hang, she thought as she came across the cordless phone. Deedee dialed Miss Katie's number.

The older lady answered and told her to hold on. She had to check if Coco was next door. Deedee waited patiently brushing her hair there and trying to find a style that fit. She was thinking of scheduling an appointment with her favorite hair stylist when she heard Coco's grumpy voice on the phone.

"Sup?" Coco asked. Deedee skipped the attitude in Coco's cold greeting.

"Guess who called?" she blurted out and immediately realized that Coco wasn't in the mood to play the guessing games with her. "Josephine called and wants us to meet her at Sixty Sixth and First Ave," Deedee quickly added.

"Wait up. Jo called, yo?" Coco asked warming up significantly.

"Yep, she called and she wants us to hang with her. We should be meeting in about an hour."

"Say word?"

"Word up, Coco. You down?" Deedee asked and Coco thought about it. She would not have said yes if it wasn't for Josephine. Deedee knew she would be down.

"Ahight, yo. I'll link up with y'all. What's the name of da place, yo?"

"There's a café there. I can't think of the name right now but we'll wait for you on the corner," Deedee said.

"Ahight, that sounds good. I'll see y'all there, yo," Coco said and hung up.

Deedee replaced the cordless and felt a warm feeling that making up with a friend brought. It shot through her and resulted in a smile on her beautiful face. She fixed her hair and stared in the mirror thinking about what to wear. This should be really great, Deedee thought and hurried from the bathroom.

THIRTY

Coco scratched her head and ass. She thanked Miss Katie just before walking out.

"Thanks Miss Katie. I'm really sorry for bothering you."

"Oh Coco, don't be silly, child. You know you're more than welcome to use the phone anytime you want."

"That's really good looking out. I'll see you later, Miss Katie," Coco said and walked to her apartment next door. Her mother and Miss Katie had been living next door for all of Coco's life. Miss Katie was the godmother she always wanted. The old lady had assumed the big responsibility of watching over Coco while her mother was in the drug rehab.

Coco showered and got dressed in her baby blue RocaWear leisure suit with matching New Balance 440 sneakers.

Outside on the streets, Coco eased into her bop and lit a cigarette. She hailed a cab as she inhaled. She knew she was pressed for time and couldn't rely on the bus. A cab pulled up next to her.

"Where to?"

"I need to make a stop and then go downtown, yo," Coco said as she jumped into the backseat. The cab driver took off and Coco immediately halted him. "Chill, yo. Can you stop right at the next block, please?" The driver pulled over. "I'll be right back," Coco said.

"No, you pay fare first. Three dollars."

"What? Look, all I'm saying is I'll be right back and you're gonna take me downtown."

"No, you pay now and I wait," the driver said. Coco handed him three dollars and he drove off as soon as she stepped out.

"You fucking bitch ass," she yelled after him but the cab

was out of earshot. She walked still cursing beneath her breath until she was at the corner of a hundred and tenth. People were standing around the outside of the building. They nodded as Coco walked by and then one joined her.

"Whatcha looking for, ma?" he asked walking next to Coco.

"Whatcha got?" Coco asked.

"I got whatever you want, ma. Whatever you want," he repeated. This time he was real close and they stopped walking. Coco turned to face him and a smile crossed his face when she pulled out the ten spot. "A dime? This da shizit. You may even want a twenty." He pulled out a bag and handed it to Coco.

"This is kinda small, yo?"

"Yo, Coco, that's da real. You know I'm a take care o' you. Deja was my man and you was his customer. Da nigga ain't around no mo' so it's up to me."

"That's why I should get choice bags, cuz."

"Ma, this is choice weed. This bag's so nice it got stretch marks on it." They were both walking down the block haggling over the size of the bag when the shouting began.

"Five-oh!"

Coco heard it all going down around her. Sneakers hit the pavement at rapid speed. The only thing she saw were elbows and asses. She wanted to run but didn't and glanced around to see the dealer she was talking with being hauled off in a police car.

"You live around here, miss?" Coco heard the question and tried not to be too conspicuous.

"I'm from two blocks over. My cousin lives here. I was getting ready to go but that guy, he was trying to kick it to me talking 'bout he a playa and all women love him. All kinda stuff, you know..." Coco began and then heard a voice that was familiar.

"Yes, she does live in the neighborhood. I'll talk to this one," he said and Coco turned to stare into the eyes of one of the detectives from Friday night. He dragged her back to the van. "I could easily toss you but I'd rather not. You don't want to be part of this. You don't wanna be caught up in a bad situation. If I searched you, would I find anything on you?"

"Nope, I don't have anything on me. Like I was telling the officer, my cousin..."

"Coco, save it. What I really want to know is, when are you gonna come forward and finger who did all that shooting and why? That's all. Now you may walk away from here with your dime bag o' weed but if you don't come forward soon, I'll see to it that you never purchase another bag of weed again."

Coco saw the stern look on the face of Detective Hall. She desperately tried to hide the shadow of fear the detective cast on her. Coco unleashed a disarming smile and started chuckling.

"Calm down, detective. You're letting your job get to ya," Coco said without batting her brown eyes. They stared at each other. Coco, still smiling, added, "Now, are you gonna arrest me or what?" she asked. It was a bluff she had decided to play out to the end. Coco was aware that she could be locked up on the possession charge if he decided to search her but he would lose a chance to bring her over. He wanted badly to break an important case open more than the need to arrest Coco.

The detective looked at her sternly. He saw that she was street tough. He could've pushed her but he needed her to cooperate so he didn't push the matter any further. Hall pushed his card into her hand as he sent her on her way.

"Not this time, Coco. Get going before I change my mind. Take care," the detective said and went stone-faced. Coco wanted nothing else but just to keep on walking. She had secured the bag of weed and that was her purpose for being on this block. Hall may have known that. Not looking back, she raised her hand and another cab stopped. Coco jumped in the cab and from the backseat, she surveyed the scene of the police raid.

"Sixty sixth and First," she said as the cab drove off. From the rear of the cab, she could see the police searching the dealers one by one. Then each was cuffed and taken into the van. Coco kept her eyes on the activity until the whole scene disappeared from her view.

As the cab ride trailed through heavy traffic on the streets of the busy city, Coco could see the early sunshine of late April. She passed by the park with its patches of green grass and flowers blooming but could not stop her mind from stressing what had just happened. Was that detective trying to harass her deliberately? Of course, she thought. He needed a way of getting at Eric Ascot the way the world wanted to get at O.J., anyway possible. Coco sat back and whistled to a jazz number piping through the car speaker.

THIRTY-ONE

It was a windy spring afternoon and the sun shone beautifully. A warm breeze rustled the branches of the trees and stirred the birds nestled in the kindling. On the corner of 66th and 1st Avenue, the streetlight changed and Deedee looked around to see if she was in the right place. She checked her watch then glanced through the crowd trying to find Josephine's face. She was trying to remember what the girl looked like when she felt someone grab her from behind, immediately bringing a scream out of Deedee.

"Josephine, is that you girl?" Deedee shouted. She heard the laughter and turned to see Jo doubled over in laughter. "Girl, you crazy. Don't you know you're in the city? You almost scared the bejesus outta me," Deedee said and fixed her hair.

"Whassup? Whassup? Whassup, Dee? You're still looking really, really fly, girlfriend. How're ya doing?" Josephine could not stop chuckling.

Hearing the compliment and knowing what she had been through trying to get dressed, Deedee smiled but deep down inside, something made her feel like wiping the smile from Josephine's lips for scaring her. Dee knew she had made the right choice in going with her black D&G jeans. They complimented her figure.

"I see your time away from the city hasn't changed you much. Once a city girl, you can never go back. You know what I mean, right?" Josephine asked and Deedee gave her a hug. They embraced like lost ones finding each other again.

"You're looking good. I mean, like you've been working out a lil' sump'n," Deedee said with a wink as they released each other from their embrace.

"I've been on the cheerleading team, been running track and playing basketball." Josephine waved her hands over her body like an artist proudly introducing his work. "When you're bored, you find a creative outlet. I was a finalist for the Hornet's cheerleading squad but then they moved outta town."

"Who are the Hornets?"

"Oh, they're the basketball team from the town where I was living."

"Get out. Josephine, that would be so you. I mean, you can dance your ass off."

"Well, I'm glad you feel that way cuz my asshole of a mother feels that it's downright disgraceful for anyone to make their living dancing."

"Really?"

"Yeah, really. Outside of ballet and that kind of stuff, she thinks all other types of dancing for money is like being a stripper. When I first brought her the application, she told me, 'You might as well tell me to sign this paper so you can be a stripper'," Josephine mimicked and Deedee made a incredulous face.

"Now, that's bad."

"It's all good though. I made her sign that shit like quick fast in a hurry. Where's Coco? That girl's still moving like a snail, I see."

"She should be here soon. I told her we'd be here waiting."

"You should never have told that girl that. Now she gonna be taking her sweet ol' time. Anyway, how ya doing, Deedee?"

"I'm kinda, you know, trying to get it together. We had a bad weekend and I..."

"That's right! I saw that shit on the news, girl."

Josephine seemed to get too excited at recalling the news. She watched Josephine closely then asked, "How long were you out in the country, Jo?"

"I'm loud, right? It's been too fucking long and I ain't going back to that boring ass place. Ya heard it here first. I'm staying in the city," Josephine proclaimed while Deedee stared in amazement. "Where's that bitch, Coco, at?"

"Here she comes," Deedee whispered beneath the chatter.

Eyes turned, riveted on the five-foot-eight, athletically built girl with smooth as chocolate skin. Something about Coco's graceful motions caused her to stand out amongst the sidewalk crowd. From across the street, Deedee and Josephine watched as Coco braced herself in anticipation of street traffic. Her mass of brown hair was an untamed Afro celebration. The tresses shadowed her determined cheekbones. Watching her glide was like listening to her lyrical flow. She was smooth action.

It was easy the way she raised her hand and waved a peace sign to a passerby. Coco's big brown eyes squinted to shield her vision from the rays of the relentless sun. Graceful, she expertly navigated traffic as she crossed the busy city street. Not waiting for the streetlight, her bop came easy when she was on the less busy side. Resplendent and breezy in her blue RocaWear leisure, her eyes sparkled when she spotted the girls. It had been a long time and none of them could hold back the excitement.

"Coco, you're looking all that and the chips. You're so cool," Josephine shrieked. She was taller in a pair of Moschino jeans and denim shirt but it was the three-inch heels that made her even sexier. Her brown eyes twinkled with delight. Coco grabbed her arms.

"Josephine, you're so crazy. You're looking really fresh, girl," Coco said. "Girl, what happened to you?"

"I missed ya, Coco," Josephine said her voice cracking, exposing the passion she felt.

Coco may have appeared to be overcome with the emotions caused by the presence of Josephine but she walked quickly past Deedee. She hugged Josephine with the abandon you have for someone special to you. Deedee smiled as she watched tears of joy roll down Josephine and Coco's faces as they screamed each other's name.

There were no more words necessary. Nothing was said for a couple of minutes while the girls embraced. Deedee watched and was drawn into their closeness. She remembered first meeting Da Crew. Since Danielle's death, Coco and Josephine had not seen each other because Josephine's parents had relocated to North Carolina.

This was spring break and Josephine's parents were on the verge of a nasty divorce. Josephine had been daddy's little girl. Now, she wasn't sure who to trust anymore. Her mother brought her back to the city to win her daughter over. These girls were the reason Josephine wanted to be back. Although Danielle had been lost, she held one of her sisters again. Deedee joined the two in their emotional squeeze. She kissed Coco's wet cheek.

"I'm never gonna leave you guys again. I missed you so much, Coco. Oh my gosh! I can't believe we're here together again." Josephine looked up to the sky, waved her arms, and shouted, "Thank you, Lord! You guys wouldn't believe this but I've been praying this day would come for like a couple of weeks now."

"What's good, girl? You're turning into another drama queen like..." Coco's voice trailed off as if she didn't want to say it. Josephine wasn't scared to so she did.

"Like Danielle? Oh no, you're not trying to compare me to her. She's probably in heaven sitting in front of the mirror with her make-up yelling; 'I didn't bring the right color. God, can you make this shade a little lighter, pretty please? They ain't got no make-up in heaven!" Josephine made a pleading face like Danielle would have and both Deedee and Coco broke into laughter. Josephine continued in jest to rag a friend who had been important to both Coco and herself. She may have been even more important to Josephine. "She would cause God to throw lightening bolts and thunders at her like, 'Danielle, you don't need no make-up in heaven. Maybe you belong on the other side'." The three teenaged girls roared in laughter hugging and giving each other five, while standing on the street corner.

They had finally met despite several earlier attempts that ended in failure. Coco had been calling and Josephine's parents hadn't allowed any messages. Now they were together again, the remaining members of the crew. They had competed together many times and had won just as many. Josephine began reliving their last performance and how happy she had been.

"Yeah, girl, I was da shit running wit Da Crew. We had so

much fun. Seems like so long ago, huh? But it was just yesterday," Josephine said and danced around. She was in great shape and really looked fine. She was flying and her high spirits were contagious. Deedee laughed more than she had in the last couple days. It had been like living in hell but now she relaxed with Coco and welcomed the effervescent Josephine.

"Let's get sump'n to eat."

"I'm good yo," Coco said immediately.

"That may be you but I ain't had nothing since earlier today."

"So what're you saying, Josephine?" Deedee asked.

"I'm saying, I'll go with you but I want all of us to go together."

"Well, Coco?"

"Why you gotta speak for me, yo? I said I don't want nothing to eat. That's what 'I'm good' means. Ghetto 101."

"Am I detecting a lil' bitty attitude here?"

"I don't know what you talking 'bout, bitch."

"Oooh, things getting hot round here."

"No, Josephine. I'm cool but come on, you can't speak for nobody else." Coco spoke directly to Josephine, all the time avoiding the look Deedee threw at her. Josephine knew there was real tension and moved to squash it.

"Ahight, we ain't seen each other in a minute. Am I gonna have to kick some ass right away to get y'all children to cooperate?"

"Nah, I just don't want anyone speaking on my behalf, that's all. I know what I'm trying to say and I wanna say it."

"Ahight, ahight. Deedee, don't speak on Coco's behalf, you heard me?"

"It ain't that simple. Some people wanna act ostentatious like they down to earth," Coco started to speak but Josephine wasn't tolerating it.

"Wait a minute. Back the fuck up, bitch. Say what? Ostentatious? When are the regents?" Josephine asked laughing.

"Coco is right. I shouldn't speak on her behalf. I'm sorry, Coco," Deedee said.

"Sounds like an apology, Coco. Can we kiss and make-up now? Damn!" Josephine said trying to make the situation light. Deedee had offended Coco and there was a grudge. Someone had to back down and Coco did.

"Deedee, look. I probably still have a chip on my shoulder so I'm just gonna say I'll be cool, yo," Coco said and offered Deedee a handshake. The girl pulled Coco forward and gave her a hug.

"Ah, alright, it's settled. Let's go eat," Josephine said and all three walked a couple of blocks to the 62nd Street Café. "Y'all hold hands cuz I have some shit to tell y'all."

"Girl, you went down south for a minute and became a southern drama queen," Coco said and Deedee broke into laughter.

"Hold up. Don't be laughing at her jokes. She was just your enemy a minute ago."

"No matter what, we'll always be girls," Deedee said.

"May I take your order?" the waiter asked once they were seated.

"What is the special for the day?" Josephine asked. The waiter answered with a smile.

"Arugula salad with poached salmon," he said. He paused and was about to add something but Josephine cut him off.

"Sounds good. I'll have that," she said returning the smile.

"And what will it be for you, ladies?"

"I'll have the soup and salad, please," Deedee said. Coco said nothing.

"And you, Miss?"

"Nothing."

"She'd like a few more minutes before..."

"Didn't I just tell you a few minutes ago not to speak for me?"

"I'll give you a few minutes and you can order then. If there's nothing else, I'll go place these orders right now. Enjoy, ladies," the waiter said and departed the table. Coco was still heated.

"Damn, what part of it all don't you understand, yo? I'll be glad to clear it up for you," Coco said to Deedee. She spoke loud enough for the waiter to turn and asked if everything was alright.

"Yes, thanks," Josephine immediately replied.

"Perhaps some water?"

"Yes, please," Josephine answered. "Could you make it very cold? Thank you," she said when she saw Coco's nostrils flare. "What is it with y'all two? Must I break y'all both off sump'n?" Josephine asked. She looked at Deedee and then at Coco before adding, "Y'all better learn to get along before I don't take y'all back out the hood. You heard me, the two of yous?"

"Whatever, bitch. I just don't need a spokesperson, that's all."

"Both of you need to stop acting like y'all ain't got no home training. Man, I miss Danielle. See, we'd be too concerned about her shit to be dwelling on this boring shit."

"Shaddup, bitch," Coco yelled just when the busboy delivered ice cold water to the table. He appeared to be startled by the ruckus.

"I'm sorry. We didn't mean to scare you, sir," Deedee said.

"Oh, now you're gonna be speaking on behalf of the whole table? I don't need anyone speaking..." Josephine started with a wink but Coco was not having a drop more of it.

"You better put that shit to rest, yo," Coco said and when she saw that the other girls were chuckling, she joined in. "Y'all are some dumb asses, okay?"

The food arrived and Deedee and Josephine ate heartily. Coco eventually ordered a root beer float. The girls settled into idle chatter as they dined and passed the time.

"You know food tastes so much better when you're hungry," Josephine said.

"You can say that again. How was your meal?" Deedee asked.

"Hmm, so-so but because I'm starving, it's all good. And yours?"

"Delicious," Deedee said smacking her lips. "How's your shake, Coco?"

"My float? It's ahight, yo," Coco answered.

"My float's ahight, yo." Josephine said mocking Coco then excitedly continuing. "Yo, lemme tell y'all. Them niggas down south, they be killing me wit their 'yo this' and 'yo that'. I thought they were all your peeps, Coco."

"There's a hood everywhere. If you think that I'm the only one speaking this way, its like saying I'm the only one who grew up in da hood," Coco said and Josephine held her hand to her mouth as if she was speaking into a microphone.

"Ladies and gents, that was Miss Coco from da hood bringing you hood facts for the day. We will not try to paraphrase the bitch cuz she ain't having it. Ha, ha, ha." Both Deedee and Josephine rocked with laughter and although Coco gave a pretentious smile, inside she was really happy to see Josephine. They kept on laughing until the waiter arrived.

"Hey, we should dip. The bill is gonna be too high," Josephine said still chuckling.

"Back in the days me, you, Dani maybe. Now? I don't think so, yo," Coco said with a wink and nodded her head in Deedee's direction. The gesture was ignored by Deedee.

"Ahight, remember when we used to do that shit? Lord, why did you have to take the craziest sister I've ever had?" Josephine's voice trailed off and tears ran freely down her cheeks.

"Jo, you're a mess girl but I love you anyway," Coco said as her eyes filled. While Deedee cried quietly, Josephine raised her glass and they all followed suit.

"To our girl, Danielle. May she rest in peace," Josephine said.

"To Danielle, she was the fiercest dancer and a dope singer. She was all that and more," Coco said.

"Here's to Danielle. May her star continue to shine on even though she's gone."

"Here, here," they all said and drank their water. It was symbolic of the bond that the girls had with their fallen comrade, Danielle. For a minute, each girl seemed to retreat into a private memory.

Their group, Da Crew, had started out with two members

and had grown to three when Coco joined up with Danielle and Josephine. Da Crew had entered and won several talent competitions which led to the finals in a citywide talent search. The winners were Coco, Danielle, and Josephine. After celebrating their win, Danielle was never seen alive again. The police had found her naked with a bullet hole in her head and a nine millimeter next to her body. The weapon had her fingerprints all over it. There was no note. Forensic tests done later revealed high amounts of cocaine and heroine in her blood stream. The experts had been baffled as to why she did not die of an overdose.

Their glasses clinked and water washed down their meal. The thought of Danielle had stirred memories that dampened their spirits. Coco saw the forlorn look on the faces of the other girls. She knew they were teary eyed and saddened by the memories. The nostalgic trip had taken its toll then Deedee broke the trance.

"Let me see that?" Deedee asked.

"See what?" Josephine retorted in a crying voice.

"The bill."

"Oh, I'm sorry, here you go," Josephine said and handed the bill to Deedee. She examined it then leaned forward and spoke to the other two.

"We can each walk as if we're going to the bathroom and then you guys..." Deedee started but the other two held their hands up.

"Whoa."

"You know you ain't built for that."

"Let's just pay this," Josephine immediately suggested as soon as she heard the attitude in Coco's voice.

"Just a thought," Deedee said and summoned the waiter. She gave him a fifty. "Keep the change," Deedee told him and smiled.

"Thanks for trickin', Dee," Josephine said. She gazed at Coco batting her eyes several times.

"Yeah, no doubt. Good looking out, Deedee," Coco said and felt the pressure of making the day a better one ease onto her shoulders. In the past, she had been the one Da Crew had always relied on. When it was time for hanging, Coco was it so she made a suggestion.

"Let's go check out a flick, yo," Coco recommended.

"Sounds good to me," Josephine said. "And I ain't fussy 'bout nothing we see either," she continued.

"Why?" Deedee asked.

"Honey, my parents had me locked away in the country for so long that anything I look at in this city is gonna be new to me," Josephine said.

"You got it bad, girl." Deedee said.

"Had it bad. I done told y'all, I ain't going back there," Josephine said.

"Oh ma Lord, what done happened to our poor chile?" Coco asked mocking Josephine. "They done turned you into Kizzie. You straight outta 'Roots', yo," Coco said. Josephine eyed her for a beat then announced.

"I can't blame my parents for wanting me out of this crack infested place. They didn't want me to be cracked up like some people we know."

"Ooh, that one was low, bitch. But at least some people you know ain't running, girl. We staying right here."

"Yeah, where all the dealers know your name, huh?" Josephine asked. Then with a knowing smile, she added, "Speaking of which, I know you got a lil' sump'n. Just tell me you got sump'n to roll."

"And if I don't then what? You gonna beat my ass or sump'n, bitch?" Coco asked with a chuckle.

"You mean to tell me you couldn't get weed down south?" Deedee asked

"I know I could but because I was new, everytime I went to get it I had to dumb-down. And Coco, you know me."

"You dumb down for no man," Coco finished.

"Not for no man but I did for sump'n to roll-up."

"No you didn't," Coco said.

"Yes I did. Coco, you know I could hold my smoke but nig- gas down there, they don't smoke wit bitches. So you gotta play ditsy like and run up on the cool looking dude and be like, 'Oh boy, don't tell me that's reefer you're smoking? Like, I've been really trying to smoke and get high but I can't get the feeling, you know?'" Josephine said as she flirted and fixed her hair while batting her eyes. "Then the nigga will get you weed until you give-up sump'n, tongue him down, let him feel on the titties, put his hands down your drawers or whatever but don't give up no ass."

"Why? I mean if you gave him sump'n, it seems he would bring you more or better."

"That's only in your head, yo."

Josephine was laughing so hard she couldn't continue talking. Finally, she was able to control herself long enough to say. "If you gave him ass, he'd stop immediately and you've got do it all again. You've got to learn him slow. Peer pressure is a bad thing." Josephine was shaking her head and giggling.

"Jo, shame on you, girl," Deedee said but watching Josephine's comical face started her laughing again.

"Hey, I needed a lil' sump'n to smoke. I was new and I didn't know any better," Josephine said.

"You're still a crazy ass."

"Shoot," Josephine said, "after awhile, word got around and I had all the boys bringing me weed. I developed my own delivery service. Never ran out unless of course I had my period. Niggas can always tell when a bitch is on da rag. They don't even have to come around. Must be in my voice."

"Jo, you lil' ho," screamed Coco.

"It's true. The day my period arrived, the weed always ran out. I'd be callin' and niggas be like, 'Nah, I ain't got none. Holla back at me next week.' I'd be thinking, 'Ain't this a bitch'," Josephine said and the girls all laughed. Coco was happy to see Josephine and Deedee needed the comic relief.

Josephine's hilarious demonstration of the lengths she had to go to get weed while she was out of the city brought fun to the setting. Her re-enactments and antics caused laughter to rock the girls' bodies. Their eruptions ended in a crescendo of guffaws that aired loudly throughout the café. The noise caused a minor disruption and other patrons threw annoyed glances in the girls' direction. Those close by either sneered or snickered at them.

"Yo, Jo, over on this side you ain't got to put out for some weed. Ahight, yo?" Coco said still chuckling.

"On that note, let's be out," Deedee said. The girls walked out of the café and left the waiter happy either about his big tip or the comedic drama. All eyes turned to see them out. Some were frowning and others smiling.

"Enjoy the rest of your day, ladies," the waiter said and bowed as they passed by him.

"What flick are we gonna catch?"

"Let's just walk until we see a movie theater."

"Alright, you're in the city now."

"So what you're saying?"

"We can't just be walking. We gotta have a destination."

"Okay, I got it. Let's go shopping and then we can check out that new 2Pac joint."

"Deedee, girlfriend, you've got to be talking window shopping. Girl, I'm so broke I can't even pay attention much less go shopping. Where you wanna go?" Josephine hurriedly asked.

"I don't think she's talking 'bout no ninety nine cents store. That means it's a wrap, yo. I ain't got it like that," Coco said.

"I got y'all," Deedee said. The response left Coco and Josephine stunned. They stared incredulously at each other. Deedee looked anxiously at both of them. "I'm for real," she said. "I'll pick up the tab," Deedee continued as both girls looked at her with their mouths wide open.

"First of all, don't be a show off cause we all know that it's your uncle and not you that's gonna pick up the tab..." Coco started to speak but Josephine cut her off.

"Nah, Coco, let her be. Deedee can be a show off. I mean, as long as nobody gets hurt, right?"

"Whatever, yo."

"C'mon, Coco, be a sweetheart today for Jo? Does it matter who picks up the tab? It ain't you, yo," Josephine said pleading with Coco.

"Why you gotta be acting all country, Jo? You switched up so much on me, girl. You used to be..."

"The devil used to be an angel."

"Whatever, bitch."

"You ain't got nothing else to do. No school and no test to study for. Hang with us, Coco."

"I said whatever, bitch."

"Still the same hardcore sista, huh?" Josephine was toe to toe with Coco. They were circling each other as if they were sparring. All they needed to do was throw some punches but only the harmless words of a friend came. "You ain't never gonna change, bitch, but today you can be...umm, nicer?"

"Yeah, bitch, you best bite your tongue."

"You can take a bitch out da hood but you can't get da hood out a bitch."

"Yeah, bitch, cuz I'm ghetto like that."

"Really? You ghetto?" Josephine was feigning disbelief but Coco was not backing down.

"That's right. Running wit da rats and roaches in dirty stairwells. That's just me getting down so the people feel my struggle cuz in the end you too will be enchanted. All I'm saying is, I ain't just another ghetto girl."

"Whatever. Coco da rebel. I ain't trying to hear you right now. Let's just hang outside the hood today and tomorrow, I promise we'll work on da rebel shit. Ahight?"

Deedee watched as Coco and Josephine cavorted on the street. It was plain for all to see that there was a bond wound so tightly that not even distance or time could loosen it. They were real friends arguing every point like sisters to the end. The way they finished each other's sentences and the amount of ribbing each took off the other were barriers Deedee knew had to be sur-mounted, especially if she wanted a real relationship like the one she craved. The fact that Coco wore a thin skin made this feat just a little bit more difficult. It was heavy on her mind when she heard Josephine speak.

"Ahight, we going shopping, y'all. What's our limit, Dee?"

"We're all entitled to one outfit."

"An outfit each?"

"I'm talking about everything." Both girls appeared puzzled by the offer Deedee had made.

"Be more specific, Dee."

"How much more specific can I get? Whatever you con-sider an outfit to be. You know like a top and bottom to match, a handbag or purse, a hat..."

"A Benz," added Josephine. "Girl, you're a wreck but I'm with it. How 'bout it, Coco?"

"Don't be throwing me into no scheme, Jo. You were the one running your mouth and making all 'em plans, yo," Coco said as Josephine moved closer to her and whispered.

"Tell me is this bitch crazy or what?" Josephine asked under her breath.

"My name is Bennett and I ain't in it."

"Whatever, Coco," Josephine said then Coco whispered back in Josephine ears.

"I think da bitch is ditsy, though."

"Why y'all taking so long to make your minds up? It's real-ly a simple deal."

"I'm in," Josephine said. "But you know how some people gotta front."

"Who's front'n, yo? I was born ready for whatever. Let's go."

"Ahight, that's what I'm talking 'bout." Josephine was excited and Deedee hoped that her exuberance would be trans-ferred to Coco who was still acting cold. Maybe Josephine's pres-ence was what both she and Coco needed after the horrific week-end they had just shared. Deedee's bid to make up with Coco was hatched with this shopping scheme.

She hailed a cab and they all piled in. The cab raced off to the shopping district of Fifth Avenue. Josephine eyes widened with anticipation as the designer stores came into view.

"This is gonna be so great," she said when she saw the Polo, Channel, Gucci, and Fendi boutiques. Josephine saw Denzel Washington walking out of Dior. "Look, it's the sexiest man alive. Denzel!" she screamed as he continued walking. The girls waved at him. He returned their wave with a smile.

"Yeah, he's the best," Deedee said.

"He was dope in 'Training Day,' yo. Matter o' fact, he killed that role."

"No kidding. He's dope in all his roles."

"Imagine getting a Oscar for a role like that? He should've received one for his Malcolm X role," Deedee opined.

"That's true, girl. He should win sump'n for every role he plays," Josephine agreed.

"I'm telling you, Coco, I cannot wait to become an actress. It'd be over. Over, ya heard me?" She acted as if she had a microphone to her mouth. "Ladies and gentlemen, the academy award goes to Miss Josephine. Yeah."

Coco looked doubtful as she watched the excited Josephine throw kisses at her imaginary crowd. Both she and Deedee jumped as the overjoyed Josephine kissed both their cheeks.

"Ugh, don't tell me you gone that way too?" Coco said feigning revulsion.

"Not hardly. Strictly-dickly, girlfriend. That's not ever gonna change but a lot of other things have," Josephine said. She was sandwiched between Coco and Deedee. Coco felt the vibe in her and knew she wanted to talk but she didn't push. Coco thought she'd let Josephine make the first move. Coco knew her friend well enough to know that she couldn't hold anything inside for very long. Eventually, she'd talk.

"Really now?" Coco said with a smile.

"I'll tell you about it soon," Josephine said as the cab pulled to the busy sidewalk curb. Deedee paid and the girls jumped out. "Ahight, we're here. What's our limit?" Josephine asked.

Deedee thought for a second and answered, "There are no limits. The rules are if you like it, you buy it but you've got to wear it all together. Like the hat, the gloves and the scarf have gotta match. The outfit has to be complete."

"Let me get this right. A complete outfit? No limits. I must be dreaming," Josephine said. "But just one outfit, right?" she asked, still unsure.

"One complete outfit," Deedee said and raised one finger.

"Got it?" Deedee asked. Coco raised her eyebrows and shrugged her shoulders.

"What are we waiting for? Let's go shopping, girls," Josephine said grabbing both Deedee and Coco by their arms.

The trio skipped across the busy street and walked into the Coach boutique on the corner. "Good afternoon, ladies. May I help you?" Not waiting for an answer, the store clerk continued, "If you see anything that I may be able to help you with, I'll be right over there." His words must have triggered a switch. The afternoon shopping spree had officially begun. Ching ching.

Early blossoms were evident all around on this late April afternoon. Here in midtown, a busy pre-season summer sale raged down Madison and Fifth. In the hours that followed, the girls covered every fancy store on Madison, expertly combing through designer outfits that caught their every fancy. Occasionally, Coco and Josephine made faces of disbelief when they glanced at some of the price tags which were displayed. Being a bit more privileged, Deedee didn't even bother to bat an eye.

"Dior makes some nice evening joints but this shit is ridiculously expensive, yo," Coco said after going through a couple of stores.

"I ain't looking at price tags. I'm keeping my eyes peeled for something sexy from Donna Karan and her boutique is close by," Josephine responded.

"What, for the prom?" Coco asked.

"Not really but that could be a secondary motive," Josephine said walking away and inspecting some dresses. Coco lingered awhile and rubbed her cheek against the silky fabric of one particularly beautiful dress.

"Girls, there are no limits. Is there anything y'all see in here that you like?" Deedee asked.

"They ahight," Josephine answered casually keeping it moving.

"Dior's style is the dopest, Coco," Deedee said as she huddled next to Coco. "I saw you had your eyes on that red outfit back there. That's cool. It would match your skin tone really well,"

Deedee continued.

Coco looked at her for sometime without answering. When she spoke, she immediately regretted it. "Why ya gotta be trying to make selections for me. I mean the dress is really nice but..."

"But what, Coco?" Deedee asked.

"I'm saying, I'm really not trying to get your opinion. The only reason I'm here playing your game is because Jo wanted to."

"I respect that, Coco. I mean I can't blame you for whatever you wanna hold against me."

"Hold against you? Do you remember that only a couple o' days ago you were calling me a hood rat?"

"Coco, I never called you that. I never did," Deedee said. Coco stared at her with fierceness of a boxer facing his challenger. "I would never call you that," Deedee reiterated in a harmless whisper uttered without retreat.

What is the plan if your opponent doesn't back out of the fight? All day long Coco had it in her mind to yell, 'To hell with Deedee because she's a phony bitch'. Now it seemed it was all just a big misunderstanding on Coco's part. Was she deliberately trying to be mean to Deedee? There was no real need to be, Coco decided. Lost in her own thoughts, she could still hear Deedee's apologetic voice.

"...I mean if I knew that's what you thought, I would've called and really tried to apologize. I would not think that of you, Coco. You're far better..."

The only question remaining was, Did Coco believe her? "So you wouldn't mind coming to visit me in da hood, then?"

"A visit is no problem. It's just that in light of what was going on at the time, I knew my uncle wouldn't let me go with you."

"Okay, maybe I was too quick to jump to conclusions. I'm sorry, Dee. How're your uncle and Sophia doing by the way?" Coco asked. She could be so cool, Deedee thought as she answered.

"They both good, I guess. Sophia went to work earlier and my uncle, he was in the studio all night doing his thing."

"That's good. I been home working on some rhymes too. Say whassup to them for me, ahight?"

"Ahight, Coco. So, do you want to get that dress?"

"I really don't know. I'll take a look in some other stores then I'll make a decision, ok?"

"That's all good, Coco."

"But Dee, how're you gonna pay for these outfits, yo?"

"I've got a card from my uncle," Deedee said with a shrug of her shoulder. "And I've never used it. It just seemed like a fun thing to do right now. Shopping with my girls," Deedee said as Josephine rejoined them.

"You got that right," Josephine said. "I've seen enough. Ladies, let's bounce up outta this piece."

"Oh, because you're through, we should?" Deedee said with a laugh.

"Nah but I can't wait for Donna Karan," Josephine said beaming which left Coco and Deedee rolling their eyes. They left the store and continued investigating all the sales. Crisscrossing from east to west, they left nothing but the pavement unturned.

As the expedition went on, the girls strolled through blocks and blocks of designer stores until they all had their complete outfit. Josephine claimed a black Donna Karan gown which really complemented her now sexy physique and Deedee sparkled with a new Versace silver dress. Coco settled for the elegant red dress by Dior that Deedee liked. It was an expensive but pleasurable time.

THIRTY-TWO

Later that afternoon, the girls cooled their heels at the trendy, Mr. Chow's restaurant.

"This is where all the hip hop stars come and discuss biz," Josephine said as she surveyed the crowd in awe.

"Yeah, the Def Jam crowd and a lot of video models are over to our left," Deedee said.

"Musicians, dancers and models all go hand in hand," Josephine said. "Oh my God! Look y'all, there goes Jamie Fox!"

"Where at?" Coco and Deedee chorused.

"Over there," Josephine said.

"Look, we're not here to sweat these industry peeps, Josephine. Can you act cool and just eat your food, yo?"

"Look, there's Show Biz and Silky Black. We met Silky Black. Think he's gonna remember us?" Josephine asked. Not waiting for a reply, she bounded across the dining room. Coco and Deedee sat with jaws dropped at Josephine's brazenness.

"Is that bitch crazy or what?" Coco asked shaking her head.

"Oh my God, she's actually talking to them and disturbing their meal," Deedee said her eyes riveted on Josephine. She turned away quickly when Josephine pointed in their direction. Coco looked up just in time to catch a wave from Silky Black. She threw up a peace sign.

"Her parents must've made her crazy. I'm telling ya they shouldn't have left the city." Coco perused the menu. Josephine strode with poise back to the table. Coco and Deedee watched as she wore a gloating smile.

"That nigga, Silky Black, was trying to kick it to a sista, ya heard," she sat and bragged.

"Well, your ass practically knocked people over trying to get at him. He probably thought you was crazy and was kicking' it to calm your crazy butt down," Coco deadpanned.

"Nah, I don't think so. He was really kicking' it. He remembered the performance and even recognized you, Coco. He said 'What's up?'" Josephine said.

"Y'all were talking 'bout me after you ran your crazy ass over there?" Coco asked.

"If you give me a chance, I'll tell you. Tomorrow evening, his album release jump off is going down and guess what?" Josephine asked.

"Ah, here we go," Coco said but Josephine cut her off.

"Coco, you can never cooperate, can you? Anyway, Deedee, he is putting us on the guest list. Ya heard me, girlfriend. We in da building, ahight," Josephine gave Deedee an unexpected high-five. "What's the matter, y'all not down or sump'n?"

"Oh, we are," Deedee said.

"Whoopty fucking doo," Coco replied.

"Told ya. This bitch just don't know when to be civil. Now, if he came over and dropped some line like, 'Yo Coco, wanna be in my video?' that would be better, right?" Josephine asked.

"Damn skippy. How many industry parties have you been to? All niggas try to do is impress each other and the chicken heads. In da morning, you know some nigga is waking up scratching' his nuts saying, 'Yo, my man, we spent all that cheddar at da bar?' And his manager saying, 'Nah, man, it was you who spent the entire budget at the bar trying to be like Jigga'. He'll be calling his other herb friends begging' for a dollar to make up for when da bill comes," Coco said.

"No way. They write it off because that's part of doing business," Deedee said. Josephine immediately took sides.

"She should know. Her uncle is in da business. They do write all those parties off as business expenses."

"Exactly, Josephine, and it's also another reason why artists end up owing a lot of dough to labels before they even drop their first CD," Deedee said.

A minor commotion and the girls looked up to see Silky

GHETTO
GIRLS
TOO

Black himself standing at their table. The girls all smiled.

"Having a bizness lunch, huh?" Josephine asked with a wink.

"Yeah, you how that goes. Listen, I would definitely like to invite y'all to a lil' jump-off for the new joint," Silky Black said to the girls and then he turned and introduced his friend. "Yo, this my man, Show Biz. He did a lot a work on the joint."

"Oh, I thought your face looked familiar," Coco said as she reached out to greet Show Biz. "I love your stuff. All them DITC joints. Classic hip hop."

"Thank you. It feels good to hear that coming from someone like you."

"Ah, you don't have to go there like that," Coco said, interrupting but Show Biz kept on.

"But I can cuz you're on fire right now, Coco."

"Wait up. You know my name like that?"

"Yo, you're one of the unsigned female rappers out there that everyone is talking about like, 'when she coming out?' People stressing for your shit to drop, Coco," Show Biz said. She stared at him wondering why a rap producer would lie to her but he really had no reason to.

"Much respect. Maybe we could do sump'n together?"

"Yo, the pleasure would be all mine, Coco. You on fire, girl," Show Biz said giving Coco a handshake.

"If Show sez it then that's what it is. That nigga knows joints and produced a lot of hot ones so take that as encouragement. You writing?" asked Silky Black.

"Yeah, all the time. I keep them pens and pads on fire."

"That's what's up," Show said and turned to Silky Black. "Yo, tomorrow we're shooting scenes from the new video. If y'all ain't busy, I'm saying y'all could come through."

"Damn, that's right. We're shooting tomorrow. Yo, call me and I'll come through and scoop you but it's gonna be kinda early."

"Exactly how early is early?" Coco asked.

"It really doesn't matter. Anytime is the right time. We'll be there because it's the experience that counts. We'll definitely be there," Josephine interrupted with a smile.

"Ahight, then it's set. We'll see y'all 'round five."

"F-i-v-e." The chorus rang out from all three girls.

"If that's too soon in da morning then y'all will make it another time or sump'n. It's up to y'all. We gonna be shooting like at six on the dot, not no CPT, feel me?" Show looked at the faces of the girls. "Yo Josephine, you got da digits. Just holla and let us know what's what, ahight. Be easy, y'all."

"Ahight, take care. Nice seeing y'all," Silk said and hugged the girls. "Keep doing your homework, Coco. Hope to see y'all in the morn."

"I'll call y'all for sure. Bye, Show Biz and Silky Black," Josephine said smiling and waving.

"Chill, Jo," Coco said as the rap duo vacated Mr. Chow's. The girls could see the flash of the paparazzi.

"Coco, I swear you need an agent. First of all, you don't think about sleeping or anything else when opportunity comes knocking. These cats fitting to drop a new video and they practically trying to push you into it, Coco. I thought this is what you wanted?"

"Look, I don't need no agent and I don't need anyone speaking for me."

Josephine and Deedee mimicked the last half and they all wound up laughing about it. The girls were happy at the prospect at participating in a big video shoot. Although the time appeared to be unreasonably early, it was an opportunity and they rejoiced. Filled with jubilance, the girls walked out the restaurant. It had been a very good day and they were caught up in the happiness.

"We still going to da flicks or what?" Josephine asked.

"I was born ready. What about you, Dee?"

"I'm with it. Just gotta make a phone call."

"Then you not really wit it if you gotta make a call."

"Whatever, Coco. Make your call, girlfriend."

"Okay, ain't no one trying to stop her."

"I'm kinda glad that you and her made up. That was so big of you, Coco. You learning," Josephine patted Coco's butt as she spoke to her and Coco jumped into action.

"Bitch, you best back up and don't be feeling on my ass.

You sure you ain't gay, yo?"

"Hmm, that's right and that bootie looking really delicious, ma. Whatcha say, huh?"

"I say you best leave my bootie alone."

"Speaking of bootie, whatever happened to that big butt buck tooth, Miss Santiago?"

"Who you talking 'bout?"

"Ya know from school."

"Oh, you talking 'bout Miss Martinez. That biddy is still nosey."

"Ain't shit change, huh?"

"I ain't trying to sweat them fools. I'm trying to graduate and get da fuck on."

"Okay, we're good and I did us a favor. I got us some tickets reserved for the 'Fast and the Furious' with Vin Diesel."

"Oh yes, he's all that and sexy too."

"Now, what if we wanted to see 2Pac's new flick, yo?"

Josephine covered Coco's mouth. She laughed then said, "This girl just don't know when to quit."

"Ahight, let's go then," Coco said when Josephine finally removed her hand from Coco's mouth.

"The movie starts soon and finishes late. We gonna have to get up early in da morning. I don't know why you told 'em that we were going, Jo?"

"Well, you can call and tell 'em you don't wanna go."

"Whatever, bitch," Coco said and her voice trailed off as the girls made their way to the movie theater. The smell of popcorn whipped through the air as couples sneaked kisses and kids hid behind video machines waiting for a new challenge. The girls walked into the theater and were greeted by the buzz of spring time celebrating the rebirth of the earth.

It was one of those magical days that started out looking bad but after all the fussing was over, everything felt right. Being around friends and enjoying new experiences made it all worthwhile. It was a good-time that left the girls wishing the moment could be bottled and stored for another day. The girls wandered into the movie theater, found some empty seats, and cooled their heels. They immediately became oblivious to everything but the screen.

THIRTY-THREE

A couple of hours later, laden with shopping bags, the girls filed out of the theater and onto the busy sidewalk. Bustling pedestrians hurrying everywhere rushed at them. They stepped back from the crowd. Coco lit a cigarette and they all shared it.

"That was decent," Josephine said, her eyes peeled on the traffic of busy people. "I love city life." She breathed in exhilaration. Both Coco and Deedee stared at her.

"Girl, you should try to get out more often, yo." Coco said sarcasm dripping from her tone.

"Didn't I tell you that my dumb ass parents had me crazy padlocked," Josephine replied, sounding a little bit annoyed.

"You could hardly tell," Deedee said laughing.

"No, for real. I'm being dead up," Josephine said puffing on the cigarette then throwing the butt away. "I'm telling y'all, I don't think I'm going back." She exhaled still exasperated. Neither Coco nor Deedee inquired any further. They quickly dismissed Josephine's ranting as normal complaining. Coco opened the belly of a cigar and rolled a blunt, pronto. She passed it to Josephine.

"Here, you do the honors," Coco said as Josephine took the blunt. Her eyes widened as she smelled it and put it to her lips. Coco and Deedee eyed her ritual. "It's chronic, bitch," Coco said with a smile.

"Choco or haze?" Josephine asked before lighting up.

Deedee, feeling the need to be down, smoked a little too. "Smoking weed always makes my eyes so red," she complained and puffed. "I don't want to be looking too high. My uncle will notice."

"That means more for me. Pass da blunt, yo."

"How is your uncle?" Josephine asked. Coco eyed Deedee as she answered.

"He's good. He's, you know, working. Getting things done. That's what he's about," Deedee said more to reassure herself than the other girls. She was aware of the problems her uncle and Sophia had been having since the evening of the shooting.

Darkness fell as the smoke rushed into Coco's lungs. Deedee and Josephine were high and staring at the clouds descending over the city. Their minds floated under the spell of the marijuana. Each had different realities that they were trying to dodge. They laughed and kissed the sky with an awareness that their lives had changed.

"Let's be out, yo," Coco said and the girls started walking. Coco tossed the roach and asked, "Where you headed, Jo?"

"Back to the hotel with my strange madre. Y'all could walk me. It's only a few blocks away."

"My feet hurt," Deedee said. "I don't think I can walk much farther."

"That's why you gotta wear comfy shoes. Put that in your hangout notes."

"Jo, I know you not talking all that yang in 'em six inch heels, yo."

"Listen, I ain't complaining 'bout nothing. I'm just sexy, y'all," Josephine laughingly said. She sashayed a bit and then languorously sauntered away.

"Whatever, bitch," Coco said running up to her and yelling in her ear.

"I can't hear ya, haters."

"Whatever."

"Look, we might as well catch a cab now. We gotta get da fuck up early," Josephine said.

"And whose fault is that, Miss Josephine?"

"Here's one," Deedee said as a yellow cab pulled to a stop. The girls got in. "Ah."

"Where to?"

"The W hotel and then to Ninety Second and Park then

ah...?"

"Hundred and tenth and Lenox."

"Got it."

Within minutes, they were in front of the W hotel. Josephine grabbed her bag and thanked Deedee for the shopping spree. "Thanks for tricking, girl. I'll holla in the morning, aight," Josephine said as she air kissed the girls before walking away.

"Don't make it too early, yo," Coco yelled before the cab jolted away. Coco and Deedee sat in the backseat as the cab made its way through the city streets. The temperature had dropped and the girls had cooled. Now all that was left were the uncertainties of their recent past.

"That detective from your place, you know the one that be acting like he's a hip hop head or sump'n? Don't shake your head. You know who I'm talking 'bout," Coco said lighting a cigarette.

"Alright, but I don't..."

"Anyway, that mothafucka, he been following me 'round or sump'n. Nigga showed up on my block."

"Get out. For real?" Deedee asked with a trace of nervous excitement in her voice.

"I'm saying, I go cop and he was right there like: 'Hello'."

"Oh, that's crazy. He's actually following you, you think?"

"I don't know. I ain't putting it past five-oh," Coco said.

"I haven't seen anyone that..."

"Matter fact, I wanted to say this," Coco said interrupting Deedee. "I know you think it's cool and it might just be but I don't want the outfit, yo. Here, the receipt is in the box," Coco said. Deedee's initial reaction was borne out of anger and at that moment she couldn't say anything without losing her temper. She pursed her lips and waited.

"Ninety second and Park," the cab driver announced. Coco glanced out the window and for a moment became confused.

"You're staying with Sophia?" Coco asked.

"Yeah but Coco, I mean, how could you wanna return the dress?" Deedee asked as she stepped out of the cab. "C'mon,

Coco, keep it," Deedee said looking at the box from Dior. She pushed it toward Coco. Coco pushed it back.

"I can't," Coco said shaking her head.

"You can't or you won't?" Deedee asked.

Coco shut the door behind her and as Deedee stood on the curb, the cab drove off. Coco was so lost in her thoughts that she didn't even notice she was home until the cab driver made his announcement. She got out and started to walk away but the driver called after her.

"Where's the fare?" He asked. Coco realizing that nobody had paid the fare, pulled out the last twenty she had and silently swore as she paid.

THIRTY-FOUR

Eric sat next to Sophia in the living room of her apartment. His arms were folded across his chest and he was struggling with his thoughts. He was trying not to squirm or move around too much. Eric did not want to appear nervous as Sophia watched him. He appeared cool on the outside but his mind was frenzied and his stomach did calisthenics trying to keep up with what he heard.

Sophia had shared some information she had gathered during lunch with her friend from the DA's office. She appeared drained and withdrawn. Eric was sure she didn't know of his or Busta's role in the murder for hire scheme. It would be his secret and he hoped Busta had not shared it with anyone else.

He took a peek at Sophia but said nothing. Eric wanted to hold her but felt the tension of her unbending silence. He still felt love for her but wondered if this was the beginning of the end. Sophia was resolute in her convictions of right and wrong, he did not know what to expect. He knew she was patiently waiting for answers. There were a lot of questions to be answered but where does one start when lives are lost at the end? He didn't want to second-guess his actions.

Sophia could sense Eric's heartbeat increasing. She watched his chest heaved with each beat. He should work at getting into better shape, she thought as she waited for him to open up. Sophia wanted him to tell her something but most of all, she wanted to trust him again. She was just about to push his buttons when the doorbell disturbed her.

Sophia sighed, got up, and checked the monitor. It was Deedee with shopping bags. She shook her head and buzzed the teenager into the building.

"It's your niece and it seems as if she's been doing some

shopping. Smart girl," Sophia added as she walked to the kitchen. Eric waited for Deedee to get off the elevator. There were tears in her eyes when she ran to him, hugged, and kissed him.

"What's the matter, Dee?" Eric asked. "Why are you crying, baby?" he asked bending over his niece in parental concern. Deedee cried for a second then spoke.

"A touch of nostalgia, I guess."

"Huh?" Eric asked. Sophia joined them seated out in the living room.

"I was with the girls, you know," Deedee said as Sophia handed her a glass of cold water. "And I was feeling down so I wanted everyone to feel better without being selfish. So, I bought everyone an outfit and Coco returned hers."

"Well, that's not so bad. Coco could get an outfit at another time, Dee," Eric said.

"But that's not it," Deedee continued. "Coco just doesn't want me to buy her anything. I told her it was okay with you, Uncle E. She thinks I'm a show-off."

"Dee, don't worry. People like Coco are ghetto. You don't have to kiss anyone's ass to..."

"Eric, how dare you tell the child such things. Deedee, listen, Coco may not want to owe you any money for..."

"But that's just it, she doesn't have to pay me back. I charged it on my new card. It was just something that I wanted to do to show..." Deedee started and exhaled in frustration. "Maybe she doesn't like me to be nice to her. Where she's from, she's not used to people giving her anything. In the ghetto, everyone is taking or trying to steal from you. No one gives..."

"What you know about being in the hood, girl?" Sophia asked with a smile.

"I mean, its poor people and people who can't help themselves so other people take advantage of them. You know the system, the police..." Deedee said.

"Not all people who live there feel that way about it and that's what you may not be seeing," Sophia said. "It's like when you accept something for itself and not anything else. Coco is probably defensive about anything anyone says about her neck of the woods," Sophia said. Deedee thought about it for a minute and for the first time, she felt like she could understand Coco.

"You know, I've never thought about it that way. I mean, I thought everyone wanted to do better and live better."

"Most people do but they don't want you to point it out to them," Sophia said and opened the box containing Coco's outfit. "It's a very nice dress," Sophia said as she refolded the dress and placed the box on the sofa. "You can always wear it or maybe one day she'll reconsider," Sophia said and winked at Deedee.

"Thanks, Sophia," Deedee sighed and bid goodnight. "I'll see y'all in the morning." She headed to her bedroom.

"You're welcome, hon. I'll look at what you bought later, alright?"

"Okay but you better come quickly because I've got to go to sleep. I was invited to a video shoot scheduled for six tomorrow morning."

"That's early."

"Yeah, that's about the time those cameras usually start rolling," Eric said.

"Whose video shoot is it?"

"It's Silky Black's. We ran into him and Show Biz at Mr. Chow's."

"Really, you were having some kind of day, weren't you?"

"Trying to," Deedee said drifting off to her room where she quickly took off her heels and flopped onto the bed. Before dozing off into a deep sleep, she could hear Eric and Sophia speaking in hushed tones back in the living room.

"I don't know how much you wanna be involved in the kinds of things that I'm talking about," Sophia said. "Eric, in order to change, you've got to want to change. I'm going to sleep. I can't do this anymore tonight."

Eric sat in the living room staring into space. He was unable to immediately react. Eric wanted desperately to convince his fiancé that there was nothing else to the killings but Sophia could hardly be swayed. He sat around nursing a beer and thinking what it would take to persuade the woman of his dreams of his innocence. A smile cursed his lips when he saw the Dior box sitting next to him. That night, he fell asleep with a strategy on how to win his Sophia back. Eric thought the plan was fool proof and couldn't wait to put it in effect.

THIRTY-FIVE

No sooner had she fallen asleep, Deedee heard her cell phone ringing. She struggled to get it from her Coach Birken. By the time she was able to get her hands on it, the ringing had stopped. Deedee pressed the missed call button and saw that it was Josephine. She closed the cell phone and plopped her head back onto the pillow. Before she shut her eyes, the voicemail indicator began to wail. She quickly grabbed the phone to retrieve her voicemail. It was Josephine, excited as ever, telling her to wake up. Was Josephine crazy? Deedee wondered before going back to snooze land.

It couldn't have been five minutes later when the phone rang again. Deedee grabbed the instrument and spoke.

"Yes, Josephine. Huh? You're downstairs? I can't believe that you're already outside. Alright then, I'll be down shortly." Deedee closed the phone and dragged herself to the bathroom to freshen up.

Downstairs, music could be heard pumping through the speakers vibrating the building. Josephine sat in a Hummer with Coco and three guys. The smell of weed and coffee saturated the interior.

"Turn down the music some. I can't hear what Dee said on the phone. I think she's coming down."

"Yo, I need some hot chocolate, some pancakes and some..." Silky Black started to say but was immediately cut off by Show Biz.

"Sounds to me like you need some breakfast but we gotta get to the shoot. These are white people we fucking wit. They ain't on that CPT, know what I'm saying?"

"Ahight, dogs. Where honey at? As soon as she brings her fine ass down, we on our way."

"Say no mo'. Here she is," Show Biz said.

Dressed in a white tee and black capri's, Deedee walked over to the Hummer smiled as she greeted everyone, "Hi, guys."

"How ya doing, ma?" Silky Black greeted the newcomer. "You look fine no matter what time of day it is."

"What's really hood? Let's bounce," the driver yelled. Deedee got in the vehicle and sat next to Coco. Coffee spilled as it pulled off.

"My bad, that's my deejay, Chop Gee," Silky Black said pointing to the driver. "He's responsible for fucking shit up." Silky Black was laughing and the girls realized he was clowning. "I mean cutting shit up."

"Whassup, Chop," Deedee chimed.

"Holla, Chop-master," Josephine yelled and smiled.

Coco and Deedee glared at a hyped up Josephine.

"What did you have for breakfast?" asked Deedee.

"Oh, we ain't even done that yet, girlfriend. They picked me up and it was like, 'No food we going straight to the shoot, homey'," Josephine said with a grin then leaned over to Deedee and whispered in her ear. "It's my time of the month and I ain't wanna eat. My stomach may stick out too much and spoil my out-fit."

"Okay," Deedee said and closed her eyes but Josephine just kept on talking.

"Me and Gee were smoking a lil' sump'n sump'n. He's kinda cute, right?" Josephine asked.

"Yeah, he kinda got it going on but he need to learn how to drive properly."

"Word," Coco said and passed the lit blunt to Deedee. She waited too long and Coco glanced at her between slits that were eyes before the weed hit. "You gonna smoke or what, yo?"

"Ah...no, I mean yes," she said finally taking the blunt and with her eyes on Coco, she puffed some more.

"Easy with the weed," Silky Black laughed as Deedee began to cough. "That's that purple haze. You know that iller shit." Deedee passed the blunt to Josephine.

THIRTY-SIX

A video shoot can be boring and bothersome. With all the retakes and hot tempers, the set is not too kind, especially early in the morning when every girl is a diva and all the guys think they're P. Diddy. Caution is the comfort zone where one can relax with a cigarette or a cup of hot chocolate. There were cameras, big and small, along with cameramen and extras. Then there were the main people, Silky Black and the Shop Crew, a quartet of fire spitting rappers from uptown, and their peeps. They sat out in the parking lot, inside their vehicles, and in the hallways. There were a lot of people up early for this shoot.

At six in morning, the whole place was jumping as the music from the album, 'Silky Black Madness', blasted from the speakers spread throughout the set. There was an early shot depicting a typical party scene where the guys went shirtless and the ladies wore next to nothing. Water sprayed onto a simulated club stage. The scene was set up in an abandoned factory. Josephine was busy getting into her party gear for the shoot. Her outfit, almost nonexistent, could better be described as under-wear. Maybe Josephine had this prearranged, Coco wondered as she saw the outfit.

"You lil' ho, how could you be thinking of wearing those strings around your fat ass?" Coco asked with a frown on her face. "That's so wack," she continued when Josephine ignored her. "Your damn thong is showing from under that short ass skirt, Jo."

"You can see that I'm wearing the damn thing? I'm think-ing of not wearing it. Furthermore, if Christina Aguilera can get down in her Dirty video then why can't I do the same in a damn Silky Black video, huh?"

"Cuz you ain't Christina."

"I heard that," Deedee said. "I'm just gonna do me," she

continued. Coco looked on as Josephine kept ignoring her and began to teach Deedee a few dance moves.

"This that New Orleans shake. Ya gotta just flow. You can't fight it. Like, you can't change your heartbeat. That's rhythm." Josephine moved with ease through some simple steps and turns. Deedee tried her best to keep up but Josephine's hectic pace kept her about two steps back.

Coco bobbed her head and watched the two with little interest. She was always first on the dance track and had been here before. Coco had other interests in mind. What stole her interest was the idea of creating a video rather than being an extra set of tits in one.

She glanced around and imagined herself starring in her own fantasy. It was a longing that she cherished and one that brought back the sparkle to her brown eyes. Coco wanted this one to come true and would do what it took to hog the limelight in the making of her own video. She wanted to be ready and her eager eyes followed Silky Black's every move. Pretty soon, the location was no longer a secret. Fans started arriving and started to go gaga over him.

When Silk and his entourage retreated to a trailer, Coco observed the way the make-up people catered to the whims of the video star. She was so lost in her private thoughts that she didn't notice that Silky Black had walked up to her. Coco didn't hear him when he spoke and failed to respond.

"Yo, ya ahight, Coco?" Silky Black asked. Coco felt cheated out of the ending to her fantasy but she managed to snap out of her flight of the imagination.

"Yeah, I'm good, yo."

"Ahight, I'm fittin' to bring you up more to camera front. Front and center where I can see you," Silky Black said as a make-up artist rushed him and started to fuss over his look. "It don't seem that way but this shit is hard work, Coco," he said before being dragged away by a posse of people. Coco smiled as she watched the spectacle. Josephine ran up to her.

"Guess what, Coco?" Josephine asked. Before Coco could focus, she continued, "BET's Access Granted is here. They just a little way off. I gotta get more make-up. Do me and Deedee and I'll do you after, cool?"

"You guys are getting scary," Coco said with a smile.

"Yes, Miss Coco, I know. You're gonna stay in the back wearing no make-up and reppin' da hood, ahight. Me and Dee here are gonna be up front in makeup and string bikinis," Josephine said as she applied more make-up to Deedee's face.

"I beg to differ..." Coco started but Josephine was not letting her finished.

"What? You know everyone is gonna be wearing mad make-up and chi-chi stringy shit so don't front." Josephine countered.

"Well, I won't be wearing that and I'll be out in front."

"Huh?" The question hadn't completely left Josephine's mouth when they heard the loudspeaker.

"Coco, report to stage right. Coco, report to stage right."

"That be's me, I believe," Coco said and sauntered over to her position leaving Josephine behind looking stunned. Deedee wore a smile as if she was in on the joke. Josephine jerked around to hear.

"All other dancers take their places."

"I swear Coco was born to get over. She always does," Josephine complained as the music hit her and she began to move. It was all action for the next fifteen minutes then they heard, "...and cut." Josephine was livid.

"Then that's the other shit. You spend hours in make-up and then you dance for only a few seconds. That's it. A few seconds," Josephine continued. Throwing her head back, she laughed out loudly on a lark and Deedee followed suit. "Cut this and cut that. Cut everything, cut you too and after I cut you, die slow all o' y'all," Josephine taunted jokingly.

"Girl, you're crazy." Deedee laughed so hard she could barely hold herself straight. Coco walked over to them seemingly hyped.

"They're gonna shoot us together as Silky Black walks through," Coco announced.

"Oh yeah? All of us?" Deedee asked.

"All of us, yo," Coco answered. A few minutes later, the camera came rolling by.

Once a video scene is being shot, the set is under the director's supervision. The video director's duty is almost pious and it would be sacrilegious for someone else to usurp that. Show Biz was the director and he was calling all the shots on this location. However, Josephine's ambition eclipsed that sacred duty.

"Hold it. Cut it," Josephine said. "I haven't had a chance to refresh my make-up yet. I can't be looking busted in anyone's video," she said. There was a loud groan from the crew. "Hey it will be only a few minutes," she countered.

"You've been all over this video shoot so far," Show Biz said.

"What? Are you complaining now?" Josephine asked in a seductive tone.

"No, I'm saying we can't wait to shoot you. We've got to do this," he said to Josephine who was steadily reapplying her make-up. Then he yelled out to Silky Black. "Yo, Silky Black, you ready over there?" Turning back to Josephine, he asked, "Is the star ready yet?"

"I'm ready," Josephine said smiling.

"All right, this is what's gonna be happening. As Silky Black approaches you beautiful young ladies, cuz that's what this about, the beautiful young ladies. So, as Silky Black approaches, bam! I wanna see your smiles and then boom! I wanna see you do your thing. Asses, loose and high in the air, shaking. You hear me? Shaking. I wanna see you drop-it-like-it's-hot, you know what I mean?"

"You don't want us to first shake-it-like-a-salt-shaker and then after that, drop-it-like-its-hot?"

"This may take about half an hour to do depending on how many takes we do. The raw footage will be edited down to about three to four seconds so we ain't gonna have a lot of time for all that. But you can certainly bring that to the album release party."

"I just have to shake it a little to loosen up."

"Go ahead but once I say action, all I want to see is what

I told you to do. Alright, ladies, lets do this."

"C'mon, Dee. You're in the scene too," said Coco pulling Deedee by the arm.

"Ah, you guys are in the scene. I'm here to watch. I mean what am I gonna do?"

"Don't play yourself. You're just as involved with this as Jo. We're just gonna be dancing around acting like we having big fun like we do in da club. That's easy, yo."

"Just don't stare into the camera and always smile," Josephine said as she finally caught up with the others. Make-up and wardrobe complete, Josephine was finally ready.

"They're gonna be shooting the scene over there," Coco said and the girls filed downstage followed closely by the camera. In a minute, they heard the commands.

"Silence on the set, please. And action!"

The music rumbled and Silky Black sauntered through the midst of the girls. He stopped to kick a few bars and turned to Coco as he continued to rap, *"...and just like Pac said it 'ya got to keep ya head up' if you don't then it's all this drama that it bring might get you wet up..."*

Josephine shook her hips and whined to the bass as Coco nodded her head to the beat and rapped along to the song. Deedee jumped up and shook her rump having fun preening for the camera. The crew loved her performance too. They shot it for about five minutes longer when they heard the order.

"Cut! That's it, guys. It's a wrap on that."

"All that and it'll be shaved to only a couple of seconds. Gee thanks, guys," Josephine yelled as the camera crew pushed off laughing. "I can't believe I got up early for that." She looked around for sympathy.

"You're such an ungrateful bitch, yo," Coco said coming up fast behind Josephine. Josephine dressed in her skivvies was much too slow in getting away from Coco. As she tried to jerk herself free, her top came loose and some guys on the set whistled and applauded.

"Yeah, ma, take it off," they cheered. Deedee laughed and Josephine attempted to put her top back together.

"Aah, come on, take it off," the crew yelled from across the stage.

"See, you caused all this fuss," Josephine said as she tried to shield her wares from public view and get back at Coco. The view interested Gee enough for him to walk over.

"Yeah, you're a wild one. I like that in my girls," he said enjoying the hunt.

"Oh, all you Spanish guys like wild women, huh?" Josephine asked all the time her eyes flirting.

"Hmm, ma, I can't speak for nobody else but I can say that I love the way you move that body." he said in a whisper. Josephine welcomed his advances. "I want a private showing."

"Oh really? And are you gonna respect me in the morning?"

"That's the least of your worries, ma. Respect first."

"Then what should I worry about?"

"My ten inches of fun."

"Yo, Gee, come over here and get on the turntables, nigga," Show Biz yelled. Before he walked away, Gee turned and nodded to everyone.

"Can't wait for that moment," he said and was gone to shoot his frame of the music video leaving Josephine holding her breath. Yet, it wasn't before long that she was singing another tune.

"I wonder why he'd wanna sweat a sista like that, huh?" Josephine asked.

"Maybe it could very well be because you were, ah, smoking with him earlier?"

"Or he just liked your video get-up," Deedee threw her two cents in.

"Whatever, bitches. I hear some hating. That's all good. Homey is just open on my sexiness."

"Did Danielle's soul creep into your body or sump'n?" Coco asked jokingly at first then realized she'd really meant it. She continued, "Cuz you ain't the Ms. Conservative Josephine I used to know. The one who used to like to keep even that boyfriend biz on the down low. Now you're talking 'bout giving brains for a blunt."

"Bitch, who's giving brains for blunts? What kinda shit you on?"

"No, bitch. It's more like what kinda shit you on? You were the one talking 'bout giving it up for smoke when you were down south."

"Oh, you mean earlier. I thought you were talking 'bout right now. I'm working in the here and now so please leave all baggage behind. That Spanish nigga is real cute. That's what's up, bitch."

"Oh, that's what's up, huh?"

"Now you feel me. Coco, we've got to really sit down and..."

"Josephine, why don't you just put your clothes back on? Throughout the video, your ass is in every shot and you only wearing a panty and bra. Titties flapping around like you some video ho."

"It's my thong and my ass but who's checking?" Josephine asked and pulled her dress over her shoulders. She had a great body and she let it go to her head. Coco was seeing a totally different side of Josephine. Heaven forbid but it was like Josephine really had adopted Danielle's ways. The thought left Coco a little mystified.

"Yo, wanna go eat sump'n when this thing is over? I'm feeling like throwing up or sump'n," Josephine said, rubbing her flat stomach.

"Yeah, I heard that. Not the throwing up part but the really hungry part," Deedee said.

"I'm so amped from being around all these cameras and the BET people got me even more hype. I don't know but that may have taken all my energy," Josephine added letting her voice trail away.

"Could be. Although last night, I was so tired that I went to sleep as soon as I got in," Deedee said as she watched Coco roll a blunt.

"Yeah, roll that weed up. Maybe that will calm my stomach down. Its doing flips right now," Josephine whined.

"Whatever, bitch. That will teach you next time to..."

"What's it gonna be ladies? Coffee, hot chocolate, or soup?" A caterer disrupted Coco as she was about to let Josephine have it.

"Soup for me," Josephine said immediately reaching for the cup. "Ooh, nice and hot. Just the way I like it. Thank you," she said holding the handle and slurping from the cup. "Ah, yeah. That's better."

"I'll try the soup also. Thank you," Deedee announced.

"Yeah, this soup is da bomb," Josephine said.

"I'll have the hot chocolate," Coco said. She was through rolling and was ready to light up when Josephine cautioned her.

"Excuse me, can we wait? Must we light up while there's company?" Josephine asked winking at the caterer.

"Don't worry. Everyone is doing that right now. Sure smells real good," he said as Coco sparked the blunt and sucked on it. She inhaled rapidly, exhaled then sipped from the hot chocolate.

"Hmm, the chocolate is good. Good looking out, yo," she said as she inhaled the smoke from the blunt. The caterer moved on smiling.

THIRTY-SEVEN

Wednesday, the detectives received the call from the hospital confirming that the man they had brought in had regained consciousness. Detective Kowalski was ready and waiting for the opportunity to turn this prisoner into a witness. He felt that whatever Lil' Long knew would be helpful if he could just get it out of him. Kowalski was confident that he could. He could either talk freely or get it beaten out of him. The choice would be his, Kowalski thought as he swung into traffic and headed for the hospital. His anticipation made him frantic enough to almost wipe out a pedestrian.

"Easy before you kill us," Hall said.

The two were a study in contrast. One wanted to show off his skill and break open a major case. The other was in no hurry to do anything but sit and have lunch. Hall also took evening classes at a local college. He had aspirations of becoming a realtor and was winding down his law enforcement career. He remembered being young and eager. Now he was just older and wiser.

Kowalski pulled to a stop and jumped from the car in a big haste to interview Lil' Long. They walked through the hospital door. "Excuse me, where can I find a patient by the name of...ah ...Michael Lowe?" Kowalski asked as he showed his badge upon entering the main floor of the hospital. The receptionist quickly examined her patient listing and answered.

"He's in intensive care on the sixteenth floor. Take the elevator on your left, gentlemen."

"Thank you, ma'am," Detective Hall said eyeing her figure as they headed to the elevator. "She's got a very good future," he said as they waited on the elevator.

"What is it about you brothers and chicks with fat asses?" Detective Kowalski asked. Hall looked his younger white partner up and down. He saw a young man living in dirty jeans doing whatever it took to bust a case wide open.

"If you gotta ask then you don't need to know," Hall said smiling as if smiling was an unpleasant thing to do.

"Let's go interrogate a perp," Kowalski said reading the sardonic grin pasted on Hall's face. The two walked onto the elevator as the doors spread open.

THIRTY-EIGHT

He had been an unruly patient, inattentive and less than eager to please anyone. The doctors noted that there was something tragic about him even in his movements. A kick to the groin of the doctor as he tried to inject serum into his post surgery bullet riddled body. He tussled with the orderlies trying to restrain him to the bed with the use of handcuffs. Lil' Long threw threatening gestures at the armed police guarding him. He grimaced when he felt the needle in his vein. His eyes rolled back and he nodded off to sleep wrapped in his blood soaked bandages.

The detectives got off the elevator and hurried to the room. The commotion had just about dwindled down to snores coming from the sleeping patient. A sweating doctor, still breathing hard from the ordeal, greeted the detectives.

"How ya doing, doc?" Kowalski asked.

"Annoyed by your patient's antics," the doctor answered as he signed off on a medical chart. "Doesn't seem like he wants to live, detective," the doctor continued as the detectives observed Lil' Long lying in the hospital bed.

"He may not wanna live but he's mine. He owes me his life and after all the fuss to get him here, he's gonna live. Right, doc?" Kowalski asked moving closer to Lil' Long.

"Well, luckily the bullets passed right through the chest cavity barely grazing his spine on exit. Ah...there is one round caught under his chest next to his spinal column that may require additional surgery...ah...he can live with this for awhile but eventually..."

"Doc, doc," Detective Kowalski said and raised his hand. "Doc, you can go ahead and explain and discuss all that medical possibilities with my superiors. The only thing I wanna know is, is he gonna be able to talk to me anytime soon?"

"All right, even though further surgery will be required to repair the bullet damages, the patient will be able to talk to you as soon as he wakes up," the doctor said, his voice becoming terse. He viewed his charts before continuing. "At the moment, all things being equal, Michael Lowe should be able to regain all normal functions." The doctor looked up to see that both detectives were busy leaving the room.

Outside the door, Kowalski spoke with the uniform on duty. "I want that prisoner transferred to the prison infirmary as soon as possible. Where's the other guy?" He asked gruffly.

"Ah, he took a smoke-break, detective," the uniformed officer answered.

"When he gets back, have the prisoner escorted and let me know immediately as soon as it's done."

"Gotcha, detective. That's a ten-four." The detectives walked away. "Asshole," whispered the uniform under his breath.

Neither said anything as they waited on the elevator. When it arrived, they got on and rode to the main floor. They walked to the end of the corridor of the hospital. The door parted and medical technicians rushed by pushing a gurney with a teen dripping blood from holes in his body. The detectives took a deep breath and casually walked on.

Dusk had drawn closer as they stood outside for a moment. Kowalski lit a cigarette and exhaled directing smoke at the sky. Hall stood next to the car and stared at the city's darkening skyline thwarted by the smog from the high rises. He could barely see the stars. Kowalski leaned closer to him. "Hall, I know you're my partner but you're lacking enthusiasm. We could bust this case wide open if you do certain things."

"Really?" Hall replied. "And just what are you suggesting I do?"

Kowalski thought about it as he puffed heavy on the cigarette. He subsequently exhaled and all the smoke temporarily hid his facial expression from Hall's curious glance.

"All you have to do is show your kid brother all the evidence gathered."

"Huh?" Hall was befuddled.

"I took the liberty of looking at the forensic report. It showed..."

"You went on my desk and pilfered those reports?"

"Yes," Kowalski said and got inside the driver's side of the car. He was nodding his head when Hall jumped on the passenger side. "Yes, you may say that. I guess you learned all them fancy words in those classes of yours, uh, Hall? Pilfer? Yeah, I looked at the report."

"Listen, I don't know how you used to conduct yourself around other partners but as the senior detective here, I'm saying to you stay off my fucking desk. Anything you need to know about the case will be supplied to you by me. Do you have that straight, Detective Kowalski?"

"Yes sir, yes sir, three bags full. Now forensic tests proved negative on our man, Eric Ascot. There was no bullet residue on his clothes according to the reports which proves what we've been saying all along. He's covering up something. Also..."

"Can I see the damn report myself?" Hall asked in a tone suggesting annoyance.

"Sure, I took the liberty of making a copy and bringing it with me just in case."

"Where is the copy?"

"Here," Kowalski said as he reached under the sun visor and tossing the papers at Hall.

"You got coffee stains all over my damn paperwork."

"I didn't say I was perfect, detective," Kowalski mocked. "Those bullets that killed the young lady from our man's apartment came from the same gun and are identical to the rounds that were used to kill our mob connect, Busta, and the two police officers they found by the roadside. They're not through searching."

"I can read, dammit!"

"That's right. What do you say we go to a funeral? I heard all kinds of celebrities will be there."

THIRTY-NINE

Funerals are supposed to be a morbid affair, a time of parting ways with loved ones, permanently. It's usually a sad time filled with tears. The death of a person is celebrated in different ways. This affair was part of Busta's last will and testament. Cars and fans lined the streets outside of Sosa's Funeral Home. The crush of crowd blocked the streets around the area of the hall as fans tried desperately to catch a glimpse of their favorite rap royalties in attendance.

The big gathering attracted people from all walks of life. It seemed like Busta, during his existence, had touched a lot of folks and they came in droves to celebrate his life. Coco, Deedee and Josephine all dressed in black, stood next to a balcony watching the turnout.

"There goes Kim from the block. What she doing up here with her coked-up half-Rican-friend, Tina?" Coco immediately asked as she recognized two of the attendees.

"Who're you talking 'bout, Coco? And what half Puerto?"

"I'm talking bout them two underdressed heifers coming through, y'all..." Coco started to say but was cut off by Josephine's sly remark.

"Do I detect a lil' bit o' hatred in that tone thurr, girl?" Josephine asked then winked at Deedee. "What do you have to say, Dee?"

"It could be..."

"Call it what it is then."

"No, I ain't hating. All that you hearing is the frustration of a young black woman. That's it, yo. You believe this bitch thinks that I knew 'bout her baby daddy and Bebop," Coco said eyeing the girls who were causing heads to spin everywhere they turned.

"Who are these girls? They dressed like dancers, Coco."

"Word Jo, they're really wack. They are dressed like they stole the clothes from the toddler's department at Macy's," Deedee said laughing. Coco and Josephine joined as the girls chuckled. Josephine continued to do some prying.

"Where did all this beef start, Coco? Really though, I ain't never hear you mention any of this before now, girl."

"C'mon, Jo, there are lots of issues that I don't really be speaking on cuz..." Coco started to speak and her voice trailed for a beat before she continued. "Jo, you know me, I don't be speaking on shit like this but this bitch had the audacity to spread my name around the way saying I knew 'bout her man and got me involved with all that killing and bs."

"Yeah? Who's her baby daddy supposed to be?"

"Remember that nigga that used to be up on Tenth Ave hustling?"

"Where you used to cop that chocolate chip?" Josephine asked licking her lips.

"Yeah, you remember that cookies an' cream."

"How could I forget? That shit was the bomb!"

"The cookies an' cream...He sold ice cream?" Deedee asked with a confused frown. Both Coco and Josephine burst into uncontrollable laughter. They laughed so hard that they had to embrace to keep each other from falling over the balcony's edge.

"Okay, what did I say that was so funny?" Deedee asked when it was safe to do so.

"Cookies an' cream and the chocolate chip that we were talking about, that was us referring to the blizack." Josephine said holding her breath to prevent from an outburst but then she glanced at Coco desperately biting her lips to prevent from laughing.

"The blizack?" Deedee asked cautiously but it wasn't guarded enough and Coco and Josephine erupted gleefully once again.

"I'm not gonna say anything else," Deedee said crossing her arms against her chest.

"No, it's just that all those names we were using, that was all weed, yo."

"You guys are soo..."

"Ah sookie, sookie, here they come," Josephine announced as Kim and Tina had somehow made their way up the stairs. They both stopped when they saw Coco.

"What's poppin', Coco?" Kim asked.

"Ain't a damn thing, Kim. Whatcha you know?"

"Struggle."

"I hear ya."

"Oh, you know my girl, Tina, right?" Kim asked.

"Yeah, how're ya doing?" Coco asked and looked at Josephine. "These are my girls, Jo and Dee," Coco said to Kim with a sneer pasted on her pretty face. "Jo, Dee, this is Kim and her girl, Tina." Somehow it got so tense that the air began to tell that this was much more than just an ordinary introduction. It was more like a show of forces. The combatants stood their ground.

"Whassup, y'all?" Josephine said. Deedee nodded ever so slightly. The stare-down continued between Coco and Kim. Then almost as quickly as they appeared, they vanished with, "I'll see ya,"

"She's kinda mean," Deedee remarked when they were out of earshot.

"That bitch is a punk ass. I'll whip her in that lil' ass skirt from here to downtown back to the baby section where they boosted that shit," Josephine said. "Yo, Coco, who was that witch's baby daddy?" Josephine asked.

"I done told ya already."

"No you didn't. You were just talking bout that nigga hustling with da black," Josephine said and squinted her eyes when she realized the person Coco was referring to was someone she knew. "You mean Deja?" she asked snapping her fingers. "He was her baby daddy for real?"

"Which one are you referring to? I don't know they were both..." Deedee started but Coco raised her hand and waved her finger like a wand.

"Kim, the bitch with da ugly mug," Coco answered.

"I mean, neither was ugly but..."

"They were two ugly stank bitches and I don't care for they asses," Josephine said.

"What do you know about his death, Coco?" Deedee asked taking cue from Josephine.

"A friend of mine from da building was found with her baby daddy," Coco said.

"Word, he was cheating on her?" Deedee asked.

"I don't know nada. If Bebop was creeping with that nigga, she kept it secret. Then after the news broke, homegirl here wanted to step to me like I was Bebop's sister or sump'n talking 'bout, 'Oh, Coco, you had to have known sump'n'," Coco said looking back at Kim and Tina. "How am I gonna know anything? Just because me an' you is cool don't mean I'm gonna be knowing every single thing you do, you feel me?" Coco asked and looked around for validation.

"That's true."

"That's real."

"Man, Busta, he really knew a lot of peeps, yo," she continued as the two young ladies pranced by again. "He must have met their asses at the strip club."

"From A to Z, everybody is here," Kim was overheard saying as she made her way through the steadily building crowd. "They even got the news camera and all out here for Busta. People showing him much love," she continued.

It was typical that the atmosphere behind Busta's last rites would be a less than somber one. Those who knew him came out to celebrate. That was the theme for the evening. It was the way Busta had wanted it all to culminate. His friends did the rest. Outside, people rushed to express their views for the cameras camped there. A crowd had formed and each person readily shared their opinions.

"He was a great friend of mine," a diminutive, dark skin man yelled when the cameras turned on him. Dressed in black pants and a tie, the man carried a bowler in his hand. He wore a white shirt and sneakers that matched.

"Yeah, alright, but who was he and who are you?" a curious reporter asked.

"He was the owner and operator of the hottest hip hop spot in town. He had a lot of talent shows and gave money to charity of which I'm requesting that you donate a nice amount to at this time. It is for a very worthy cause," Rightchus added as he passed the bowler through the gathered crowd.

"Hold up. Before we give to any causes, who are you? You related to him or sump'n?" An onlooker had questions but Rightchus came ready with answers.

"Related? I'm Rightchus," the man said as he passed the cup around. *"Holy terror delight, everywhere I go them haters and suckers want to fist fight. They know that I'll bust everything in my sight, don't need no six guns. I got my knuckles. I see you and sump'n comes over me. 'Tween me and you, that must be love. You to me is the only one that can keep from around drugs. I swear it must be love, baby, ah-ah-ah... You feel me?"*

"Yeah, here is a dollar. Start taking some rap classes," one guy said and dropped a dollar bill in the bowler. Others took heed and handed over their bucks. The detectives rolled up as the hat was brimming with dollars and Rightchus was smiling with happiness from ear to ear.

"Five-oh," Kowalski announced. "Everybody break it up. Stand back," he yelled. The crowd dispersed. "Hey, if it ain't Rightchus, my main man," Kowalski said as he hugged Rightchus. "Let's go talk somewhere private." The detective walked with his arms about Rightchus' shoulder. "So tell me, my man, what're you doing out here today?" He asked as Rightchus tried in vain to shove all the dollar bills into his pocket while fixing the hat on his head.

"Yo, I was just spitting my fire for the crowd and they feeling me," Rightchus said showing the detective his dance moves.

"That's it? Spitting your fire?" Kowalski asked.

"Looks like your fire was well received, huh, Rightchus?" Hall asked.

"Yeah, sump'n like that. You know I gots da mad skillz and it ain't no joke. Peeps just gotta respect. With all them hip hop peeps in there, I gotta get a deal or my name ain't..."

"Who else is in there that isn't hip hop?" asked Hall. Rightchus thought for a minute then answered.

"Ah what's his face, the godfather...ah, Maruichi, he was up in there..." Rightchus' voice faded as he thought more of who went inside the funeral home. The detectives exchanged quizzing glances when Rightchus continued, "Eric Ascot and his fiancé, that's peeps, you know? They up in da building." Hall whipped out a five dollar bill and stuffed it into Rightchus' pocket.

"See ya later," he said and walked away.

"That's how we want Lil' Long to be once he gets out of the hospital. Who helped turned Rightchus?" Kowalski asked.

"I have a friend in parole," Hall said as they reached their Caprice.

"I guess we'll wait here," Kowalski suggested but Hall had other ideas.

"You can stay here if you want. You're not dressed well enough. I'm going inside to take a look around," Hall said as he walked away. Kowalski lit a cigarette, pulled out a pen and pad and started to record license plates.

FORTY

Coco, Josephine and Deedee saw it all go down. Restless from waking early for the video shoot, the contact between Coco, Kim and Tina had made them all grumpy. The girls went down the stairs and wandered out of the assembly area. The three looked around before they found a spot that was quiet. There they sat where they could easily see who was approaching without being seen. The girls shared a cigarette away from the crush of people.

"Trifling ho's," Coco exhaled.

"Later for them."

"Folks had mad love for Busta."

"What! You see all these stars that came out. Like peeps from Japan and all?"

"Who you kidding? I ain't even known the nigga, Busta, was that large, yo."

"And I mean large." Josephine was sucking on the cigarette when she thought she recognized another face. "Yo, ain't that the guy who plays on 'The Wire'? Ah sugar, now he's cute."

"Which one?"

"The light skinned one? He's a real cutie."

"Yo, why y'all OD'ing on these celebrities, yo?" Coco asked in a tone that revealed annoyance. Deedee and Josephine turned to look at her as if she had just cursed at them. "I'm saying, we here to pay respects to Busta and all you two have been doing is playing name that celeb. Y'all bugging," Coco continued in an irritated manner.

"Can I get some of the cig, Coco?" Josephine asked ignoring her attitude. Coco puffed and stared at her then passed the cigarette. "What can I say? You're absolutely right, Coco," Josephine said as she inhaled. She exhaled and continued, "We're kinda acting a little gully."

"A little?" Coco asked shaking her head. "How about extremely gully?"

"Look! Mef n Red, y'all." Josephine yelled excitedly and handed the cigarette back to Coco.

"Oh my god, where?" Deedee asked.

"You see 'em, Coco?" Josephine asked.

"Nah, I don't see 'em but I do spot a DT," Coco said.

"Where at?" Deedee asked.

"Heading toward the hall," Coco said as she puffed.

"Now I know Busta was huge. I mean, even po-po is showing up at his funeral. That's big," Josephine said and took the cigarette from Coco who continued to watch Detective Hall.

"I know them cops ain't here on Busta's account. They probably just here to see who's here," Coco said as the dapper Hall moved into the assembly area.

"Coco, that nigga is five-oh?" Josephine asked.

"Hell yeah, that nigga five-oh. Can't you smell him, yo?"

"That nigga is too fly to be five-oh. I'm saying he could arrest me anytime."

"You bugging. That's it. I'm going back inside," Coco said and threw the butt away.

FORTY-ONE

The hall was huge and surrounded by a balcony. The amount of people in attendance made the place appeared smaller and crowded. Inside, people mingled easy under the hue of a purple light. Most were dressed in black but judging from the glad-handing, there was little or no sadness. Others sipped wine from long stemmed glasses while video clips of Busta's life were displayed on a huge flat screen on the wall.

In the center of the room was a table covered in purple suede. On top of it was a golden urn. No one had opened the lid and everyone assumed that Busta's remains rested peacefully inside. Light chatter circulated around the place and filtered throughout the atmosphere. The denseness of the crowd was made more oppressive by the presence of large floral arrangements.

Everywhere one turned, someone was air kissing someone else or there were people locked in an embrace. The whole scene was overbearing and pretentious and reminiscent of the opening night of a Broadway play rather than a funeral. There were the famous and infamous pretending to get along. It was easy to spot the real gangsters, they were all decked out in dark gray striped suits. It was as if they not only shared the same barber but the same tailor. There were gentlemen escorting ladies and ladies looking for rich gentlemen to escort them.

The common people stood milling around. Those without celebrity status were only allowed inside if they were related in some way to the deceased. They turned out to say their final goodbyes to Busta's enigmatic personality from the world of entertainment. Some could have been close relatives judging by the way they wailed and cried.

'Oohs' and 'ahhs' were heard as the shielded face of different celebrities passed through to pay their respects. Most raised their shades when a parade of ladies, some Asian, some Spanish and some White sauntered to the casket and laid hands or lips on it before they turned away, only to be greeted a few steps later by waiters and waitresses serving chilled champagne.

Eric and Sophia stood side by side wondering whether this was the kind of celebration Busta had in mind or was this concocted by some crazy relative. They were deep in discussion when Francisco Maruichi, with two buxom blonds on either side and a bunch of bodyguards behind him, stopped by to greet Eric.

"Busta must've left the instructions for this in his last will and testament," Sophia was critiquing when she noticed the group of people congregated in front of where she stood.

"Mr. Ascot, how are you doing, my friend? Is this the Misses? She's a doll," he complimented as he gave Eric a firm handshake.

"Mr. Maruichi, how're doing? Yes, this is the Misses. This is my fiancé, Sophia Sullivan," Eric said as he accepted an embrace that ended in a handshake. "Everything is going well, you know."

Maruichi extended a hand to Sophia. When she reached out, he bowed and kissed her hand.

"It's all my pleasure," he said. Suave in a striped black suit, Maruichi presented the courteous and clean shaven side of him.

"Eric, I've got a lot of old friends here so I'm gonna run and make my rounds. Why don't you give me a call in a couple of days and we'll talk. I may have something that you might like. Nice to meet you, Sophia. You're a very beautiful woman. Goodnight."

"Thank you, Mr. Maruichi."

"Call me Frankie. Let's keep things light." Maruichi walked away his entourage in tow.

"What an interesting friend you've got there, Eric."

"He was Busta's man, Sophie."

"So does that make him your friend, too?"

"Oh please. What're talking about? He stopped by to say

hi. C'mon, Sophia. Don't start up with that bullshit again."

"Bullshit, huh? All I'm trying to do is find out what kind of friends you've been keeping just in case."

"Just in case of what?" Eric asked his tone seething with anger. Sophia turned to give him an evil stare but was greeted by Herb Thai, the newest rap sensation from Japan and the accompanying flash bulbs. Sophia was forced to check herself and remain cool on the exterior but as she extended her hand and smiled, she was boiling on the inside.

"Hey, Eric, what's good?" A suited member of the rapper's entourage asked.

"Ain't nothing, Rob. You know, still trying to do this damn thing. How's things with you, man?" Eric asked as he gave the immaculately dressed man with that familiar bling of success an embrace. "Rob, I'd like you to meet my fiancé, Sophia. Sophia, Rob. He's competition so be careful," Eric added as Sophia shook Rob's hand.

"Nice to meet you, Rob," Sophia said.

"I heard your new man spit. He's nice," Eric said.

"Yeah, Thai really got sump'n, sump'n. I think he's working with some shit. Why don't you come down to the studio tomorrow, E-money? We'll be there all day. I'll let you hear some new joints. See if you really feeling the kid," Rob said.

"I'll definitely try to pass through."

"C'mon, E, how long have I known you? Just come through, don't front."

"Okay, okay," Eric replied laughing.

"Nice to meet you, Miss. Take care y'all," Rob said and his group moved on.

The stars popped out as the evening wore on. Each one paid the ultimate respect to the ashes in the urn. Some walked directly to the table on which the urn sat and touched it while others planted light kisses against the edge. Above the urn, stood a life sized picture of a young Busta. An announcement was made and several people began to eulogize and honor the memory of Busta.

Eric was called upon to give his tribute. Dressed in his

black Armani suit with black shirt, sporting no tie, he slowly made his way to the center of the gathering. Sophia looking beautiful by his side resplendent in a black Helmut Lang dress, her head held proudly, she cupped her hand in his. Eric looked at Sophia before he began to speak.

"I want y'all to know that my good friend, Busta, was the most loyal person I've ever known. We came up together, Busta, my brother, Dennis, and I. I was the baby and right now, I'm the only one still standing." Eric's voice wavered and his eyes became watery when he mentioned his brother's name.

"You're a survivor," an audience member yelled. Eric dabbed at his face and squeezed Sophia's hands ever so tightly as he continued.

"When I was six years old, my brother and Busta were best friends. They were both twelve years old and all they used to talk about was who was gonna have more cars than the other, who's gonna have the most houses and most women when they got older. About six years ago, I buried my brother and now I'm doing the same thing for his best friend. They both couldn't have died in vain. Not from the same thing...bullet wounds. We've got to start growing old and dying of old age cause ain't too much of us around and the kids are really going wild."

Sniffling was heard coming from all over the place as Eric continued his tribute to his fallen comrade. People were genuinely moved by what he had to say. With tears in his eyes, he glanced around at the attendees. There were hardly any dry eyes by then. Eric felt the love shown for Busta. "In a couple of weeks, we are gonna continue with something Busta started. 'Reach for the Stars' will feature all of the finalists from the talent show that he ran for our teens over the past ten years." There was thunderous applause and whistling when Eric made the announcement. Slowly, the applause died and Eric called on a surprised Coco to say a few words.

"Ooh, I think we got to get closer," Josephine said and pushed her way through the throng of mourners and pretenders. "Excuse us, we've got to get up front...Excuse us...Sorry, don't mind us," Josephine said as the girls made their way to the front next to the urn. She moved closer to Coco. The crowd stared brazenly at the girls. Some of the people present wore confused expressions and wondered, 'Who were these girls?' Coco broke the awkward silence.

"Hi," Coco said greeting the crowd. "Me and my crew, Josephine and Danielle, may her soul rest in peace, we did a lot of battles sponsored by Busta and we won a lot of those battles. Busta always looked out for the kids from the get go. He always had a kind word for all of us. He truly understood us...we're really gonna miss him."

"Peace y'all. I'm Jo and I just wanna let y'all know that we'll be performing at the event mentioned by Mr. Ascot. So come on out and support. Show us some love," Josephine interjected. Coco and Deedee hugged her and they all waded back through the crowd.

Eric called on some other people to say a few words. Some were long winded while others short and to the point. There were even a few who sang their condolences. The benediction was announced by someone introduced as a priest.

"I hope they have a real priest and just not some nigga who comes in and is like: 'My bitches call me Priest' cuz I'm gonna be like: 'Nigga get the fuck outta here wit that juvenile bullshit. This is grown folks affair'."

"Kim, I don't think Busta would be having any front'n ass nigga who passes himself off as a priest, ahight, so take a chill pill. You been on that shit since we left the babysitter."

"I'm just saying, for as much as that brother did for our community, they should have a real mofucking priest or bishop or a reverend or sump'n cuz this ain't no real funeral."

"Kim, chill, I got it," Tina said.

Busta may have departed the earth but his friends turned out in huge numbers to make sure that his memory was not forgotten. It went down like that, ashes to ashes dust to dust. It was a gala affair more befitting the opening of a play or movie than an actual ending of someone's life. Busta's ashes remained in the golden urn as the crowd thinned out. Celebrities went on their way, discussing business and forgetting what the function was really about.

"Come out to the after party at my place," a pimp dressed in gold told another. "If you think this was sump'n, you just wait and see when I make that heavenly trip."

"Amen, brother. I'll see you there."

FORTY-TWO

Eric and Sophia walked past the waiting pimps and was greeted by scattered evening showers. With the girls running in front, they made their way to the Range Rover. All hopped inside. As he was about to peel away, he could hear tapping on the window. Eric lowered it and saw Rightchus standing outside the Range clutching a forty ounce.

"Yo, yo, what's good my peeps?" Rightchus said, his eyes glossy as if severely under the influence. Eric nodded.

"How can we help you?" Eric asked but Rightchus cut him off.

"I know you not gonna be akkin like we ain't never met? Remember your boy, the dearly departed? May his soul rest in peace...Busta introduced us. You know me. I'm like a rapper's delight, you feel me? I was kicking sump'n for you and Busta, remember? You were like you wanna work wit me an' all. You was feeling all that fire I was spitting," Rightchus said and moved closer when he saw the confused look on Eric's face. "Busta, me, you outside...I rapped...you liked it and..."

"Yeah, sure I remember. And what did you say your name was?" Eric asked still unsure.

"Yo, yo, yo ahight. I'll spit it fo' you. Huh, what, one time, check it and huh, hear me now... They call me Rightchus, holy terror delight..." Rightchus rapped as Coco and Josephine dropped a beat box sound for his impromptu accapella.

"...suckas think I won't bust a grape in fruit fight but I surprised 'em hurr-where I go same suckas hugging da wall all tight...don't wanna see me cuz I will fight...busting hurr-thing in my sight...and I don't need no six guns, just me an my knuckles I'll shoot a fair one...c'mon man see me an I'll wobble you an' I still ain't done..."

"Whoa," Josephine yelled.

"That's enough right thurr, Rightchus. Ahight!" Coco yelled applauding.

"Yeah, yeah say no more, dogs" Eric said and handed Rightchus a fifty dollar bill. "You good now, right?" Eric asked as Rightchus jigged when paper touched his parched hand. He whirled, elated when he glanced at the numbers.

"Oh baby, today was a blessed day for me. God bless you, my brother. Coco, I see you my girl. Who's that next to you?"

"You remember Jo from Da crew?" Coco asked. Rightchus thought for awhile.

"Sure do, sure do. Your face did look familiar, ma. You're back in da city, huh?"

"Yes, finally," Josephine answered.

"Welcome back. Ya know Rightchus ain't got nothing but love for y'all."

"Ahight, Rightchus," Coco yelled.

"Take care of yourself," Eric said. Rightchus moved closer and gave him a handshake.

"Drive safe. There are cops all over the place, ya heard?"

Eric gunned the engine and they were out. He steered the vehicle into traffic as he watched Rightchus in the rearview mirror. Eric could see two men speaking to Rightchus from a gray Caprice. Probably the police chasing Rightchus off the street for panhandling, Eric thought and kept driving.

"I'm hungry. Anyone else?" Eric asked.

"I'm kind a famished too. Oh, Uncle E, I wanted to know if I could attend this album release party. It's on Friday," Deedee asked.

"I really don't see why not. Whose album is dropping?" Eric asked.

"Silky Black's new joint," all three girls echoed then laughed. Eric chuckled and eyed Sophia sitting next to him. She continued to stare straight ahead.

"I guess all three of you were invited, huh?" Eric asked smiling.

"Uh huh," all three girls chorused once again.

"Did anyone have any suggestions in mind about what to eat?" Eric asked.

"Could you drop me at my place, please, Eric?" Sophia asked abruptly putting to rest the buzz Eric had created regarding food. All of a sudden, you could hear a pin drop.

"Why, do you wanna get...?" Eric started to ask as he recovered from the surprise of Sophia's request. It wasn't so much the request but the manner in which it was made.

"I've got some paperwork that I've got to catch up on," Sophia said. When she saw the disappointment shading his doubt, she added, "Eric, you know this weekend was hectic and today was the worst."

Eric drove in silence to Sophia's place. She got out of the vehicle and Eric spoke to the girls as he followed her into the building.

"Give me a few minutes and I'll be right back," he said.

"Josephine, nice to see you and Coco again and Dee, I'll be seeing you later. Goodnight," Sophia said.

"Goodnight. Take care. Nice to see you again," Josephine smiled and waved.

"Don't work too hard. You hear me, Sophia?" Deedee blew her a kiss.

"Ahight, Sophia, I'll see you," Coco said then Sophia waved and walked away with Eric by her side. From the car, the girls could see them walking close but couldn't hear what was being discussed.

"Yo, she's stressed," Josephine said, watching as they went through the entrance. Inside, Eric waved at the doorman.

"Good evening, Paul," Sophia said and then checked her mailbox. Eric waited on her. "Oh, Eric, there's no reason for you to ride up with me. The girls are waiting and I'll be..."

"I've got a surprise for you," he said moving closer to Sophia.

"Please, I've had enough of your surprises to last all eternity, Eric. No more, please." Sophia was busy protesting and didn't notice as Eric unveiled a small jewelry box. He opened it and when the sparkle from the diamonds hit her face, her mouth fell open but sound failed her. Eric stood with the oblong shaped black box opened to reveal the glow of perfect diamonds. Sophia gasped

"Oh...oh my...oh my...this is beautiful. What? Why?" The diamonds glittered and Sophia struggled with her words.

"It's for you. Take it," he said. Sophia reached out and touched the necklace laced with diamonds.

"Oh my, this must have cost you a fortune, Eric," she said as he reached behind and clasped it around her neck. That maneuver placed them face to face with each other and Eric could see her tears in her eyes. "Even when I'm trying to hate you, you make it difficult," Sophia said. Tears rolled down her cheeks as the elevator arrived and they both stepped inside. She pressed twelve and then hugged and kissed Eric harder than she had planned. It wasn't easy for her to withhold anything from Eric. He was trying to be someone and go somewhere with his life. Emotionally, she wanted to stand by her man but there was the professional side that could not be avoided. Should she open up to him and ask the tough questions? The impetus of her fear came from the information she received from her trusted friend and business associate, Michael Thompson. Sophia slowly realized that she was reluctantly approaching an impasse in her life and a future with Eric depended on her decision.

"I love you and I know sometimes I make it difficult but that's what's gonna make us stronger as a couple."

They kissed at length. The door to the elevator opened on her floor and slowly started to close. Eric used his foot to block it. As the door started to close a second time, they laughingly jumped off just in the nick of time.

"We were almost taken for a ride, huh? Goodnight, Eric," Sophia said dreamily walking to her door but Eric was right behind her and she fell once more into his arms. They kissed long and hard again until he could only smell her scent. Riding on a sudden resurging cloud of romance, Eric floated into Sophia's apartment.

"What about the girls?" Sophia asked as Eric planted his lips on hers cutting off her speech. "You've got to go and make sure the girls are home safe, Eric. Call me later, all right?"

"Alright, I'll call later," Eric said on his way out the door.

"Thanks so much for my gift. It really cheered me up," Sophia said and hugged Eric.

"You're welcome, love," he said then she closed the door after him. He whistled all the way down to the lobby and waved at the doorman as he went by. "Have a very good evening," Eric sang as he exited through the front door. Outside, the girls sat in the car and saw the swagger that accompanied Eric's gait. It was a little past ten and they were all hungry and looking forward to dining out.

"Your uncle is looking kinda happy, yo."

"Yep, looks like homey gonna have it his way tonight. Get him some trim tonight."

"You guys are soo bad. I can't believe you're just sitting here and talking about my uncle and his fiancé like that," Deedee said looking out the window as her uncle approached the vehicle. "You could be right, though. He does look kinda happy," she said then got out and went to sit in the front.

"Same thing I was saying," Josephine said when Eric entered the Range Rover and slammed the door. Deedee giggled.

"What happened? Something funny happened while I was away?" Eric questioned.

"Yeah, you kinda missed it," Deedee said looking back at both girls. "You had to be here."

"Yeah, that's all good but the real deal is, have you ladies decided where we're going to go eat or do you want the man to make the decision?"

"Sure Uncle E, that would be fine by me," Deedee said. "What about y'all? I mean, whatever works, right?"

Eric turned up the volume as Tupac's clever rhymes raced to the front of the foray. Coco, Deedee and Josephine joined the chorus. After a few bars, Eric couldn't resist the mood. Maybe Tupac was right so he rapped along too.

...*What you won't do ...you do for love...*

...*you tried everything but you don't give up ...*

They rapped along with Pac until Eric pulled into a parking spot.

"Uncle E, tell me, you really gotta make moves?" Deedee asked.

"I do but we've got some time to spare," he said laughing now. He parked and they walked to Carmine's, famous for its Italian cuisine and favorite of Sophia's. Once seated, Eric and the girls chowed down with much gusto on appetizers, salad, and plenty of pasta. They sat relishing their feast. After Eric ordered pasta and salad to go, he turned to find out if anyone had room for dessert.

"There's a little space reserved for a slice of cheese cake," Josephine suggested.

"Damn, what you keep in your stomach? A shredder?" Coco asked. Deedee and Eric laughed.

"It's all good. Some people have healthy appetites," Eric said smiling.

"Uh huh and those people usually get fat. Look at her, she's already busting out o' them jeans." Coco was getting at Josephine, clowning like they always do. Deedee was used to the act by now. Each of them would say what she really felt about the other but it always had to be done in a comical way.

"Don't matter whatcha say. I'm still charming and petite," Josephine said and stood to take her bow. Deedee applauded and Eric smiled amused by the antics.

"Sit down, Jo. Don't embarrass yourself, girl. Petite is not another name for ho'," Coco said.

"Oh no, you didn't go there, Coco. At least I know my sexual preference."

"Who's that? Anyone with a light?" Coco asked jokingly.

"You know, I'm never singing back-up on any of your joints again and watch if you ever go number one."

"I don't need you to sing back up. I took all your verses out." The girls were clowning and high fiving.

"No you did not just say that. You a dirty low down..." Josephine and Coco went at it like sisters did. It was a familiarity that developed after knowing a person intimately for some time. Eric wanted to use the same energy to bring Sophia around. The diamond necklace from Harry Winston, though expensive, had softened her up a bit. He had made a note to order food to go for her and added her favorite bottle of vino to make her simmer.

The waiter brought dessert for the girls and coffee for Eric. He sipped and thought about what else he could do to save his relationship with the woman he loved.

"By the way, I remember that you guys won the first place in that last contest and I'll be putting up the first prize. Part of that prize is a recording deal. Along with that, there is the prize money," Eric said. He looked at Coco and Josephine's shocked faces and pulled out a check. "This is the actual check and I hope you guys remember who brought you this."

"Ah, you did?"

"No, Busta did. Back in the days, he and my older brother, Dennis, built a record label from scratch. Although Busta went off and did other things, he stayed close. After I graduated from college, Dennis brought me into this indie music market. Right now, we got the support from about three majors. We work with everyone from R&B to hip-hop, rap, rock, and jazz...It doesn't really matter. We trying to do it all. Our next venture will be to score films. I'm currently negotiating on a deal right now."

"Wow, Uncle E, that's really good."

"Word? That's great, yo."

"You've got to keep it moving. Makes no sense sitting on the pot unless you gonna do the damn thing."

"With all these moves coming into effect...Ah, do you, um...Do you have any job opportunities?" Josephine asked with curiosity.

"I don't see why not. We're growing and the opportunities will exist for interns and other positions. But you guys want to be signed as artists."

"True dat, true dat," Josephine chirped and struck a high fashion pose.

"I think they got enough of you, video-ho," Coco whispered.

"Does anyone else feel the sweat or is it just that I smell haters?" Josephine said. She became distracted as Eric pulled out another check. "Uh oh, is that money I see?" Josephine said.

Eric handed her an American Express check for ten thousand dollars. "Ohh yess! Is it all mine?" she finally recovered enough to ask.

"Here you are, Coco," Eric said and passed a similar check to Coco. She first looked at him as if he had just done the worse possible thing to her. The look of disbelief that slowly appeared on Coco's face transformed to an immense grin when she glanced at the paper in her hand.

"All this? Is it real? Thanks, good looking out. Yeah, yeah! Finally, I can show my mother sump'n that I got from this music thing, yo," Coco said and reached over to hug Eric. Deedee was overcome with emotion and shed tears of joy. Josephine walked around the table and threw her arms around Eric too. Deedee eventually joined as the rest of the patrons close enough to hear applauded.

"Now, there is another check here for the same amount. It's for the third member of your group. Ah, sadly to say, she's not here with us but I wanted y'all to decide what to do with her share," Eric said, looking at both Coco and Josephine.

"That should be easy. We could just give it to her through her parents," Josephine immediately suggested.

"Yeah, I'm with that. I mean, they could decide what they wanted to do with her share better than we can," Coco said, looking at Josephine.

"Deal," Josephine said as she threw a high-five to Coco. "We could take it to her parents place tomorrow. I know their address," Josephine said.

"Just don't make it too early, ahight Jo," Coco said.

"Okay, okay. I'll call that lady, your neighbor."

"Miss Katie."

"Yeah, I'll call Miss Katie at about noon or so."

"Okay, that'll be good," Coco said nodding to Josephine.

Not long after, they left the restaurant and all enjoyed a happy ride home. Not only were their stomachs filled but Coco and Josephine both had American Express checks with ten thousand dollars and their names written on them. Deedee smiled with glee that she had been a part of it all. The idea that led to the prize money being split evenly for the members of the group belonged to her.

FORTY-THREE

About an hour after dinner, Coco found herself back at home. She hurriedly went through the mail, then examined the check she had received. She rolled a blunt and started enjoying the herbal lift. There came a knock on her door. "Who is it?" she asked not expecting anyone but knew it had to be Miss Katie.

"It's Miss Katie, Coco. Are you up?" Coco clipped the blunt, hid it under the ashtray, and looked around for the can of air freshener.

"Hold on Miss Katie," Coco said when she found the aerosol can. She ran around the apartment spraying everywhere as she yelled, "I'll be right there, Miss Katie. Just give me a sec and I'll be there." She prayed and sniffed. Finally, she opened the window and walked over to answer the door.

"Hey Miss Katie how're you?"

"Just fine. I mean, I could give you the long list or the short one," Miss Katie said and walked a little way into the apartment. "You burning paper or sump'n Coco?" she asked as she glanced around. Without waiting for the answer, the old lady continued. "Two people from the Social Services came here to see where your mother lives but I wasn't able to let them inside."

"Really? What time was that?"

"I don't know exactly. Could've been around six or so. You know those damn social workers always coming late."

"What did they say? Are they coming back?"

"Oh yes. Here, they left this note for you. They'll be coming back tomorrow at three o' clock," Miss Katie said still looking around. She saw the run down sofa and the small television screen sitting atop a center table. "I guess that means your mommy will be home soon, huh, Coco?"

"I guess so, Miss Katie. I mean you and I..." Coco appeared

confused for a second. "We both did our best to let her know that she should stay in a little longer but after the shooting..."

"What shooting are you talking about, Coco? Who done got themselves shot this time?" Miss Katie asked getting excited. "Got the cops crawling up and down the roof to the streets. That's probably why they shot that child last week. They probably nervous like myself, Coco. I don't know why your mother would want to come back to this," Miss Katie rambled and when she waved her hands, Coco was unsure if she was talking about the apartment or outside. She was too tired to ask for any further clarification.

"I'll come and see you in the morning. You have a good night," Coco said and then turned as Miss Katie was about to walk away. "Oh Miss Katie, guess what. You'll never guess so I better tell you," Coco said with so much excitement the eyes of the old lady bulged with curiousity.

"What, child? What is it you wanna say so badly? Spit it out already will you?" Miss Katie was herself getting excited again. "This too much for my ol' heart. Lemme sit." Miss Katie sat on the clean side of the sofa, which was further from the door. Coco retrieved the check and showed it to her. "What is this? A check?" Miss Katie squinted and asked. "I can't see so well without my glasses. What does it say?" She saw the smile spread across Coco's lips.

"It's my prize money. Ten thousand dollars," Coco said, waving the paper in the air. She did a dance move and struck a pose. Miss Katie smiled and commended the proud teen.

"Oh, God's blessings have reached you, Coco. Oh, this is such a beautiful thing. It is a great start. I'm so proud of you." Miss Katie jubilantly leapt up and embraced Coco.

"This is hopefully the start of more good things."

"I wish you all the best. You deserve all the blessings." The old lady was moved to tears as she framed the young girl's face with her hands and planted a kiss on each cheek. "God bless you. You're gonna make your mother so proud."

"Thank you. I wanna make her proud."

"You will, child. You will," Miss Katie said smiling.

"I've got to open a bank account. Can you help me?" Coco

asked as she looked at the check.

"Sure thing, as a matter of fact, my Roxy works in a bank. She's a manager or sump'n like that."

"Oh, your daughter does?" Coco asked. "That'll be cool. We'll go in the morning and do it." Coco couldn't stop staring at the check. "I'm really happy about this, Miss Katie."

"You've got every right to be Coco. You're applying your God-given talent and improving your life. I imagine it's a great feeling."

"Sure is," Coco said beaming but she still looked a little down. Miss Katie sensed that something must be awry.

"If it's the social workers you worried about, you don't have to report anything to them just yet."

"Nah, that's all good. I just hope that my mother will be proud to know that her daughter has some kinda talent."

"Oh she will, Coco. Don't you worry 'bout a thing. God willing, she'll be here to see you shine like the star you truly are. She'll be so proud of you, she won't stop talking. She'll be bragging all day long," Miss Katie said like it was her most profound wish. It was in her unselfish nature that she wanted nothing to spoil the rise of Coco's star. She watched Coco smile and Miss Katie silently thanked God.

"Goodnight, Coco. Don't forget about tomorrow morning, dear. Sleep tight," the old lady said and happily went next door.

"Goodnight, Miss Katie and thanks a lot for all you've done," Coco said and thought about buying a gift for Miss Katie. She closed the door and glanced at the note from the social service's office. She shook her head and then said aloud, "My mother is bugged, yo." Coco retrieved the clip and relit it. She inhaled heavily and held her breath. She walked to her bedroom, exhaling slowly. "I might as well get lifted in my crib. Mommy ain't here so she won't find out," Coco said to the streets. I've got real money. I'm rich. Maybe I can help move my mom out the hood, she thought as she stared out the window and blew smoke rings at the people below.

"That Coco, she smokes too much," Miss Katie said back in her apartment. The infant boy watching television rolled his big eyes and gave her a huge smile. "But I'm so happy for her. That's right, my baby boy, Roshawn," Miss Katie said playfully throwing kisses at him. Roshawn continued to cackle and smile. "Where's your mommy?" Miss Katie teasingly asked the jovial toddler.

Next door, Coco stared out the window and saw a patrol car on the street corner. The occupants were busy in conversation with two other officers on the corner. She observed how they all turned their heads when Kim and Tina got out of a cab. One of the officers walked a little closer to where the ladies stood. He shook his head as they both walked away from the cab after paying the tab.

She lit a cigarette and pulled out her pen and pad. Slipping a CD into the player, she nodded her head as the beat flooded the apartment. Coco sat on the edge of her bed and began to write her rhymes.

> Huh, huh, how many times I done told y'all
> I'm here till it's over, I ain't neva gonna fall
> slip and slide till the day I drop and leave y'all
> waiting for the next hero at ground zero
> Coco up in this piece, who wanna test
> Nah, who wanna mess with the raw lyricist
> Wit the ill flow, uh try to blast me wit that weak shit
> I thought you'd know by now it ain't happening I'm a
> realist, you can't see me

Coco bobbed her head to the beat as her rhymes fell from her pen. She was a slave to the discipline as she puffed and tried to compose the perfect rhyme. The weed and the dollar amount on the check added to the euphoria, sending her in a zone.

FORTY-FOUR

He woke up as if he had been falling down a cliff in a nice dream that had somehow gone bad. Lil' Long felt himself still shackled but no longer to the bed. He was able to sit and let his feet touch the floor. The chain dangled easily from both his ankles. He was able to move around and was no longer cuffed.

A smile broke out for this seemingly small victory. Lil' Long surveyed his new digs and realized he must have been transported from the hospital while he was still unconscious. He saw bars and his worst nightmare slowly dawned. He was alive in a jailhouse infirmary. Here, as in all prisons, inmates were expected to wear the clothes the prison officials issued them. Lil' Long had somehow remained in his hospital issued which covered his front but not his backside. Making a run was not out of the question but it was a little risky. He sat up in the bed thinking. The correction officer at the end of the corridor watched him curiously. Lil' Long decided to strike up a conversation with her.

"Yo, CO, you mind tellin' me what this hellhole is called?" he asked. She moved closer to him, her hips gyrating as he walked. Lil' Long felt the immediate pang of a hard-on just from watching her walk. "My shit's working again. Oh baby!" he screamed as she got closer. He could tell she was in her thirties. Lil' Long sized her up. When she was close enough to smell her perfume, he whistled. "Hmm...hmm. That fragrance you're wearing sure smells damn good." Lil' Long smiled. Now he could see that her face wasn't all that but there was plenty of junk in the trunk.

"Good luck with your conversation. Where you think you're going to get with that cheap talk is beyond me. I could tell you though that tomorrow you'll be upstate in prison." There was the sound of a door opening and shutting in the hall.

"What's your name?" asked Lil' Long, peering to catch a glimpse of her name tag. She was heavy in the hips and her sides showed some fat but Lil' Long decided since he was on lock down, he might as well push-up on her.

"It's Officer Torres, scum bag," she said acidly, her eyes shooting daggers at his wounds.

"Yo, ease up. You don't know me like that, Officer Torres. Why I gotta be a scum bag? Haven't you heard of innocent till..."

"Not for you. You're the violent type. The type that doesn't mind killing innocent people. You should be stripped naked and beaten until you get sick and die from it."

"Well, at least I know you got my interests at heart," Lil' Long said, nastily licking his lips. He felt her eyes lock onto his erection and made no attempt to conceal it.

"Keep that in mind and do something about waving your dick around before someone does you, boo," Torres said and turned. Before she could walk away, Lil' Long pressed further.

"Whadya suggest?"

"Miss Thumb and her four friends," she said and then walked away leaving Lil' Long to admire her rear. She stopped at the door and spoke briefly with another correction officer. Lil' Long eased back onto the bed wearing a smile on his face. He threw a glance down the hallway hoping to catch her eyes. Feeling groggy, he closed his eyes and pretended to sleep until the other officer walked away.

He reached under his hospital gown and grabbed the shaft of his dick and began to stroke it up and down. Lil' Long knew she would be watching so he continued. She wasn't just watching. Officer Torres gawked at the size as it grew and smiled as he exploded above his head.

"You better clean all them skeet marks off the damn floor and window," she yelled as the other prisoners who had witnessed the incident laughed. Some honored him with adorations.

"I can't believe he jerked off for her."

"Seems like she enjoyed it."

"Nah, he's gonna be getting some additional charges put on him."

"That nigga must have a death wish."

Later, Lil' Long was escorted by Officer Torres and a male officer to the transport van where he was the only occupant.

"Ain't y'all supposed to give me some clothes? Damn, how y'all expect a nigga to sit on this hard ass seat in my bare ass?"

"You'll figure it out and make the appropriate adjustments necessary," Torres said smiling. She slammed the door and walked away. The movement of the van left him sprawled uncomfortably against the hard interior as the van jerked away. He rode uneasily as each bump in the road brought a howl from him.

"Fucking bitch, she knows I'm supposed to get real clothes issued to me. Yeow! I'll get that fat bitch for doing this shit to me," he yelped. The ride continued and sometimes, it was if the van jerked back and forth purposely trying to throw his barely dressed body against the metal and hard plastic seats.

FORTY-FIVE

Coco woke to a loud banging on her door. She rushed to put away all the cigarette stubs left over from her long night of composing and opened the window. Miss Katie must be feeling antsy today, Coco thought as she opened the door in her pajamas. She was greeted by two women dressed like Jehovah's Witnesses. Coco rubbed the surprise from her sleepy eyes before she spoke.

"Look, I think you've got the wrong address," she said coldly and was about to close the door when the ladies addressed her.

"Good morning. I'm Miss Cook and this is Mrs. Smalls and we're from the social service office. Are you Ms....?"

"Oh, my bad. You were here yesterday, right?"

"Yes, we were and spoke to, ah, Miss Katie. She told us that you'd be here today so we just stopped by. The reason we're here is to assess your home. Your mother will be released from her program in a few days and we'd like to take a look at her place of residence."

Coco could see Miss Katie coming up from behind and immediately tried to prevent the visitors' entrance to the apartment.

"Here she comes right now," Coco said as she walked out and closed the door. "Miss Katie, here are the social workers from yesterday."

"How're you doing, ladies?" Miss Katie asked with a pleasant smile.

"Miss Katie helps my mother so maybe you should assess her apartment," Coco said but the workers wanted to see where Rachel Harvey called home.

"Now, Miss Katie could be a collateral resource for your mother but I'm afraid we've got to see the apartment where she receives her mail."

"I'm not her collateral. I've never used any illegal drugs so I can't possibly be her co-nothing." Miss Katie took offense until the worker smiled and raised her hand.

"No, I'm sorry. That's not what I meant. Collateral is a term used by the Department of Social Services to identify some-one who has known the family and is able to provide information that will assist us in helping the family."

"Oh," Miss Katie said with a chuckle, "Well then I'm sorry because I didn't know."

"That's quite alright," the social worker said. She then turned to Coco.

"Can I have a few minutes to clean up?" Coco asked. "Like, can y'all go grab breakfast and come back in a few?"

"Coco, these are busy people and it..."

"We really would like to see the place. You don't have to worry about the mess. We understand how messy teenagers are. It will only take a few minutes."

"Okay then lets go see the place," Coco said leading the way. They paraded through the one bedroom. The social workers made stops and took quick glances here and there. After viewing the bathroom, they passed next to where Coco had previously sat generating lyrics. Things seemed like they were going well up until that point and then the bomb exploded. One of the social workers bent over and picked-up a small plastic bag.

Coco saw the whole thing occurring as if she was in a dream. The slow motion of it all made her want to scream, to say something to stop or divert the social worker from putting the bag closer to her face. As she sniffed and examined it, Coco's mind did laps trying to come up with the appropriate excuse but there was only a strained silence in the room. Miss Katie saw the social worker pour the contents onto a sheet of paper and fold the paper.

"I'm not sure but I do believe that this substance is mari-juana," she announced.

"Lemme see that," Coco said and reached for the bag. The social worker did not release it.

"I think we should take this back and have a more complete analysis done but I'm almost sure it is marijuana." The silence increased such that the social worker sounded as if she was making an announcement for the entire world to hear. "We'll be getting back to you as soon as we speak with our supervisor." They were both heading out the door. Coco caught up with them before they were completely outside.

"But ah...I don't even know what it was doing there. I mean, it could've stuck to the bottom of my sneaks or sump'n."

"That's an unlikely story."

"But what could happen though?" Coco asked frantically.

"Well, for one thing you'll have to attend a drug rehab for your addiction."

"Addiction? You can't be serious, yo," Coco said, anger slowly seeping into her tone.

"At this time, we're going to ask that you say nothing else until you hear from us, okay?"

"When will that be?" Coco asked anxiously. "I mean, are you gonna be talking to my mother or..."

"We've got to go. We're late for another appointment. We will give you a call on Monday and let you know then. We've got Katie Patterson's telephone number as the number to contact you," one of the social workers said. "Good day. You'll be hearing from us." Both ladies left with so much haste that their departure left Coco and Miss Katie gasping for air.

"But wait a minute now," Miss Katie hollered as they went off down the stairs. There was no stopping them. The social workers were gone before Coco could think of another question.

"Uh," she muttered as Miss Katie gave her a wide eyed stare.

"I don't know what to make of it," Miss Katie said. Coco remained speechless. "Coco, only you and God know how that reefer could've gotten into your mother's place. I mean, your mother isn't here at the time and that puts a lot of blame on you," Miss Katie said in a sympathetic tone.

"But they're saying I'll have to go to rehab. I'm not going to any place for addicts. I'm no addict," Coco said, her hand on her chest. "I'll just refuse to go. That's all to it," she said with her head held low and her eyes downcast.

"Coco, it's just like the social workers said. You've just gotta wait till Monday when they call. Don't make no sense you worrying right now. Pray now that everything will be alright."

"Prayer, Miss Katie?" Coco asked skeptically.

"You got that right. Prayer. That's what we tend to forget. Only God can make things right," Miss Katie preached as she looked up toward the ceiling. "Only God can. Coco, go on and get yourself together before we're late for your appointment," Miss Katie said courteously.

"What appointment?" Coco asked and then answered herself. "Oh, that's right. The one at the bank," she said remembering the check. Coco felt some relief as she thought of the check.

"That's right. Let's go," Miss Katie said and walked back to her apartment.

"I'll be ready in a minute." Coco walked back inside the apartment. This had to be her lowest and highest at the same time. Coco quickly showered and dressed in her Baby Phat warm-up suit. She twisted her curls under a baseball hat. Miss Katie was ready and waiting when Coco rang the bell.

"C'mon in, Coco, and have a cup of hot chocolate before we go," Miss Katie said ushering Coco into her apartment.

FORTY-SIX

Josephine got up with the sound of the television blaring in her ears. She could hear the sound of Usher and danced out of her hotel bed. She headed straight to the bathroom and played with her bangs before sitting and urinating.

"Jo, you're up?" she heard her mother shouting.

"Damn, she's here?" Josephine mumbled to herself and took a deep breath before answering her mother. "Yeah, I'm up. What's new?" Josephine deadpanned. She could hear her mother's footsteps getting close. Josephine looked in her wallet and made sure the checks were still there. She would call Coco and make arrangements to drop one of the checks off to Danielle's parents. That was a good thing Eric did. He was alright, thought Josephine as her mother called her name again. "Yes? Why do you insist on calling me so often when you want absolutely nothing?" she asked her mother in a most callous manner.

"Josephine, if you can take time to get off your high horse and realize that I'm your mother..."

"So what? Does that give you the right to harass me?"

"I'm not going to go there with you, young lady. Just keep this act up and I'll send you to your father's. You think his sweetheart is going to want you around, uh? He has no time for you and that's why we're here together back in this hellhole of a city."

"I didn't tell you to leave dad," Josephine responded as she walked out of the bathroom.

"Your father did not want us. That's why he went out and got himself a bimbo from his office."

"How could you say that?" Josephine asked, tears rolling down her eyes. She was sobbing now, shoulders heaving and crying hard. Her mother reached out to hug her but she turned away.

"I'm all you got, girl. I didn't leave your father. He left us.

You're going to have to face that hard fact of life. Your father and I are getting a divorce as soon as possible because I refuse to be the other woman." Josephine heard what her mother said but refused to acknowledge any of it. She kept her head down until her mother left her alone and went into the bathroom. Josephine sneered when she heard the door slam.

"You're a fucking witch and that's why dad ain't with us," Josephine said between her sobs. She opened her Coach wallet and pulled out the checks. A smile slowly returned to her face. Josephine picked up the phone and dialed Miss Katie's number. The telephone rang through to an outgoing message. Josephine waited and left her message. "Hi, I'm trying to reach Coco. This is her friend, Jo. Please tell her I called and I'll call again later. Bye," she said then hung up the telephone to discover her mother standing next to her. "What do you want, mother?" she asked tersely. Her mother took a deep breath before she replied.

"Josephine, as much as you may want to deny the facts, they are there for you to see." Josephine remained quiet, not looking at her mother's face. She didn't want to hear the excuses but she let her speak. "Honey, you're bitter right now. I wanted the marriage just as you did. I fought for the family but your father wanted something else. He selfishly took me along for the ride." Josephine could hear the emotions straining the tone of her mother's voice but she never looked up. She didn't want to see anymore tears. There had been an ocean of them since the separation, Josephine thought as her mother cried then continued. "I wanted a family. I wanted to be loved and respected as a wife. I wasn't going to compete with that bitch from his office. Your daddy made his choice. You're grown enough to know that if he wanted his family then he would've chosen us over that two timing slut."

Josephine heard her mother's voice rise then trail off but she still held her head steadfast away from her mother's view. She was angry and knew that facing her mother would bring about an explosion in her.

"I know you wanted the family or maybe you wanted to be with your father but...You know whenever there's a break up,

everyone involved gets hurt. I know you're hurting as much as I..."
It was then that detonation occurred.

"You may be my mother but you really don't know how much I hurt. I love daddy and I wanted a family but now that's not gonna happen. I'm..."

"Josephine, why do you insist on saying..."

"I gave you your time to speak. At least respect me and give me equal time. Despite the problems you and dad were having, going around and telling everyone didn't do anything to solve those problems so why do it? Because you wanted sympathy and everyone on your side. That's why you did it."

"Josephine, you know that's not true. I was in therapy and the therapist's secretary spread the news like it was gossip. That's why he had to fire her and..."

"Mommy, the reason she got fired is because you told the therapist that you think daddy was boning her."

"Young lady, I did not accuse that woman of 'boning' your dad. They were seen on camera leaving the Holiday Inn."

"Yeah, by a private detective that you hired to stalk and frame dad so you could get a better alimony." Out of nowhere, Josephine felt the slap against her cheek. As she whirled, she saw her mother's arm getting ready to deliver another smack across her face. Josephine ducked in the nick of time and ran to the bathroom where she slammed and bolted the door. "You better leave me alone or I'm gonna call 911. I swear, I'll call BCW on you if you hit me again," Josephine screamed from behind the bathroom door. "I know why you mad at me. I know why. It's because I know your secrets. I'm your daughter, remember? I know your secrets, mother."

Josephine wept from the confines of the bathroom. The teenager stood at the sink and examined her face in the mirror. Josephine, tears still streaming, saw that her cheek bore the marks of the slap. "I should call the police on her," she whimpered. Josephine turned each cheek to compare the amount of swelling. I've got enough money. I could leave now, she thought as she tried her best to use make-up to cover the redness on her face. The wound was more than skin deep and would take time to heal.

From the other side of the door, her mother shook her head and wandered through the sitting area. She turned on the television and looked around the hotel room. She found the mini-bar then poured some scotch in a cup. After a sip, she lit a cigarette and sat on the sofa smoking. A few minutes later, her daughter emerged from the bathroom.

"I'm sorry Josephine. I'm sorry. I never meant to cause you any harm," she said with a slight slur. This was no time to forgive and Josephine picked up her wallet and kept on walking right out the door. "You're just like your father. Go ahead and walk out. See if I care." Josephine could hear her mother yelling. She slammed the door shut and didn't hear her mother whisper, "I hope you never ever have to go through a divorce."

While on the elevator, Josephine held her tears back but as she felt the rush of wind on her face, she cried softly. The hurt came from deep within. She once had a family and now it seemed that she had lost both parents. Her father had stayed back at the house the family had bought. He had given them the reason that his job had him supervising an important project and he couldn't take the time off.

Josephine had known it was due to the pending divorce and he just didn't want to be with her mother. After all, why would anyone want to be with someone if you're trying to get rid of that person? Josephine thought. She knew her father loved her and maybe he wanted to be with her but she couldn't understand why he hadn't returned her calls. The latter was the cause of her unhappiness. She found a coffee shop and sat in a corner sipping coffee.

FORTY-SEVEN

"Now that was a good thing you did, Coco. Opening a new bank account is something worthy of remembering. I remember when I first...ah, yeah," Miss Katie said with a smile as she walked with Coco from the bus stop. They dodged traffic and Miss Katie waited until she was safely on the other side before resuming. "Yeah, I couldn't have been more than ten years old. My parents took me to the Credit Union and I opened up my first account. Fifty eight years later, I still have that account. Done raise my children and sent them to college off that," Miss Katie said with a laugh. She nudged Coco. "I cheated a little though. I used to take all my hubby's money and spend that on the bills. Then I'd put my lil' ol' checks into my secret account," the woman said and both she and Coco laughed as they walked briskly into their apartment building.

Moments later, Josephine dialed Miss Katie's number and this time, the old lady picked up. "Hello, this is Josephine. May I please speak to Coco?"

"Oh hello, Josephine. This is Miss Katie. If you can hold a minute, I'll go get Coco," Miss Katie said as she opened her door and saw Coco. She pointed to the instrument in her hand. "She's right here, Josephine," Miss Katie said and handed the phone to Coco. "It's your friend, Josephine."

"Yeah, what's good, Jo?" Coco asked. She listened and nodded her head. "Oh yeah, that's right. I'll meet you there then. See ya, Jo." Coco handed the cordless back to Miss Katie and said, "That was my friend, Josephine. We gotta go do sump'n for Da Crew. Remember that other girl, Danielle? Well Eric Ascot gave Josephine her cut of the prize money."

"What's that?"

"She gets ten grand also but because she's dead and no

longer with us, we're gonna take her share to her parents."

"Well that's a good thing, Coco. See, all that hard work paid off in the end. Of course, it's really too bad for her but I'm sure her parents will find sump'n to do with that money. You're leaving now?"

"Yep, as a matter of fact I am. I'll see you later, Miss Katie."

"Okay, let me know when you get back in. I should still be up. God travel with you girl," Miss Katie said and waved at Coco. The teenager was down the stairs in a flash.

FORTY-EIGHT

They met at the rendezvous just the way Josephine had called it. She was the first to get there. Josephine stood rooted to the spot thinking about the fun she'd had with Danielle. 'Mama Loca' she liked to call her. They had been opposites. Danielle always used to wear wild outfits like sarong skirts with no underwear and short shorts. Danielle was extravagantly untamed from the first time they had met. Josephine had felt an immediate attraction to Danielle. She was fun to be around. Josephine knew that Danielle's parents were going through a divorce and that was somehow linked to Danielle's wilder side.

"What's good, Jo?" Coco asked as she approached Josephine.

"Oh shoot." Josephine seemed to be startled by the sudden appearance of Coco.

"You look like I scared da shit outta you. Didn't mean to scare ya, girl. You ahight?"

"Yeah, I'm good. I was just sorta reminiscing on Danielle a lil' sump'n and I got caught up. How're you?"

"I'm chilling, yo. We catching the bus or sump'n?"

"No, we can ride down in a cab. It's not far at all."

"Ahight, let's do this," Coco said and the girls waved for a taxi.

"Yo, Coco, what did you really think of Danielle? I mean..."

"I hear you. I catch your drift, yo. What did I think of her?" Coco glanced outside then back at Josephine. "At first, she was sorta like this wild bitch and then next, she's the sweetest person. She was real with her shit though. If she ain't like you, you knew about it quick fast," Coco said.

"She was crazy. Danielle was my girl but she was soo crazy."

"You mean like she was seven thirty, yo?" Coco asked and as Josephine was about to answer, she looked out the window and suddenly yelled at the driver.

"Stop please! That's where Danielle lived," she said. The taxi's brakes screeched as the girls dug out money to pay the fare. Moments later, Coco and Josephine stood outside Danielle's parent's apartment door. "This is where her mother lives," Josephine said sounding unsure.

"You sure this is it, yo?" Coco asked. Josephine glanced around before she answered.

"Yep, this is it. This the one, 4B," Josephine said and rang the doorbell. "Yep, I've been here before." There were voices coming from the other side of the door. The door swung open and a young white guy answered. The girls were taken by surprise.

"Ah...Hi, we're trying to find a friend...Her parents live here. This is 4B, right?" Josephine asked, still looking at the person at the door incredulously when he began to speak.

"I feel for ya, baby doll. What's your friend's name?" he asked.

"Her name was Danielle. She died some months ago and..."

"Oh, so that's da dealie, yo? Yo, I'm saying, dogs, I don't know da peeps but I'm sayin' da apartment was on da market an' my ol' man hollered at me to cop it. You know what I'm sayin'?"

Josephine looked at Coco with her mouth wide open in disbelief. "Ahight, tell me what just happened ain't just happen," she said.

"I'm trying to digest it all," Coco said looking at the young white guy at the door then back at Josephine.

"All I'm sayin' is she ain't here. She probably dipped on y'all or sump'n," he continued.

"Thanks," said Josephine.

"Good looking out, my nig," said Coco. Both girls walked away laughing.

"Peace, fam. I'm outtie," he shouted.

When they were out of the apartment building, Coco and Josephine were still laughing.

"Yo, that white boy was like any ol' nigga on da corner, ya know?"

"Whatcha fit'n to do now, Coco?" Josephine asked. Coco looked at her and saw the sadness on her face. She knew there was something else to the question but teased her anyway.

"Why nothing, cousin Kizzie. Ya think we should run away from Massa's house today? We paid niggas now, cuz."

"I ain't playing around, Coco. I'm for real girl. You wanna go get lunch or a snack?" Josephine asked. Coco stared at her intently.

"Sump'n is bothering you?"

"Either that or my period," Josephine said.

"You better do sump'n about that," Coco said.

"I will. I will. I'm a go buck wild with that nigga."

"Josephine, I'm talking 'bout your period. Take Demerol or sump'n like that for the pain." They both laughed and Josephine quickly added.

"Ya gotta make yourself clear, Coco."

"Whatever. You always have sex on the mind, that's all."

"Whatever, Coco. I've got Danielle's parents home number somewhere in my hotel room though. Hopefully, they ain't changed it. I'll call and set up the appointment for me and..."

"Nah, yo. You just call them and let them know you're gonna bring the check to them." The girls discussed the possibilities as they walked into a café on the corner. They found a booth and sat down. A busboy immediately brought two glasses with water to the table.

"Why you gonna front, Coco? You don't wanna meet her moms and them? I think her parents are divorced. Maybe that's why they sold their apartment to that wigga."

"See, now you buggin' calling him a wigga. You're crazy girl," Coco said and they both laughed until the waiter came to take the order.

"I'll have scrambled eggs with home fries and orange juice," Josephine said.

"I'll have the cheese sandwich with ice tea," Coco said.

"Make mine fried soft, please. The scrambled eggs, that

is," Josephine said and sipped some water. "You got smokes?" Josephine suddenly asked as if it was an emergency.

"Nah, I'm fresh out and shit, if I tell you what happened this morning, you'd see why," Coco said rolling her eyes.

"It's that bad?"

"What? I'm telling you, Jo. I was in the bedroom with two social workers and don't you know that one of them found a bag a weed in my room."

"You let them know that that was some of your mother's shit, right?"

"Man, they grabbed that shit and ran like they was fiends."

"Oh, you mean they were gonna smoke that shit?"

"I'm trying to tell you, Jo. They ran out the apartment as soon as they put their hands on the smoke."

"Well, fuck it. What're you gonna do?"

"I don't know. I guess I could wait until Monday."

"That's when they gonna try to tell you that they want you to go to a drug program."

"Bitch, I ain't going to no druggie place."

"Yeah but ain't your mom in one of these places, Coco?"

"Yeah but that's my mother. She needs that counseling and shit. I don't. I ain't hooked on nada."

"Sounds like you already made up your mind so I guess you'll wait till Monday. So that means you can't smoke?"

"I'm gonna do what I wanna do. Nobody's gonna threaten me."

"They already found the bag of weed on you."

"No, they found that shit on the floor," Coco said emphatically.

"Ahight, so they found the shit. The point is, is you gonna smoke or is you not?"

"You sound like you gonna cop."

"Yep, you got that right. I'm fitting to cop like a fifty and call it a day," Josephine said.

"I heard that," Coco said with a smile.

"You wanna chip in?"

GHETTO
GIRLS
TOO

"Why I gotta chip in when you now have money coming out da ass? You can't buy a fifty sack dolo?" Coco answered.

"Ahight, ahight. You get the food and I'll buy the weed. And that includes the tip, bitch," Josephine said and the girls shook hands on it.

"Jo, where you gonna cop?"

"I know this spot that Geo told me about."

"Word, where is it? Cuz five-oh be waiting on me to do sump'n, you know?"

"What're you? America's most wanted? I got the info in my cell phone," Josephine said producing the instrument.

"You gotta call 'em and let 'em know you're on your way or sump'n like that, right?"

"Nope, I call this number and put in my special code and they'll deliver in about ten to fifteen minutes." Josephine dialed the digits and gave her location. Like she said, a delivery was immediately dispatched to meet her at the café.

"Get out, Jo. How you gonna come back to the city and get connections like that before I do, yo?"

"Don't worry. Once they come by and see you, you're down. Being that you my girl and all, I'll verify for you."

"Stop playing, yo. They coming to deliver to you right here?"

"Right here at the café in about another ten minutes. Coco, don't sweat it. The 'dro will be here, ahight," Josephine said and sipped orange juice.

"If you say so, bitch. I gotta wait and see this," Coco said as she slapped Josephine a high-five.

"So, Coco, what's up with you and Dee?"

"What you mean?"

"Like she wants to be your friend but you won't let her."

"Nah, it aint even like that. She's just a show-off. Quick to let you know she got dough and all."

"Her uncle's got dough."

"Yeah but at times, the bitch be flaunting like she's soo fucking rich. Pisses me off, that's all."

"Damn, girl, I didn't think it was that serious."

"It ain't that serious but she be doing shit when I'm around and it just irritates me is all."

"Shoot, I heard that but she's kind hearted and likes to help."

"Yeah, that's true but sometimes it's too much. You know, back up some and stop sweat'n a sista. You feel me?"

"I smell you, girl."

"Shit's irritating."

"Ahight, Coco, be nice. Our food is here."

"I can't wait for the weed to come. I've got to see this."

"Just wait a while, you'll see. You'll see what I'm working with."

FORTY-NINE

He felt the uneasiness of his confines. After being processed, Lil' Long was issued an orange jumpsuit by prison officials. Lying on his back in his bunk, he could hear the alarm ring for mess. He had sauntered through to this isolated cell without interference and remained sleeping until now. He opened his eyes, briefly struggling to deal with his reality. Although he was hungry and still woozy, he refused to budge and stayed horizontal. The impact of the ride had left him nauseous. He lit a cigarette to chase his thoughts away. Later, Lil' Long awoke to the prodding of a CO. He strained to snap out of his sleep.

"Yeah, what da fuck is da deal?" he asked.

"You got some demerits to work off. There's no smoking in bed."

It was Torres, the bitch from sickbay. Fucking bitch, what she want from me? Lil' Long's mind became activated as he stared at the curvaceous officer.

"Whatever. Why you busting my chops? You love me or sump'n? I know you saw the size o' my dick. You probably fantasizing 'bout it and all. I got it right here for you, baby." Lil' Long grabbed his crotch and thrust his hips.

"You should be very careful. I wouldn't move around like that if I were you. The doctors left a bullet close to your spine, the one they couldn't remove. If you move too much, the bullet may become lodged in your spine. A couple of days later, you won't be able to walk and you may not be able to move anything below your waist. So like I'm saying, be very careful."

Lil' Long stared at her face trying to read something in the grin she bore on her mug but he only drew a blank. In the end, he didn't know whether what she had just told him was the truth or not. There was no trust in him for the system. He waved his arms. "I don't give a fuck," he said and closed his eyes. She waited awhile before hitting his leg.

"You need to get up. You got some important visitors." He slowly hunched his back trying to stretch and flopped back onto the bunk.

"I can't stand so tell 'em if it ain't about money, I'll see 'em another time," he said casually.

"Don't make me call for assistance. I don't think you'd like it too much," she replied. Lil' Long stared at her for a moment before he answered.

"Who came to visit? My peeps don't know I'm here."

"They said to tell you that they're your guardian angels, that's all," the officer said blankly. Lil' Long again tried to read something in her expression but could not. He got up and left the cell escorted by the officer.

When he arrived in the visitor's area, he was pulled into a side office and the door slammed. "Here's your man, officers," was all she said and he knew that this was not going to be a happy visit.

"Sit," Detective Kowalski ordered. "Good to see you finally recovered," he continued as Lil' Long sat down and looked around. He immediately identified Hall and his partner, Kowalski. They were probably here to try and juice him for info. He cast a sneer their way when he spoke.

"Can I smoke a cig, detectives?" Lil' Long asked and the detectives looked at each other.

"Can he smoke?" Kowalski reflected aloud. "I guess you can do anything you wanna do, within limitations of course, on the condition that you provide us with all we need to know about this past weekend and all that led up to it."

"Does that mean I can light up?"

"It certainly means that if you light up, you start talking," Hall said as he sat down and pulled out a recorder. "Go ahead. Light up, my man."

Lil' Long put the cigarette to his lips and Kowalski lit it. The prisoner inhaled hard and blew rings before he opening his mouth to speak. "So whatcha wanna hear, detectives?" Lil' Long asked as he took another puff.

"You can start with explaining why the guns that were found in your hands were used to commit multiple murders?"

"Ah, that was simple. Give me a harder question, man." The detectives stared at each other befuddled by Lil' Long's remark.

"C'mon, we don't have time to play around," Kowalski said. "You mess around and you'll be eating that cigarette soon, homeboy," he continued. "Now talk to me."

"I'm saying, man, that shit's real simple. All I did was walk up in his crib and I get blamed for all these murders and shit. C'mon, even Ray Charles could see through that. I was set up." Lil' Long sucked on the cigarette then spit while exhaling.

"Why did you 'walk up in his crib' in the first place?"

"Listen, first of all, I didn't know whose crib it was. All I knew was that I wanted to talk to that bitch, Kamilla."

"Why?"

"Cuz that bitch knew who killed my man. She was s'pose to be wit da nigga and da nigga got shot so I wanted to know what she knew. You feel me? I gets to the place and we started arguing. They tell me to get out. I kept arguing. They began shooting and somebody shot me and the girl. She dead?"

"Yes, she's dead. Who was your man that was shot?"

"Ah, that would be Vulcha. You know 'bout him?"

"So you're saying Eric Ascot framed you for all these murders just because you walked up to his apartment and started arguing with one of his guests? Did he know you were coming?"

"No, I mean, yes, he had an idea. He didn't know exactly when I was gonna be there but he knew I was coming."

"So, you get there and all the other guests were there. Did you know anyone else who was there?"

"Yeah, I knew some o' the others. I mean, everybody heard of Coco and all the Crew members..." Lil' Long's voice trailed off. The detectives focused their attention on his body language. He was still relishing his cigarette. Lil' Long appeared relaxed as he sprawled in the seat.

"So, you see Kamilla and you start asking her what?"

"I mean, I don't remember word for word what I said but I

know we were going at it. I was angry and I wasn't trying to hear her bullshit, you feel me?"

"So, at one point or the other, the argument may have gotten out of hand?"

"That's what it is. I got up but I wasn't gonna hurt da bitch. I just wanted to know 'bout my man and all. That's when all the shooting took place. I gained consciousness to find that I had possession of weapons with bodies on 'em. Ain't that a bitch? What am I doing with all 'em weapons, uh?" Lil' Long asked and the detectives looked at each other.

"You may have to testify to this in a court of law. I mean, is this all of the truth or is there more to it?"

"Look, detectives, I ain't gonna further waste your time. Why don't you just have the mothafucka take a lie detector test and we'll see who's on the up. I mean, I ain't trying to tell you your jobs but just because the mothafucka rich don't mean he can't be down with illegal shit too. The poor man ain't always the guilty one."

"How's your stay so far?"

"What can I say? I'm locked down and my man, Vulcha, is dead. Things ain't so good, you feel me?"

"We gonna have to check this story and see what we can do. By the way, you may have to sign a sworn statement before we can even begin to think of letting you out. In the meantime, you'll stay put."

"Yo, I'm saying, ask that nigga to take that polygraph and watch what happens. He stuntin'."

"We'll see, we'll see," said Hall. After Lil' Long was ushered from the room, Hall spoke again. "You know what, his story is more plausible than Eric Ascot's."

"There you go with them two dollar words again," Kowalski said in disgust. "Are you saying that our prisoner turned song bird has a better story regarding the murders?"

"Yep, that's what I guess I was trying to say," answered Hall.

"Well, for the first time, you and I are on the same sheet of music," Kowalski said.

"That's scary."

"No, what's scary is thinking the court's gonna buy this. We gotta go out and prove that story. Any suggestions on how to make this stick, college boy?" Kowalski asked.

"While I resent you calling me college boy, I also resent being your partner. Anyway, dodo brain, a good start would be at the beginning with Mr. Ascot."

"Damn, that's twice in a row. I'm thoroughly in agreement." Kowalski laughed as they walked out of the room. They could see Lil' Long going back into general population. "I pray what he said had at least one ounce of truth."

"Do you really, Kowalski? Or as you like to say, 'I just wanna bust this case wide open'."

FIFTY

Lil' Long slowly made his way back across the passage to his cellblock. On the way, he was bumped twice by two different inmates wearing red bandanas. He took offense at the third bump.

"Hey, any one of y'all blood niggas can get it," Lil' Long said. One of the inmates who had bumped him walked right up to him.

"You talking' to me, sun?" he asked.

Without answering, Lil' Long slammed his fist hard into the face of the inmate then followed with another hard right, a left and another right. He felt himself restrained by some officers. Lil' Long found himself face down on the floor.

"Alright, break this up, now!" a correction officer yelled out. There were six of them now on scene. Chaos took a calm turn. "What happened here?" one CO snarled.

"They jumped my man," someone said. Lil' Long turned to see who had spoken. The voice had a familiar ring. They must have believed him because they released him immediately. "All right, gentlemen, let's not have anymore of this or everyone will be on lockdown."

"What's good, nigga?" Lil' Long said and exchanged pounds with the other inmate. "I know you from somewhere, right?" They drifted away from the area.

"Nigga, you know me from around the way. Maybe because I got bigger and all. I'm Nesto, nigga," the inmate said then hugged Lil' Long.

"Oh shit, that's right. Nesto from da heights, right?"

"No question, my nigga. Whatcha doing here, Lil' Long?"

"That's da sixty-mothafucking-four dollar question. I have no clue. They trying to frame a nigga so a nigga can't eat.

You feel me?"

"I hear you. How's shit on the outside?" Nesto asked.

Lil' Long glanced around and noticed all the eyes on him and Nesto. "Shit's crazy, man. Po-po got everything on lock. Mothafuckas wanted me out the game and all that so they put bullet holes in me."

"Yo, what happened to your man you used to run wit?"

"Oh, they done killed my man. They ambushed him and tagged him with bullet holes."

"Get da fuck out. Who did that, sun?"

"Evidently the same mothafuckas who set my ass up."

"Huh, that's bad, bad news. Vulcha was a cool mo'fucka. He ain't fuck wit no one."

"I'm saying, they made sure he was stiff on his back. I'm gonna get who did that shit, though."

"You know who did that?"

"I got an idea but I ain't gonna say right now."

"Mothafucking Lil' Long," Nesto said as they both walked. "Yo, I want you to meet some people who run things round here," Nesto said as they made their way to another side of the jailhouse.

"I remember your peeps from da heights, Carlos and Manny," Lil' Long said. "They seen how big you got, dogs?"

"Hell yeah. Them niggas be here all the time visiting a nigga, you know. Nesto's peeps ain't desert him, you heard?"

"I hear that but who these other peeps you dealin' wit?"

"Oh, these some big dogs. These mothafuckas run this place and when I say run, I mean run," Nesto bragged.

"Maybe they could take care o' that big ass CO who keeps fucking wit my ass."

"Who? Torres? Wait until she sees this. She'll be licking your balls soon."

"Stop playing, nigga."

"I'm a show you, sun. I'm dead-ass."

"Ahight, take me to meet these mothafuckas then."

"Say no more, Lil' Long, we'll be on our way in a minute," Nesto said, reaching down underneath his bunk and unveiling an envelope filled with marijuana. Nesto quickly crushed the weed up and wrapped it neatly in a Philly blunt and lit it. "Light a ciga-rette," he said as he inhaled. Lil' Long watched in amused antici-pation. "Go ahead, sit on down," Nesto said pointing to a milk crate in the corner of the small cell. "Pull that seat up and hit this, nigga."

"Yo, you da real, you hear me? You da real mothafuckin' man, Nesto. That's how my ghetto soldier was. Real, you feel me?" Lil' Long said as he smoked. Nesto took the cigarette and puffed.

"You're talking 'bout Vulcha?"

"Yeah, dogs, he was my soldier, my right hand."

"His end kinda came quick."

"Yeah and that made my target list grow longer. Feel me? Two months after I met the nigga, the streets were mine. You know wha' I'm saying?"

"That's fucked up, sun. That nigga should be living."

"Yeah but its saddle and boots time. Ride or die time. I don't care where these mothafuckas be at. If they dead, I'm killing myself to go after them. Where ever they be at, I'm going hunt-ing for they asses and kill 'em one by one. You heard?" Lil' Long said as he passed the blunt to Nesto. They stole a smoke and Lil' Long felt the connection to Nesto, not only for being from the block but for being ballsy with the weed.

"Lemme know if I can help you, sun," Nesto said as he put the smoke out.

"Yo, that's real. You're ahight wit me. You know you my man and all that," Lil' Long said as he glad-handed with Nesto. They walked out of the cell and down the corridor to the other side of the jailhouse.

"Come with me, Lil' Long. I'll introduce you to the peeps that run the whole joint," Nesto said as he walked ahead.

FIFTY-ONE

Eric Ascot smiled when the salesman revealed the price. He glanced at the Porsche Cayenne and shook his head. Nice, he thought, but too busy and a little too large for her. He stood inside the Porsche dealership contemplating which model to buy the girl of his dreams. Sophia would love this roadster. She was a racing enthusiast and could appreciate the style and grace of a Boxter S. At his wits ends, he wondered as he slowly sipped the champagne and explored the possibilities.

There were more important questions. Such as whether Sophia would buy his philanthropic behavior as one of the spur of the moment variety or would it be seen as another attempt to get on her good side. Eric sipped the champagne and scrutinized the cars. It should be the Boxter S, he decided. On cue, the salesman wandered back over.

"Enjoying the view, Eric?" he asked.

"Sure am. I want the Boxter S, fully loaded. Clarion speaker system and all the trimmings," Eric said.

"That's an excellent choice. For a while, I thought it would be the Cayenne but you fooled me. You said you want it in silver and just cause you're you, I'm throwing in the Anniversary Edition package. Now, is this where you want it delivered? You said Sophia Sullivan and I've got the address right here. Oh, and I'll throw in the DVD player free of cost."

"It's not really free though. I'm sure it's neatly wrapped in a hidden cost somewhere."

"No, absolutely not the truth. Everything is set so we just need to set up a delivery time. How're you paying for this?" Eric threw down his American Express Black card and the discussion ceased. "We'll have it prepped and ready for delivery later today.

She's a very lucky woman," the salesman said with a grin.

"You can say that again," Eric said and shook the sales-man's outstretched hand.

"So nice to have done business with you, sir. Goodbye and don't you worry. Everything will be taken care of down to the red bow around it, sir. You'll be pleased," he said, practically eating out of Eric's palm.

Eric Ascot strolled through the Porsche dealership admir-ing the new cars. The 911 Turbo looked good but he was confident that he had made the right choice. He jumped into his Range Rover and rolled out of the parking lot thinking that he had done the right thing. He had just set himself back over fifty thousand dollars trying to get back in favor of the woman he loved.

Would've been cheaper to tell her the truth, he thought as he drove along with the afternoon traffic. Suffice it to say, Sophia had definitely been impressed by his altruism so far but would it blow up in his face? As he pulled to a stop, Eric felt confident that he was doing the right thing. Judging from the way they spooned as they slept last night, he felt Sophia's resistance was wearing down. Even though she didn't eat the food or drink the wine, she did take the pasta salad for lunch. That fact made him smile as he walked into the studio.

FIFTY-TWO

"You saw that? The sonofabitch just bought a hot car for his fiancée. Just wait until we send her our little package," Kowalski said looking over at his partner. "He's gonna freak out." Both detectives laughed as they hurried across the street to the Porsche dealership. Flashing his badge, Kowalski asked to see the manager.

"Who's the salesman that just handled the customer that just left?" he asked when the man appeared.

"Which customer?" the manager asked.

"Eric Ascot," Kowalski replied.

"Mr. Ascot was tended to by Ernie Fryer. What seems to be the problem, detectives? Maybe I could be of some help to you? I'm always doing what I can to help out the law."

"The car he bought, which is it and who is it being delivered to?" Hall asked.

The manager scanned the sales log and looked at the detective. "Mr. Ascot bought a Boxter S. It is being primed to be delivered to his fiancé, a Ms. Sophia Sullivan," the manager said. "We checked out his card and everything was cleared with his credit card company. I mean, we did everything on the level, detectives. I'm afraid..."

"Here's what we need you to do," interrupted Kowalski. He gave the manager a big brown envelope with detailed instructions. Before they walked away, Kowalski added, "Make sure that it is done before the car is delivered. Do you understand?"

"Yes, sir, I do. A very minor thing for a citizen to do, detectives. Good day," the manager said as they left the office.

"I'm quite sure his lawyer girlfriend is gonna want some kind of explanation to go along with that video and snapshots of her man with his two dancing girls," laughed Kowalski once they got back outside.

"It really tickles your funny bone, huh?" Hall sarcastically asked.

"Whenever uppity black guys get too big for their britches, I just want you to know that old Kowalski here is ready to put their no good black asses back in place and if that means sending them to jail, it makes me sleep oh so much better."

"I'm sure it does," Hall said as he glared at his snickering partner. How did this guy get on the job? He's such a bigot, Hall thought as they drove to the station house. "Do me a favor," Hall said.

"Sure, anything, partner," Kowalski answered.

"Stay the fuck off my desk. Don't let me have to repeat myself."

"I gotcha back, bro. I'll stay off your desk." Kowalski reached out to shake his hand but Hall walked past him and into the stationhouse. No sooner had he sat down when he heard the chief hollering his name.

"Hall, get in my office right now and bring that crazy partner of yours with you," the chief said. Hall immediately detected a lot of anger in the chief's tone. He knew he was about to be rimmed. He called for Kowalski, who was busy chatting up a secretary a few desks down.

"Kowalski, get your narrow ass over here right now. The chief wants to see us. Now, Kowalski," Hall yelled when he saw Kowalski not budging. Finally, he walked over to where Kowalski stood and yanked him by the arm.

"I must go, hon. Until later. I'll see ya around nine, ya hear," Kowalski said as Hall pulled on his sleeve. "Can't you see I'm making moves? You know, getting my groove on."

"You need to groove into the chief's office, lover boy. I can't believe you're trying to run game on a black woman," Hall said just before they walked into the office where the chief of detectives sat looking at reports and photos.

"Baby got back," Kowalski said as he entered the office.

"Shut the door. Shut yer yaps and siddown because I

don't wanna be saying what I'm about to say twice. This case needs to be wrapped up immediately, gentlemen. Everyone's looking for answers. There were officers gunned down, politicians are talking, and when they talk, we better be listening. I want suspects brought in. I want to shake this thing up. Bring people in, knock on doors. I'm giving you two a couple more days to wrap up this investigation and indict someone. Geez, what else do we need? We got the smoking guns and we got positive ID's from the boys at the lab. Do we have any corroboration? Do we have motives?"

"Chief, we're onto something that could blow the case wide open."

"Yeah, that's right, chief, we're onto a strong lead."

"I don't wanna hear that kind of dribble out of either of you. Feed the press all that verbiage. Bring some closure to this damn case and don't drag it out too long. We can hardly spare the manpower around here. Now, get outta my office and go arrest someone for these murders."

"Yes, sir," they both replied and left the office with great haste. They had laid the bait for Eric and knew he would take it once the delivery was made along with the car. Both detectives knew that somehow they would have to get either Eric or Lil' Long to cooperate totally. They figured it would be Eric Ascot.

FIFTY-THREE

Eric wandered easily through the yard. From the front, the house was huge and as he reached the front door, he realized that it was actually a mansion. Security seemed lax. There were men standing around seemingly doing nothing but talking about baseball. A closer look revealed that they were wore heavy artillery and bullet proof vests under their sweaters. He was directed into the main hall of the mansion and remained surprised at the many guests inside. He took a glass of champagne along with cashews and sipped as he walked around. He overheard the whining of what he thought was a child, but when he turned, he saw a well developed beautiful brunette.

"Did you record the episode of Montel?" she asked the young man next to her.

"Yes, I know he's your fav so I did. How was your trip from Martha's Vineyard?"

"Much too long. My ass is still sore from the plane ride."

"Excuse me, I'm trying to locate Mr. Maruichi. Do you know where I can find him?" Eric asked politely. They both stopped and stared for a minute. The brunette looked him up and down. Finally, the guy spoke.

"That line over there leads right to him. I guess there are about...oh, lets see, hmm, about twelve people in front of you. You'd better hurry over because most of the folks are really here to see dad," he said. They turned away and continued with their conversation.

"Thank you. Oh, by the way, why the celebration?" Eric asked before they walked away. Both kids gave him an incredulous stare after which the girl smiled and replied.

"It's my brother's seventeenth birthday and dad thought

he would throw him a party. Okay, Mr. Whoever you are? You were obviously invited. Otherwise, you would not have been able to put your foot through the front door. My dad's in his study. Please excuse us," she said easily.

"Well, happy birthday," Eric started to say apologetically but the kids had enough of him and were ready to party.

Eric walked around slowly and watched them as they danced around with other kids. Obviously Maruichi's kids, he thought as he reached the area and saw some of the familiar faces from his first visit with Maruichi. Eric took another sip of champagne and wondered why the man had invited him here. He paced, anxious to see the shock on Sophia's face when that Porsche was delivered to her apartment. He tried to reach her cell phone but the phone just rang through to her voicemail. Eric tried to contain his excitement when he spoke. "Give me a call when you can," he said and closed his cellular.

That's a nice gift, Eric thought as he watched the bustle of the place. There were a lot of people, mostly Sicilian looking. Wine was flowing freely and people danced around singing. Eric remembered when Mariuchi had first invited him. There was no mention of a celebration. The invitation was more along the lines of business, not his son's seventeenth birthday party. Eric continued to pace as he monitored his cell phone in anticipation of Sophia's call.

FIFTY-FOUR

She was clearly surprised. Flabbergasted even after walking around the car several times, crying in disbelief. "Oh my, oh my," Sophia sang as the doorman joined her.

"That's a very classy car. Fits you very well. What the hell, it's a perfect fit for you, Ms. Sullivan. The person who sent you this must really think you're very special. It's gotta be love."

"It is love," Sophia crooned and danced around the silver car with the big red bow. The top was down and it was the perfect evening for a ride. She swooned and hugged herself as she looked at the car. "Oh my, I love that man," she whispered slightly into the wind. The doorman moved closer and offered to help her remove the bow. "I don't know, Paul. I wanted to wait until Eric gets here."

Deedee walked up to the entrance and saw Sophia swooning over the car. "Uncle E has lost his mind," she whispered as she ran toward the car. "That's for you, Sophia? Oh God, I love it. It's a Porsche. A real Porsche," Deedee chanted as she hugged Sophia and they danced in the street. Paul stood back and enjoyed the view. Deedee was wearing a mini skirt that easily raised up to reveal her panties as she danced around merrily. He used the occasion to show off his knowledge of cars.

"Yes, it is a Porsche," he said getting the ladies' attention. "Built from the 550, the Spyder was the first Porsche designed for racing. This," the doorman said, "is the Boxter S. Anniversary edition at that."

"Oh really? Let me find out," Deedee said smiling at Paul. "Let me know you're moonlighting as a car salesman on your time off."

"No, it's a fantasy I've had ever since I can remember."

"What's that?" Sophia asked.

"Oh, to own one. To own a Porsche."

"Wow, well I guess my fantasy has been achieved," Sophia beamed. "Eric Ascot, you're gonna make me love you."

"So are we going for a spin, Sophia?" Deedee asked. Sophia scratched her head.

"I was waiting on your uncle to call me back. He hasn't yet," Sophia said.

"Oh, come on, Ms. Sullivan. You've got the keys. Do you have the guts to experience this baby go from zero to sixty in under six seconds? Then hop in. What're you waiting for? I'm sure Mr. Ascot bought this for you to have some fun in, albeit without him right now but you'll enjoy the experience I'm sure. Just don't try to go too fast. This baby can burn."

With the doorman and Deedee encouraging her, Sophia heeded their advice and hopped into the driver's seat. Deedee skipped around and sat in the passenger seat. When Sophia turned the key in the ignition, she felt the power of the car rush through her. It was a heady sensation and she smiled like a kid with a new favorite toy.

"It sounds awesome and so powerful, Sophie. I can't wait. Let's get moving," Deedee yelled with her hands in the air.

"The top folds down when you press that knob right there. Go ahead and take this baby for a spin. Enjoy the fabulous pure Porsche performance," Paul said. Sophia needed no further assistance. She took off with Deedee hooting and hollering.

"Take care and have a safe ride," Paul shouted and waved. Sophia stopped at the light briefly then she hit the gas and the car was quickly out of sight.

"We've got to give this car a name," Sophia yelled, triumphantly speeding down the road with the top down. Both Sophia and Deedee were enjoying the ride as the wind blew their hair out of place. "I better get used to having my hair tied up when I'm rolling in my drop top."

"Yes, you sure do," Deedee yelled. She reached out and turned on the car stereo. "Uncle E sure hooked you up, Sophia," Deedee yelled above the music. Sophia manipulated the vehicle like she was used to it. "You handle this well," Deedee said as she looked on and saw the smile of happiness on Sophia's face.

"I love the way it handles, Dee. It really feels good. This is me," Sophia said as she stared ahead at the city's evening traffic. "Are there no empty streets?" she asked.

"Not at this time of the day. This is rush hour traffic," Deedee opined.

"Well, too bad. I got a tank full of petrol and I'm ready to roll," Sophia said with a wink to Deedee.

"Oh, because you got a new car, you gonna try and rhyme?" Deedee asked.

"Nah, I don't think so, Dee. Leave that for Coco," Sophia said.

"Yep, you're so right. She's the real rapper."

"How's she doing?" Sophia asked then pressed on her horn. "Be careful. Don't try to get too close to this baby. I'm definitely going to have to get garage space. In this city, forget about it," Sophia said and then remembering, she asked again. "So, how's Coco?"

"She's cool especially now that Jo is back."

"Who's Jo?"

"Oh, you remember Josephine?"

"Dee, I've been so stressed since last weekend, I can't even remember me sometimes."

"You got it bad. Jo is one of the group members from Coco's rap crew."

"Oh that Jo. I do remember her. Sort of nervous type."

"She's lost the nervousness and now she's crazy. But she seems to keep Coco balanced," Deedee said staring at the traffic jam in front them.

"You mean like sisters do?"

"Yeah, I think...like that, yeah," Deedee said finally.

"I don't like this part of driving. All this traffic..."

"I guess this contains the video and the driver's manual," Deedee said picking up a brown envelope from the floor.

"Please, anything to do with the car I'll just go ask Mr. Porsche himself," Sophia joked.

"Who, the guys at the dealership?" Deedee asked.

"No, I don't have to go that far."

"Oh, that's right. You can just go ask your doorman."

"Bingo," Sophia announced as Deedee opened the brown envelope and blinked hard when she first saw the snapshots. She became distracted as she leafed through the pictures quickly and failed to notice that there was a DVD inside the envelope until it came crashing out.

Sophia had glimpsed Deedee's reaction through the corner of her eye but made nothing of it until the DVD fell to the floor. "Hmm, everything from your home appliances to your car comes with a DVD nowadays. Manufactures don't trust the consumer will have time so they send you this so you can slip it into your DVD player," Sophia said as she braked suddenly to avoid hitting a car in front of her. "Ah, I best be a little bit more careful," she started to say then noticed the DVD player. "Cool, I've got a DVD player right here. Dee, pass me the DVD so I could learn something about this car."

Deedee was nervous when she saw the pictures and tried to ease them back into the envelope but then the DVD fell out and now Sophia wanted to view it on her DVD player. This was not going to be good, Deedee thought as she glanced over at a concerned Sophia.

"What's the problem, Dee?" Sophia asked growing impatient.

"No, I don't think this is the correct DVD. These are some...ah...this is not...ah...."

"Dee, what's wrong? You look as if you just saw a ghost," Sophia said growing suspicious. "What's in the envelope, girl?" Sophia asked.

Deedee could hear the nervousness in her tone and was reluctant to give the answer. Sophia guided the car to side of the busy road. Her cell phone rang twice. "Dee, what is it that you don't want me to see? I'm going to have to see it anyway. The package is in my car," Sophia demanded as she answered her cell phone. "Hello, Eric, can you hold a second please?" Sophia turned her attention to Deedee who appeared nervous beyond a doubt.

"What's going on Dee? Am I in any kind of trouble?" Sophia asked before she attempted to wrest the envelope from Deedee's hand. She spoke into the phone. "Eric, there was a brown envelope in the car and for some reason, Dee refuses to release it or even tell me what's inside. Will you talk to her, please?" she said and handed the cellular to Deedee. "Here, speak to your uncle because I don't know what's the matter with you," Sophia said. Deedee took the phone and began to speak.

"Uncle Eric, the envelope has nothing to do with the car. It's..."

"Just give her the damn thing, Dee. It's alright," he said.

"No it isn't. The pictures are..."

"Give 'em to her, sweetheart. I know what I'm doing."

"But the pictures are of...ah, you know, they're dirty."

"Huh? What're you talking about?" Eric asked but Sophia was successful in getting the envelope from Deedee's grip.

"No, nothing. They're probably just pictures of the guy who delivered the car, I guess."

"What kind of pictures are these?" Sophia asked and the first snapshot she saw caused her to lose her voice as her heart jumped into her throat. She quickly scrolled through the rest as Deedee tried unsuccessfully to retrieve the envelope. Again, the DVD fell to the floor. This time, Sophia placed it into the machine and the screen was filled with slurping sounds of tongues against flesh. Sophia's eyes watered as she tried to focus. The volume on the DVD player was tuned up high and she could see Eric's dick sliding in and out of the mouth of two women. Sophia watched speechless as her fiancé squirted all over them. She saw the look of satisfaction on Eric's face then broke down and sobbed. Eric could hear the commotion in the background but was totally unaware of the cause. He felt Sophia's anger.

"You're nothing but a lowdown good for nothing man. How dare you, Eric Ascot?" Sophia screamed into the phone. Eric was still unsure of what was going down. He asked the same thing over and over until there was just a dial tone.

"What did Dee do? What's happening? Did you hit someone? The car is insured..." When he realized he was speaking to a

GHETTO
GIRLS
TOO

dial tone, Eric redialed but couldn't get through. He was summoned to see Mr. Maruichi but couldn't put away the phone.

"Mr. Maruichi will see you now, Mr. Ascot," a warm voice said. Eric's face only registered alarm.

"Can I come back? I'm afraid..."

"I'm sorry, Mr. Ascot, but you'll have to come right away."

"Okay, let's not keep Mr. Maruichi waiting," Eric said and went along, completely oblivious as to what had just occurred. He knew Deedee would call back. He set his ring tone on vibrate as he entered the study.

"Welcome Eric," Mr. Mariuchi said from behind a huge mahogany desk. The place was well lit and there were sofas lining the walls. Mr. Maruichi joined Eric on the sofa. "What's the matter? You seem upset?" Maruichi asked and continued without waiting for the answer. "What I'm about to say will put you in a very good mood," he said and examined Eric's features. "Tell me what's wrong, Eric?"

"I don't know. I went out and bought my fiancé a sports car and she just called really happy at first. Then she got a package from my niece. My niece either gave her the package or didn't but Sophia snapped. I mean, I just bought her something nice from Harry Winston..."

"That's class," Mr. Maruichi said then he asked, "What kind of sports car did you get the lady?"

"A Porsche Boxter S."

"Hmm. You must really love this lady. Is that the one I met at the shindig for Busta?"

"Yes, that's the one."

"She's a very lovely woman. A very beautiful woman. That means lots of money and lots of problems. I know, I know."

"Man, Mr. Maruichi, sometimes I don't know if I'm coming or she's going," Eric sighed.

"Affairs of the heart are very difficult to understand. Nothing is cut and dry."

"I wish I understood what she was dealing with, you know. A man has got to love you to send you a Porsche and give you diamond necklace from the best jeweler around. Come on already.

What else is a dude to do?"

"Eric, my boy, I can tell you to have patience. Women love power. Power equals money. The more money one obtains, the more power he'll have. When she sees the type of dough you're rolling in, she'll want to come around. You'll see, Eric." Maruichi got up and poured Eric a drink from a bottle. "Chase that with some of this Cognac," he said.

Eric slung it back and took another shot. After repeating the process another time, Eric felt the alcohol burning his throat and loosening the knots the phone incident with Sophia had left in the pit of his stomach. He heard Mr. Maruichi laughing.

"Ha, ha, ha, Eric we're embarking on a journey that I hope will be long and productive. I want you to know that I thought this out carefully with my advisors and we all agreed that it should be profitable," Mr. Maruichi said. "Best of all, it could kick off tomorrow or whenever you say. There's a half a million dollars coming your way. All you've got to do is accept three million dollars into your account over the next couple months and you may see your business rise to about one hundred million. Your company gets half a million dollars on every ten mill we deposit. That will be quite a hefty sum by the end of the year, I'll say," Mr. Maruichi said, sounding pleased with himself as if the deal had been already done.

Eric Ascot had lost all interest in the deal and was preoccupied with the thought of the earlier incident on the phone. What could've possibly gone wrong? I bought a diamond necklace worth one hundred grand, a damn car that's worth over fifty thousand, what more does she want from me? Eric wondered as Mr. Maruichi continued with his business proposal. Eric listened to everything he said but was retaining nothing and could've saved time by telling that to Maruichi. Instead, he nodded his head, occasionally feigning interest. After a few more minutes of this and Mr. Maruichi, sensing Eric's distraction, relieved him by curtailing the meeting.

"It's my son's birthday and I've got to see a couple more folks. Everyone has their own unique problems and they come to hear my perspective on them. Mr. Ascot...Eric," Maruichi said, rising and shaking Eric's hand. "You take care of your fiancée. Make sure everything is alright. She seems like such a beautiful lady."

"She's all that and more to me. Listen, I'll give you a call and um, I wish you and your son the best on his birthday, Mr. Maruichi. I'm afraid I've got to run. You'll hear from me, I promise." Eric quickly shook hands with Maruichi and was almost running out the door while dialing his cell phone. He spoke to the voicemail again. "Sophia, will you please give me a call? What's wrong? This is Eric," he said then closed the cell. Deedee was with Sophia. She's probably still with her, he thought as the key hit the ignition. Eric dialed his niece as he slipped into his safety belt. "Dee? Deedee...can you hear me?"

"It's very difficult. We're outside. Sophia and I..." That's all he heard and Eric noted that there was a bad connection.

"Outside? Outside where, Dee? I'll come get you. Is everything alright?" The phone disconnected before he had a chance to continue the conversation. Eric was unsure of where they were. However, he was happy to hear they were still alive. The fact that Sophia had not picked up on his attempts to reach her still gave him reason to be concerned. Eric drove and pondered his next move. He was completely unaware of the detectives following him.

FIFTY-FIVE

"Alright, it seems the brother is moving on up. Hey, did you know he was that close with Maruichi? Man, only real close friends get invited, not just any brother from the hood," Kowalski said with a smile.

"Do pipe down before I slap that snicker off your face."

"Aw c'mon, you're just talking, old-timer. Let's not fight. Let's do something useful and pull this sucker over."

"For what possible reason?"

"Well, I'm sure you could think of some. He's probably listening to rap and smoking a blunt. Shit, he might just have that forty stuck between his legs. He didn't stop long enough at the last street sign. What da fuck? Do we really need a goddamn reason? We're the police. We represent the law and I betcha your next paycheck that that cocksucker is up to something illegal. Now can we pull him over, pretty please with sprinkles on top?"

"No, I can't agree with you. Yes, he's probably up to something illegal but why rush in? I say we wait and see what other fish he's frying besides his music thing and now his obvious involvement with a known mobster. I say we wait and give him a couple days. His fiancé should've received the package by now and had ample time to examine the photos," Hall reasoned.

"Spoken like a true college boy. Anyway, I still think we should put more pressure on the bastard. Pull him over and toss him but I actually think you're right. You know when his fiancé sees our handiwork, she may help us out after all," Kowalski said and winked. Hall could see the devious smile on Kowalski's face.

"What are you up to and what do you mean by 'our handiwork'?" Hall's curiosity peaked when he noticed that Kowalski was unable to contain his enthusiasm and broke into a wide grin. "Look, I'm letting you know now, if we're going to bring the man

down we're going to be fair about it. Now tell me what exactly is
'our handiwork'?" Hall was at his boiling point. The tailing car
swerved excessively.

"Okay, okay you might as well know."

"Know? Know what?" Hall yelled as he became really furious. "I just hope you've not done anything to fuck this investigation up. I'll file a complaint against your white racist ass so fast
your head will be in a spin."

"No need to get emotional. I don't think what I did will
fuck up this investigation. I suspect it will speed up the investigation," Kowalski said in a serious tone.

"Okay, let's hear it."

"I simply replaced his head with some other guy's body
who's already fucking a girl. So, when she looks at the porno
shots from the strip club, she'll be convinced that he's fucking..."

"Around on her with some other chick."

"Yeah...Wham-bam. It's a knock-out. You like it?" Kowalski
was excited.

"No, I don't like it. I think it stinks. What if she can identify that it's not him? You know the woman just might know what
her man's private shit looks like. How do you account for that?
That's why it's a dumb plan. No way its going to work."

"What will you tell me if I say I can guarantee that it will
work?"

"I'll say stay off the internet and most importantly leave
the photo work to the experts," Hall said dismissing Kowalski.
"Your guarantee that it will work is based on nothing."

"I don't have the scientific data to back this up but I bet
after she sees the actual pictures of her man at the strip club getting expensive lap-dances and free feels, she'll already have it in
for him. Now when she puts that DVD in, she's not going to want
to see the whole thing. One headshot will be enough."

"You're saying she's just going to be looking at his face
and that's it?" Hall asked sounding confused.

"No, she's going to see his face and then see the face of
another woman making out with her man."

"You did what?" Hall sounded infuriated then a smile

spread over his face. "You're banking on the fact that she'll be too pissed to notice nothing but his face and another woman's face. Is this woman really giving it up to him? I mean on the DVD?" Hall asked.

"That DVD is hotter than R. Kelly's."

"Are you bootlegging this DVD? I got to see how this one works out," Hall said.

FIFTY-SIX

After she saw the snapshots of Eric, her eyes clouded with tears. When she slid the DVD into the car's system and saw what came on the screen, she was so shocked she immediately pressed the eject button. She put all the contents of the envelope back and cried as she stared at the paper as if she expected it to start apologizing. Deedee hugged her but it was not enough and Sophia cried harder. After a few minutes, she bit her lip and drove slowly around before she started to head back in the direction of her apartment. Deedee held her hand and saw the look of determination in Sophia's eyes as she drove. It was a look that Deedee had never seen before and she tried to make sure that Sophia was in the right frame of mind to be driving. The car picked up speed and Deedee got nervous.

"Sophia. Sophia?" She spoke softly so as not to startle the driver. She wanted to cause as little distraction as possible. Sophia turned up the music and kept switching the radio channels manually as she navigated through evening's traffic. From the corner of Sophia's eyes, Deedee could see her tears blown over her hunched shoulders by the wind. "What do you want to hear, Sophia? The remote is right here," she said. All the time, she had a keen eye on Sophia.

"Oh, how about some jazz?" Sophia seemed unsure. "Maybe R&B? No, I don't want that. Whatever you want, Dee. Just make sure it's loud. You know this car is really fast," Sophia said as the car shot through the streets. Her cell phone rang but Sophia didn't bother to look at it. Deedee was happy for that and picked up the ringing phone. She saw 'Baby Bear' on the caller I.D.

"It's Baby Bear," Deedee said. "Should I answer it?"

Sophia grappled with the question. After biting her lip several times, she still didn't answer. It really didn't matter because the phone had stopped ringing. They were stopped at a red light. Sophia seemed to be holding up well despite the circumstances, Deedee thought. I guess Uncle E is going to have to have some explaining to do, she thought as she heard the phone ring again. She picked it up. Once again, the caller ID registered 'Baby Bear'.

"It's that same person. Do you want me to answer it?" Deedee asked.

"Baby Bear is my nickname for your uncle. Give me the phone, Deedee," Sophia said with a certain assurance. Her voice revealed nothing but confidence as Deedee passed her the cell. "Eric, I just want to tell you that you're the dirtiest and your niece is next to me so that's the reason I'm going to tell you not to call me anymore. Dammit..." screamed Sophia. She had kept her cool act up until the last part of the conversation when she suddenly screamed. Deedee watched Sophia fight back the tears without realizing what the screaming was really about until it was too late. "Oh my God!" Sophia yelled as she gripped the steering wheel. Deedee felt the car swerve suddenly. She looked up and immediately after, she heard the bang and felt the thud. She saw the car slowly avoid a head on collision with a pedestrian but in doing that, Sophia managed to hit a fire hydrant.

A burst of flowing water greeted both as the bump caused the hydrant to send a spray of water smashing into the windshield. The cabriolet style top of the Porsche was down and water descended on both Deedee and Sophia. "Oh my God, are you alright, Deedee?" Sophia spat water from her mouth as she spoke.

"I'm okay, Sophia. Let's get out of here before the cops come, Sophia."

"Good thinking, Dee. Makes no sense staying for a traffic ticket," Sophia said but was met by flashing lights as she started to move off. "Oh well, here comes the cavalry," she said. Deedee turned to see the welcome wagon carrying two officers.

"Just act ditsy and cute and we'll be alright," Deedee suggested. The officers walked coolly to the car.

"Good evening, ladies," the one close to the driver's side said.

"Officer, I was trying to avoid hitting this man and his dog and I lost control," Sophia said as the officer looked on with disinterest.

"Your license, registration and insurance forms, please." The officer closest to the driver took the forms from Sophia and then both officers walked back to their car.

"I swear this has been one of the worst days of my life," Sophia said as she watched the officers get in their patrol car. "The damn man and his damn dog. He should've waited for the light to change to red. Oh, what else could go wrong?" she asked as the police officers spoke into their radio.

"...a silver Porsche Boxter S registered to Sophia Sullivan. It's clean and legal..."

Detectives Hall and Kowalski stared as if transfixed by the radio. Kowalski grabbed the radio and started to interrogate the operator. "Operator, this is Detective Kowalski. Can you tell me the location of that accident?" he asked, nodding and writing as he looked at Hall. After a couple minutes, Kowalski put the radio down and shouted, "Hurrah for justice! She fell for the trap, hook, line and sinker." Kowalski pumped his fist while Hall drove steadily following Eric's Range Rover.

FIFTY-SEVEN

Frankie Maruichi called his favorite whipping boy close to him. "Get my son, Eddie, over here right now," he told him with a voice that was used to having men follow his orders to the letter. A few seconds later, Eddie, decked out in a Sean John velour warm-up suit, made his way quickly to Maruichi's side. There he stood glued, only nodding periodically in confirmation that he understood his duties. Eddie was a foot soldier on the rise and all who were close to Maruichi knew that whenever Eddie walked quickly, there was something urgent to be done. Maruichi's oldest son was fat and normally did not move very fast.

Eddie ran to three other guys dressed in similar warm-up suits. Two of them got into an SUV while the others jumped into black sedan and peeled out. Inside the SUV, Eddie was busy barking out orders.

"I specifically want to say, do not, I repeat, do not under any circumstances kill this mug, alright? Scare him. The key word is scare cause dad wants it that way. Now, everyone knows what it is they've got to do, right?" Eddie asked.

"Right," was the unanimous response.

"Alright. As much as I think dad is getting soft, I believe that there's nothing to stop him from kicking my ass all over this great city," Eddie said as both cars with liscense plates hidden joined the traffic in hot pursuit of Eric's black Range Rover. The mission was a simple one, the plan to bring Eric into the folds of the mob might be complicated. How this would turn out depended on how much fear was instilled in Eric. Maruichi figured the police would not be involved. He did not second-guess himself.

FIFTY-EIGHT

They jumped out of the tow truck that had just pulled to a stop in front of Sophia's apartment building with her wrecked Porsche in tow. Both thanked the truck driver. "Anytime, ladies. But where do you want me to leave your vehicle?" he asked. Sophia glanced around. She saw Paul, the doorman, and an idea took shape.

"Paul, guess what?" Sophia asked as she approached the doorman. He was standing looking pitifully at the wrecked Porsche.

"What?" he asked, sounding heartbroken.

"How would like to own a Boxter S Anniversary Edition? It's new but it's got a dent on the left front side," Sophia said to the doorman who stared at her in surprise.

"Miss Sophia...oh, I'd love that but I can't afford..."

"Then it's a done deal. Congratulations, Paul. Enjoy your Porsche," Sophia said dropping the keys in his hand and walking away. "Paul, please do me one major favor, please. Do not let anyone up to see me, thank you. One more thing. The brown envelope in the seat, please make sure Mr. Ascot gets it. Thanks again and goodnight Paul." Deedee walked next to Sophia and they made their way to the elevator.

"Okay, will do. Goodnight, Ms. Sullivan." He heard the words come out of his mouth but did not know how he formed them. Paul stood rooted to the ground watching the tow truck driver unhook the silver vehicle with the cracked up front. She must have had a wee too much to drink. She doesn't even know what the hell she's doing right now. Women drivers, he thought shaking his head as the car fell on the black top. He heard himself again, "Hey, man, take it easy. Can't you tell that that's not just any car, it's a Porsche." Paul drove the car into the garage and walked back with the keys on the inside of his top pocket and the Porsche emblem showing on the outside.

Moments later, Eric rolled up. He looked around trying to see any evidence of what had gotten Sophia so upset. He saw nothing, not the Porsche, nothing. Eric walked to where the door-man was standing

"Hey, how're you doing?" Eric asked Paul.

"Good evening sir. I'm doing just fine, just fine right now," he said smiling.

"Hey, you know Sophia, right?" Eric asked.

"Do I know her? C'mon, she's the best person in the whole world. Of course, I know her."

"Did she get a delivery?" Eric asked.

"Yep, sure did." He whistled. "A pure performance Porsche, I saw it. Helped her cut the ribbon myself."

"Oh good," Eric said. "So she was happy?"

"Very happy. Then she went for a spin with another young lady and..."

"She went for a spin with Deedee and what happened?"

"She made it back but the car...Ah, the Porsche suffered slight damage but the ladies were fine."

"I'd like to go and see."

"Well, I'm afraid you can't do that at this time, sir. She's not having visitors up."

"My name is Eric Ascot. I'm Miss Sullivan's fiancé," Eric started to speak but the doorman raised his hand and stopped him.

"Sir, she left this package for you, sir," Paul said and Eric had an incredulous look on his face. He stared at the brown enve-lope in Paul's hand then snatched it without a 'thank-you' and walked away.

Eric stopped in the street and glanced up as he waited for traffic to go by. He looked at the brown envelope in his hand, pulled out his keys and deactivated the alarm to the Range. He made his way slowly to his vehicle and hopped inside. He opened the envelope and allowed the contents to fall onto his lap. Flabbergasted, he glanced at each of the Polaroid shots.

They were photos of him from the night at the strip club. The Geisha twins were prominently featured. So this was the cause of Sophia's fit, Eric thought then he slid the DVD into the player. He was astounded by the images on the screen. "This is not me! This is some bozo playing a fucking trick on me," Eric screamed. He glanced up toward the apartment and dialed the number. "Come on Sophia, pick up the damn phone," he said, looking up at Sophia's window.

Eric saw the vehicle coming from the wrong side of the street but he didn't care. He was too busy trying to reach Sophia. He let the phone ring and the SUV continued to drive down the one way street. Suddenly, there was a flash and he heard the bang. Eric jumped to the passenger seat and stayed close to the floor for what seemed like an eternity. The Range Rover was suddenly being strafed by automatic weapon fire.

Sweat poured down his back as he tried to reach for the 9mm under the driver's seat. Eric struggled before he loosened the Velcro strap holding the gun in place. Without looking, Eric held the gun above his head and attempted to fire. He heard the SUV skid off and fired the gun anyway. Eric was surprised by a series of orders.

"Toss the gun out then get out of the vehicle." Eric heard the request but did not comply. "This is the police. Do as you're told. Toss the gun out the window now." Eric did not budge.

"How do I know you're not the same people trying to kill me?" He asked instead.

"It's Detective Kowalski and my partner and I are going to pull out our badges and walk to you. Do not try to shoot," Detective Kowalski said.

Once he was outside his vehicle, the detectives began reading Eric his rights. "You have the right to an attorney..."

"Hey, I still don't understand what the fuck is going on! They tried to kill me coming down a one way street and you're trying to arrest my black ass? That shit don't make no kinda sense," Eric protested.

"Watch your head," Kowalski said. Eric was handcuffed and driven to the precinct where he was escorted into an interro-

ANTHONY WHYTE

gation room. He spent the next fifteen minutes alone staring at an empty desk. Eric was not aware that he was being watched by the chief along with the two arresting detectives. "Is this our man? Hall? Kowalski? Will one of you answer me, dammit," the chief demanded.

"Yes that's Eric Ascot, music producer linked to underworld crime figure, Frankie Maruichi. We picked him up just now after a shoot out in front of his girlfriend's upscale building."

"What, trouble now follows that guy around like he's Tupac? What kind of criminal background did you dig up?" the chief asked.

"Well, ah, sir, chief, what I'm trying to say is..."

"The guy's a good, hardworking citizen and no jury would convict him or believe either of you over him. What else we got besides the gun charge?"

"Sir, he's somehow connected to Maruichi and if we could get something linking him and..."

"No, I don't want either of you fucking with Maruichi. Why? It's none of your concern. You just follow orders the same way I do. Maruichi is off limits. I don't want to hear that either of you is snooping around him. I do and I'll have your badge. That's fair warning. If you can somehow get a witness to place him at anymore shootings, we may have an airtight case. Let him make bail and go on the gun charges. He'll mess up again. Until then, find a damn witness to put him at the shooting. Boys, I'm afraid that's the only way it's going to stick," the chief said. Hall and Kowalski looked at each other with raised eyebrows.

"Let's go find a damn witness then," Kowalski said as all three walked away.

FIFTY-NINE

Hours later, after being processed and making the perp walk for all the media to witness, Eric was released on bail. He adamantly refused to cooperate with the police even with proper legal representation. He was also in no mood to address members of the media who had gathered. Instead, Eric's attorney made a public plea urging the public not to judge him and that he was not guilty. When asked about the weapon and the purpose for Eric Ascot having it on him, he stared right into the cameras and said, "The criminal justice system as you know is not perfect and oftentimes it does more harm than good." The attorney was very convincing. That's why Maruichi had sent him to represent Eric. He was able to discredit the police without mentioning anything Eric had done. It seemed like just another police fabrication. The truth would prevail, the attorney promised as he and Eric walked to a waiting limousine. Eric dialed Maruichi's number.

"Thanks," he said then listened for awhile. He handed the phone to the attorney who had joined him in the limousine. "It's Maruichi. He wants to talk with you," Eric said. The attorney grabbed the phone.

"Hey, things worked out perfectly. Shouldn't be a problem. Ok, see you later." He returned the phone to Eric who immediately dialed Sophia's number. Deedee picked up.

"Uncle E., are you okay? The doorman said your car was ambushed outside," Deedee said sounding worried.

"It was but they were lousy shooters. They missed. The Range was shot up pretty bad but I wasn't hit. How're you doing, Dee?"

"Worried, Uncle E. I thought you had been shot or...I just feared the worst but I'm glad to hear your voice and know you're alive. Why didn't you pick up your cell phone?"

"I didn't have it. It's a long story. Did Sophie leave for work?"

"Yes, she did. She was involved in some litigation or something but she said to call her at her office."

"She's still mad, huh?"

"You gave her a lot of reasons to be angry. I mean Uncle E, those pictures and the video were really awful."

"Look, the pictures are real. I was in the club but someone switched my head up with someone's body."

"Really? Oh, you mean like they did with R. Kelly?"

"Precisely," Eric said. Deedee felt a little better after hearing the explanation.

"Call Sophia, Uncle. She's probably worried."

"Okay, I'll do that after I hang up from you."

"Will I see you later, Uncle E?" Deedee asked.

"Yes, you will. Take care."

"You do the same. Don't forget to call Sophia."

"I'm on it right now. I'll be seeing you, Dee. Goodbye, honey," Eric said and pressed the speed dial to Sophia's office. "Hi, may I speak to Sophia Sullivan, please?" Eric said then followed with a 'Thank you'. He held the cell to his ear and waited. Moments later, he spoke again. "Hi Sophie, how're you?"

"I'm fine Eric. How're you? I'm happy that you called but I'm in the midst of something important right now and I'll have to talk to you another time. Please, please be careful out there. I've really got to go, Eric. Bye." Eric heard the click at the other end and tried to say something but she did not hear.

"Sophia, Sophie," he said but there was no response. He redialed. "I was speaking with Ms. Sullivan and we were disconnected. Could you put me through once more?"

"I'm afraid I can't, sir. You're going to have to leave a message and I'll make sure she receives it. Is that alright?"

"It's Eric Ascot, her fiancé."

"I'm sorry, sir, but she cannot be disturbed at this time."

"Thanks a lot," Eric said.

"You're welcome. Have a nice day."

He put away the cellular and gritted his teeth. "You can't give some people a job. It's like they wanna run the whole damn company. She could've gotten up off her fat ass and gotten her,"

Eric said to no one in particular but the attorney was listening all the time and not saying anything. Eric exhaled hard. "Do you have a cigarette?"

"Sure," the attorney said. "There are lots of changes occurring at this point in your life. It's understandable for you to be upset," the attorney said then gave Eric a light before adding, "We all have those days in our lives, Mr. Ascot." Eric inhaled hard and exhaled a roomful of smoke. He sat back then stared straight ahead, visibly upset.

SIXTY

Coco woke up to the knocking on her door. "Coco? Coco, wake up girl. Are you okay?" It was Miss Katie and it was still early. This wasn't a school day and Coco had stayed up writing songs all night and wanted to get some sleep. She knew she had promised to catch up with Josephine. That girl wanted to go shopping but it was still too early, Coco thought as she struggled to open the door.

"Good morning, Miss Katie," she said greeting the old lady while trying to wipe the sleep from her eyes.

"Coco, did you see the news on the TV? They arrested that man, Eric ah..."

"They arrested Eric Ascot for what?"

"Oh Coco, it was on the news," Miss Katie said pushing her weight past Coco. "It was on all the channels, Coco." Miss Katie reached out to turn on the television. "It's on every single one of the channels in the city," she said getting anxious when the screen remained blank. "Coco, is it plugged in? How come there ain't no picture?" Miss Katie asked.

"It's old and has to warm up, Miss Katie. What was Eric arrested for?"

"Oh girl, they got him for guns and shooting. He had a shoot out with rivals, the news said. Go get ready and come by. Oh, by the way, Josephine said to tell you she's on her way."

"Thanks, Miss Katie. I'll come over in a minute, alright?"

"Okay Coco. That man... Oh Lord, help him." The door slammed cutting off Miss Katie's prayers.

"Oh shit," Coco exclaimed as her television had finally come on. "I gotta buy mommy a television for Mother's Day," she whispered. She sat down and attentively watched the news cast.

...Music mogul, Eric Ascot, was released from jail where

he spent the night after what police described as a wild shoot out in the city last night. Mr. Ascot was arrested on a possession of weapons charge as well as reckless endangerment charges. Both charges carry stiff penalties. This is what his attorney had to say earlier today...

The scene shifted to Eric Ascot being led out in handcuffs then changed to outside Central Booking where his attorney was being shown jawing with the media. Eric was shown being escorted to a waiting limousine. The scene is reverted to the newsroom. *...His attorney said that his client was being framed by the police and promised that the truth would come out. Police said they are investigating the shooting. Mr. Ascot's SUV was riddled with bullets when, at about eleven o'clock last night, police were called to the scene of a gang-style shoot out. An NYPD spokesperson reported that the first officers on the scene were greeted by a hail of gunfire coming from the direction of Mr. Ascot's vehicle and rival gang members. We'll keep you posted with up to the minute broadcasts as the case develops. Elsewhere...*

Coco turned the shower on and stepped in. She let the water beat on her shoulders as she digested the news she had just received. Lil' Long was released already? She wondered. No, couldn't be. He's still supposed to be locked down. Maybe he had his boys doing the dirty. Maybe it's them crooked cops fucking with Eric. Coco's thoughts flowed freely along with the water. Later, she dressed and went to see Miss Katie.

SIXTY-ONE

Lil Long walked into the workout area where Nesto told him he would be. It was plain to see that Lil' Long didn't belong. He moved between big bulges of biceps and quads. He spotted Nesto surrounded by some other prisoners. They were all working out, lifting heavy weights. Lil' Long ambled over to their corner of the gym.

"Yo, y'all mad diesel on this side here," he said and embraced Nesto.

"Sup, Lil' Long," Nesto replied. "You look like you may wanna join me and my peeps here. Everyone, this Lil' Long, the cat from around the way. Don't tell me you forgot? Nesto just mentioned that shit less than an hour ago."

"You up, Nesto. It's your set, baby," a man with huge biceps said.

"Excuse me here, daddy. This the last set I'm doing. These Russians ain't gonna kill Nesto," he said then put himself in position to lift the weight. Lil' Long watched Nesto hoist the barbell filled with big round plates of steel. Lil' Long was getting dizzy after the fifteenth rep but he could hear the grunts as Nesto hefted the barbell again and again. After the twentieth rep, the weights slammed down.

"Whoa, hold up. You da fucking man. How much weight was that?" Lil' long asked as he gave Nesto a pound.

"Yo," Nesto said gasping. "That was what? Five fifteen, five twenty and change?" Nesto huffed. "Ya gotta do that shit twenty times, daddy," he said as his breathing slowly returned to norm.

"Shit, that's a lot. Neva ketch me doing no shit like that. No way, baby. The only thing I'm lifting up is da four pound... Desert Eagles, kid." Lil' Long laughed and Nesto joined him as they walked away.

"Let's go blaze sump'n, my nigga. I wanna tell you 'bout my son. Daddy you know Tina?"

"Which Tina?"

"You gotta see her. She da bomb, kid. Got da fatty with long black hair. Nice pair o' tatas too."

"Yeah, she sounds like a dime. I must've seen her in da hood. Where she hang?"

"She be uptown all da time on da Eastside. Her peeps Puerto Rican." As Nesto painted the picture, Lil' Long realized exactly who he was referring to and tried not to seem shocked when he heard Nesto saying, "She got my shortie, my little man. Nesto Junior, that's my heart, daddy. C'mon, let's blaze this and I'll show you a picture of him, sun." Nesto swaggered with confidence to the cell block and found the picture. He made himself busy rolling the blunt as Lil' Long took a look at the photo. He recognized the beautiful woman as Tina from around the way. This was a chick he had dogged many a night. A smile consumed his demeanor.

"You got a lovely fam, man," Lil' Long said with wink.

SIXTY-TWO

Josephine walked up the stairs because she was familiar with the place. She had been to Coco's home before and even though it wasn't her favorite, she climbed the stairs knowing that she and Coco would hang out and chit chat. She also wanted to go shopping. Coco may not dress the part but she knew all the hot spots and had an unbiased taste in style. If it didn't look good on you, she'd let you know immediately. Unlike my boring ass mother who's always saying everything looks good on you and buy what you want. Josephine was deep in thought when a couple of kids ran by her.

"Huh! Damn, you guys scared me. Take it easy before you fall, little bad ass boys. Where are your parents?" she asked aloud as she knocked on Coco's door. Just then the elevator door swung open and two girls, one pushing a stroller, got off. Josephine remembered their faces but she couldn't recall their names. She knew one was Deja's baby mother. This must be their floor also, she thought as they walked toward her.

"Hi, remember me from Busta's thing?" one of the girls asked.

"Yes, right. That's where we met," Josephine said and knocked again. She heard rustling from within. "It's Josephine. Is Coco inside?" Coco opened the door and saw the crowd in the hall.

"Chill, Jo, you crazy ass. Oh, what's good, Kim. Hi, Tina," Coco said nodding at the girls. Josephine turned around and smiled. "You remember my friend, Jo, right?" Coco asked.

"Yeah, we were about to..." Josephine started to say when the door adjacent to Coco's opened and Miss Katie peeked out.

"Why, everyone is here," she beamed. "Hey, Coco and...?"

"Hi, Miss Katie. This is my friend from school and the singing group, Josephine," Coco said.

"Josephine," Miss Katie repeated. "Your face seems familiar. How're doing, Josephine? Any friend of Coco is a friend of mine. Hey, Roshawn, are you coming to spend the day with Grandma Katie?" Miss Katie bent over and picked up the infant boy.

"Yes, Roshawn is here to spend the day. I appreciate it so much, Miss Katie," Kim said. "Did you ever meet my friend, Tina?"

"Bring his carriage inside. Nice to meet you, Tina," Miss Katie said to Kim and Tina. Then she smiled and said, "Coco and Josephine, I'll see you all later, ya hear. Gotta go take care of my cute boyfriend. Hey, Roshawn, whatcha up to, baby boy, smiling with them big eyes?"

"Bye y'all," said Josephine as she waved.

"See y'all. I'll talk to you later, Miss Katie," Coco said before Josephine walked into the apartment and the door closed behind her.

"I don't think she heard ya. She was too busy with that kid. Is that what's-his-face's baby?" Josephine asked excitedly.

"Who is what's-his-face? That's Deja's son."

"Yeah, that's who I meant, Deja. Deja has such a cute little boy," Josephine said then she glanced around the place. "Damn, Coco, you need to fix this place." She laughed.

"Very funny, bitch. What ol' hole did you crawl out from?" Coco asked.

"Whatever, bitch." Josephine answered and flipped her middle finger.

"Whatever, bitch," Coco responded unveiling both her middle fingers.

"You know what? It's all good cause I'm rich."

"Speaking of rich, did you get the number for Danielle's mother?" Coco asked and when Josephine hesitated, Coco continued. "You forgot, right?"

"I wasn't even thinking about that shit when I got home. All I could..."

"Think? You didn't need to think. You're walking around with a ten thousand dollar check. What is there to think about?"

"If your mother was riding you all day long then..."

"That's just excuses, bitch. Speaking of mothers, I need to buy my mom a lil' Mother's Day sump'n, sump'n before I forget."

"Oh really? What're you getting her? Furniture would be nice. Maybe a nice living room set. Hmm, just what the doctor ordered."

"See, you're asking to be kicked out."

"No, I'm just making gift suggestions."

"I suggest you keep your damn suggestions to yourself. You brought da weed, yo?"

"Thought you'd never ask. You're gonna roll, right? Cause you know me when it comes to rolling a blunt."

"Yeah, I know. You'd rather give brains before you roll."

"You just take shit I tell you and throw it back in my face. Here, roll this shit already," Josephine said and threw the bag of weed at Coco. She examined the bag for a few seconds too long for Josephine who stood staring anxiously, awaiting Coco's approval.

"Aw shit, my girl got the purple stuff. Ahight, Jo. This that shit, yo," Coco said happily. "We ready for the party tonight, yo. We got enough weed here to last a minute. How much did you spend?"

"I guess it meets your standards, huh, Miss Weedology," Josephine deadpanned. Coco ignored her and was busy breaking up the buds from the stalk. She slit open a cigar, emptied the tobacco and replaced it with the finely ground from between her fingers. "Anyway, who said I spent shit? That's from Geo's stash," Josephine continued with a smile.

"Oh, don't tell me that nigga already boned you, girl?" Coco said as she licked the blunt-wrap and sealed it.

"I won't tell you cuz he ain't. I wish but I got my period."

"Thank God cuz I know you'd already give up the chocha," Coco said as she got down to the business at hand. She ran her fingers over the outside until the blunt was smooth and dry. "Let's go by the kitchen window and take a few puffs."

"Look at you. Let me know you smoking in da crib now," Josephine said as she joined Coco by the window.

"This my spot right here. Madukes ain't around so I might

as well stunt in my own crib."

"Word," Josephine said as she watched Coco open the window then light the blunt. She saw someone who had become more important to her while they were apart. Josephine realized she missed not only the camaraderie of the group but the individuals too. Danielle was gone forever, Josephine thought as she watched Coco suck on the blunt, hold her breath then exhale a cloud of smoke. She'd come to cherish more the time spent with Coco. "How does it burn, Coco?"

"Oh, it's purple haze and it's good, yo. This da shit. Here, see for yourself," Coco said holding her breath and speaking at the same time. The whole time smoke flowed in and out of her mouth. It was a difficult act that Coco had mastered. Josephine appreciated it as she tried to do the same thing and wound up choking instead.

"Oh, oh..." Josephine started to speak but ended up in a coughing fit. "You're right, Coco," she finally said. "This da shit." Josephine started to cough again.

"I'll get you sump'n to drink, Jo," she said and reached for a glass. She poured the girl some cherry flavored Kool Aid and handed the glass to her.

"Hey," Josephine said taking the glass. "I'm official in da hood now. Weed and Kool Aid. Thanks, Coco," Josephine said and gulped.

"You're welcome, bitch, and don't get the blunt tip wet. I hate that shit. You ever smoke wit niggas and they gotta slob all over the blunt then try to pass it to you? I be like, you can keep that shit. I'll be mad if da weed's da bomb though."

"Shit, I ain't trying to smoke wit no nigga that slob. Cuz if you gonna smoke wit him then he's gonna wanna know why he can't slob you down?"

"See, you getting ready to start talking all that freaky shit. Just in case you forgot, I'm Coco and not Danielle. You and her might be into that freaky nastiness but I am not," Coco said. "Look, you let the blunt go dead. I'm a put my sneaks on and then let's bounce up out this piece and go shopping."

"Coco, have you heard from Dee?"

"No but did you see that shit about her uncle on the news?"

"What shit?"

"He was arrested on some gun charges and shit, girl."

"Word?"

"It was on the news all morning. You been under a rock or sump'n, yo?"

"I went home and fell out alright. I put earplugs in my ears and slept with blinders on," Josephine said. As Coco slipped on her sneakers, Josephine relit the blunt. She puffed and gazed out the window. After a few puffs, she began to speak. "There are a lot of people in this city," she said. "I wonder what would happen if I go. Nobody would know. I mean, nobody would care."

"Jo, get away from the window and pass the blunt," Coco said walking to the window. She took the blunt from between Josephine's fingers. "Why you bugging and talking all that BS, yo?" Coco asked taking a drag. "Of course, people would care if Miss Josephine Johnson died, yo," Coco said and went back to making sure the laces on her sneakers were just right. Josephine's mood was unchanged by what Coco had said. She gazed from the window and saw the mad dash of people seemingly running off to nowhere. Buses, cabs and dollar vans were transporting them with faces of gloom like they were going to their doom. We're all hypocrites, she thought. She turned to see Coco puffing away.

"Nobody would care, Coco."

"You're just saying that because, right now, you mad at your parents, Jo. I'm quite sure they'd at least care about..."

"My mother and father, they're too concerned about what each other is gonna gain from this divorce," Josephine said. She reached for the blunt. Coco hesitated in passing it.

"You sure you can handle this, yo?" she asked.

"Word, it's too strong for me. I don't need anymore," she said. Coco continued to puff. "Yo, going through this divorce thing with my parents is like a fucking game. You don't even know. Wanna see two adults who are supposed to be sensible act the fool? Just get married and after living together over eighteen years, tell the other, 'You know what? I don't think this marriage is working.' Then after awhile, you'll see what's it all about. 'Well, if you're gonna leave then I want this and I want that' and back and forth. It boils down to damn material shit and money. That's why I say they wouldn't give a shit if I died today. They too busy with their own shit to even so much as care."

"Here," Coco said handing Josephine the blunt. "You might need this after all, yo."

"Yeah, I probably could use some more," Josephine said and took a pull. She exhaled and realized Coco was standing closer and watching her keenly. "What, I'm violating puff-puff-pass?" she asked Coco and saw her shaking her head. "What? What is it, Coco? My make-up? What's wrong with it?" Josephine asked.

"I would care, Jo. I would give a fuck if you died today," Coco said and the girls embraced.

"That's sweet, Coco. I know we like sisters but you're not just saying this because of the weed, are you?" Josephine teased. They both laughed.

"Yes, I must admit the weed's got sump'n to do with it but..."

"You bitch, you," Josephine said interrupting.

"If you let me finish my statement."

"Speak to the hand, bitch," Josephine said and thrust her hand in front of Coco's face.

"See, you gonna make me have to whip your counchy ass."

"Counchy, bitch? The word is country, okay."

"Whatever. Let's bounce, yo."

"Yeah, let's go shopping plus I'm getting hungry."

"You haven't eaten breakfast? Me neither."

"Yo, Coco, there goes your girls. Who're they again, Fifi and Dodo?"

"Where? What're you talking 'bout, girl?"

"Here, out the window trying to get a cab," Josephine said and Coco walked back to the window.

"Oh, Kim and Tina. What did you call 'em?" Coco giggled. "Their dresses are so tight, I know they can't breathe properly,"

Coco said as she and Josephine watched from the window.

"Yeah but they don't care. The men love that shit."

"Exactly and that's why they be akin stupid, yo. Walking around switching they asses. They just straight up hos," Coco said as cabs raced from all over vying to get to Kim and Tina.

"See, she can't even get into the cab without drawing a crowd cuz her dress is too tight. They thongs are showing."

"Yeah, but some men think that's sexy."

"Who cares what skuzzy men think?" Coco asked and pointed Josephine's attention to a group running to get the cab door for Kim and Tina. "Do you know that Kim and I used to have a fight every single day for about a month when we were in grade school?"

"Get out," Josephine declared with a smile. "Did you whip her ass?" she asked as they gathered everything and walked out the door.

"Let's just say we respect each other's ability to throw down," Coco said and locked the door. The girls bounded down the stairs and out to the street. They saw the crowd of people milling across the street from the apartment building. "Oh, there goes Rightchus doing his thing," Coco said as they walked by. Some guys whistled while others nodded as Coco and Josephine walked through the block.

"What's he doing? Giving away government cheese?"

"That nigga up to sump'n. Sometimes he be looking out for the dealers and all."

"Yo, Coco, what's popping?" Rightchus ran toward Coco and Josephine.

"Yo, let's see what this fool wants, Jo. You remember him from over by...?"

"How could I forget? He used to be a pest, always begging for dough and running his bullshit ass con games. I have no time for trifling niggas."

"You sound like he took you for sump'n."

"What? He sold me and Danielle some fake ass shit for weed. My ass was pissed. It cost me five dollars. We was going in on a dime and this lil' short ass blue black mothafucka stole our little bit a money," Josephine said and walked away as Rightchus approached.

"Yo, Coco, your friend ain't got to go anywhere. She ain't got to be scurred o' lil' ol' me," Rightchus said with a chuckle. "Yo, sweetness," he shouted at Josephine then he turned to Coco and said, "She ain't trying to hear the pimp in me, huh?"

"Nah, uh uh. Leave that alone. It's her time o' the month," Coco said with a wink. Rightchus gave her dap.

"Ah, I get your drift. So, what da deal? Your man shooting up da place and all that mess last night?"

"Yeah, ain't it a shame how they let Lil' Long out already. I know he was doing some shooting but the cops gonna be hiding that because he a snitch," Coco said.

"Nah, Coco, it wasn't that nigga. Lil' Long still locked up."

"Stop playing, yo," Coco yelled. Rightchus nodded affirmatively.

"Yo, Coco, I'm telling you, the devil keeps the people illiterate because that's the only way he can use them as tools and make 'em slaves. You feelin' me?" Rightchus was about to fall into a groove but Coco knew she was on another mission when Josephine gave her the eye.

"I ain't got time to chit chat, Rightchus. I'll holla at you another time."

"Coco, I'll walk wit you to da corner. Niggas busting guns and you and your friend might need some security," Rightchus said as he walked along with Coco. They both walked to where Josephine stood. "Goddamn, your friend is fine. That's a sexy ass bitch right there, Coco. Hmm, hmm, hmm. Them jeans hugging those hips oh so right. Oh, it's ah, what's-her-name from 'Da Crew'?"

"It's Josephine, nigga."

"Easy now, sis. Why you wanna jump down a nigga's throat like that?" Rightchus asked, surprised by Josephine's reaction.

"Rightchus, what did I say? You don't listen, do you? We just had this conversation so leave her alone, yo. She don't wanna be talking to anyone right now."

"No, I'm not talking to..."

"Josephine, chill."

"I'm chill. I'm waiting on you, girl. We got places to go." With that, she walked away.

"Rightchus, I gotta be out, yo."

"Yo, Coco, I'm telling you. Keep your eye out for da jakes. They called Starsky and Hutch, them hip hop po-pos. They down the block right over there," Rightchus said as he took the cigarette from Coco's hand.

"Oh, that's how it's going down? Fuck da police. I seen 'em around da weed spot on the south side. Fuck 'em. I'm out," Coco said.

"Ahight, peace and tell your friend to be cool when she comes around my part of town," Rightchus said but Coco was already down the block trying to find Josephine.

SIXTY-THREE

She walked into the store just as Josephine was emerging with a sack full of goodies including a newspaper, soda, chewing gum, and a pack of cigars.

"Here, I bought you a Pepsi."

"You my girl, Jo. For real, I was just about to say where my girl at? And if she's in the store, I hope she..." Coco was addressing Josephine when a voice cut into her flow.

"Hey, Coco, going to cop some of that chocolate? Don't waste your time going down the South Drive. We busted all their fucking asses. You cop somewhere else and we'll bust their asses anywhere you go. Coco, we coming for 'em. You might as well let your boys know they going to jail if they sell you any weed." Coco and Josephine looked at each other. Neither turned to see the face of the person making the threats but Coco already knew it was Detective Kowalski. She heard the Caprice peel out before she moved.

"Who...what da fuck was that about, Coco?" Josephine asked rolling her eyes.

"Just a couple of fucking dicks. Let's get a cab, yo."

"Lemme know if I'm hanging' wit Amerikaz Most Wanted, you hear? I want to be ready to spit back lead at jakes. You heard me, Coco?" Josephine joked as a taxi pulled to a stop in front of them.

"You be bugging, yo. What you looking around for, Jo? Get in the damn cab already, will you?"

"I don't want anyone to sneak us from behind. Real gangsters always watch their back at all times."

"Get real, Josephine. You need to get in this cab before the driver thinks we're trying to play with him or sump'n."

"Take us to the mall at one-two-fifth," Josephine said and with that, the cab whisked them away.

"I'm ready to party tonight, Coco," Josephine said. "Not go to jail so be on your best behavior. We don't want the police following us around, okay?" Josephine said. Suddenly, she leaned forward and whispered, "I'm dirty. I've got more of that purple haze stashed in my panties."

"Oh, Jo, must you be saying all that? Keep all that shit to yourself."

"Just letting you know, girl."

The cab sped along with the rest of the traffic transporting the girls to a shopping expedition at the Mall. They paid and jumped from the cab. "Ready to get your shop on, Coco?" Josephine asked.

"Yeah, I'm ready," Coco replied as the girls, accompanied by glances of most of the single men in the immediate vicinity, easily made their way through the mall. They shopped for outfits for the night's party then ate, chatted, and shopped some more. "Coco, there goes another cutie, girl," Josephine said as the girls moved from store to store.

"Let's go check out some of those Van Dutch joints, Jo," Coco responded and grabbed Josephine by the arm, curtailing her from following the handsome youth all the way through the Mall. "I swear you're a bug out, girl."

"Coco, I'm trying to get mine, girl. As long as I've known you, you ain't never had a boyfriend, Coco," Josephine said walking so close to Coco that it seemed as if they were joined at the hip.

"I ain't got time for a nigga's shit." Coco answered as they walked into the store. They were greeted by another store clerk.

"He's good looking, Coco. Push up a little sump'n."

"We here to shop for outfits, not pick up guys, bitch."

"Coco, you shy or sump'n, girl?"

"May I help you ladies?" the clerk asked.

"And he has manners. Ah, yes, me and my girlfriend were wondering if you're an Aries or a Leo. Now, I was telling her by the curve of your nose that you were definitely a Leo. Am I right?"

"You're right, I am a Leo. Let me know if you see anything you like and I'll get you a nice price," he said smiling as he walked away.

"See what I'm talking 'bout? You could have a fan club at your beck and call, Coco," Josephine said waving her arms around the store. "Don't you want a boyfriend? Damn girl, you a virgin or sump'n?"

"I have a feeling if you continue this conversation, you're gonna go to this party with either my foot wedged in your ass or be stuck in surgery with a doctor trying to remove it."

"Whatever, bitch. Let me find out you muff diving or sump'n," Josephine said and her grin was met by the flare of Coco's nostrils. This was her signature move before she hit the boiling point. "I'm gonna be so scared in another second." They continued to shop throwing jabs at each other like any sisters would do.

SIXTY-FOUR

They sat around a table sipping from shot glasses. Eric, along with the attorney, listened as Maruichi outlined the details of their agreement. One of the main points was that Eric would receive protection. At a cost, Eric would have real muscle and real security. He was about to be provided with a two-man security team that would not draw attention to him or them. They would be able to blend into the environment, Maruichi had explained. That was earlier. Now they sat around and sipped Cognac, toasting the deal.

"May our agreement be bulletproof, Eric," Mr. Maruichi said and raised his glass.

Eric sipped but his mind was still on the outrageous events from last night. From the time Deedee had called until the time he was arrested, his life had been reduced to a series of mishaps. He nodded, raised his glass, and sipped but all the time, Eric wondered what Sophia's next move was. He knew she didn't want to talk to him. He'd heard it in her voice. Sitting downstairs from where his troubles with the photo had begun, he wanted to talk to Maruichi in private about it. Now, he wouldn't be surprised if Sophia threw the engagement ring at him the next time they were face to face. "You still have problems with your fiancé, yes?" Maruichi asked as he cozied up to Eric.

"You could say that," Eric said after sometime.

"It is such a beautiful thing to be in love, isn't it?"

"Yeah but right now, the view isn't so lovely. Not from where I'm sitting, Mr. Maruichi. It ain't such a pretty picture," Eric said and pulled out a cigarette.

"Apparently someone sent pictures and a doctored videotape with the car," the attorney added. "I had someone look into the dealership. They're straight. Our informant told us that the envelope contained pictures from the...ah, club."

"Upstairs?" Maruichi asked, pointing to the ceiling. The attorney nodded. "We got a dirty rat in this place?" he asked violently bringing the glass down against the table. The action caused some of the cognac to spill out onto the table. "How long have you known about this? Where's Eddie? Tell Eddie to get his nose out of the card game and get over here now," Maruichi shouted. "Why wasn't I told immediately?" he asked. He turned to Eric and said, "I'm sorry you've got to be a witness to this outburst but if your problems were a result of someone leaking information from the club then that mess must be cleaned up right away. I'm sure you can appreciate the expediency and efficiency that will be used to eliminate this minor hitch."

Eddie Maruichi appeared at his father's side. After a brief conversation with the attorney, he walked away.

"Eddie I want to know when you find them," Maruichi called to his son then Eddie was off again. After that, the meeting ended. Eric walked out with a confident feeling about his security but was uncertain about his relationship with the person that mattered the most. He dialed Sophia's cell as he drove. No answer. He listened to the outgoing message and realized how much he needed her. Along the way to the studio, Eric stopped at a florist and placed an order for a dozen roses to be sent to her office everyday for the rest of the month. There were still twenty four days left in this month. From there, he drove to the recording studio where he could hide behind the blues he felt and drown his sorrows in the creation of the better beat. It was now the only place where he still had the presence to exert his full influence with no questions asked.

SIXTY-FIVE

Couple hours after the meeting at the back of the pizza bar, Maruichi received a call from his son, Eddie. He was told that the leak was found and he should come on down to the address given. With driver and bodyguards in tow, Maruichi left his haunt immediately. They raced through the streets like a fire truck to a fire. They pulled to a stop on a lonely street lined with a row of private houses. Maruichi was greeted by Eddie. They spoke briefly then he and Eddie went up the stairs with two of the body-guards.

At the foot of the stairs, they stopped and Maruichi knocked on the door. An older lady answered the door. She was the mother of the girls known as the Geisha twins. Looking torn, they finally came out and spoke to Mr. Maruichi. They all sat in a bleak living room. The dark hue of the leather sofa did nothing to brighten the dullness of the place.

"Hey, girls, how're you doing? I understand we had some problems the other night, uh?" Maruichi said as he eyed both girls. "There was a breach of security, a lapse in judgment, but nothing that cannot be corrected. I'm afraid that in order for us to take the necessary steps to correct the problem, we're going to have to get information from every single worker. You're includ-ed in this family network," Maruichi said smiling. "So I wanted to ask you girls in the presence of your mother, did you give anyone or provide anyone with anything because they threatened you with arrest or maybe wanted to pay you extra money for any type of pictures. That information would be necessary to bring a law-suit against this person as they're trying to harass my employees. Also, this is not the first time it has occurred. We must end this by punishing these people to the fullest extent of the law."

"Mr. Maruichi, we know the name of one such person. He said he'd arrest us if we told anyone but he gave us money."

"Really, what's his name?" Mr. Maruichi asked and his ears perked up the way animals do.

"His name is Michael Johnson. He gave us money and told us we were helping him to catch a criminal," one of the ladies said. They were both a little nervous but had taken the reassurances that Maruichi offered as real. They spilled their guts and explained how Michael Thompson, on the pretense of catching a criminal, had paid them to take pictures of Eric or Busta, who had been a favorite client of theirs. Maruichi listened with no visible signs of rage but inside, he fumed to the point of revulsion.

Maruichi was a member of the old order. Family unity began with loyalty and silence was golden. He openly smiled when the dancers nervously told him of their transgressions and how it all started with a simple request by Michael Thompson. He had asked the girls to take pictures of all of Busta's friends. The pictures would fetch the girls five hundred a piece. That it was enough incentive for his workers to betray him was, in itself, repulsive to Maruichi. He tapped his feet as he decided their fate then he said, "I can't forgive you but I understand that you need to work, just not with me. We cannot tolerate employees doing things behind our backs that could sabotage the company or our clientele. That would be deadly to our future growth, you understand?" At that point, Maruichi signaled to Eddie. "Pay these ladies the usual severance and I'll recommend you ladies to whoever is going to be your future employer," he said as Eddie counted out three thousand dollars. "It's fifteen hundred apiece," he said and waved goodbye to the Geisha twins and their mother. They sobbed a little as their former boss and his entourage departed. At the foot of the stairs, the man some called Chi glanced up at the apartment before walking out.

"I want someone efficient to set this rat trap on fire. And I want you to check out this Michael Thompson. Find out his angle."

"Yes father. Done, sir," Eddie said and looked at his father again then asked, "Burn it all?" Eddie asked uneasily. His father gave him a cold stare before the answer came.

"Anyone who comes against you and causes you sorrow

must be completely eliminated. That includes all of their family members," Maruichi said and patted Eddie's dome. "Burn it all. I want them dead by nightfall," he said as he got into his car and drove away. Eddie turned to the three guys left standing with him and smiled.

"We got a job to do by nightfall, guys. Let's get to it," he said and the group departed in two cars.

Later that evening, fire trucks were called to the scene as flames caused by electrical damage ravaged the row of houses destroying everything and killing all the occupants. Included in the list of casualties were the Geisha Twins and their seventy-two year old mother. Maruichi wanted the lesson to be clear. Those who cooperate with the police will not only die but their family members will also meet the same fate. Frankie Maruichi had not earned a reputation on the street for being Mr. Nice Guy. From day one, he had set out to make sure everyone knew exactly who was in charge. Burning down a house with all its occupants was just another way Maruichi enforced his power.

SIXTY-SIX

Coco and Josephine were both dressed and ready to be a part of the party scene honoring the new rap album from Silky Black. The girls stood in Miss Katie's apartment and examined their appearances in a full length closet mirror. Coco was stylish and cool in a denim Baby Phat jumpsuit and stilettos while Josephine heated things up with a sleeveless denim blouse and real short denim skirt and heels. She threw a red leather racing jacket over her shoulder while Coco went with the black. The girls took turns dancing and profiling for each other in the mirror.

"You think my ass looks too big in this?" Josephine asked.

"Your ass looks just right, girl. Stop buggin'," Coco said.

"Whatever. This mirror is another thing you need up in that place of yours, Coco," Josephine said as she twisted and arched her body in an attempt to admire every inch of her body in the mirror.

"Bitch, I mean..." Coco said to Josephine then she glanced around to see if Miss Katie was in earshot. She was not far away and could hear the chit chat between the girls. Coco smirked at Josephine then continued to speak. "Listen, Jo, I ordered a sofa and a new television that cost me nearly what?" Coco asked.

"Only three thousand dollars but remember, you got the lamps and the end tables for free."

"Free? Don't you know by now that there ain't nothing for free in this world, yo?" Coco said and turned to the old lady who was pretending to be busy with Roshawn. "Talk to her, Miss Katie. Let her know sump'n," Coco continued as she smooth down her tresses.

"Miss Katie, tell her it will be a great Mother's Day gift," Josephine countered as she tugged at her short skirt.

"Oh, listen to both of you sounding just like sisters. That's very good," Miss Katie said. "So ah...where is this party that you're going to?" The circumspection was not lost on Coco. Josephine, not used to the wily old lady, gave the innocent answer.

"It's at this lovely hotel..." Josephine started.

"No, what she meant is that the club is located in the hotel, Miss Katie, in the same building but two different places. Alright, Miss Katie?" Coco said and glared at Josephine.

"Oh," Miss Katie murmured.

"Yeah, the party is gonna be with...ah, you know a lot of other kids."

"It's getting to be that time," Coco said, preventing Josephine from putting her foot in any deeper than she already had.

"Ah...Gotta go now, Miss Katie," Josephine said as she felt her arm tugged by the Coco. "Goodnight, uhm...Roshanny."

"Oh, you mean Roshawn. Tell her your name, baby. He's so shy. Goodnight and you be careful. Don't you hang out too late, okay?" Miss Katie planted a kiss on Coco's cheek.

"See ya later, Miss Katie. Bye, Roshawn," Coco said as the girls grabbed the rest of their belongings and were out the door.

SIXTY-SEVEN

Sophia sat in the restaurant and listened to Eric wing it. She felt trapped in a nightmare but she had gotten there by following someone else's dream. Now she wanted the truth and listened to Eric's variation of it. Sophia wanted to know the truth about Busta and Eric's collaboration and whether it had anything to do with the fact that one of them had been murdered. She had questions and really feared for her life. Sophia wanted to be with Eric but did not want the violence she had seen to dog her. Between her salad and the main course, she had let Eric know exactly how she felt. The waiter had emptied the table and they sat facing each other, holding their glasses. Sophia's explanation had started mildly enough but took on a definite turn.

"You're not some street thug, Eric, but if you want to be treated like that, people will accommodate you and the police are constantly..." Sophia explained but Eric ended it with an outburst.

"Fuck the police and I don't give a fuck about people. This is between me and you," he said forgetting that their table was located in the middle of a restaurant. Sophia watched Eric carefully. She could tell at once that he was getting really angry. His face seemed to shake with fury while registering an astonishment that the woman he loved thought so little of him. She saw that he was hurting but could do nothing to comfort him.

"Eric you're going to have to start taking responsibility for your own actions. Nobody else can. You're grown and..."

"And what? I've got to go run to crooked cops every time something goes wrong, Sophie? Is that what you're saying?" Eric asked becoming more frustrated. She expected him to throw a tirade but he fell silent as his perspective on his life suddenly coalesced into the cynical visage like a drug dealer peddling crack in a schoolyard.

As darkness fell and lights descended on them, all of their

troubles seemed to become illuminated. Eric was at a loss and searched for the right thing to say. He had hoped to make things better but couldn't find exactly what it was that he had to say to accomplish his goal. He felt frustrated by the fact that he didn't want to tell her the truth because he might run the risk of making her an accomplice. Eric was silent as his thoughts flooded his mind. He felt himself sinking, drowning while trying to find the solution. Then he heard what Sophia was saying and knew this was the end.

"I can't go on like this. My job, my career is in jeopardy while you're running around with known mobsters. I can't keep following my heart. It's going to lead me into further trouble because I care too much about you and I realize you're going to have to make your own mistakes. I refuse to sit back and see if you're going to die or be sent to prison, Eric. I really can't bear to watch." Sophia broke down and sobbed. Other patrons threw sympathetic glances in their direction. Eric tried to console her but not even the gentle rub he applied to her shoulders could stem the flow of her tears. Sophia stood and hurriedly made her way to the ladies room.

Eric sat in silence and directed his focus on the table of food in front of him. Neither had touched much of their meal. Eric thought it would be a waste to tell her that he'd put a contract on someone's head and that it had led to the death of Busta and the shooting incident in his apartment. He felt better now that he had decided to let Maruichi give him protection. Eric knew that Maruichi was a mobster but he figured this was the better deal. He could chase his dreams of producing both music and films. It was a better situation but it came at a huge price, he thought as Sophia returned to the table.

The moment she sat down, he could see that her eyes were red and swollen. Maybe she convinced herself that everything that had gone wrong was her fault or some failure on her part. Eric wanted to soothe her but how do you tell someone you love that you're involved in the death of several people? Busta had died with this knowledge and silently Eric vowed to take this to his grave.

Sophia could scarcely believe the fact that Eric would not open up to her. She was convinced that he was involved in something illegal with Busta. This was his chance and he lied. Tears flowed when she realized she could no longer trust him and that she would have to leave him. He looked serious and concerned when she opened her mouth.

"Eric you're not going to change so I've got to look out for myself. I want to call the engagement off," Sophia said and took the ring off. She threw it on the table and started to run away. Eric reached out for her but she shrugged him off saying: "Don't bother yourself with caring about how I feel about any of this," she said and left. Eric got up, picked up the ring and quickly followed behind her.

"Let me take you home, Sophia," he said when he finally caught up to her. "I wanna know that you're home alright."

"Eric, there's a cab waiting for me outside. I called for one when I went to the bathroom," Sophia said and walked away, leaving Eric staring at her behind. He felt like shouting at her but couldn't bring himself to lie to her anymore. Eric knew that in order for Sophia to come back, he would have to reveal the truth to her. He turned dejectedly and walked back to the table with a heavy heart.

SIXTY-EIGHT

"Yeah, Coco, this party looks like it's off the rack, girl-friend," Josephine said as the taxi came to a stop and they glanced out at all the patrons making their way into the gala affair. "Niggas dressed like they upscale, huh?"

"You can tell from the way niggas is dressed up that this is strictly a baller's affair, Jo," Coco said. They paid the cab and made their way through the throngs of people and were ushered in through the VIP entrance. "Dee would have loved this affair."

"Oh, Coco, she called me. Deedee left a message that she wasn't gonna be able to make it. I forgot…"

"Oh, you heard from her then?" Coco asked as they entered the club. The girls took a fleeting look around and saw that from the windows to the wall, the jump-off was hopping. Coco and Josephine both rocked their bodies as Usher and Lil' John yelled 'Yeah!' Like fish to water, the girls caught the groove immediately. The lights flashed and Coco and Josephine knew it was time to shine.

"Yeah," Josephine screamed as the volume of the music pumped loud in the club. "Coco, shit's krunk in hurr, girl."

"I could feel that. Shit's like wall to wall already, yo."

"Let's get a drink and go work it on da floor," Josephine suggested and the heavy bass seemed to twirl her around.

"It don't seem as if you need anything else."

"Coco, roll up da weed, bring out the drinks and bring on the ecstasy cuz I'm ready to party hard like I'm a rock star," Josephine announced and broke for the dance floor to the sound of Petey Pablo's: *Raise up.* "Let's party, Coco," Josephine said gaily and dragged Coco to the dance floor. They partied and danced merrily for each other. A couple of guys cut in on the duo and they shared a dance for a few songs. Out of nowhere, others joined them in their jig on the floor but when things got too hot, both girls excused themselves to check on their jackets and get a drink.

From the bar, Coco saw Silky Black and his entourage drinking. They hollered at her and offered her a glass. "Yo, Jo, I think Silky Black is over there sipping champagne and blazing. I'm gonna join 'em, yo. You coming?" Coco asked.

"Yeah, let's go." The girls made their way past a few tables and found the guys and girls sitting at a long table covered with champagne bottles. Josephine immediately recognized Kim and Tina sitting amongst the famous faces of rap. "They get around, don't they?"

"Yep, they probably here for the main entertainment. You know them stars gotta have they groupies for the after party up in da telley, lasting till six in the morn," Coco said nodding at Kim and Tina.

"Till six in da morning?" Josephine joked.

"Six in da morn."

"I think we've arrived, Coco," Josephine said with a smile.

"No, you've arrived. Me, I'm just gonna chill and watch how these stars live it up, yo. I don't wanna make the same mistakes when it's my turn to burn so don't get too drunk, bitch. I don't wanna have to carry your ass out. It's too big," Coco said with a smile.

"Whatever, bitch." Josephine said and waved at everyone. She threw a kiss in Kim and Tina's direction. A frown was tossed her way.

"That bitch is such a diva show-off wannabe cuz she hanging wit her bitch, Coco," Kimberly whispered to Tina.

At the table, Coco and Josephine took seat next to some of the music industry's bigwigs. They laughed, shook hands, swigged champagne, and smoked until their lungs hurt with no other care in the world. About an hour or so later when things got a bit too tipsy, Josephine disappeared from the table leaving Coco leaning with a blunt in her mouth and a glass of champagne in her hand.

A few moments later, Coco saw the fracas on the dance floor and knew immediately it had to be Josephine. The girl had danced her way into every male's heart when she got down and let her thong show. But Josephine didn't stop. She couldn't and so she shook it again and again. Coco walked over with the others who enjoyed the show. Kim and Tina observed Josephine's dance routine.

"Wha' I told you. Da bitch ain't nothing but a copy cat ho. Let's show her how to shake this," Kim said and joined Tina on the floor.

Within minutes, the floor was in frenzy as the dancers shook and ground. Josephine was up to the challenge and made moves that left grown men spellbind. Then Coco joined in and her moves transformed minds into doubts as she waged war against gravity going with spins, flips and shakes that left the whole club chanting in her wake:

Go, Coco. Go, Jo...Go Coco, Go Jo...

"Let's get off this dance floor, yo," yelled Coco as she heard the crowd chanting for more. She was greeted by cheers as she flopped into a nearby chair.

"Here's some Mo, Coco. You were killing it, girl."

"Yeah, you all that. You got moves like water, girl. Say, how'd you like to be in a video? Call me tomorrow. Shooting starts next week and bring your friend, too."

"We're not just friend. We partners, too, and since this is biz...I'm Josephine, her partner. Nice to meet you again." They sat at the table for a moment before Josephine disappeared again. Coco glanced around to see her climbing the stairs to the deejay booth.

The party raged on and after more drinking and smoking, Coco looked around for Josephine. The girl was nowhere to be found. I hope she didn't leave and not tell me, Coco thought as she headed outside to take a look. Josephine was not there so Coco decided to check the deejay booth. It seemed a long way up as the alcohol and weed did their job on her judgment. She climbed the stairs carefully and slowly. In the booth sat Josephine with her legs wrapped around Geo's waist. They were kissing so hard that neither heard when Coco walked into the booth. He continued with his tongue in her mouth as Coco decided to grab the mike and start kicking rhymes.

> *Ah, gimme the mike and nobody move*
> *or get hurt die at the sound of my words,*
> *cuz I'm Coco, deadly and loco-*
> *my motive is to leave emcees*
> *with their tongues to their knees*
> *leaving em doing verbalistic calisthenics*
> *they don't wanna see me*
> *gimme da mike...*

"Oh that's you, Coco?" Josephine asked, coming up for a breath.

"Who be spinning when you get down like that, yo?" Coco asked.

"Shit's on auto pilot. Whassup, Coco?" Geo asked.

"Ain't nothing. Makes no sense me asking you that, right, Gee? I can see."

"I'm waiting for my boys to come back and start packing up. They got my truck. Can't go nowhere without the Caddy, you heard?"

"Who?"

"Here they are. Took y'all forever to get that food, dogs. Time to pack up. I gotta drop Coco and Jo to their homes then I'll shoot over by..."

"Aw man, you on some kinda mission already, sun? You know it's a wrap for the night. If anything, we'll see you tomorrow," one of the guys said.

"Oh, before I forget my manners. Coco and Josephine meet Carlos and Mannie. They supposed to be helping me but they disappeared all night."

"Nice to meet you officially. Me and my man here were checking y'all out at the video shoot," Carlos said and extended his hand.

"Yeah, y'all definitely did your damn thing," Mannie concurred.

"Oh, now they gonna try and be nice. Y'all got workers to

supervise and make sure this thing gets done right."

"I know you ain't gonna be running your mouth like that. We just do what you normally does. You get to the event and pull a Houdini. You know that's your steeze, so don't front," Mannie said.

"That shit is dead ass, sun. Stop front'n," Carlos laughed.

"It don't matter what neither of you say. Just make sure the equipment is safe. You got a whole crew working for you. I'm out," Geo said and threw his deejay bag across his shoulder.

"Take care, fellas," Josephine yelled.

"Nice to meet y'all," Coco said and walked out.

"Y'all ain't gonna stay and smoke some o' this dro?"

"Nah, we good," Josephine said.

"Yeah, we tapped out for good," Coco said.

"Ain't nobody wanna smoke wit y'all Spanish asses. Mira, we out."

"Look who's talking."

They made their way back slowly down the steps. At the foot of the stairs lurked Kim and Tina. They said nothing as Coco, Josephine and Geo walked right past them. From behind, they could see Geo's hand all over Josephine's ass as the trio made their way out the club. Both Kim and Tina looked at each with a surprised grin.

"Oh no she didn't."

"He wasn't..." Tina started to say then bit her lip. Then they both burst into laughter. "That nigga is playing my cousin like that right in front of me. I will have to drop dime on that bitch ass," Tina said. "You know us Latinas, we going out for our man."

$IXTY-NINE

It was early morning. Three am to be exact. Darkness shrouded the city except for the usual streetlights and all night candy stores. Geo guided the Escalade through the city and headed uptown. Coco was in the rear while Josephine was up front, hands all over his erect package. Geo swerved to avoid Rightchus and his fellow crackheads wandering the streets. "Oh shit, you scared me," Josephine said.

"You know ain't nobody but them damn crack fiends out here at this time. Cops and fiends," Geo said as he steadied the vehicle.

"That's da nigga, Rightchus, and his disciples, yo. That nigga is crack itself."

"Coco, you're around here somewhere, right?" Geo asked slowing the ride down.

"Yeah, just a couple more blocks up then left, yo," Coco said as she kept her eyes on Rightchus and his friends. She watched as they went to the corner store. "They gonna re-up on beers and whatever," Coco continued watching Rightchus.

"Why they all following Rightchus?" Josephine asked.

"Cuz he got the rocks," Coco said still looking at the small throng.

Coco watched as Rightchus yelled to his gang of about ten loyal crack followers. They hoofed it in a zombie-like state, following the leader to the grocery store. It was easy to figure that Rightchus had the supply for the night since the others followed him the way rats followed the pied piper through the dark.

Rightchus stood outside the all night corner store. He waited while the other fiends bought cigarettes, beer, and an assortment of candies. A police siren sounded and about ten people scattered like roaches under the siege of bright lights. "Hey, Rightchus, don't run. We wanna talk to you." It was the hip hop cops. Coco watched as Rightchus got in the car and the Caprice took off.

"Good looking out, Geo. Drive safely. And, slut, call me later."

"Get in safe, bitch," Josephine said. "Call you later."

The moment Coco waved was the signal for Josephine and Geo's lips to become locked again. They stayed that way touching as the vehicle sped down the block.

SEVENTY

Rightchus sat in the back of the Caprice staring wide-eyed at both detectives. He could not believe what he had just heard. They were planning to set him up as the next drug kingpin if he turned over Eric Ascot.

"Well, I know that him and Busta was up to no good..."

"You said Busta? You can connect him to Busta?" Kowalski asked excitedly.

"Man, let me speak. Lemme tell you sump'n and this is strictly on the hush, hush end. Really down low. Eric and Busta, they hit up Lil' Long and Vulcha."

"Why? Tell us why." Kowalski was beside himself with excitement. "This is what we needed all along, Rightchus, you..."

"Let him talk," Hall said cautiously. "Rightchus, why did they wanna get even? Drug turf?"

"Nah, it wasn't even none o' that. You know E-money just about da beats and the music. He not into no drug deals."

"So, what was the war about?" Hall asked.

"It wasn't no war. Nah, it started when Lil' Long and Vulcha pushed they stinkin' dicks up in my man's niece's guts. They raped her. They raped Deedee and that pissed off my man so much, he brought it to the wrong peeps. Deja, may his soul rest in peace, was killed on account of that bullshit."

"By who? Killed by who? Who did it?" Kowalski asked. He pulled out a bag filled with crack vials. "Look, you're gonna be smiling all day for the rest of your life." Kowalski threw the bag in Rightchus' lap. It had to contain over five hundred crack vials. "Talk and we'll let you live high off the hog, Rightchus," Detective Kowalski said.

"It's all simple, guys. Eric's niece was raped and he didn't want to fuck wit y'all. Y'all did him and his brother wrong so he got his man, Busta, to do the dirty deed, you hear? That's it, two bodies."

"So who shot da cops?"

"Probably Lil' Long. I know it wasn't Vulcha cuz he was toe-tagged already. I feel it's Lil' Long."

"But it could've been Eric Ascot. Why couldn't he have them murdered also? They could've pissed him off just the same."

"I don't know. I ain't sayin' it couldn't happen that way but I personally believe it was Lil" Long."

"Alright, we heard enough. Listen, you stick around and don't go anywhere too far, alright? You're our star witness, boy." The car sped off and stopped in front of Rightchus' building. "Okay, star witness, you take it easy, now." They rode off leaving Rightchus feeling great. He snuck a look into the bag and grinned from ear to ear.

"One man goes down and the other rises." Rightchus pranced into the building where he was met by the super.

"Hey, Rightchus, when you gonna pay me the rent for the past three months for that room of yours?" the super asked, blocking Rightchus' entrance to the elevator.

"Jose, my main man, what's going on, papichulo? Listen, give me couple a weeks and I'll pay you all that," Rightchus said shifting from leg to leg.

"You told me that last month. You told me that the month before that. When are you gonna come up with the damn rent? I'm gonna have to evict you."

"My word is my bond and my bond is my life. I'll give my life before my word."

"Listen, Rightchus, save all that preaching for them people who don't know no better. I want the rent. Money talks, bullshit walks."

"Ahight, my word will not fail, Jose. I'll have all that rent for you, my man."

"I'll believe it when it happens. But you will be out as soon as I get the eviction papers," Jose said. As the elevator arrived, he got in and smiled. "It'll happen," he said and stepped off the elevator and into his apartment. He searched for a little until he found his pipe, sat back, and lit it. "Ah yesss," Rightchus hissed as he exhaled.

SEVENTY-ONE

They lay on his bed, she on her back and he between her legs. She sucked his lip into her mouth while they made out. Their lips crushed each other's, filling the room with the sounds of slurping and moaning. Josephine wrapped her legs around Geo and ground her body into his. She smiled when she felt his dick pressing harder against her thighs. The slurping continued as he held her tightly in his arms. They rocked back and forth then rolled around on his huge bed.

"This bed is major. I mean, you can't fall out," Josephine slurred as the weed and alcohol served to relax her past the point of inebriation. Josephine giggled as she felt the tingling when he unbuttoned her shirt. She moaned loudly when Geo removed her bra and began licking her nipples. "Ohh, my...that feels so good. Yeah, Geo."

Josephine began sliding the tip her of tongue up and down Geo's throat. Her tongue played with his Adam's apple, sending crazy sensations through his entire body. She used her wet lips to rub against the hollow of his throat. He slowly licked her areola in a circular motion. Switching from side to side, his head traveled from nipple to nipple until both were rock hard and appeared on the verge of bursting at the seams. Geo cupped both breasts and moaned when he felt Josephine's soft, moist mouth on his neck. He set her desire afire when he bit both her nipples hard. Her legs kicked uncontrollably and her toes curled.

He got up out of the bed and slipped out of his pants. He was now fully naked with his spear ready for the plunging. With Geo on his back and Barry White humming softly in the background, Josephine caressed Geo's full package. She licked and sucked his dick until the shiny head pointed rudely to the ceiling. She continued to rub the tip against her soft open lips. Josephine heard the moaning and saw the excitement crawling across Geo's face. "Ah...ugh, yeah, yeah, ah... baby, you're doing it right." He groaned harder and louder then his face began contorting. She sucked harder and moved up and down. She felt his body bucking then Geo exploded, squirting cream over her face and hair. "Ah-ho-ooh, oh yes, Jo," he yelled caressing her face gently as she slowly licked his dick, her fingers massaging his balls.

"Oh no, your skeet messed up my hair," she laughed after awhile.

"Are you ready to give up da chocha, now?" he asked excitedly reaching underneath her skirt. Josephine held him against her. She could feel his dick pulsing against her and caressed it gently.

"You got yours. I mean, do we really have to do the nasty?" she asked.

"Baby, yeah, hell yeah, we got to do it. I got to get some of that now. You can't leave a man like me hanging like this," he said pointing to his hard on.

"I... I got my period and all. You know how a woman is."

"Baby, I could hook it up anyway. A quick shower and bam, it's over. Have you ever had it in da culo before?" Geo asked wishing.

"In my ass? Hell no, we ain't doing that. You too big. That shit would be too painful, Geo," Josephine said with a frown. "Maybe another time."

"I'll be real careful. It won't hurt. I got some KY jelly and Vaseline," he said, getting up and going to the bathroom while Josephine fidgeted with her hair. He returned with condoms and lubricants. Josephine glanced around the small studio big enough for a futon, a television, his electronic games, and his DJ equipment. She wanted to stall.

"Where's the bathroom?" she asked. Geo pointed and Josephine crawled out of the bed. "You've got towels ready for me that I can use?" Josephine asked. She figured she could take a warm shower and try to clean up her period for a couple minutes as she slammed the door shut.

She busied herself wiping stains from her hair. She turned the water to the shower on and could not hear the commotion as it was going down outside. She was examining her hair and make-up in the bathroom mirror when she realized that there was loud talking going on in the other room. Josephine put her head closer to the door and it swung in, knocking her backwards onto the toilet seat.

"What da fuck is going...?" Josephine started to scream when, all of a sudden, four girls descended on her. They came swinging fists and shoved her hard against the bathroom wall. She fell and hit her head. It was difficult for Josephine to fathom what happened next but she tried in vain to get back up. The tiles of the bathroom were slippery and every time she thought she would make it up, she would slip and felt everything from belts to shoes being used to beat her. There was blood coming from everywhere and although Josephine fought back, she was easily overpowered by these girls. They dragged her outside into the elevator and carried her to the lobby. A fist hit her real hard and she fell out cold.

She recovered to find herself on the lobby floor wearing her jacket and skirt but no shirt or bra. She peered outside from beneath her swollen eyes. Her head hurt but she recognized the raindrops outside the front door and knew that it was pouring. What Josephine wasn't aware of was the tremendous beating she had just suffered at the hands of four girls. She remembered seeing the faces and getting hit by Kim and Tina.

There were two other girls with them, both Spanish. She did not know who they were but she was sure that one of them was a jealous girlfriend and she was sure that Geo had not told her the truth. He had not mentioned a girlfriend. Josephine's head pounded and there was blood on her clothes coming from her lips. She struggled to her feet when she saw the patrol car and ran outside waving at the vehicle. The officers stopped and told her she had to go to the precinct to make a report then called an ambulance.

Josephine couldn't focus long enough to remember the

apartment where the incident took place. The police told her there was nothing else that could be done at this time and left immediately when the ambulance came. A few minutes later, she passed out inside the speeding ambulance.

SEVENTY-TWO

The following morning at about nine, Josephine awoke and sobbed when she felt the bandages on her face and head. She had slept for hours and felt rested even though there was a light ringing in her head. Otherwise, she was able to get out of bed and walk to the bathroom. She peered out of her bloodshot eyes, which were still swollen. She heard footsteps and saw that a nurse had walked into the room.

"Finally," the nurse said. "You're awake, sleeping beauty. How do you feel?" the nurse asked.

"I feel okay. A little sore but I'm okay. How long have I been sleeping?"

"Since you came in. What happened? Did you have a fight with your boyfriend?"

"Nah," said Josephine reflectively. She looked at the nurse.

"Okay, we need to get some contact information from you. You've been in the hospital since early Saturday morning. You had multiple wounds around your eyes, earlobes, and swollen lips. What happened to you? Tell me if your boyfriend did this terrible thing to you. He should be punished to the fullest extent of the law if he did this to you," the nurse said. Josephine stared at her for a second as if she did not comprehend. "You're safe now. You can tell me, did your boyfriend..."

"I heard you," Josephine snapped recalling the beat down she suffered. "No, it wasn't my boyfriend. He didn't do anything," Josephine said framing each syllable carefully. "I was jumped by some girls I don't even know," Josephine said looking at the nurse. She was met by the nurse's astute stare.

"There're a lot of girls ganging up on other girls and real-ly fighting like boys do," the nurse said shaking her head. "Things getting real violent. Ah, what is your name?" the nurse asked.

"Josephine, Josephine Johnson. Did you try to call my mother, nurse?"

"You had no ID on you so I don't think anyone has. Plus, you were sleeping for so long we wanted to let you get as much rest as possible," the nurse continued and asked Josephine all the pertinent information. Josephine did not want her mother informed as to where she had spent most of her weekend.

"You don't have to call my mother, do you?"

"Is your father here in the city?"

"No, but I have got friends who..."

"We'll have to notify your relatives because you're still a minor, not your friends. Hospital policy, Josephine," the nurse said. "But we'll also call your friends nonetheless and let them know where you are," she said finally. Josephine grudgingly gave the nurse the required information then dialed Miss Katie. After a couple rings, she heard the familiar voice of Coco. Josephine was happy.

"Coco, whassup? You gotta come and get me, girl," she said immediately.

"Oh thank goodness, we were tryin' to find out what the hell happened to you all day yesterday. Oh, your mother called, yo. Where are you? You ahight?"

"Yes, I'm ahight but I need you to come down here and get me now."

"Where?"

"In this hospital at Twelfth Street and Seventh Ave. Come now, Coco please."

"Whatcha doing in a damn hospital? Don't tell me that nigga had an accident or sump'n?"

"Nah, nah, it wasn't even that. Coco, come down now, please, and we'll talk. Do me a solid and bring some clothes for me. I'll see you in a little while."

"It's done. Ahight yo," Coco said and hung up the phone.

The hospital provided little comfort to the fact that she

had been beaten up. Josephine watched from her bed as nurses moved through the hallway. The shock of finding herself a patient was still coursing through Josephine. She lay back in her bed reassured with the fact that Coco was on her way. She looked in her pocketbook but it was empty except for her lipstick, a condom, and some gum.

SEVENTY-THREE

About an hour later, a nurse came in with Coco and Deedee nearly running in behind her.

"Damn, Jo, what happened?" Coco asked when she saw her friend banged up with bruises all over the facial area. Josephine wore a weak smile that did nothing to conceal how angry she was.

"Bitches jumped me," Josephine said.

"What? Get da fuck..." Coco started but her shouting brought the nurse back into the room. Coco realizing she was in the hospital, regrouped. "Hold up, Jo, who da fuck?"

"If you're going to scream and use profanity, I'm afraid I'm going to have to stop your visit at once," the nurse said.

"I'm sorry," Coco started to apologize but the nurse walked out the room. "I brought you a pair of sweats," Coco continued.

"That's good. Y'all could come a little closer. I promise I won't break," Josephine said with a grin.

"Man, it's so messed up that someone robbed you," Deedee started to say.

"I probably look a lot worse than I feel," Josephine said then ushered her friends closer. "It was Kim and that bitch, Tina, and some of their friends," she whispered. "Yo, it was like them bitches waited until I was in the bathroom and then...then they just jumped me," Josephine continued with a strain in her voice.

"So they must have seen you with Geo and then called his girl or sump'n. Man, no way that nigga shoulda played you like that," Coco said, staring at Josephine with sympathy all over her face. They were close and it was sad to see Josephine beaten up like this for a guy. She could hear Josephine giving him pardon.

"Nah, we went to his crib to fool around and after that, I went to use the bathroom. They came in when I went to the bathroom. They kicked the door in and then jumped me." Josephine unveiled the salacious tale, often softening the details with a smile but there were tears beneath the scabs forming on the bruises around her eyes. Josephine, with help from Coco and Deedee, eventually got dressed just in time for Josephine's mother's arrival to the hospital room.

"Oh, my God, Josephine, what happened?" Mrs. Johnson yelled. Josephine gave her a very curt look.

"Mother, stop with the drama already. These are my friends. Coco and Deedee, this is my mother," Josephine deadpanned.

"I met Coco and Deedee earlier. I went to their homes looking for you. I want to know what happened to you, Josephine."

"I was coming from a party and got mugged and robbed, mother."

"But why? Why?" Mrs. Johnson asked.

"I don't know. They just felt like robbing me, that's all. You should know. Shit happens in da city, mother."

"That's why you've got to go back with me. You stay here in this city and you'll die. I mean, I was worried about you."

"Mother, please stop it. Just because I got mugged don't mean I changed my views," Josephine started. "When did you begin worrying about me? Just leave me alone," Josephine said and turned her head away from her mother. The woman broke down sobbing. Coco looked at Deedee with raised brows.

"Drama," she whispered then she spoke to Josephine. "Josephine, I know you done told everyone that you're not going back but I'm your friend and I think you should go back with her and stand by your mother," Coco said. Josephine looked at Coco with a dumbfounded expression.

"Coco, you out of everyone here ought to know, this is a stressful thing that I'm going through with my..."

"I feel you but we only get one mother, Jo."

"Yeah, but you don't have to suffer under her. I mean, I need to be me. I can survive on my own."

"Yeah, but you're gonna need an education and a high school diploma and money."

"What about interning with Eric and making songs with you? Working on that album and doing videos and all the things we talked about, Coco? I could make it," Josephine said. She was right. If Eric Ascot gave her a position as an intern and they worked on the album, maybe the money would not be a problem. Coco knew there was something wrong but she was stumped on what to say when she heard Deedee speaking.

"Jo, you've got to go back with your mom. Please do as she sez because not only is Coco right that you're gonna need all that stuff but Uncle Eric is not ready to take on any interns right now," Deedee said and Josephine squinted to stare at her. "He told me personally that all that will be set up for the summer and that means after you're out of school. Go back with your mom and in a couple of months, it'll be summer and you'll graduate. Then..."

"And remember you told me what I could get my mother for Mother's Day and I did it. Now, I'm telling you to do what we're saying and it'll still be all good, yo," Coco said. Josephine stared at both Coco and Deedee then glanced at her mother.

"Ahight, ahight, you guys. I heard y'all. I guess you're right. Look, I wanna get away but I gotta be patient because in the end, like you said before Coco, 'You only get one mom.' So I'll go back with mine and try to enjoy the southern hospitality while it lasts," Josephine said and the girls all hugged. Josephine embraced her tearful mother and they both cried softly.

"This is a great Mother's Day gift," Mrs. Johnson said. "Let's go pack, Jo."

"Okay," Josephine said, still sobbing quietly.

"Can I give you a ride?" Deedee asked as everyone filed from the hospital room.

"Sure," Mrs. Johnson replied.

"Oh, Jo, you've gotta see this. She's even got a chauffer," Coco said with a wink.

"That was my uncle's idea," Deedee said and the girls slapped high-five.

The Range Rover splashed through the puddles in the streets. It had rained for most of the day and as the Range Rover pulled to stop outside the hotel where Josephine and her mother stayed, a zip of lightning struck and occasionally, thunder rumbling in the distance. The girls kissed and hugged as they said their goodbyes.

"Stay sweet as you are, Dee, and you, Coco, I love you like a sister," Josephine said and embraced each one more time before she and her mother stepped out of the vehicle. "See you in the summer," Josephine yelled and her mother waved as they made their way into the hotel.

"Bye, Jo, take care and I'll see you in summer," Deedee said as she threw kisses.

"Stay strong, Jo, and call me. I'll give your number to Dee, okay? Bye," Coco yelled and waved.

SEVENTY-FOUR

A sudden downpour of rain once again flooded the streets as the Range made its way uptown. "Dee, that was good that you were able to know about the intern stuff and all."

"Who said I did. My uncle hasn't told me anything about his plans. I just made that up cuz it sounded like the right thing to say at the time."

"Whatever works and it did the job. Hopefully we'll see Jo's crazy as in da summer, yo. She's off the hook."

"Yes, she is," Deedee laughed. "She's fun though. She and her mother need to make up quick fast. I'm sure they definitely love each other," Deedee said as she continued to watch the raindrops outside the window. "It would be a nice Mother's Day gift if I could find my mother, Coco," Deedee said and Coco looked at her.

"If you're serious, I'll do everything I can to help you, yo."

"Thanks, Coco. I know I can count on you. With the police harassing my uncle, I don't know when he's gonna be able to be a parent or have anytime for me. He's too busy with his own situation."

"I hear that. You just gotta go find Madukes, that's all."

"True, I wish it was that easy though."

"It could be. You won't know until you've tried."

Coco and Deedee saw the yellow cab stop in front of them. They saw two girls getting out. It was easy to identify the hunky curvaceous Kim and the equally endowed Tina.

"Coco, look, there goes the girls Josephine said attacked her," Deedee exclaimed.

"Yeah, I see 'em bitches," Coco said and watched the girls

enter the building. The afternoon was still soggy even though the downpour had stopped. Coco got out the Range at her building. Kim and Tina were walking inside. "She's probably gonna get her son from, Miss Katie. Trifling ho's," Coco said and walked inside. Deedee got out and ran behind her.

"Coco, you left your wallet on the seat," Deedee said but realized that Coco was caught in a stare down. Deedee slipped the wallet inside her pocket and waited next to the lethally silent Coco. She could feel the tension and decided to ride up with them just in case. All through the ride, the air was thick enough to knock any brave soul out. Deedee hung in there standing by her friend. Then, as the elevator door opened, all hell broke loose. It started with a shove in the back of Deedee. She turned to hear Tina already winding up.

"Bitch, you gonna let me off or what?" Tina asked Deedee.

"You could get by..." Deedee began but Coco intervened.

"You gotta move completely, Dee. Can't you see the bitch's butt's as big as her fucking head?" Coco opined and Kim immediately jumped in.

"Yo, Tina, these bitches want some o' what they diva wannabe friend got."

"Yes," said Coco immediately, "you got some to spare, bitch?" Coco said and pushed Kim from the elevator. They were all getting out on the same floor. Kim and Tina were on their way to get Roshawn from Miss Katie. Kim returned Coco's shove then Coco kicked her in the crotch and punched her on the lip. As blood trickled from Kim's mouth, Tina took a swing at Coco but Deedee saw her first and blocked the blow. She then executed a perfectly timed roundhouse kick that dropped Tina. Coco saw that and belted a fist to the midsection of the slowly recovering Kim. She followed that by a swift kick and then another. Tina reached to pull Coco's hair but again Deedee intercepted her by the arms and flipped her over with ease.

The resulting noise from all the activity had tenants peeking out of half opened doors. Some were cheering as the girls threw down in the hallway and yelled, "Give her what she deserved, Coco." "Rock her world, Coco." The noise brought Miss Katie carrying Roshawn to her door. When she realized what was happening, she started shouting.

"Stop it! Stop this damn fighting! Break it up! Coco, please stop," the old lady cried. The whole the time, she had Roshawn in her arms. Just as she was about to put him down, Deedee who had been beating on Tina, suddenly screamed.

"Look out, she's gotta gun. She's gotta gun..."

It was too late for anyone to get out of the way. Tina held the tiny pistol in her hand and pointed it.

"You fucking bitches! Wanna fuck wit me now, huh?" she screamed as she closed her eyes and pulled the trigger.

Total chaos broke out. The explosion erupted in the hallway causing panic and the crowd that had gathered took off running madly and screaming everywhere. Noise and pandemonium spread like brushfire through the hallway as visitors ran down the stairs and residents closed their doors.

An eerie silence followed. It covered the place the way dark clouds do prior to the rain. Asses and elbows were all that were seen as people scattered or took refuge in their apartments. All that was left were echoes of their fear. When the smoke had cleared, the ominous sound of a baby's howl was the only clamoring left to this bizarre episode.

To be continued...

GHETTO GIRLS 3
$OO HOOD

Trained eyes searched for any suspicious acts easily over-looked by the ordinary. P.O Ward had ended his day at the office several hours earlier. Now he sat in a department car and got ready to bite into his gyro.

"Ahh shit!" he uttered aloud. Ward began picking at pieces of onion. "I told those people at that damn Greek deli no fucking onions." Ward spoke looking out the car window. He could see activity over at the legendary Rucker but no one could hear him swear. He preferred it that way. Ward liked the peace and calm of his position but most of all he liked things his way. "How many times must I tell them the same damn thing over and over? No onions," the veteran parole officer pondered aloud.

Ward had ten years under his belt in the parole division. He was a hard driving and tough senior officer. He was particu-larly hard with his current parolee, Michael Long aka Lil' Long. It was just his way of repaying society, Ward thought as he unrav-eled the soft-shell of his meal. He meticulously removed the onions from his sandwich and delicately rolled the sandwich together. This is the way decent people get rid of the riff-raff of society, Ward thought as he threw the onions from his parked car. He eyeballed the sandwich before taking a bite, chewed quickly then took another bite. He sipped cola as he continued his visual reconnaissance of the area. After finishing off the food, Ward reached into his pocket for an antacid. Quickly swallowing then letting out a burp, he lit a cigarette and watched the specks of sunlight that splashed onto the windshield of his navy Chevy Caprice. He slipped on his Ray Bans, easily shielding his eyes.

P.O. Ward had arrived early and driven the entire perime-ter before settling on a spot on the uptown side of West 155th street. By skillful utilization of his front and rearview mirrors, he was able to see in all directions. Ward knew he was dealing with a parolee. Not just any ordinary one but a dangerous person, one who killed at will. This fact sent his mind racing and made him even more cautious. Why did I agree to meet with him? I should bring his ass to the office and ship him upstate, Ward pondered as he second-guessed himself. He quickly checked his service weapon and replaced it in the holster then felt for the gun strapped to his ankle. He always carried two guns just in case. Ward felt ready to deal with any type of shadiness that Lil' Long would exhibit. From the moment he had agreed to meet with the hardened criminal, Ward had steeled his mind to handle and put to an end any drama that jumped off. He was prepared to deal with this thug single-handedly, Ward thought.

Parole Officer Ward was on a mission to root out criminals who hid behind the system. He was known for constantly violating his parolees and sending them back to prison until their time was completely served. The word was clear: Mess with Ward and you'll be back upstate in a flash of his signature.

Herb Cliff Ward was a former high school basketball star and the proud father of two boys. He had two years of junior college under his belt and served in the Marines. Married for ten years, he and his wife, a schoolteacher, were raising their two children to be law-abiding citizens in a middle class neighborhood. He was a man with a keen sense of devotion and not only did he want to succeed but he also wanted to be the very best example for his family.

It was with this vigilante approach to his duties that the parole officer sat in his car parked just beyond the Holcombe Rucker Playground and waited for Lil' Long's arrival. Ward casually observed the basketball game while his vision steeled the perimeter. He believed that the street thug had backed himself into a deadly corner and now needed his help. Well, he's got to give up some necessary info, Ward thought as he surveyed his perimeter then returned his attention to the game.

The game was West Coast fast breaks with an East Coast man-to-man defense. The mere act of passing was done with so much pizzazz that offensive moves were poetry in motion at one end and a brawling hardcore defense at the next. Young basketball players were living with the hope of becoming street legends, sacrificing limbs and minds with acts of athleticism and machismo that defied gravity. Every dunk or spectacular lay-up etched that player into the collective conscience of the street-ball hall of fame.

The crowd roared after each dramatic play. Fans bet their dollars on players with names like Shane the Dribbling Machine, Half-Man Half-Amazing, Hot Sauce and I B Right Back. On the court were street ballers blessed with immense skills, each player living up to their own billing. Another spectacular dunk and Half-Man Half-Amazing sent a buzz through the crowd. His legend grew with every utterance from the lips of elated fans. A pass zipped to an open man and after a tantalizing part dance, part dribble. Shane, the Dribbling Machine was born. The game went by but in the back of his mind, Ward kept track of the cars coming and going.

Ward looked closer and saw young guys whipping Benz's and Bentley's into illegal parking spots. There were street people festive in baggy blue Enyce and RocaWear jeans with white tees and white sneaks. Thugs were throwing down hundred dollar bills in bets of wanton proportions on the outcome of the game. Music blasted from DJ Lodose as the crowd cheered in appreciation of the skills on display.

"Goddamn hip-hoppers," Ward uttered shaking his head. Probably ninety percent of the crowd was out enjoying the activity compliments of the parole board, thought Ward as he watched with disdain.

He checked his cell phone. No calls. That Michael Long must be on colored people time. Ward shook the idea by watching the non-stop frenzy of the basketball game as it happened. He waited patiently and clicked stills of who's who from his disposable camera. Before long the applause, shrieks, and loud screams that accompanied each sensational play captured the parole officer's attention. Everyone was jubilant and participated in the experience of a breath taking, tomahawk dunk.

The crowd was too joyous to notice Lil' Long smiling as he crept to the side of the lawman's car. He heaved a friendly wave at the suspicious parole officer. Across the street at the Rucker there was an outburst of cheer from the crowd as Hot Sauce brought the house down with another scintillating dunk. At that same moment, Lil' Long pulled out his guns and began mouthing off. Ward flinched and reached for his gun sitting in his lap. He wasn't fast enough and fumbled when he heard the litany coming from Lil' Long.

"In order for me to remain immortal, a-a-all w-we-weak m-m-mothafuckas must di-di-die," he proclaimed stuttering loudly.

From corner to corner on 155th street, the cheering basketball fans filled the summer night's air drowning out any other sound in the immediate vicinity. The crowd was noisy, raucous and wild as Shane, the Dribbling Machine broke a few ankles. They held collective breaths as he wove his way through the porous defense of his opponent. Before any opposing player could recover from the mesmerizing crossover display, Shane pulled up, faked the jump shot, and then shot a clean pass to the Main Event. He rose, clearing the pack from beneath the basket and sent down a roaring slam. The orange ball bounced high above the rim.

"Get da fuck up out here!" he yelled as the referee blew the whistle signaling the end of the first half. The ball continued to bounce and life returned to the air. Pandemonium broke loose. The sound of rap music resonated through the air as the crowd cheered the final bucket before half time.

At the same time, about twenty feet away Lil' Long squeezed both triggers. Fifteen rounds from his twin Desert Eagles went flying faster than the speed of sound. Shattered glass scattered all over from the explosion. Tumultuous noise echoed as the parole officer tried to recover his gun but all he saw were pieces of glass shrapnel coming at him. Ward attempted to duck but even getting low he could not avoid Lil' Long's deadly aim.

READ MORE IN: GHETTO GIRLS 3: SOO HOOD
by ANTHONY WHYTE

WHERE
HIP-HOP
LITERATURE
BEGINS...

AUGUSTUS
PUBLISHING

Augustus Publishing was created to unify minds with entertaining, hard-hitting tales from a hood near you. Hip Hop literature interprets contemporary times and connects to readers through shared language, culture and artistic expression. From street tales and erotica to coming-of age sagas, our stories are endearing, filled with drama, imagination and laced with a Hip Hop steez.

Hard White: On the street of New York only on color matters
Novel By Anthony Whyle Based on the screenplay by Shannon Holmes

The streets are pitch black...A different shade of darkness has drifted to the North Bronx neighborhood known as Edenwald. Sleepless nights, there is no escaping dishonesty, disrespect, suspicion, ignorance, hostility, treachery, violence, karma... Hard White metered out to the residents. Two, Melquan and Precious have big dreams but must overcome much in order to manifest theirs. Hard White the novel is a story of triumph and tribulations of two people's journey to make it despite the odds. Nail biting drama you won't ever forget...Once you pick it up you can't put it down. Deftly written by Anthony Whyte based on the screenplay by Shannon Holmes, the story comes at you fast, furiously offering an insight to what it takes to get off the streets. It shows a woman's unWlimited love for her man. Precious is a rider and will do it all again for her man, Melquan... His love for the street must be bloodily severed. Her love for him will melt the coldest heart...Together their lives hang precariously over the crucible of Hard White. Read the novel and see why they make the perfect couple.

$14.95 // 9780982541531

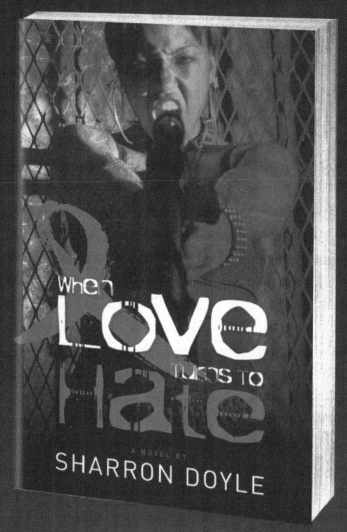

When Love Turns To Hate
By Sharron Doylee

Petie is back regulating from down south. He rides with a new ruthless partner, and they're all about making fast money. The partners mercilessly go after a shady associate who is caught in an FBI stin and threatens their road to riches. Petie and his two sons have grown apart. Renee, their mother, ha to make a big decision when one of her sons wild-out. Desperately, she tries to keep her world fron crumbling while holding onto what's left of her family. Venus fights for life after suffering a brutal phys ical attack. Share goes to great lengths to make sure her best friend's attacker stays ruined foreve. Crazy entertaining and teeming with betrayal, corruption, and murder, When Love Turn To Hate is mixed with romance gone awry. The drama will leave you panting for more.

$14.95 / / 9780982541517

Street Chic
By Anthony Whyte

A new case comes across the desk of detective Sheryl Street, from the Dade county larceny squad in Miami. Pursuing the investigation she discovers that it threatens to unfold some details of her life she thought was left buried in the Washington Heights area of New York City. Her duties as detective pits her against a family that had emotionally destabilized her. Street ran away from a world she wanted nothing to do with. The murder of a friend brings her back as law and order. Surely as night time follows daylight, Street's forced into a resolve she cannot walk away from. Loyalty is tested when a deadly choice has to be made. When you read this dark and twisted novel you'll find out if allegiance to her family wins Street over. A most interesting moral conundrum exists in the dramatic tension that is Street Chic.

$14.95 // 9780982541500

SMUT central
By Brandon McCalla

Markus Johnson, so mysterious he bare[ly] knows who he is. An infant left at the doo[r] step of an orphanage. After fleeing his re[f] uge, he was taken in by a couple with [a] perverse appetite for sexual indiscretion[s] only to become a star in the porn industry[.] Dr. Nancy Adler, a shrink who gained a peculi[ar] patient, unlike any she has ever encountered. [A] young African American man who faints up[on] sight of a woman he has never met, havin[g] flashbacks of a past he never knew existed. [A] past that contradicts the few things he know[s] about himself... Sex and lust tangled in a web s[o] disgustingly tantalizing and demented. Some[thing] thing evil, something demonic... Somethin[g] beyond the far reaches of a porn stars min[d,] peculiar to a well established shrink, leavin[g] an old NYPD detective on the verge of solvin[g] a case that has been a dead end for years... a[ll] triggered by desires for a mysterious woman[.]

$14.95 // 9780982541586

Dead And Stinkin'
By Stephen Hewett

A collection of three deadly novellas, Dead and Stinkin' invokes the themes of Jamaican folklore and traditions West Indian storytelling in a modern setting.

$14.95 // 9780982541555

Power of the P
By James Hendricks

Erotica at its gritty best, Power of the P is the seductive story of an entrepreneur who wields his powerful status in unimaginable — and sometimes unethical — ways. This exotic ride through the underworld of sex and prostitution in the hood explores how sex is leveraged to gain advantage over friends and rivals alike, and how sometimes the white collar world and the streets aren't as different as we thought they were.

$14.95 // 9780982541579

America's Soul
By Erick S Gray

Soul has just finished his 18-month sentence for a parole violation. Still in love with his son's mother, America, he wants nothing more than for them to become a family and move on from his past. But while Soul was in prison, America's music career started blowing up and she became entangled in a rocky relationship with a new man, Kendall. Kendall is determined to keep his woman by his side, and America finds herself caught in a tug of war between the two men. Soul turns his attention to battling the street life that landed him in jail — setting up a drug program to rid the community of its tortuous meth problem — but will Soul's efforts cross his former best friend, the murderous drug kingpin Omega?

$14.95 // 9780982541548

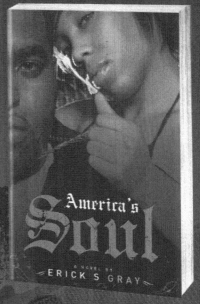

GHETTO GIRLS

Young Luv

ESSENCE BESTSELLING AU[T]

ANTHONY WHY[TE]

Ghetto Girls IV Young Luv
$14.95 // 9780979281662

Ghetto Girls
$14.95 // 0975945319

Ghetto Girls Too
$14.95 // 0975945300

Ghetto Girls 3 Soo
$14.95 // 0975945351

THE BEST OF THE STREET CHRONICLES TODAY, THE **GHETTO GIRLS SERIES** IS A
WONDERFULLY HYPNOTIC ADVENTURE THAT DELVES INTO THE CONVOLUTED MIND
OF CRIMINALS AND THE DARK WORLD OF POLICE CORRUPTION. YET, THERE IS
SOMETHING THRILLING AND SURPRISINGLY TENDER ABOUT THIS ONGOING
YOUNG-ADULT SAGA FILLED WITH MAD FLAVA.

Love and a Gangsta
author // **ERICK S GRAY**

This explosive sequel to **Crave All Lose All**. Soul and America
were together ten years 'til Soul's incarceration for drugs.
Faithfully, she waited four years for his return. Once home they
find life ain't so easy anymore. America believes in holding her
man down and expects Soul to be as committed. His lust for
fast money rears its ugly head at the same time America's mus[ic]
career takes off. From shootouts, to hustling and thugging life,
Soul and his man, Omega, have done it. Omega is on the
come-up in the drug-game of South Jamaica, Queens. Using
ties to a Mexican drug cartel, Omega has Queens in his grip. His
older brother, Rahmel, was Soul's cellmate in an upstate prison.
Rahmel, a man of God, tries to counsel Soul. Omega introduces
New York to crystal meth. Misery loves company and on the roa[d]
to the riches and spoils of the game, Omega wants the only ma[n]
he can trust, Soul, with him. Love between Soul and America is
tested by an unforgivable greed that leads quickly to deception
and murder.

$14.95 // 9780979281648

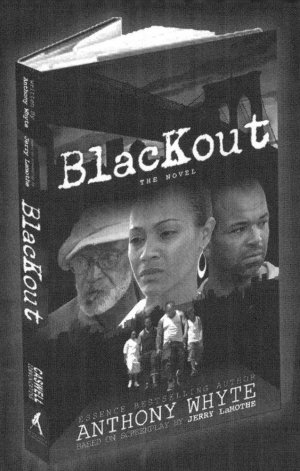

The lights went out
and the
mayhem began.

It's gritty in the city but hotter in Brooklyn where a small community in east Flatbush must come to grips with its greatest threat, self-destruction. August 14 and 15, 2003, the eastern section of the United States is crippled by a major shortage of electrical power, the worst in US history. Blackout, the spellbinding novel is based on the epic motion picture, directed by Jerry Lamothe. A thoroughly riveting story with delectable details of families caught in a harsh 48 hours of random violent acts, exploding in deadly conflict. There's a message in everything... even the bullet. The author vividly places characters on the stage of life and like pieces on a chess-board, expertly moves them to a tumultuous end. Voila! Checkmate, a literary triumph. Blackout is a masterpiece. This heart-stopping, page-turning drama is moving fast. Blackout is destined to become an American classic.

BASED ON SCREENPLAY BY **JERRY LaMOTHE**

Inspired by true events

US $14.95 CAN $20.95
ISBN 978-0-9820653-0-3

CASWELL
COMMUNICATIONS

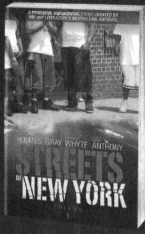 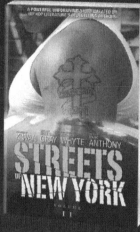